Palgrave Studies in Nineteenth-Century Writing and Culture

General Editor: **Joseph Bristow**, Professor of English, UCLA

Editorial Advisory Board: **Hilary Fraser**, Birkbeck College, University of London; **Josephine McDonagh**, Linacre College, University of Oxford; **Yopie Prins**, University of Michigan; **Lindsay Smith**, University of Sussex; **Margaret D. Stetz**, University of Delaware; **Jenny Bourne Taylor**, University of Sussex

Palgrave Studies in Nineteenth-Century Writing and Culture is a new monograph series that aims to represent the most innovative research on literary works that were produced in the English-speaking world from the time of the Napoleonic Wars to the *fin de siècle*. Attentive to the historical continuities between 'Romantic' and 'Victorian', the series will feature studies that help scholarship to reassess the meaning of these terms during a century marked by diverse cultural, literary, and political movements. The main aim of the series is to look at the increasing influence of types of historicism on our understanding of literary forms and genres. It reflects the shift from critical theory to cultural history that has affected not only the period 1800–1900 but also every field within the discipline of English literature. All titles in the series seek to offer fresh critical perspectives and challenging readings of both canonical and non-canonical writings of this era.

Titles include:

Laurel Brake and Julie F. Codell (*editors*)
ENCOUNTERS IN THE VICTORIAN PRESS
Editors, Authors, Readers

Colette Colligan
THE TRAFFIC IN OBSCENITY FROM BYRON TO BEARDSLEY
Sexuality and Exoticism in Nineteenth-Century Print Culture

Dennis Denisoff
SEXUAL VISUALITY FROM LITERATURE TO FILM, 1850–1950

Laura E. Franey
VICTORIAN TRAVEL WRITING AND IMPERIAL VIOLENCE

Lawrence Frank
VICTORIAN DETECTIVE FICTION AND THE NATURE OF EVIDENCE
The Scientific Investigations of Poe, Dickens and Doyle

Jarlath Killeen
THE FAITHS OF OSCAR WILDE
Catholicism, Folklore and Ireland

Stephanie Kuduk Weiner
REPUBLICAN POLITICS AND ENGLISH POETRY, 1789–1874

Kirsten MacLeod
FICTIONS OF BRITISH DECADENCE
High Art, Popular Writing and the *Fin de Siècle*

Diana Maltz
BRITISH AESTHETICISM AND THE URBAN WORKING CLASSES, 1870–1900

Catherine Maxwell and Patricia Pulham (*editors*)
VERNON LEE
Decadence, Ethics, Aesthetics

David Payne
THE REENCHANTMENT OF NINETEENTH-CENTURY FICTION
Dickens, Thackeray, George Eliot and Serialization

Julia Reid
ROBERT LOUIS STEVENSON, SCIENCE AND THE *FIN DE SIÈCLE*

Ana Parejo Vadillo
WOMEN POETS AND URBAN AESTHETICISM
Passengers of Modernity

Palgrave Studies in Nineteenth-Century Writing and Culture
Series Standing Order ISBN 0–333–97700–9 (hardback)
(outside North America only)

You can receive future titles in this series as they are published by placing a standing order. Please contact your bookseller or, in case of difficulty, write to us at the address below with your name and address, the title of the series and the ISBN quoted above.

Customer Services Department, Macmillan Distribution Ltd, Houndmills, Basingstoke, Hampshire RG21 6XS, England

Vernon Lee

Decadence, Ethics, Aesthetics

Edited by
Catherine Maxwell and Patricia Pulham

palgrave
macmillan

First published 2006 by
PALGRAVE MACMILLAN
Houndmills, Basingstoke, Hampshire RG21 6XS and
175 Fifth Avenue, New York, N.Y. 10010
Companies and representatives throughout the world

PALGRAVE MACMILLAN is the global academic imprint of the Palgrave Macmillan division of St. Martin's Press, LLC and of Palgrave Macmillan Ltd. Macmillan® is a registered trademark in the United States, United Kingdom and other countries. Palgrave is a registered trademark in the European Union and other countries.

ISBN 13: 978–1–4039–9213–0   hardback
ISBN 10: 1–4039–9213–4   hardback

This book is printed on paper suitable for recycling and made from fully managed and sustained forest sources.

A catalogue record for this book is available from the British Library.

Library of Congress Cataloging-in-Publication Data

Vernon Lee : decadence, ethics, aesthetics / edited by Catherine Maxwell and Patricia Pulham.
        p. cm. – (Palgrave studies in nineteenth-century writing and culture)
    "This collection of essays stems from an international conference 'Vernon Lee: literary revenant', organized by Catherine Maxwell and Patricia Pulham, and held in London at the Institute of English Studies in June 2003"–Pref.
    Includes bibliographical references and index.
    ISBN 1–4039–9213–4 (cloth)
    1. Lee, Vernon, 1856–1935–Criticism and interpretation. 2. Decadence in literature. 3. Aesthetics in literature. 4. Feminism and literature–Great Britain–History–19th century. 5. Women and literature–Great Britain–History–19th century. 6. Aestheticism (Literature) I. Maxwell, Catherine, 1962– II. Pulham, Patricia, 1959– III. Series.

PR5115.P2Z89 2006

2005055349

10   9   8   7   6   5   4   3   2   1
15   14   13   12   11   10   09   08   07   06

Printed and bound in Great Britain by
Antony Rowe Ltd, Chippenham and Eastbourne

For Vernon Lee

'...and he's a *friend*, and it doesn't matter, does it, how long ago friends may have been born and died, they always know and love each other when they meet!'

Vernon Lee, *Louis Norbert: A Two-fold Romance* (1914), 85.

Contents

Art and Argument

List of Illustrations

Preface and Acknowledgements

This collection of essays stems from an international conference 'Vernon Lee: Literary Revenant', organized by Catherine Maxwell and Patricia Pulham, and held in London at the Institute of English Studies in June 2003. Famous for her penetrating intellect and breadth of culture during the late nineteenth century, the writer and critic Vernon Lee (Violet Paget, 1856–1935) is one of many 'lost' and neglected women authors now being rehabilitated for a modern audience. However, as the author of forty-three volumes which reflect her diverse interests in fiction, aesthetics, philosophy, history and travel writing, she is remarkable for the sheer range and quality of her oeuvre.

As research on Lee has developed over the last twenty years, readers have become increasingly aware of her as a major literary figure and leading European cosmopolitan intellectual whose substantial contribution to the literature and culture of the Victorian *fin de siècle* and to an emergent twentieth-century modernism stands in need of urgent reassessment. From the appearance of her *Studies of the Eighteenth Century in Italy* in 1880, an astonishingly assured and erudite monograph for a young writer of twenty four, and in her works on the Italian Renaissance, *Euphorion* (1884) and *Renaissance Fancies and Studies* (1895); in her fiction – the short stories collected in *Hauntings* (1890) and *Vanitas* (1892), the controversial novel *Miss Brown* (1884), or her fascinating historical detective novel *Louis Norbert* (1914); in the philosophical dialogues *Baldwin* (1886) and *Althea* (1894); the polemical essays in *Gospels of Anarchy* (1908); the daring pacifism of *The Ballet of the Nations* (1915) and *Satan the Waster* (1920); the innovative literary theory of *The Handling of Words* (1923); the important and still largely unassessed work on empathy and on physiological aesthetics found in *Beauty and Ugliness*, co-authored with Clementina Anstruther-Thomson (1912), *The Beautiful* (1913), and the detailed Introduction to Anstruther-Thomson's *Art and Man* (1924), through to her last volume, *Music and Its Lovers* (1932), an original experimental study of how individuals respond to music – in all these many works one sees the tremendous confidence and reach of an extraordinarily sophisticated, imaginative and agile mind. Fluent in four languages, astoundingly well-read and with an enviable mastery of current intellectual thought,

Lee was one of the pre-eminent critics and thinkers of her time. Reading her now in the twenty-first century, one is struck powerfully by the fact there is no need to apologise or make a special case for her work, and many of the concerns thrown up by her writing – sexuality, identity, vision and imagination, the presence of the past – are those which speak to the readers of today.

Over the last decade publication on Lee has increased considerably and there has been a steady stream of articles on those aspects of her work which have most interested modern critics: her use of the supernatural, her interpretation of the Italian Renaissance, the importance of Italy and the sense of place to her work, her extensive knowledge of art and music, her relations to late nineteenth-century aestheticism and Decadence, her controversial pacifism as voiced during World War I, the way in which her 'lesbian' identity informs her imaginative and other writings, and her influence on later literary figures such as Virginia Woolf.[1] These diverse critical responses have begun to reshape our understanding of the literary and cultural landscape of the late nineteenth and early twentieth centuries, a landscape which, until recently, seemed to be dominated by the figures of male writers and intellectuals. Lee's unusual compass of so many varied fields of scholarship during this period means that she is becoming an increasingly conspicuous figure. Critics working in art history, intellectual history, lesbian and gay studies, women's studies, aesthetics, literary theory, musicology, politics, travel writing, late-Victorian literature and the transition to modernism have begun to find that she demands and then considerably rewards their attention and careful evaluation.

The 2003 conference marked a turning-point in the revival of interest in Lee, bringing together for the first time established academics and younger scholars from the United Kingdom, America, Canada, Australia, Italy, France and Germany, all with their own particular investments in her work. Coinciding with the arrival of two important monographs by Vineta Colby and Christa Zorn, the first book-length publications on Vernon Lee since Peter Gunn's biography of 1964,[2] the conference played an important part in consolidating Lee's writing as a key area for critical enquiry. In gathering together revised and extended essays from the conference into this, the first collection focusing on Lee, the editors aim to continue that process of consolidation, by demonstrating her extraordinary range of intellectual interests and emphasizing her central importance in the literary and cultural history of the late nineteenth and early twentieth centuries. The knowledge that other works on Lee are in preparation confirms our belief that Lee's reputation continues to strengthen and that this volume will play a significant role in introducing her work to a widening audience.[3] Aware that some members of that audience will not be familiar with Lee's life and major publications, we have included a short explicatory chronology which precedes the introduction proper so that readers can gain a sense of the original context of her work.

In preparing this volume, we would like to acknowledge use of material from the Vernon Lee Archive in Colby College Special Collections, Waterville, Maine, and also to express our thanks for the use of material from the Harry Ransom Center, Austin, Texas, the University of Reading Modern Publishing Archive, and the Tate Gallery Archive, London. We should also like to thank Professor Hilary Fraser of Birkbeck College, London, who read and assessed our original proposal for Palgrave Macmillan, for her warm support for this project and Professor Joseph Bristow, editor of the series Palgrave Studies in Nineteenth-Century Writing and Culture, for his very helpful and detailed comments on our manuscript. Many thanks to Queen Mary, University of London, for meeting the cost of the permission fees for the illustration on the jacket cover to this volume, to the Institute of English Studies for hosting the conference 'Vernon Lee: Literary Revenant' which provided the incentive for this collection, to Queen Mary, for its financial support of this event, and to all who attended, especially our contributors.

Notes

1 See, as examples, the publications by Gillian Beer (1997), Angela Leighton (2000, 2003), Hilary Fraser (1999, 2001, 2004), Martha Vicinus (2004), Kathy Alexis Psomiades (1997, 1999), Dennis Denisoff (1999, 2004), Sophie Geffroy-Menoux (1998, 1999, 2001), Richard Dellamora (2005), Catherine Maxwell (1997, 2003), and Patricia Pulham (2002, 2003).

2 See Colby 2003, Zorn 2003, Gunn 1964. 2004 saw the publication of Mary Patricia Kane's study of Lee's early fiction.

3 The first critical edition of Lee's fantastic fiction *Hauntings and Other Fantastic Tales*, co-edited by Catherine Maxwell and Patricia Pulham, is due out from Broadview Press in 2006, while critical monographs by Patricia Pulham and Sondeep Kandola are also in preparation. The international conference 'Vernon Lee e Firenze settant'anni dopo', held in Florence in late May 2005, with a particular focus on Lee's Italian context, demonstrated that Lee cuts an increasingly important figure not just in Anglo-American literary and cultural criticism but as a continental and cosmopolitan public intellectual. An edited collection of its proceedings is also promised.

Notes on Contributors

Laurel Brake is Professor in Literature and Print Culture at Birkbeck College, University of London. Her research interests take in all aspects of nineteenth-century print culture. She has published on journals, gender, Walter Pater, and the sociology of texts. Her books include *Subjugated Knowledges* (1994), *Walter Pater* (1994) and *Print in Transition* (2001). She has co-edited *Walter Pater: Transparencies of Desire* with Lesley Higgins and Carolyn Williams (2002), and *Nineteenth-Century Media and the Construction of Identities* with Bill Bell and David Finkelstein. She is currently writing a biography of Walter Pater and, with Julie Codell, has co-edited *Encounters in the Victorian Press*, a volume on nineteenth-century print journalism (2004).

Jo Briggs is a PhD student at Yale University. She completed a degree in the history of art, and a Masters in nineteenth-century British art at the Courtauld Institute of Art. Later she undertook a Master of Studies degree in Women's Studies at Oxford University. Her doctoral dissertation considers artistic protests against the Boer War (1899–1902) in European mass media.

Grace Brockington, formerly Junior Research Fellow at Wolfson College, Oxford, is currently a British Academy Postdoctoral Fellow at Clare College, Cambridge. She read English at Pembroke College, Cambridge, before doing an MA in the History of Art at the Courtauld Institute, London, and a PhD in English and the History of Art at Oxford. Her doctoral thesis (completed 2003) examined artistic and political debate among pacifists in Britain during the First World War. Publications include ' "Tending the Lamp" or "Minding their own Business"? Bloomsbury Art and Pacifism during World War', *Immediations: The Research Journal of the Courtauld Institute of Art* (2004); 'Jacob Epstein: Sculptor in Revolt', for *Art and Architecture* (2004); and a biographical article on Annie Constance Smedley (1876–1941) for the *New Dictionary of National Biography*.

Stefano Evangelista, formerly Junior Research Fellow at the Institute of Hellenic and Roman Studies, University of Bristol, is currently Fitzjames Research Fellow in English at Merton College, Oxford. He has published various articles on Walter Pater including contributions to

Walter Pater: Transparencies of Desire, ed. Brake et al (2002) and *Anglo-German Affinities in the Nineteenth Century*, ed. Rüdiger Görner (2005). Forthcoming articles on the legacy of Ancient Greece to nineteenth-century England and aesthetic Platonism at the *fin de siècle* will appear respectively in *Journal of British Cultures* and *The Yearbook of English Studies* in 2006. He is currently working on a book on Walter Pater, Aestheticism and the Greeks.

Dennis Denisoff is Ryerson Research Chair in the English Department and Graduate Programme in Communications and Culture at Ryerson University, Toronto. His areas of specialization are sexuality, visuality, British literature and culture from 1850 to 1950. He is the author of *Aestheticism and Sexual Parody: 1840–1940* (2001) and *Sexual Visuality from Literature to Film: 1850–1950* (2004), as well as co-editor of *Perennial Decay: On the Aesthetics and Politics of Decadence* (1999).

Catherine Maxwell is Reader in Victorian Literature at Queen Mary, University of London. She is the author of *The Female Sublime from Milton to Swinburne: Bearing Blindness* (2001) and the editor of *Algernon Charles Swinburne* (1997). Her monograph *Swinburne* in the British Council series Writers and Their Work is forthcoming in 2006 from Northcote House. She has published articles on Robert Browning, Dante Gabriel Rossetti, Christina Rossetti, Thomas Hardy, George Eliot, Ruskin, and Swinburne and two articles on Vernon Lee: 'From Dionysus to Dionea: Vernon Lee's Portraits', *Word & Image* 13: 3 (July–Sept, 1999), and 'Vernon Lee and the Ghosts of Italy', for *Unfolding the South: Nineteenth-Century British Women Writers and Artists in Italy 1789–1900*, eds. Alison Chapman and Jane Stabler (2003). With Patricia Pulham, she has co-edited a collection of Vernon Lee's stories *Hauntings and Other Fantastic Tales*, forthcoming from Broadview Press in 2006. She is currently writing a monograph for Manchester University Press on the visionary tradition in late Victorian literature.

Patricia Pulham is Senior Lecturer in Victorian Literature at the University of Portsmouth. Co-editor with Catherine Maxwell of a collection of Vernon Lee's stories *Hauntings and Other Fantastic Tales*, forthcoming from Broadview Press in 2006, she is currently working on a monograph, *Aesthetic Forms and Transitional Objects in Vernon Lee's Fantastic Tales*, under contract to Ashgate Press. She has published a number of articles on Vernon Lee including 'A Transatlantic Alliance: Charlotte Perkins Gilman and Vernon Lee' in *Feminist Forerunners: (New) Womanism and Feminism in the Early Twentieth Century*, ed. Ann

Heilmann (2003), and 'The Castrato and the Cry in Vernon Lee's Wicked Voices', *Victorian Literature and Culture* 30: 2, (2002).

Margaret D. Stetz is Mae and Robert Carter Professor of Women's Studies and Professor of Humanities at the University of Delaware. She has published more than fifty articles on women's literature and on nineteenth and twentieth century literature, culture, and film history. She is the author of *British Women's Comic Fiction, 1890–1990* (2001) and the co-author with Mark Samuels Lasner of *England in the 1880s: Old Guard and Avant-Garde* (1989); *England in the 1990s: Literary Publishing at the Bodley Head* (1990); and *The Yellow Book: A Centenary Exhibition* (1994). She is also co-editor with Bonnie B. C. Oh of *Legacies of the Comfort Women of WWII* (2001), and in 1999 she produced the reissue of the Victorian feminist novel *A Writer of Books* by 'George Paston' for Academy Chicago Press. She also serves on the editorial boards of the scholarly journals *Nineteenth Century Studies*; *Iris: A Journal About Women*; and *Victorian Literature and Culture*, as well on the board of Palgrave's Nineteenth-century Writing and Culture Series of monographs. In 2000, she received the National Association for Women in Catholic Higher Education's 'Wise Woman' biannual award for Women's Studies service and scholarship. Her latest book is *Gender and the London Theatre, 1880–1920* (2004).

Catherine Anne Wiley is a Visiting Assistant Professor at Temple University in Philadelphia, PA. She completed her doctorate in January of 2002, and the chapter in this collection is based on ideas explored in her thesis, entitled *'Amphibious Creatures': Essayism and Tranformative Play in Walter Pater, Vernon Lee, and John Addington Symonds*. Her work explores intersections among late-Victorian and modernist aesthetics, essayistic writing, and negotiations of gender and sexuality in identity formation. A forthcoming article on Walter Pater is due to be published in *Journal of Modern Literature*, and she is currently working on a study of the influence of female aesthetes on modernist writers. She is also a psychoanalyst in training.

Christa Zorn is an Associate Professor of English and coordinator of Women and Gender Studies at Indiana University Southeast, New Albany, where she teaches Victorian literature and culture, modernism, and critical theory. She holds a Master's degree in English and History from the University of Hamburg (Germany) and a PhD in English from the University of Florida. She is the author of *Vernon Lee: Aesthetics, History and the Victorian Female Intellectual* (2003) and has published several articles on Vernon Lee and on Lou Andreas-Salomé.

Vernon Lee: A Brief Chronology

1856   Vernon Lee (Violet Paget) born 14 October in Boulogne-sur-Mer, France to Matilda (née Adams) former wife of Captain James Lee-Hamilton (deceased) and Henry Ferguson Paget. Family maintains a nomadic lifestyle, at times moving twice a year. The first five years of Vernon Lee's life are spent mostly in Germany at Frankfurt, Baden, Wiesbaden, and Kissingen with a short sojourn at the Swiss resort of Thun.

1862   Lee visits England for the first time, spending summer with parents on the Isle of Wight.

1866   The Paget family becomes acquainted with the Fitzwilliam Sargents of Philadelphia in Nice, South of France. Vernon Lee's first meeting with John Singer Sargent. In succeeding years Sargent's mother, Mary (Mrs Fitzwilliam) Sargent, introduces Lee to the world of culture, history, music, and art that was to prove her inspiration.

1868   The Pagets and the Sargents spend the winter in Rome together. The Pagets are introduced to American artistic circles that include Harriet Hosmer and William Wetmore Story.

1869   Lee and her mother return to Switzerland for the summer. The poet Eugene Lee-Hamilton, Lee's half-brother (child of Matilda Paget's first marriage), is appointed to the Diplomatic Service, training at the Foreign Office in London. He begins to take an increasing interest in his sister's education.

1870   Lee's first literary work, 'Les Aventures d'une pièce de monnaie', is published in *La Famille*, a Lausanne periodical. Written in French, the story employs the narrative device of a coin, bearing the image of the emperor Hadrian, which relates its journey as it passes from hand to hand through various historical periods. June: visits Eugene in Paris.

1873   First signs of Eugene Lee-Hamilton's debilitating illness. The Pagets settle in Florence.

1878   Meets Mme Annie Meyer in Florence with whom she forms her first passionate friendship.

1880   *Studies of the Eighteenth Century in Italy*, an erudite collection of essays on Italian music and culture and *Tuscan Fairy Tales*, a volume of Italian folk stories translated and embellished by

Vernon Lee. Sends copy of *Studies* to John Addington Symonds. Meets Mary Robinson at 'Casa Paget' at 12 Via Solferino, Florence.

1881 *Belcaro: Being Essays on Sundry Æsthetical Questions* (dedicated to Mary Robinson), Lee's first treatise on aesthetic philosophy commenting on music, sculpture, and the nature of art. Visits Mary in London. Meets Robert Browning, Edmund Gosse, William Morris, Walter Pater, William Rossetti, Henry James and, among others, Oscar Wilde. John Singer Sargent paints her portrait.

1882 The Pagets move from Via Solferino to 5 Via Garibaldi, Florence.

1883 *The Prince of the Hundred Soups*, a puppet-play in the form of a story, enjoyed by the youthful Maurice Baring and Virginia Woolf; *Ottilie: An Eighteenth-Century Idyll*, a novella that centres on the lives of siblings living in a small German town and charts the sister's unhappy sacrifices for, and devotion to, her younger brother. Stays in London with Bella Duffy. Visits Sir Frederick Leighton's home, Leighton House, in Kensington and G.F. Watts's studio.

1884 *Miss Brown*, Lee's first novel (dedicated to Henry James), a scathing satire of the Aesthetic movement and its London devotees; *Euphorion: Being Studies of the Antique and the Mediæval in the Renaissance*, a volume gathering together essays, written over a period of years, on the history of Italian mediaeval and renaissance culture; *The Countess of Albany*, a historical novel (dedicated to the memory of Annie Meyer) based on the life of Princess Louise of Stolberg who, in 1772, married the Count of Albany, formerly known as 'Bonnie Prince Charlie'. Satirical content of *Miss Brown* offends prominent members of her social circle.

1886 *Baldwin: Being Dialogues on Views and Aspirations* (dedicated to Eugene Lee-Hamilton), a discussion of religion, literature, morality and aesthetics, presented in dialogue form.

1887 *Juvenilia: Being a Second Series of Essays on Sundry Æsthetical Questions*, a volume of impressionistic essays on music and art addressed to her friend, the Florentine scholar, Carlo Placci. August: Mary Robinson becomes engaged to James Darmesteter; Lee meets Clementina (Kit) Anstruther-Thomson. Suffers severe attack of neurasthenia.

1888 Kit visits Vernon Lee in Florence. Lee still unwell. August: Mary Robinson marries James Darmesteter. November: Lee travels with Evelyn Wimbush to Tangiers and Spain for her health.

1889   The Pagets lease Villa Il Palmerino in Maiano, in the hills above Florence.

1890   *Hauntings: Fantastic Stories*, a collection of four supernatural tales: 'Amour Dure: Passages from the Diary of Spiridion Trepka', 'Dionea', 'Oke of Okehurst' and 'A Wicked Voice'.

1892   *Vanitas: Polite Stories*, containing three short stories including 'Lady Tal', a study of literary rivalry, set in fashionable Venetian society, which features Jervase Marion, a character based on Henry James. William James visits Vernon Lee at Il Palmerino.

1893   *Althea: A Second Book of Dialogues on Aspirations and Duties*, a companion volume to *Baldwin* (1886) maintaining the dialogue form of the earlier book. Lee is introduced to George Bernard Shaw. Meets the composer, Ethel Smyth, at a dinner party at Windsor Castle and the critic and novelist, Maurice Baring, in Florence.

1894   July: Walter Pater dies. November: death of father, Henry Ferguson Paget.

1895   *Renaissance Fancies and Studies*, a sequel to *Euphorion* (1884), comprises historical essays on art and literature and includes Lee's 'Valedictory' for Walter Pater.

1896   March: Matilda Paget dies; Eugene Lee-Hamilton recovers from his illness and leaves Il Palmerino for America.

1897   *Limbo, and Other Essays*, a collection of impressionistic writings, predominantly on travel and Italy. August: sends galley proofs of 'Beauty and Ugliness' (Part I), later published in the *Contemporary Review* in October (and repeated in *Beauty and Ugliness* (1912)) to Bernard Berenson. Receives reply from Berenson accusing her and Kit of plagiarism, resulting in long-term feud.

1898   Eugene Lee-Hamilton marries the novelist, Annie Holdsworth. Kit leaves Il Palmerino to nurse another friend, Mrs Christian Head.

1899   *Genius Loci: Notes on Places*, travel essays set in France, Germany, and Italy. Kit spends six months of the year with Lee; six with Mrs Head. Meets Ottoline Cavendish Bentinck (later Lady Ottoline Morrell) at Il Palmerino.

1900   Mary Darmesteter (née Robinson) marries Emile Duclaux. Final break with Kit.

1903   *Ariadne in Mantua*, musical drama of unrequited love set in the late Renaissance; *Penelope Brandling*, historical fiction set on the Welsh coast in the eighteenth century, charting the life of a young girl who unknowingly marries into a family of wreckers. Lee's niece, Persis, daughter of Eugene Lee-Hamilton and Annie Holdsworth is born.

1904 *Pope Jacynth, and Other Fantastic Tales*, compilation of supernatural tales that includes 'Prince Alberic and the Snake Lady' originally published in the *Yellow Book* in 1896; *Hortus Vitae: Essays on the Gardening of Life*, personal impressions, written in the essayist tradition, on a range of subjects including reading, hearing music, and the nature of relationships. Begins friendship with H.G. Wells. March: meets Edith Wharton who visits her at Il Palmerino. October: Lee's niece, Persis, dies.

1905 *The Enchanted Woods, and Other Essays*, imaginative travel writings on locations in France, Italy, Switzerland, and Germany.

1906 *The Spirit of Rome*, subjective essays on her responses to the city and its history during the period 1888–1905. Lee buys Il Palmerino.

1907 September: Eugene Lee-Hamilton dies. Lee travels to Greece and Egypt.

1908 *The Sentimental Traveller*, collection of travel writings on European locations; *Gospels of Anarchy*, a volume of essays on contemporary social issues.

1909 *Laurus Nobilis: Chapters on Art and Life*, a collection of essays on art and aesthetics.

1911 Meets Irene Cooper Willis, who later becomes her executor. Lee opposes the Italo-Turkish war.

1912 *Vital Lies*, a volume of philosophical essays; *Beauty and Ugliness*, studies on psychological aesthetics based on collaborative work by Vernon Lee and Clementina Anstruther-Thomson.

1913 *The Beautiful*, a treatise on psychological aesthetics focusing on physiological and empathic responses to art.

1914 *Louis Norbert: A Two-Fold Romance*, Lee's last novel linking two love stories: one set in the Edwardian present, the other in seventeenth-century Italy; *The Tower of Mirrors*, a collection of evocative travel essays. August: World War I begins. Lee is unable to return to Italy after summer in England. Her pacifism loses her friends and publishers and she is accused of harbouring pro-German sympathies.

1915 *The Ballet of the Nations: A Present-Day Morality*, allegorical play commenting on the horrors of war. First edition carries illustrations by the British artist, Maxwell Armfield. Lee becomes a member of the Union of Democratic Control.

1920   *Satan the Waster: A Philosophical War Trilogy*, includes the text of *The Ballet of the Nations* to which Lee adds an introduction and explanatory notes. Returns to Florence. Reconciled with Bernard Berenson.

1921   Death of Clementina (Kit) Anstruther-Thomson.

1923   *The Handling of Words*, a collection of critical essays on literary style and reader-response theory.

1924   Lee collects and publishes Clementina Anstruther-Thomson's papers on aesthetic experimentation in *Art and Man*, for which she writes a long introduction. September 20: University of Durham confers on Lee the degree of Doctor of Letters.

1925   *The Golden Keys, and Other Essays on the Genius Loci*, Lee's final volume of travel essays; *Proteus: or the Future of Intelligence*, philosophical treatise on the history and prospects of intellectual thought. Death of John Singer Sargent.

1926   *The Poet's Eye*, a short comparison of the techniques of prose and poetry which appeared in 'The Hogarth Essays' series.

1927   *For Maurice: Five Unlikely Stories*, a collection of fantastic tales dedicated to Lee's friend Maurice Baring.

1932   *Music and Its Lovers*, a major study of musical response and appreciation, compiled from research amassed over a period of twenty years.

1934   Lee's last visit to England. Taken ill and returns to Italy.

1935   Vernon Lee dies at Il Palmerino on 13 February after a series of heart attacks. After cremation, her ashes are buried with Eugene Lee-Hamilton in the Allori cemetery in Florence.

Introduction

Catherine Maxwell and Patricia Pulham

From 1881 onwards, the young Vernon Lee, already esteemed for *Studies of the Eighteenth Century in Italy*, her monumental critical work on Italian opera and culture which had appeared the previous year, was a regular visitor to England. Leaving behind her parents and half-brother at home in Florence, her summers were spent visiting friends but, perhaps more important, moving in literary circles in London where she could promote her work, make important contacts and establish her reputation as a leading writer and critic. There is no doubt that this strategy was successful and that Lee, who met and fostered relationships with luminaries such as Robert Browning, Walter Pater, and Henry James, achieved literary celebrity during the 1880s and 1890s for an ambitious and impressive stream of productions which included collections of short stories, novels, historical biography, philosophical dialogues, volumes on the Italian Renaissance, travel writing and numerous essays on ethics, aesthetics, art and music. Back home in Italy she was also the pivotal figure in the gatherings of the leading cosmopolitan intellectuals who lived around or visited the cultural centre of Florence – critics and men of letters such as Carlo Placci, Enrico Nencioni and Karl Hillebrand, the sculptor Adolf von Hildebrand, the poets Peter Boutourline, Katharine Bradley and Edith Cooper (the two women who wrote as Michael Field), and the novelists Anatole France, Paul Bourget, Ouida (Louise de la Ramée) and Eliza Lynn Linton. During the last two decades of the nineteenth century Lee was recognized by the educated reading public as a writer and thinker of note, one of a number of prominent intellectuals whose works informed the significant debates of the day.

Although probably better-known by repute than by a large readership, Lee continued to be held in high regard into the early twentieth century, although thereafter her standing began to decline for a number of reasons. Her increasing concentration on abstract and philosophical concerns, as can be seen in her writings on physiological aesthetics, lost her a wider audience, while that work itself was imperfectly understood. It is still true today that her books on this subject, along with her pioneering studies of reader-response theory in *The Handling of Words* (1923) and her analysis of the modes of musical listening and hearing in *Music and Its Lovers* (1932), are still largely unknown and unappreciated. This last volume is only likely to receive full criticism when the fields of literary criticism and musicology are in closer dialogue.[1]

Other factors contributing to Lee's decline include her 'unpatriotic' pacifism in the face of World War I and the supposition that her writing was dated and irrelevant, a relic of a bygone age. 'Fresca was baptised in a soapy sea / Of Symonds – Walter Pater – Vernon Lee', wrote T. S. Eliot dismissively in the cancelled draft version of 'The Fire Sermon' from *The Waste Land* (Eliot 1971, 26, 27, 40, 41), and the new generation, keen to embrace what Perry Meisel has called 'the myth of the Modern', relegated Lee along with other supposedly embarrassing late Victorians, like Pater and John Addington Symonds, to the lumber room of literature (Meisel 1987).[2] Of course this dismissive gesture concealed the fact that the modernists were deeply influenced by the writers they claimed to despise. Meisel has shown how Pater was central to Eliot, James Joyce and Virginia Woolf (Meisel 1987 and 1980), and, on reading Woolf, it seems, in spite of her appalled sense in July 1909 that Lee was a 'garrulous baby' (Woolf 1975, I. 400), that the earlier writer in many ways anticipates and probably influences the later writer's experiments with consciousness and style.[3] Twenty years later, in *A Room of One's Own* (1929), Woolf more generously shows her perception of Lee's significance when, in a passage which acknowledges the intellectual contributions of modern-day women, she places 'Vernon Lee's books on aesthetics', alongside 'Jane Harrison's books on Greek archaeology' and 'Gertrude Bell's books on Persia' (Woolf 1929, 119.).

We have now begun to appreciate that Vernon Lee's work, far from being irrelevant to modernism, is crucial to its development. To take just one perspective: the flexible experimental treatment of sexuality, gender and identity, which characterizes the writing of female modernist writers such as Virginia Woolf, H. D., and Mina Loy and is also present in male writers such as James Joyce and Eliot, is no innovation but is clearly anticipated in the work of a number of late-Victorian writers such as Algernon Charles Swinburne, Pater, Michael Field, Simeon Solomon, Symonds, and, of course, Vernon Lee. In the supernatural and fantastic stories for which she is still best-known today, in the controversial *Miss Brown* (1884), and in the multiple layered identities of *Louis Norbert* (1914), Lee represents sexual desire as complex, violent, contradictory, and perverse, cryptically expressed through personae who dramatize but are often themselves unable to apprehend their own erotic drives and impulses. Same-sex desire in particular is often represented obliquely, fractured, split or shifting between ostensibly heterosexual characters caught in ambiguous triangular relationships.

Such fictional love triangles often reflect the real-life entanglements of Vernon Lee's desires. In the triangular relationship between Anne Brown, Walter Hamlin, and Sacha Elaguine in *Miss Brown*, for example, one may perhaps detect a melodramatic, and ostensibly heterosexualized, version of Lee's first romantic attachment to Annie Meyer, wife of John Meyer, to whom she was introduced by mutual friends in the late 1870s.[4] Similarly, Lee's tale 'A Wedding Chest' (1904) depicts a violent triangle of desire featuring a beautiful boy, Troilo (suggestive of 'troilism'),[5] whom Martha Vicinus reads as partly symbolic of 'Lee's personal anguish (and anger) in regard to the various women who deserted her for marriage' (Vicinus 1994, 107).

Among such women is the poet Mary Robinson (later Darmesteter and then Duclaux), to whom Lee refers in a letter dated 18 August 1904 as 'the first great ... love of my life'.[6] Robinson met Vernon Lee in September 1880 when she visited the Paget household in Florence. The relationship soon intensified: Lee spending her summers with the Robinsons in London, Robinson spending each autumn with Lee in Italy. Vineta Colby describes their partnership as a 'Boston marriage', a socially acceptable romantic friendship 'defined by devoted companionship and often open expressions of affection' (Colby 2003, 51). Despite her sanitizing strategy, and her reluctance to confront the issue of Lee's sexuality, it seems that Colby is not entirely convinced by her own argument, since she later writes: 'Mary offered a release for her [Lee's] long repressed hunger for love and reciprocal affection. That their relationship was and remained nonsexual in the physical sense is beyond doubt. But physical desire was not absent, at least on Violet's part' (Colby 2003, 58).

It is not entirely clear why it should be 'beyond doubt' that Lee and Robinson's friendship did not have a physical dimension. Possibly, Colby has chosen to accept Irene Cooper Willis's stark statement:

'Vernon was homosexual but she never faced up to sexual facts. ... She had a whole series of passions for women, but they were all perfectly correct. Physical contact she shunned' (quoted in Gardner 1987, 85), or perhaps her assertion is based on Ethel Smyth's comment that Vernon Lee's 'lesbian tendencies were repressed; the most a *culte* [adoring fan] could expect was a kiss which one of them, unnamed, described as having been of the sacramental kind. You feel you had been to your first communion' (quoted in Colby 2003, 176). Yet, as Vicinus proves, it seems that Lee did not shun all physical affection, nor was such contact always entirely devoid of sexual tension. In a tender letter to Mary Robinson dated 27 February 1881, Lee reminds her: 'once at Siena ... you said you had become mine, because you kissed me & I had held you tight' – a comment which suggests that they experienced mutual pleasure in each other's touch (quoted in Vicinus 2004, 272, n. 78). Equally, it is evident from Colby's own research that others suspected this to be the case. In her biography of Lee, Colby cites Havelock Ellis's suggestion (in consultation with John Addington Symonds, Robinson's friend and mentor) that Vernon Lee and Mary Robinson 'might serve as a possible case-history for the section on Lesbianism in *Sexual Inversion*' (quoted in Colby 2003, 51), and Lee's 'lesbian attachment' to Mary Robinson was the subject of discussion among acquaintances such as Lucy Rossetti (wife of Michael Rossetti) and Marie Spartali Stillman.[7] We can be certain, at least, that their relationship, whether sexual or platonic, was deeply passionate and that Lee was emotionally devastated by Robinson's sudden engagement to James Darmesteter (the Jewish professor who later became her first husband) in the summer of 1887, since Lee subsequently succumbed to a severe nervous breakdown.

It was in the aftermath of this event that Lee formed an attachment to Clementina (Kit) Anstruther-Thomson a Scottish 'semi-painter, semi-sculptor' in whose home she was staying when she received Mary Robinson's letter announcing her engagement (Gunn 1964, 118), and who later collaborated with Lee on a number of intellectual projects during a friendship that lasted 33 years. The romantic phase of this second major relationship began with Kit's attempt to console Vernon Lee, in the days following the unwelcome receipt of Robinson's news, with the touching gift of a white rose. In her commonplace book for the period 1887–1900, in an entry dated 28 August 1887, Lee relates how, upon undressing for bed, she found the flower on her pillow: 'It was a rose, scarcely more than a bud, lying very gently, white on whiteness. The scent of that rose will cling, I believe, as long as I live, in the corners of my soul'.[8] Lee was to preserve that rose till her death in an envelope marked '*Neue Liebe, Neues Leben* (New Love, New Life)' (Mannocchi 1986, 132). In her examination of Lee and Anstruther-Thomson's relationship, Phyllis Mannocchi refers to them as 'friends, lovers, co-workers, and co-authors' (Mannocchi 1986, 129) and her assessment of their collaborative work on physiological and psychological aesthetics in the articles of 1897, compiled in book form as *Beauty and Ugliness* (1912), and the later *Art and Man* (1924) has informed recent studies by Kathy Alexis Psomiades and Diana Maltz. For Psomiades, these works represent 'a theory of the aesthetic grounded in the congress between female bodies' (Psomiades 1999, 21) while Maltz focuses more particularly on the codification of lesbian desire in Lee's observation of Anstruther-Thomson's body as she gazes at art objects, and on the adoration of the affluent young women who supposedly expressed same-sex desire through aesthetic appreciation (Maltz 1999).

This focus on Lee's 'sexual dissidence', whether supported or disputed, has its foundations, as Jo Briggs explains in her chapter in this volume, in Burdett Gardner's 1954 Harvard dissertation, published in 1987 as *The Lesbian Imagination (Victorian Style): A Psychological and Critical Study of 'Vernon Lee'*. Using Freudian analysis, Gardner explores Lee's lesbian sexuality in order to determine what effect her 'neurosis' had on her writings (Gardner 1987, 28). Despite its dated and reductive nature, Gardner's book includes interesting interviews with a number of Lee's friends and acquaintances, and provides a wealth of useful information on her works. Nevertheless, its focus on Lee's sexual proclivities has influenced contemporary scholars who refer unproblematically to Vernon Lee as Kit Anstruther-Thomson's 'lover' without seeking to qualify, or complicate, this term (Maltz 1999, 21). Finding ways to write in the present about sexualities that, in their own time, had yet to be fully defined, is increasingly difficult. Do we apply modern terms such as 'lesbian' to these expressions of same-sex desire? Or do we attempt to 'purify' such relationships under the heading of 'romantic friendship'? As indicated by the title and contents of Vicinus's recent book, *Intimate Friends: Women Who Loved Women, 1778–1928*, there are no easy answers to these questions (Vicinus 2004). In the absence of satisfactory definitions, such critical scrutiny of Lee's writings through the lens of sexuality might best be served by an acknowledgement of ambiguity, by a contextualized and more inclusive use of the word 'lesbian', and by an acknowledgement that interest in Lee's sexual inclinations forms only part of a larger discourse on her extraordinary body of work.

This present volume has selected essays on the basis of certain key themes which we find pervasive in Vernon Lee's extensive canon of writing. While this can be only a partial appreciation of her rich and diverse oeuvre, it offers a broadly chronological movement across her life, starting with her important relationship with her half-brother Eugene Lee-Hamilton. After an exploration of her affiliations with Walter Pater and his circle with particular focus on the publication of *Miss Brown*, subsequent chapters examine a succession of works by Lee – *Euphorion*, 'Oke of Okehurst' from *Hauntings*, her studies of the Renaissance, 'Prince Alberic and the Snake Lady', *Louis Norbert*, *The Ballet of the Nations*, her writings on physiological aesthetics and *The Handling of Words* – explaining the context for each work, its significance in illuminating a key aspect of her thought or creative temperament, and its larger contribution to literary and intellectual culture or to our understanding of the historical moment of its production.

Readers of this volume will notice that the chapters which deal with Lee's creative relationships, conflicts and influences feature only men. This is no accident. Although Lee's intellectual circles in both England and Florence included many women – in addition to her intimate friends the poet Mary Robinson and the artist Clementina (Kit) Anstruther-Thomson, one thinks, for example, of Mary Ward the novelist, the painter Evelyn Pickering (afterwards Evelyn de Morgan), Eugenie Sellers Strong, classicist and founder of the British School at Rome, the poet Amy Levy, the composer Ethel Smyth, Margaret Brooke, the Ranee of Saràwak, and in Italy the writers Linda Villari and Countess Maria Pasolini to name but a few – there is, as yet, no evidence that any of them was a significant influence on Lee. Moreover, as is the case with Robinson and Anstruther-Thomson, there does seem to be evidence that Lee, as the stronger intellectual energy, was herself a definite shaping influence on her female companions, on the young women who admired her prodigious mental powers, and on subsequent writers such as Woolf. In spite of Mrs Paget's intention of rearing her precocious daughter as another Madame de Staël, it seems evident that with the important exception of her mother – to whom Lee pays warm tribute in *The Handling of Words* (1923) – her primary influences were male. Furthermore, it appears equally the case that the young Violet Paget saw herself as entering a predominantly male field of scholarship armoured by a suitably androgynous pseudonym.[9]

Chapters in this volume by Laurel Brake and Stefano Evangelista feature Walter Pater, the dominant influence on Lee who was the only writer he is said to have acknowledged as a disciple. Although Pater proved to be remarkably accommodating of Lee, other male writers regarded her in a less than generous spirit. In his analysis of her relationship with that other historian of the Italian Renaissance, John Addington Symonds, Evangelista also indicates the hostility shown towards Lee by male critics who regarded her as a female interloper in the properly masculine field of historical scholarship. This hostility, as her biography makes plain, can be seen in a series of subsequent attacks by various men including the philosopher Bertrand Russell, the artist and essayist Max Beerbohm, and the art critic Bernard Berenson, all of whom seemed to resent Lee's confident assurance of her own powers. Jo Briggs's chapter, which compares and contrasts Lee and Berenson, dispenses with the now infamous charge of plagiarism levelled by Berenson at Lee, to concentrate instead on the ways in which the lens of gender studies has shaped and arguably malformed our understanding of her as an eccentric 'lesbian' aesthetician while leaving Berenson untouched as a disinterested and unimpeachable male scholar. Other chapters by Catherine Maxwell and Margaret Stetz show variously how Lee's complex relations with her half-brother, the poet Eugene Lee-Hamilton and with Oscar Wilde mark her own fictional writing in terms of imagery, plot and style, while Grace Brockington's chapter on Lee shows how her ethical beliefs about war and aesthetic practice set her strangely at odds with Max Armfield, the illustrator of her pacifist allegory *The Ballet of the Nations* (1915), whose elegant and often inapposite designs have an aesthetic agenda of their own.

Lee thus becomes identified with a group of men who variously in one way or another were seen as associated with or influenced by late nineteenth-century literary and artistic Decadence. This elite and avant-garde literature emerges out of the larger cult of aestheticism, or art for art's sake, which became recognizable in the 1870s for its focus not on the objective or material world but rather on the artist's impressions of it. By comparison, Decadent art, known by that name in Britain by the 1890s, is characterized by its choice of rarefied, arcane, unorthodox or controversial subject matter which in turn gives rise to the cultivation of new, unusual and extreme sensations, perceptions and emotions, ideally communicated in correspondingly concentrated, highly-wrought, refined forms of expression. It is axiomatic that the Decadent artist seeks to find, celebrate and communicate the beauty of subjects which the conventional majority would find emotionally and morally unacceptable or repulsive. Many men prominently linked with

Decadent art and literature were sexual outsiders, a noticeable proportion of whom were homosexually inclined; this outsiderism, and
male same-sex desire in particular, at once pushed them to the margins
of Victorian mainstream society, made them a significant deviant
minority, and provided them with an immediate if covert subject
matter. The three perhaps more obviously identifiable 'Decadent' men
just mentioned – Pater, Wilde, and Symonds – fall into this category.
Pater, though actually appalled by his association with Decadent
experimentation, was seen as a founder of the English movement on
the basis of his provocative 'Conclusion' to *Studies in the History of the
Renaissance* (1873) with its apparent invitation to seek and savour new
sensations and experiences. Wilde, whom the *National Observer* in 1895
called 'the High Priest of the Decadents'[10] and who popularized the
notion of Pater as a hedonist, baited Victorian moral complacency and
earnestness, and successfully promoted the notion of style and artifice
over naturalness and sincerity. Symonds, poet, essayist and historian,
whose wife, Henry James recorded, regarded his books as 'immoral,
pagan, hyper-aesthetic' (James 1987, 25), produced in his *In the Key of
Blue and Other Prose Essays* of February 1893, a collection of lush
impressionistic essays on art, culture and sense of place that Holbrook
Jackson, in his classic study of the *fin de siècle*, thought 'so typical in
some ways of the Nineties that it might well have been written by one
of the younger generation' (Jackson 1922, 39). Many of the studies in
Symonds's collection, including the title piece, have a marked homoerotic undertow. Like Pater and, to a certain degree Wilde, Symonds
found in his exploration and evaluation of earlier periods of historical
culture, such as Ancient Greece or the Italian Renaissance which
accommodated same-sex desire more easily, an imaginative if cryptic
space or field of manoeuvre for fuller self-expression.

The heterosexual Berenson, Lee-Hamilton, and Armfield have different Decadent affiliations. Berenson, a passionate admirer of Pater since
he had encountered his writings at Harvard, cultivated an aesthetic
self-image, and on his first visit to England was keen to meet decadent
writers such as Lionel Johnson and Wilde. While Berenson was vigorously heterosexual and, in later life, a practitioner of free love, he was
alert to male beauty and proud of his own good looks, boasting of
himself as possessing a 'delight in the beauty of the male that can
scarcely have been surpassed ... with an almost unfortunate attractive-
ness for other men', and declaring that 'Young as I was, I made homo-
sexuals mouths water' (Samuels 1979, 64, 63). His ideas, first expressed
in *Florentine Painters of the Renaissance* (1896), concerning the role of

physical sensation in the appreciation of art, ideas which, Jo Briggs explains, like Lee's, probably share a common source in the work of Carl Lange and William James on the physical changes which condition emotion, could also be seen to derive from a particular kind of reading of Pater which understands him as valuing 'Greek sensuousness' or the immediacy of physical sensation.

Vernon Lee's half-brother Eugene Lee-Hamilton, although he vigorously attested his dislike of certain leading Decadent writers such as Baudelaire and Swinburne, was in many ways by force of circumstance a Decadent artist par excellence; bed-bound for nearly twenty years and cut off from normal life by an invalidism which, at its worst confined him to a darkened room, he experimented with poetic forms such as the sonnet and the dramatic monologue, adapting them to his own purposes, and filled his poetry with a lurid phantasmagoria marked by sex and violence, using images drawn from myth, art and history to express his thwarted desires. By comparison, the artist and illustrator Maxwell Armfield, born in 1881 and thus considerably younger than the men listed above, is nonetheless marked by his training in an era in which Decadent art held sway, as can be seen in his early paintings of *femme fatales* such as Salome and Swinburne's Faustine. His adherence to art for art's sake, one of the key tenets of aestheticism borrowed by Decadent art and literature, set, as Grace Brockington shows, his illustrations for *The Ballet of the Nations* at variance with Lee's text and her stated belief in art for life's – not art's – sake.

Lee claimed to be repelled by Decadent formulations and to disapprove of their unwholesomeness and lack of moral health. Stefano Evangelista neatly demonstrates that in the 'Valedictory' to *Renaissance Fancies and Studies* (1895) – where, a year after Pater's death, Lee considers his literary career and achievements – she in many ways can be seen to remake him in her own preferred image. Thus she esteems the late seemingly more austere Pater of *Plato and Platonism* over the Pater of *The Renaissance*, although she claims that he was always governed by 'an inborn affinity for refined wholesomeness' (1895, 258). As this somewhat wishful revisionism implies, Lee's own work, like the work of many fascinating writers, can be characterized by a tension between design and imagination. In the conclusion to her chapter Catherine Maxwell indicates that Lee intended her novel *Miss Brown* (1884) to attack the literary and artistic cult of Decadence but instead found herself arraigned for writing a book which many found morally repulsive. In spite of herself Lee seemed to be attracted to topics which were less than 'healthy'. Her early essay on 'The Elizabethan Dramatists' in *Euphorion* (1884), which Catherine Wiley analyzes so astutely, shows Lee replicating an attraction she describes as both glamorous and morally dubious. If Elizabethan writers invent Italy as a place of exotic evil onto which they project their fantasies of alluring decadence, then the 'unbridled writing' that Lee exhibits in this extraordinarily intense essay seems to participate in this fantasy, allowing her to unleash and to discharge her own powerful emotions. As Wiley points out, in her 'Valedictory' of 1895 Lee reflects on her writing of this earlier essay: 'the second discovery of the Renaissance by Englishmen has spiritual consequences so similar to those of the first, that ... I analyzed the feeling of the Elizabethan playwrights towards Italian things in order to vent the intense discomfort of spirit which I shared with students older and more competent than myself' (1895, 248). Here Lee seems to identify the nineteenth-century rediscovery of the Renaissance as a site of enquiry which is, in itself, potentially dangerous and decadent, a threat that she then asserts has since abated with the cultivation of a cooler, more disinterested (dispassionate) scholarship. However, when commenting on that previous 'discomfort', she says: 'This kind of feeling has passed away among writers along with much of the fascination of the Renaissance' (1895, 248), the wistfulness aroused by the mention of loss makes it hard to believe that she would like to see the Renaissance diminished in its fascination. Indeed, that 'unwholesome' fascination shines out in Lee's own tales of Renaissance Italy such as 'A Wedding Chest', or the tale of Domenico Neroni narrated in 'A Seeker of Pagan Perfection', or the ghost story told variously by Boccaccio, Dryden and Byron, and which Lee purports to translate from an old document in 'Ravenna and Her Ghosts'.[11] All of these stories are marked by a chilling brutality and violence which is all the more disturbing for being related in a detached documentary matter-of-fact manner.

Moreover, Lee's feeling towards what she more generally called 'Italian things' also partakes of the Decadent spirit. Three of the supernatural tales in *Hauntings* (1890) are set in Italy, and in these stories sensitive male narrators explain how the present is violently invaded by the Italian past. Two of these stories have feminine revenants: Medea da Carpi is an enigmatic and fascinating spectre of the Renaissance in 'Amour Dure', while the pagan cult of Venus-Aphrodite is revived in the eponymous and exotic Dionea. In 'A Wicked Voice' the spectre is feminized rather than feminine in the form of Zaffirino, an eighteenth-century Venetian castrato singer, whose decadent strains aggressively ravish the consciousness of the young composer who narrates this tale. Dennis Denisoff in his chapter on Lee's tale 'Oke of Okehurst', the only story from *Hauntings* which is not set in Italy, notes that the identity of the English manor-house owned by the Okes does not reflect contemporary British values but derives from the preservation of distinctly Italian qualities from the past. In his chapter Denisoff identifies two kinds of Decadence in Lee's tale: 'a more traditional manifestation of Decadence, which she genders feminine and characterizes by historical sensitivity and empathy' and a negative 'particularly aggressive, masculine Decadence marked by an obsession with a productivist ethos.' Alice Oke, the mysterious lady of the house who claims to see ghosts, is associated with this first feminine form of Decadence while William, her husband, and the painter who narrates the tale are associated with the second.

Empathy with Italy and her past is also displayed by the young hero of Lee's later fantastic tale 'Prince Alberic and the Snake Lady'. Lee told Maurice Baring that she had Massa Carrara in mind when she invented the Duchy of Luna which figures in this tale, and the idyllic country scenes clearly reflect an idealized Italian pastoral. In her chapter Margaret Stetz suggests that this tale of forbidden love and cruel imprisonment published in 1896 in the Decadent journal the *Yellow Book*, after the trial and indictment of Oscar Wilde for sodomy the previous year, reflects Lee's sympathy for Wilde's plight. What makes this particularly convincing is Lee's use of a lush Decadent style which distinctly echoes that used by Wilde himself in his own fairy stories.[12] (Stetz also detects other elements of Wilde's social comedy entering into some of Lee's earlier texts of the 1890s such as the infamous 'Lady Tal', the story which cost her what was a valued friendship with Henry James.) Stetz's suggestion that Lee takes up Wilde's Decadent aesthetic style in 1896 implies that it occurred just after the point in 'Valedictory' where, as Stefano Evangelista observes, Lee 'makes it clear that for her, in 1895, the aesthetic critic has nothing left to write.' Lee wrote her acknowledgments to *Renaissance Fancies and Studies* in April 1895, a month before Wilde was indicted. Did the subsequent events of that year make her consider her position so that she as a lover of her own sex took up her pen to write a fiction in the best aesthetic and Decadent manner?

Lee's sexual identity may also motivate the action of her detective novel *Louis Norbert* (1914), another exercise in what Denisoff, in his chapter, calls 'transhistorical empathy', in which two contemporary protagonists investigate the past of two young lovers from seventeenth-century Italy. In her chapter Patricia Pulham argues that this complex tale of thwarted heterosexual passion has a homosexual subtext with this desire expressed through the portrait of the mysterious and hauntingly beautiful Louis Norbert. She shows that this novel, which depicts the breaking of codes as the latter-day lovers struggle to reconstruct the cryptic exchanges between Norbert and his secret love, Artemisia, may also encode Lee's feelings for other women but in no simple or reductive way. Like so many of Lee's leading protagonists, Norbert apparently suffers a violent end, murdered at Pisa. Desire, it seems in Lee, is always a risky business, all too often bringing death and destruction in its wake.

The empathic relations between the two sets of lovers in *Louis Norbert* highlight the permeability of boundaries – historical, sexual, and national – that characterizes Lee's oeuvre: a phenomenon that is perhaps more clearly understood by examining Lee's focus on 'empathy' throughout her career. Lee is credited with having introduced the concept of 'empathy' (translated from the German *Einfühlung*) into British aestheticism and she returns to the subject in a number of her works. In *Beauty and Ugliness, and Other Studies in Psychological Aesthetics* (1912) she outlines the German origins of the word and defines it for the British reader:

> This word, made up of *fühlen*, to feel, and *ein* (*herein, hinein*), *in, into*, conjugated (*sich einfühlen*) with the pronoun denoting the reflective mode – this word *Einfühlung* has existed in German aesthetics ever since Vischer and Lotze ... . *Sich einfühlen, to transport oneself into something in feeling* (the German reflective form as a sense of activity which to *feel* does not give ... *sich einfühlen into something*, or *into someone*, has in ordinary German the meaning of *putting oneself in the place of someone, of imagining, of experiencing, the feelings of someone or something:* it is the beginning of sympathy, but in this primary stage the attention is directed entirely into the feeling which one attributes to the other, and not at all to the imitation of that recognised or supposed feeling which is the act of sympathising (German *mitfühlen*). (1912, 46)

This theory of 'empathy', or 'feeling into' as she later terms it, underpins Lee's experiments in psychological aesthetics which she understands as a form of 'aesthetic Empathy' (Introduction to Anstruther-Thomson 1924, 73). Yet this idea of 'feeling into' something, or someone, might also account for Lee's relationship with the past (particularly in her fantastic tales), for that exquisite sense of place that defines her travel writing, for the suggestiveness of her art criticism, for her pacifist rejection of a partisan position during World War One, for her conscious or unconscious literary interaction with male writers such as her brother Eugene, Walter Pater, John Addington Symonds, Oscar Wilde, and Henry James, and even, perhaps, for that conflict between design and imagination which we referred to earlier.

In her discussion of the artistic bond between Lee and Eugene Lee-Hamilton, Catherine Maxwell defines the empathic relationship between brother and sister as one of mutual influence feeding their aesthetic productions. In doing so, she identifies a communion in which the source of intellectual power becomes increasingly indistinct. While Eugene, as the older sibling, clearly influences Lee's education, their subsequent congress and similarity of interests suggest a two-way flow of ideas and concerns that, as Maxwell observes, the critic Horace Gregory understands as a form of spiritual synthesis when he asks 'Did she become possessed by him? Or he by her?' (Gregory 1954, 17). Maxwell offers examples of such 'possession' in the resonance between the subject matter of Eugene's poetry and Lee's fantastic tales. Yet it is clear from this collection that at least one of Lee's non-fiction works is also echoed in Lee-Hamilton's sonnet on Baudelaire published in *Sonnets of the Wingless Hours* (1894). Quoting from *Juvenilia*, Dennis Denisoff refers to Lee's description of a north-eastern skyline of 'innumerable chimneys faint upon the thick brown sky, faintly reddened with an invisible sun' and of the Tyne River fed by 'foul little streams, vague nameless oozes, choking with their blackness, staining with their deadly purple and copper colour and green and white' (1887, 13–14): images that mirror the aestheticized Parisian townscape in Lee-Hamilton's sonnet. Maxwell contends that the siblings' work is marked by a tension between morality and immorality, and, according to Denisoff, Lee's attempts to resolve this conflict were informed by her socialist ethics resulting in those two models of Decadence – feminine and masculine – mentioned above.

The critic Lois Agnew suggests that such ethics also entered Lee's 'appreciation for subjective criticism' which, she argues, 'co-exists with a social conscience that leads her to insist that artistic appreciation is ultimately an ethical act' (Agnew 1999, 134). Lee's empathic response, her 'feeling into' the social climate of discontent, marks an increasing concern with 'ethical' or 'moral' art – a concern which, as we have seen, informs her revision and 're-formation' of Pater, and erupts in her severe condemnation of aestheticism and its followers in

Miss Brown. Such criticism, as Laurel Brake asserts, seems somewhat unexpected from one acknowledged as Pater's devotee, and from someone whose empathic response to him figures in her art-historical writings and in her fiction where their kindred interests in alternative sexualities, expressed through art, place, and time are made manifest in a kind of intellectual osmosis similar to that which Lee had already experienced with her brother Eugene.

Lee's ethical stance is pursued in *Miss Brown* through the character of her eponymous heroine, Anne Brown, who sacrifices herself in marriage to the decadent aesthete Walter Hamlin thus hoping to saving him from further transgression. For Lee's early biographer, Peter Gunn, Anne Brown (herself, like Lee, an outsider in the society that adopts her) is a 'lay-figure for Vernon Lee to clothe with her own emotional, moral and sociological preoccupations and prejudices' (Gunn 1964, 101–2). It is hard to argue against this view and, in fact, one might go further and suggest that, in a sense, Lee 'marries' aestheticism in order to 'reform' it, to reshape its moral framework. The 'failure' of this enterprise was brought painfully home to Lee in the reaction to *Miss Brown*. On its publication the novel received mixed reviews. Most were politely favourable, some critical. Among the latter was a review by Lee's friend, W. C. Monkhouse who, while acknowledging its merits found her *roman à clef* with its thinly disguised characters 'needlessly painful and unpleasant' and the book as a whole 'very nasty' (quoted in Colby 2003, 104; quoted in Gunn 1964, 102). As Laurel Brake shows, several of Lee's other acquaintances were equally disturbed: Pater delayed his verdict for some weeks, Henry James (her dedicatee) took months to respond, and Lee's former contact W. J. Stillman, incensed by Lee's satirical representation of his wife in *Miss Brown*, penned a review of *Euphorion* (published in the same year) in which he pronounced Lee's work immoral.[13]

In his tardy assessment of the novel, Henry James makes a similar point, though couched in kinder terms. In a letter dated 10 May 1885, James located the 'imperfection' of the book in 'a certain ferocity'. He accuses Lee of taking 'the aesthetic business too seriously, too tragically, and above all with too great an implication of sexual motives' and tells her 'your hand has been violent, the touch of life is lighter … perhaps you have been too much in a moral passion!' (James 1980, III. 86). It is ironic that Lee's 'moral passion' elicits an effect which is diametrically opposed to its intention. Wiley's identification of 'unbridled writing' in Lee's essay on 'The Elizabethan Dramatists' in *Euphorion* finds its emotional corollary in the 'unbridled (im)morality' of *Miss Brown*. 1884, the year in which both these works were published, seems to signal a spiritual crisis in Lee that is never fully resolved. What James identifies as her 'violent' hand finds its way continually into her fiction, into her criticism, and especially into her 'war-play', *The Ballet of the Nations* (1915). Grace Brockington's perceptive discussion demonstrates the problematic nature of the conflict between art and ethics, a conflict that is figured in Lee's resistance to Armfield's illustrations. *The Ballet*, subtitled 'A Present-Day Morality', employs the allegorical framework of the mediaeval morality play. However, as Gill Plain elsewhere has observed, it is a 'play' complicated by its liminal status, a 'drama-as-text' whose 'production is an impossible one' (Plain 2000, 12), absorbed as it is into the longer companion piece *Satan the Waster* (1920), written five years later, where it is framed by a long introduction and copious notes. In her chapter Brockington highlights the violence in *The Ballet*. The smallest nation is pounded into a mat, while the other countries attack each other in an orgy of blood, dismemberment, and savaged flesh.[14] From the introduction to *Satan the Waster* we learn Lee's rationale for including such violent scenes. She writes:

> A European war was going on which, from my point of view, was all about nothing at all; gigantically cruel, but at the same time needless and senseless like some ghastly 'Grand Guignol' performance. It could, as it seemed to me, have been planned and staged only by the legendary Power of Evil; and the remembrance of mediæval masques naturally added the familiar figure, fiddling and leering as in Holbein's woodcuts, of a Ballet Master Death. (1920, vii)

For Lee, the unbearable horrors of war can only be borne if viewed as a performance with ethical implications. Similarly disturbing imagery infiltrates Lee's journalistic work at this time, and Brockington notes that 'The image of society as a body corrupted by Satanic possession recurs in Lee's non-fiction writing about the war'. The use of 'possession' in this context suggests a warped form of 'empathy' and it is clear from Lee's introduction to *Satan the Waster* (1920), that her own understanding of 'empathy', and its close relation 'sympathy', required reiteration in the aftermath of World War One:

> As regards intensification and enlargement of sympathy, that has doubtless taken place towards those fighting on one's own side; but it is more than counter-balanced by the addition of anger and

vindictiveness on one's own, and the utter inability to recognize the bare human nature of those to whom one's sufferings are attributed. Thus the women of every belligerent nation seemed to forget that there were mothers, wives and sisters on the enemy side; much as the air-raided Londoners crying for reprisals on the 'Baby-killers' forgot that there were babies in Rhineland towns and that Allied bombs must surely kill some of them. (1920, xix)

It seems that Lee's acknowledgement of the dangers of selective empathy and sympathy results in a contradiction that Plain attempts to resolve in her reading of *Satan the Waster* in which *The Ballet of the Nations*, despite its origins in a humanist and inclusive empathy, is presented, Plain observes, in a style resembling that of Bertolt Brecht's epic theatre and that, like Brecht, Lee employs an alienation strategy which 'discourages empathy and facilitates the recognition of otherness, enabling people to gain a new perspective and recognize their manipulation by the puppet masters of war' (Plain 2000, 14).[15] Consequently, she argues, it appears that 'Lee's philosophy ... exists in a dialectical opposition to the concept of empathy', a shift that appears paradoxical in the writer known for introducing this concept into British aesthetics (Plain 2000, 15). By way of explanation, Plain asserts that this tells us something 'about what was considered appropriate for a woman writer' in a period 'when women were still fundamentally associated with emotion and set in opposition to the public world of (supposed) rationality and political affairs' and that it is 'the very "appropriateness" of the association of the woman writer with empathy that prevents commentators from noticing that although she [Lee] may have mobilized the concept, it is a notion completely alien to her literary practice' (Plain 2000, 15).

As anyone with knowledge of Lee will know, she could not, despite her name, be described as a 'shrinking violet' who hugged 'empathy' close to her bosom in the hope of writing acceptable prose, nor was it her reluctance to enter into public debate that led Max Beerbohm to write on the fly-leaf of his copy of *Gospels of Anarchy* (1908):

'Oh dear! Poor dear dreadful little lady! Always having a crow to pick, ever so coyly, with Nietzsche, or a wee lance to break with Mr. Carlyle, or a sweet but sharp little warning to whisper in the ear of Mr. H. G. Wells, or Strindberg or Darwin or D'Annunzio! What a dreadful little bore and busybody! How artfully at this moment she must be button-holing Einstein! And Signor Croce – and Mr James Joyce! (Quoted in Gunn 1964, 3)

If anything characterizes Vernon Lee, it is her fearlessness in the face of controversy and her insistence on the validity of her opinions. This self-assurance is exemplified by both *The Ballet of the Nations* and, more particularly, by *Satan the Waster*. It is possible that, rather than abandoning 'empathy' as Plain implies, Lee chose to 'feel out of' rather than 'feel into' the sentiments of individual countries in order to indulge that wider perspective that was hers in her role as 'outsider'. She indicates that this is the case in the passage that follows her reevaluation of empathy in the introduction to *Satan the Waster* in which she writes:

> And now let me come to the things which, to my belief, my not *being in* has allowed me to see. Chief among these are the circumstances and feelings by which certain facts concerning the war, or rather concerning all the belligerents engaged in it, were hidden or disguised from the recognition of those who, unlike myself, *were in*. (1920, xix)

Clearly, by 'not *being in*' she feels that she sees and understands so much more. Nor is the concept of 'empathy' entirely missing from *The Ballet* despite the 'alienation effect' that is seemingly adopted as a dramatic strategy. As Lee declares:

> The thesis summed up in my allegory and brought home to me by the war's prodigious waste of human virtue, is that the world needs rather than such altruism as is expressed in self-sacrifice, a different kind of altruism which is the recognition of the other (for *alter* is Latin for *other*), sides, aspects, possibilities and requirements of things and people. (Introduction 1920, xlvii)

Vernon Lee's words seem prophetic. Our own twenty-first century recognition of 'otherness' is marked by an implicit empathy – a 'feeling into' the history, rights, and culture of other peoples. In *Satan the Waster*, Lee is not rejecting empathy per se, but the unthinking and selective response that feels empathy only with its own side. Similarly, despite Plain's claim that empathy was 'a notion completely alien to her literary practice', a claim easily refuted by any serious reader of Lee's work, Christa Zorn deftly illustrates that it was a concept central to her literary criticism. *The Handling of Words and Other Studies in*

Literary Psychology (1923) brought together essays written over a thirty-year period which cover the aesthetics of writing and the psychological relationship between writer and reader. Anticipating close-reading methods expounded in I. A. Richards's *Principles of Literary Criticism* (1926) and *Practical Criticism* (1929), and foreshadowing Roland Barthes's consideration of 'author-function', *The Handling of Words* has been unfairly neglected. In her introduction to this volume, Lee writes:

> the efficacy of all writing depends not more on the Writer than on the Reader, without whose active response, whose output of experience, feeling and imagination, the living phenomenon, the only reality, of Literary Art cannot take place. This fundamental fact of literary psychology, indeed of all psychological aesthetics, appears to me both so all-important and so universally neglected that I am quite content that the make-up of this volume out of disconnected essays and lectures, should have resulted in the repetition thereof half a hundred times and in its exhibition from half a dozen angles. (1923, vii–viii)

In her chapter, Zorn studies Lee's engagement with 'empathy' in a literary context. For Zorn, *The Handling of Words* illustrates 'Lee's behavioural study of reading', her investigation of 'the sensory aspect of the reading process, tracing a writer's style and linguistic patterns as symptoms of mental habits which may or may not harmonize with those of the reader'. For Lee, this treatise represents an attempt to explain 'the phenomenon of a creature being apparently invaded from within the personality of another creature' (1923, 22). Here, we once again find an implicit reference to that 'empathy' which constitutes a 'feeling into' or 'possession' of someone or something; in this instance the invasion of the reader's subjectivity by that of the writer. Such a phenomenon brings a whole new meaning to the sense of 'absorption' one feels when reading a good book, and reinforces the transgression of boundaries that marks Lee's own work. Zorn reads Lee's literary criticism as a form of 'spiritualism', a desire to recover from the space between reader and writer, those 'unseen' energies that reconstitute the writer through the reader's response. It appears that the 'transhistorical empathy' which informs so much of her fiction finds its echo in her literary criticism. Lee's desire to experience the past is translated in *The Handling of Words* into a desire to experience past writers.

However, as so much of Lee's fiction makes clear, the past and the dead can possess, and overwhelm the present, and such recovery always carries its own risks. It is perhaps this fear of 'possession' that led Virginia Woolf to dismiss Lee as a 'garrulous baby'. In the trampling of Baby Belgium featured in *The Ballet of the Nations*, Lee perhaps unwittingly foretold her own future at the hands of modernist forces. Yet it is important to remember that in a literary career that began in 1880 and ended in 1932, many of Lee's works prefigured and contributed to the artistic, philosophical, and psychological concerns of modernism. The essays brought together in the present volume serve as a timely reminder of a writer who valued her 'outsiderism' and whose works transcend the calcified categories of 'Victorian' and 'Modernist' periodization.

Notes

1 An interesting partial approach to this subject is Caballero 1992.

2 In her editor's note on this line (note 3, p. 127), Valerie Eliot writes, 'The critics of the Renaissance, the source of Fresca's "culture", are satirically linked together as aesthetics' [*sic*].

3 Letter 495 to Violet Dickinson, early July 1909, in Woolf 1975, I. 400.

4 Anne Meyer herself had been involved in other triangles as her husband reportedly had brought mistresses into the conjugal home, and 'forced his wife to consort with his "beastly" Russian friends' (Vicinus 2004, 154).

5 The word 'troilism' is defined as 'sexual activity in which three persons take part.' OED 2nd edn (Oxford: Clarendon Press, 1989).

6 Vernon Lee to Clementina Anstruther-Thomson, Vernon Lee Collection, Colby College, Waterville, Maine.

7 See Thirlwell 2003, 248.

8 Entry; 'Charleton Aug 28 1887', Commonplace Book; New Series III–XIV 1887–1900, edited 1920, Vernon Lee Collection, Colby College, Waterville, Maine.

9 Further exceptions might be the tutelary presences of the novelists Mrs Cornelia Turner and Mrs Henrietta Jenkin whom Lee met when she was an adolescent and aspiring writer.

10 *National Observer* of 6 April 1896, quoted in R. K. R. Thornton 1983, 67.

11 'A Wedding Chest' was first published in *Pope Jacynth and Other Fantastic Tales* (1904). First published in the *Contemporary Review* in 1891 as 'Pictor Sacrilegus: A. D. 1493; Life of Domenico Neroni', 'A Seeker of Pagan Perfection' was subsequently collected in *Renaissance Fancies and Studies* (1895). 'Ravenna and Her Ghosts, appeared first in *Macmillan's Magazine* (1894), and then was collected in *Limbo and Other Essays to which is now added 'Ariadne in Mantua'* (1908).

12 Lee would again use this full-bodied sensuous style in her story about Don Juan, 'The Virgin of the Seven Daggers', first published in periodical form in 1909 and reprinted in *For Maurice* (1927), which is a distinctly picaresque, amoral and decidedly Decadent fantastic tale about the legendary seducer.

13 Stillman's wife, Marie Spartali, recognized herself in the character of the Greek society hostess, Mrs. Argiropoulo, in *Miss Brown*.

14   See Lee's Notes to the *Ballet* in *Satan the Waster* (1920) in which she directly identifies the smallest nation with Belgium: 'Small buffer-states like Belgium can indeed, alas, be subjected to the worst of war's horror's without any such choice ... They keep out of war until war comes to them' (1920, 247).

15   Vineta Colby also notes that Lee's *The Ballet of the Nations* 'anticipated the revolutionary developments in the theatre of the 1920s like expression-ism, the use of film and recorded music for dramatic effects, and the combination of dance and dialogue' (Colby 2003, 305).

1
Vernon Lee and Eugene Lee-Hamilton

Catherine Maxwell

Both Eugene Lee-Hamilton and his half-sister Vernon Lee were drawn to images of disinterment and discovery. In one of his earlier sonnets 'Sunken Gold', Lee-Hamilton pictures submerged treasure – 'In dim green depths rot ingot-laden ships' – a treasure which he compares, as he frequently does, with his own gifts and hopes wasted by the illness which afflicted him from 1873 to 1893 when he began his recovery:

> So lie the wasted gifts, the long-lost hopes,
>   Beneath the now hushed surface of myself,
> In lonelier depths than where the diver gropes.
>   They lie deep, deep; but I at times behold
> In doubtful glimpses, on some reefy shelf,
>   The gleam of irrecoverable gold.
>
> (Lee-Hamilton 1884, 131; 2002, 123)[1]

MacDonald P. Jackson's excellent new edition *Selected Poems of Eugene Lee-Hamilton (1845–1907)*, published in 2002, is appropriately timely in its subtitle *A Victorian Craftsman Rediscovered*. At this moment when many scholars are busy unearthing and rediscovering the life and work of Vernon Lee, it also seems right to fathom the strange biography and the long-neglected work of Lee-Hamilton, to recover the poetic wealth of a writer skilled in his handling of the dramatic monologue and the sonnet form, and to excavate something of the private history which informs so many of his poems. In this chapter I offer a brief overview of the complex personal and creative relationship which existed between Eugene Lee-Hamilton and Vernon Lee. In his Introduction to Lee-Hamilton's poems, Professor Jackson has written that 'material for many of Lee-Hamilton's macabre poems was furnished him by Vernon Lee' (Introduction in Lee-Hamilton 2002, 27), but I would want to suggest that the influence is reciprocal, with Lee taking as much from Eugene as she gave him, particularly in her early years. This early debt is immediately signalled in her borrowing part of his name for what was supposed to be a *nom de plume*, but which in fact became the name by which she preferred to be known.[2]

Eugene Lee-Hamilton was seven when his father died in 1852 and his mother, a woman of independent means, subsequently married his tutor, Henry Paget in 1855. Violet Paget, the future Vernon Lee, was born a year later when Eugene was eleven. The redoubtable Matilda Paget had a habit of sidelining her husbands once they had provided her with children, and Henry quickly disappeared into the background and a life of outdoor pursuits, occasionally surprising visitors who were not always aware of his continuing existence. At first, Eugene was the apple of his mother's eye while the young Violet was entrusted to a succession of governesses, but as her daughter began to show her precocious talents, Matilda took more of an interest, although she maintained an unusually close-knit relationship with her son. However, as he grew older and attended Oxford and then entered the Diplomatic service, Eugene took upon himself a tutorial role, bossily giving advice to Matilda about Violet's education. A series of pedagogical letters sent from Paris, where he was attached to the British Embassy, direct his sister's reading and the formation of her taste.[3] After a brief Diplomatic career, Eugene was forced to retire in 1873 due to ill health, and the Paget family, who, up till then had travelled extensively throughout Europe, settled in Florence, eventually buying 'Il Palmerino', the villa at nearby Maiano where Vernon Lee would live the rest of her life. The nature of Eugene's illness was obscure, and was later diagnosed by the famous physician Jean-Martin Charcot in the language of the day as 'cerebral-spinal neurasthenia', though more recently Jackson has suggested Chronic Fatigue Syndrome; in any case it certainly had a large psychosomatic element, allowing Eugene to remain unseparated from his beloved mother. This is not to diminish the debilitating nature of his illness which kept him bed-bound for twenty years. During this time, when his health permitted, he enjoyed conversation with the many intellectual and literary figures who visited the house, dictated his poems, and was taken out for carriage rides on his wheeled bed.

Eugene's illness made him the focus of the family, his mother and sister tending to his every need and organizing the household around him. When he was well enough, Lee spent hours reading to him or taking down his poems for him. In 1874 she writes to the novelist and family friend Mrs Jenkin: 'I am employed on Eugène's article, copying out and doing the fill up work for him, as he is too ill to apply himself much to anything' (29 September 1874; 1937, 40). This enforced intimacy with a personality as demanding as Eugene's and the sense of being her brother's agent and proxy must have made it difficult for the young girl not to feel encroached upon or subsumed by him. Vineta Colby, Lee's most recent biographer, cites a letter she wrote to Kit Anstruther-Thomson (24 June 1902): 'I remember when I was young the extraordinary feeling of being squeezed out like a lemon by the mere fact of sitting constantly in the same room and under the eye of my brother' (Colby 2003, 147). As the younger sibling, she felt overwhelmed, drained by his surveillance, and certainly in terms both of pedagogy and simple autocratic demands, he continued to exert a considerable influence on her. Horace Gregory, the editor of a collection of her short stories, writes:

> there can be no doubt that he upheld for her, by demanding that she read to him aloud, the standards of Walter Pater's aesthetics, an admiration for Pater's essays on the Renaissance, that he transfused to her a hatred of war, a distrust of many things which were German and yet reserved for her an appreciation of Winckelmann and Goethe.

> (Gregory 1954, 17)

In later life Lee would declare to Irene Cooper Willis that she felt detached from other people: 'I *am* hard. I *am* cold ... I *cannot* like, or love, at the expense of having my skin rubbed off' (Colby 2003, 150). Such a statement, belied by her intimate and deeply-felt relationships with Mary Robinson and Kit Anstruther-Thomson, seems to be a defensive reaction, perhaps stemming from that time when she felt the borders of her self were all too easily breached by Eugene. But she also may have absorbed – again perhaps as a combative form of self-protection or as a defensive measure – something of her brother's demanding temperament or what Maurice Baring called his 'robust egoism'.[4] Although one should now be wary of Burdett Gardner's 1954 unsympathetic and rather crude neo-Freudian study of Lee's work, his claim that Lee had 'a compulsive masculine super-ego, adopted from Eugene in her childhood' does have a certain ring of truth to it, suggesting that Lee took from her brother more than just part of his name

(Gardner 1954, 316). Gregory makes an allied observation when, commenting on the closely merged identity of the siblings, he asks:

> Did she become possessed by him? Or he by her? Neither can be proved – except that as a writer she was the stronger of the two; she visibly outgrew him and lived to write fiction in which the forces of divine good and satanic evil act out their drama, in which the themes of dual personality and demonic possession are the main-springs of action.

(Gregory 1954, 17)

Gregory's characterization of Lee's fiction aside, readers often note that all the narrators in Lee's *Hauntings* (1890), her first and most important collection of supernatural tales are male. While this ploy allows her to distance and thus intensify and make more enigmatic the spectral femininity that teases, allures and eludes these men, it also intimates that Lee felt confident about masculine impersonation. Notably two of her narrators, Magnus in 'A Wicked Voice' and Spiridion Trepka in 'Amour Dure' are romantic, impressionable, hypersensitive young men, prone to nerves, morbidity, and imaginative reverie. It could be that Lee is exploring something of her own character in these men, but it seems likely that she may also have been drawing on her brother's personality which she had had plenty of opportunity to observe. If, by such acts of reflection Lee internalized, contained, and then transcended Eugene's ego, then, as Gregory says, she helped herself outgrow him. Certainly as the youthful Violet Paget matured into adulthood, her personality became increasingly dominant and the balance of power began to shift. While she took considerable pains during her annual summer trips to England to promote Eugene's work and secure publication for him, she was a forthright critic of his poetry, candidly praising or blaming as she saw fit, as in a letter of 29 June 1882 concerning the proposed contents of his collection *The New Medusa*, where she tells him baldly: 'The *Elegy*, fine in parts, completely lacks interest, & there is a great air of pedantry about it. It seems to me a thousand pities to put it in, as the philosophical ideas are now too commonplace to be interesting' (1937, 94). In October 1888, she commented on Eugene's newly published *Imaginary Sonnets*: 'I like them *immensely* although I don't care for sonnets as such; and the only thing that worries me in the book is that too much is crammed into it, so it leaves a confused impression & the recollection of one sonnet is likely be intruded on by the presence of another' (15 October 1888; 1937, 292).

Also noteworthy is the way she takes it upon herself to suggest appropriate subjects for her brother's poems. Eugene, restricted by his illness to a very limited sphere, had little opportunity to seek out new sights for inspiration. His sister, with a feeling for what might interest him, seems to have kept a look-out for suitable subjects. In a letter written to her mother from Paris on Saturday 23 June 1883 she writes:

I saw at the Louvre a very beautiful & singular thing, which I recommend to Eugène as a possible sonnet subject. It is a torso, half draped, of a Venus, found on the seashore at a place in Africa called Tripoli Vecchio – somewhere near Carthage, I presume. It has evidently been rolled for years & years in the surf, for it is all worn away, every line & curve softened, so it looks exquisitely soft and strange & creamy, hand, breasts & drapery all indicated clearly but washed by the sea into something soft, vague & lovely (1937, 117).

Obviously inspired by his sister's suggestion, Eugene quickly produced a fine sonnet, published the following year in his *Apollo and Marsyas, and Other Poems* (1884). Titled 'On a Surf-Rolled Torso of Venus, Found at Tripoli Vecchio, and Now in the Louvre', the sonnet, which shows Eugene's own strong imaginative characterization, is nonetheless in its sestet still clearly indebted to Lee's description:

ONE day in the world's youth, long, long ago,
　　Before the golden hair of Time grew grey,
　　The bright warm sea, scarce stirred by the dolphins' play,
Was swept by sudden music soft and low;
And rippling, as 'neath kisses, parted slow,
　　And gave a new and dripping goddess birth,
　　Who brought transcendent loveliness on earth,
With limbs more pure than sunset-tinted snow.
And lo, that self-same sea has now upthrown
　　A mutilated Venus, rolled and rolled
For ages by the surf, and that has grown
　　More soft, more chaste, more lovely than of old,
With every line made vague, so that the stone
Seems seen as through a veil which ages hold.

(Lee-Hamilton 1884, 133)

However, in the manner of the smoothing action of the sea he had described, Eugene continued over time to smooth and polish the poem, producing another version which he included in *Sonnets of the Wingless Hours* of 1894, now titled 'On a Surf-Rolled Torso of Venus. Discovered at Tripoli Vecchio':

> ONE day, in the world's youth, long, long ago,
>   Before the golden hair of Time grew gray,
>   The bright warm sea, scarce stirred by dolphins' play,
> Was swept by sudden music strange and low;
>
> And rippling with the kisses Zephyrs blow,
>   Gave forth a dripping goddess, whose strong sway
>   All earth, all air, all wave, was to obey,
> Throned on a shell more rosy than dawn's glow.
>
> And, lo, that self-same sea has now upthrown
>   A mutilated Venus, roll'd and roll'd
> For centuries in surf, and who has grown
>
> More soft, more chaste, more lovely than of old,
>   With every line made vague, so that the stone
> Seems seen as through a veil which Ages hold.

(Lee-Hamilton 1894, 44)

This slightly more sophisticated version notably omits the title reference to the torso's location in the Louvre, which the invalid Eugene could not have visited in his own right, and thus somewhat diminishes the ostensible debt to his sister's firsthand account. Apart from details such as smoothing out the rhythm by removing the superfluous 'the' in line 3, or changing 'soft' (one of Lee's words) to the more magical 'strange' in line 4, Eugene strengthens the portrait of the goddess Venus by evoking in lines 5–8 images from Botticelli's *The Birth of Venus* (*c.* 1485–6) in the Uffizi Gallery, Florence – a well-known picture he could easily have seen in reproduction or viewed before his illness. Part of the work of refinement was to stamp Eugene's own poetic personality more firmly on the poem.

Eugene's use and evocation of his sister's prose inevitably calls to mind Wllliam Wordsworth's use of his sister Dorothy's Journal, the difference being that in this instance Lee quite deliberately chose to describe a specific subject expressly for her brother's use. That she was so readily able to identify and describe a subject that would appeal to him and that he could easily develop indicates the degree of creative sympathy that existed between them. While I have not been able to find another instance of Eugene's poetic recasting of his sister's words, her letters record other examples of her seeking out materials that might furnish him with opportunities for composition. For example, she dispatches a book on 'Mediæval Myth' with the hope that 'E. may find something in it' (15 July 1886), sends him a cutting about the sinking of the *Victoria* – 'wonderfully magnificent & tragic' (29 June 1893) – and while staying in Wimbledon with Margaret Brooke, the Ranee of Saràwak, notes (9 September 1893) that her friend 'is type-writing a lot of Borneo superstitions & legends for Eugene: I thought they might interest him' (1937, 222, 348, 366). For his benefit she also relates a 'picturesque' anecdote about a confession of atrocious deeds made by a respectable man fearing shipwreck, produces 'another ballad subject for him' (Catalina de Arrazo's plight in the Morisco revolt of 1569), and suggests he writes a play for Lady Archibald Campbell: 'something antique but fantastic & spectacular. What of Orpheus?'[5]

However, the relationship was obviously complex and stirred up conflicting feelings. In 1883 (the same year as her letter about the Louvre torso), Lee published *Ottilie, An Eighteenth-Century Idyll* in which the heroine devotes her life to her selfish half-brother who throws up a career in the university. Putting his needs and desires before her own, she is forced to sacrifice her own opportunities for happiness. While it would be unfair and reductive to see more than a superficial likeness between the novel and Lee's domestic situation – Lee was not the saintly type and also enjoyed plenty of opportunity to pursue her own interests – it is hard to dispel the feeling that the story does seem to be coloured by some resentment. There is no doubt that Eugene could be imperious and petulant, taxing Lee for what seemed to him a reluctance to promote his work as energetically as she might do. Writing home to her mother in 1881 during a summer spent in England, Lee complains about his inability to understand her relatively limited powers: 'Eugène cannot be expected to understand how entirely London literary society is merely a thing shewn to me through a grating' (9 July 1881; 1937, 74). She tries to explain, for example, that she feels herself unable to introduce his name 'in the midst of an (at the utmost) twenty minutes of conversation on platitudes with a shy or supercilious man like Gosse, or Watts', and she attempts to communicate the competitiveness of the literary marketplace, noting 'the appaling [*sic*] number of poets, and what is worse, very fairly good ones about here' (9 July 1881, 12 July 1881; 1937, 74, 76).

In spite of these irritations Lee nonetheless continued to be influenced by her brother's ideas. Her first collection of philosophical dialogues *Baldwin* (1886) is dedicated to him: 'To my brother Eugene Lee-Hamilton, I dedicate this book of views and aspirations, grateful for all he has done in forming my own.' Peter Gunn, like other commentators, identifies the character of Baldwin with Lee herself, but his observation that 'Her thought at this time owed much to her half-brother, Eugene', hints that Baldwin may also be determined by Lee-Hamilton (Gunn 1964, 112). If this is the case, it is interesting that by the time Lee published her second set of dialogues in *Althea* in 1894, the character of Baldwin is given a comparatively minor role to that of Althea, who, it has been suggested, is modelled on Lee's companion and intimate friend Kit Anstruther-Thomson to whom she dedicated the volume. As Lee began to gain her reputation as a writer and to assert her independence, she began to distance herself from her brother. Certainly towards the end of their shared life she despaired of having to be responsible for Eugene – 'Good Lord, I shall always have him on my hands, I fear', she complained to Kit in a letter of 1895, a year before Eugene made his full recovery.[6]

Matters had not been helped by Eugene's earlier intervention in Lee's romantic relationship with the poet Mary Robinson which ran into difficulties when Mary suddenly announced her engagement to the disabled scholar James Darmesteter, Professor at the Collège de France. Lee, egged on by her brother, opposed the marriage on eugenicist grounds, stipulating that it should only take place if the couple resolved to abstain from physical relations. Looking at the evidence it is hard not to think that Eugene was attracted to Mary himself. Certainly with Mary spending her autumns in Florence with the Pagets from 1880 onwards, the three young people had enjoyed an intense relationship. In Mary's later recollection of her Florentine vacations, 'In Casa Paget', produced in commemoration of Eugene after his death in 1907, she writes: 'We were so young, Violet and I – more than a dozen years younger than Eugène – that we had mixed so little with life, that he fell naturally enough into the position of our guide, philosopher and friend' (Duclaux 1907, 936).[7] Mary was close enough to Eugene to suggest corrections to his poems; in July 1884 Lee records her friend reading and marking up a piece by him: 'Some things, she says, really can't pass in it; but she admires it very much as a whole. I will send a list of lines for correction' (23 July 1884; 1937, 157). Eugene dedicated *The New Medusa* (1882) to her and a poem in this collection entitled 'A Letter to Miss A. Mary F. Robinson', which details the picturesque delights of Tuscany, reminds her of a promise 'to return and spend/A while with us ere Tuscan leaves be sere', and ends with the recollection 'I told you once that you were like a ray/Of sunshine' (Lee-Hamilton 1882, 98–102). A poem in *Apollo and Marsyas* (1884), 'An Ode to the Travelling Thunder', carries the bracketed explanation 'Suggested by a line in the magnificent description of Miss A. Mary F. Robinson's "Janet Fisher"' (Lee-Hamilton 1884, 114–17).

I would suggest that when Eugene learnt the news of the engagement, he deeply resented her attachment to another man, particularly one who, like himself, suffered physical disability. His interference seems to have made a difficult situation worse and helped compound his sister's intense emotional and mental distress. Again the boundaries had become uncomfortably blurred. It is noticeable that Eugene seemed to latch on to his sister's close women friends in one way or another as a matter of course. Kit Anstruther-Thomson, who had a gift for nursing invalids, was instrumental in helping him recover his health. Moreover, it seems that during her absences from home, absences which naturally relieved her from having to care for her brother, Lee, as her letters show, was often on the look-out for suitable young women to take on the job of being Eugene's secretary, a role she had herself played in earlier days. The names of various women friends are suggested as possible contenders for this role: Amy Levy (2 October 1888), Clementina Black (9 October 1890), Dorothy Blomfield (7 March 1891), Mabel Price (15 August 1893).[8]

Eugene finally recovered his health after the death of his mother in 1896 and subsequently married the novelist Annie Holdsworth in 1898. Lee thought it a good idea for him to marry but, believing him to have a weak constitution, advised him against having children, which seems forgivable in the light of his own former views on the matter. Eugene did in fact produce a daughter, Persis, whom he adored, but who died before her second birthday. Lee's biographers have made much of the fact that, in a bitter letter written shortly after the child's death, Eugene berated his sister for her lack of affection towards the child and have given the impression that this incident caused a lasting rift between the two.[9] But this is far from the truth. A few days after his outburst, Eugene wrote again in response to a letter from his sister stating that 'There is no resentment, nor could be across the Baby's grave', and concluding with the words 'Don't stay away from the house. The pain is buried with the hope; and now I only remember our love for one another.'[10] While Lee would later admit to Maurice Baring that she found it hard to feel anxious about her brother's failing health when he succumbed to Bright's disease (Colby 2003, 149), further letters in the Colby College Archive show that she continued to see and correspond affectionately with him and his wife and to offer him financial assistance, and after Eugene died in September 1907, she generously helped his widow while his financial affairs were being settled by paying the costs of the funeral and offering to pay any arrears left by her brother.

Lee and her brother thus experienced a long-lasting relationship which had its pains and frustrations as well as its strengths and loyalties. It is fascinating to see how similar they were in many ways both as writers and personalities, and to note how certain themes, ideas and images frequently recur in their work and in their lives. We could start with an early letter, written by Vernon Lee to her mother from Paris in July 1870, which tells how she and Eugene visit Mrs Jenkin the novelist, a family friend, and fall into a conversation about singing which causes both young people a certain amount of embarrassment and anxiety. Lee relates the experience as a comic dialogue, referring on occasion to Eugene by his pet name – 'Bruder':

> Mrs. J. "At St. Roch one sometimes hears the most extraordinary voices! You know that Pius IX has forbidden women to sing at churches here. I heard a man there once, I declare I could not believe his voice came from a man's mouth." *Eugène.* "A woman's voice?" *Mrs. J.* "Yes, the most wonderfully high one too. He stood up and I saw him quite well. He had a beard so he was a *real* man, he couldn't be ..." *Bruder and I* (shaking nervously and getting most uncomfortable) "Oh yes, yes."
>
> Mrs. J. (perfectly naïve and heedless of the interruption) ... "he couldn't be a woman dressed up." *Bruder* (most miserable wishing the man, his beard, and his voice at Jericho) "No."
>
> (28 July 1870; 1937, 12)

Lee goes on to relate how Mrs Jenkin is only made to abandon what she and Eugene obviously regard as an unfortunate conversational topic by a request to play the piano 'little guessing in the simplicity of her soul, that we desired the playing more as a negative than a positive, i. e. to keep her quiet' (1937, 12).

What interests me about this scene is the immediate compact between the savvy fourteen-year-old Lee and her twenty-five-year-old brother. Both are sophisticated enough to recognize a reason why the male vocalist might sing like a woman; both instinctively dread hearing that reason spoken aloud. Such is their anxiety that they still wish to drop the subject even when it becomes clear that their initial suspicions are groundless and that the bearded singer must (presumably) be a counter-tenor. Underneath the ostensible conversation is another one in which brother and sister conspire to change the subject, tacitly acknowledging that their shared superior knowledge is a source of discomfort to them, yet retrospectively, from Lee's point of view anyway, enjoying the comedy of their friend's naïveté, a comedy which is shared with their mother who becomes the knowing reader. The incident, of course, has a fictional parallel in Lee's wonderful tale 'A Wicked Voice', from *Hauntings*, in which the young Norwegian composer Magnus is terrorized by the shade of the eighteenth-century singer Zaffirino. The whole story takes place without Lee's narrator once indicating that the reason for Zaffirino's extraordinary androgynous voice is his castration. The word 'castrato' is never mentioned and the sophisticated reader is supposed to deduce it from the resonant descriptions of the timbre of Zaffirino's voice and from the engraving of his 'wicked woman's face' (1890, 207). When Magnus sings his parody of eighteenth-century music at the beginning of the story, he notes how 'the only thing which remains distinct before my eyes [is] the portrait of Zaffirino, on the edge of that boarding house piano; the sensual, effeminate face, with its wicked, cynical smile, keeps appearing and disappearing as the print wavers about in the draught that makes the candles smoke and gutter' (1890, 207).

This 'appearing and disappearing' of the evidence as it is waved, perhaps somewhat flirtatiously, before the reader, later seems to become a principle for Lee's understanding of the supernatural. Three years after the publication of *Hauntings*, Eugene writes his sister a letter in which he warmly praises her story 'Dionea'.[11] However, he adds some criticisms, noting that 'in your method of telling through allusion you are often bewildering and half your readers won't understand you.'[12] Eugene's delay in responding to her collection was due to his poor health which, at its worst, had prevented him from reading on his own, and Lee takes this into account in her reply:

> As regards obscurity in the narrative, I think that if you read it three months hence that would not strike you; for you will regain a habit of twigging suggestions and of easily following tortuosities of narrative which is the habit of consecutive reading. You will then, I think, agree with me that such a story requires to appear & reappear

& disappear, to be baffling, in order to acquire its supernatural quality. You see there is not real story; once assert the identity of Dionea with Venus, once show her clearly, & no charm remains.

(31 August 1893; 1937, 363)

Definition here is the enemy of the supernatural. Like the fact of Zaffirino's castration, the identity of Dionea with Venus, once made plain, would diminish the power of the story. Lee had explored this in more detail in a fine early essay on the supernatural, 'Faustus and Helena', in which she explains that ghostly effects are only brought about by suggestion and not embodiment: 'paint us that vagueness, mould into shape that darkness, modulate into chords that silence – tell us the character and history of those vague beings ... . What do we obtain? A picture, a piece of music, a story; but the ghost is gone' (1881, 94).[13] In the letter she writes to Eugene, we can also see Lee confidently reversing the dynamic of the tutorial relationship she had with her brother who had called her by the pet name of 'Baby' and directed her youthful reading. In this letter Lee reminds her brother about how one reads.

In fact, Eugene, unused as he may have been to reading independently, was already quite aware of the principle of appearance followed by disappearance as a principle of the supernatural as can be seen in two of his most striking dramatic monologues, 'The New Medusa' and 'The Mandolin'. In the first of these poems, which is set in the seventeenth century, the male speaker begins to be troubled by suspicions about the mysterious young woman whom he has rescued from the sea and has thereafter become his lover. After many wanderings, the couple take up temporary residence in an isolated ruined castle, and the speaker tells how, lying beside his partner at night, he twice dreams he is being strangled by snakes and wakes to find himself tangled in her hair. Brooding on this incident and on his lover's strange origins, he wonders if she might be a Medusa but tries to banish the thought from his mind. A month later, lying awake, he hears his lover's breathing quicken as she starts to murmur in her sleep:

> Methought she lay not well,
> I stretched my hand to slightly raise her head;
> But what my hand encountered was, O hell!
> No locks of silky hair: it met instead
> A something cold which whipt around my wrist
> Unholdable, and through my fingers fled.

I groped again and felt two others twist
    About my arm; – a score of vipers twined
    Beneath my hand, and, as I touched them, hissed.
There is a horror which leaves free the mind
    But glues the tongue. Without a word I slipt
    From out the bed, and struck a light behind
Its ample curtain; then, unheard, I crept
    Close up and let the light's faint radiance hover
    Over the Gorgon's features as she slept.
The snakes were gone. But long I bent me over
    Her placid face with searching, sickened glance,
    Like one who in deep waters would discover
A corpse, and can see nothing save, perchance,
    The landscape's fair reflected shapes, which keep
    Balking the vision with their endless dance.
It seemed to me that in that placid sleep,
    Beneath that splendid surface lay concealed
    Unutterable horror sunken deep.
And, seeking not to have the whole revealed,
    I fled that fatal room without a sound,
    And sought the breeze of night with brain that reeled.

            (Lee-Hamilton 1882, 21–2; 2002, 50–1)

Unhinged by the experience he takes off and roams around outside on the rocky sea-shore losing all track of time and taking no rest or refreshment. When he finally returns to the bedroom, perhaps after a gap of several days, he convinces himself that he sees clearly for the first time the writhing serpentine hair of his lover, and he decapitates her while she sleeps, only to find that when he holds up her severed head the snakes have disappeared:

I held the dripping trophy by the hair,
    Which now no more was snakes, but long black locks,
    And scanned the features with a haggard stare.
And, like to one around whose spirit flocks
    Too great a crowd of thoughts for thought to act,
    I fled once more along the moonlit rocks.
Then Doubt, with his tormentors, came and racked.

            (Lee-Hamilton 1882, 27–8; 2002, 55)

In 'The Mandolin', set at the very end of the sixteenth century, an ambitious Roman cardinal wishes to marry off his pretty niece to a wealthy Duke. She however falls in love with a skilful but low-born mandolin player whom the cardinal subsequently has murdered. She curses her uncle before starving herself to death, and thereupon, the cardinal finds that whenever he tries to sleep he is haunted by the sound of a mandolin.

> But he, the cause of all,
> I know not how, has risen from the dead,
> And takes my life by stealing sleep away.
>   No sooner do I fall
> Asleep each night, than, creeping light of tread
> Beneath my window, he begins to play.
>   How well I know his touch! It takes my life
>   Less quickly but more surely than the knife.
>
>   Now 'tis a rapid burst
> Of high and brilliant melody, which ceases
> As soon as it has waked me with a leap.
>   And now a sound, at first
> As faint as a gnat's humming, which increases
> And creeps between the folded thoughts of sleep,
>   Tickling the brain, and keeping in suspense
>   Through night's long hours the o'er-excited sense.
>
>   (Lee-Hamilton 1882, 93–4; 2002, 85)

Maddened by sleep deprivation, the Cardinal still believes he may be elected Pope but his monologue ends as he is apparently smothered by his attendants. Both 'The New Medusa' and 'The Mandolin' – a poem Lee thought 'the strongest ... in the book' (29 June 1882; 1937, 94) – depend on an intermittent appearance and disappearance for their supposed supernatural effects, effects which seem, as in Lee's stories, to have strong psychological determinants. Indeed, 'The Mandolin', with its theme of phantasmal music seems an evident influence on Lee's 'A Wicked Voice' in which Magnus is menaced by Zaffirino's singing in revenge for abusive remarks made about eighteenth-century music. Notably this motif of a phantasmal musical revenge does not come into Lee's earlier version of this story, 'A Culture-Ghost: or, Winthrop's Adventure', published the year before Eugene's poem in 1881.[14] More-

over, when Magnus in 'A Wicked Voice' hears the music, it is introduced on one occasion by 'little, sharp, metallic, detached notes, like
those of a mandoline' and on another again by 'chords, metallic sharp,
rather like the tone of a mandoline' (1890, 210, 232). As the development of these ghostly sequences makes clear, Zaffirino, like Rinaldi in
'Winthrop's Adventure', accompanies his singing on a harpsichord,
but, by first evoking a mandolin Lee seems to go out of her way to
show the echoes of her brother's poem. The Cardinal's description of
the fatal effects of the mandolin music – 'How well I know his touch!
It takes my life/Less quickly, but more surely, than the knife' – is also
powerfully revised by Lee into the image of music as a vicious, perhaps
castrating, knife-blow. At the end of 'A Wicked Voice' Magnus hears
the voice 'swelling, swelling, rending asunder that downy veil which
wrapped it, leaping forth, clear, resplendent, like the sharp and glitter-
ing blade of a knife that seemed to enter deep into my breast'
(1890, 235).

To return to Lee's letter of 31 August 1893: immediately after her
remarks about suggestion in supernatural writing, she gives Eugene
an example. Let me repeat her initial remarks which are then given
literary illustration:

> As regards obscurity in the narrative, I think that if you read it three
> months hence that would not strike you; for you will regain a habit
> of twigging suggestions and of easily following tortuosities of nar-
> rative which is the habit of consecutive reading. You will then,
> I think, agree with me that such a story requires to appear & dis-
> appear & reappear, to be baffling, in order to acquire its supernatural
> quality. You see there is not real story; once assert the identity of
> Dionea with Venus, once show her clearly, & no charm remains.
> The *Venus d'Ille* of Prosper Merimée (there are improper passages,
> so read it to yrself) by far the finest story of the *Dionea* sort, is quite
> as obscure and baffling, at least I think so in remembering it.
> (1937, 363)

A number of things are noteworthy about this response, the first being
that Lee instructs Eugene to read a text which he must surely already
have known well. What Eugene's biographer, Harvey T. Lyon, calls his
'Venus-worship' (Lyon 1955, 104) and his interest in the legends about
the goddess are apparent even in *Poems and Transcripts* (1878), his
earliest collection of verse, which contains two poems about statues
of Venus.[15] Eugene's preoccupation with the figure of Venus clearly

predates Lee's similar interest as expressed in her later stories such as 'Dionea' and 'St Eudæmon and his Orange-Tree'.[16] Secondly, in Lee's concern that Eugene read the story to himself rather than have it read to him by a female amanuensis, we again sense her anxiety about a potential impropriety. In the earlier episode with Mrs Jenkin it is Eugene's embarrassment which is paramount and it is he who takes the responsibility for changing the conversation, while here it is Lee who acts to contain impropriety, thus preventing an innocent party from possible corruption, and reminding us that, in the words of her biographer Peter Gunn: 'she had the strongest aversion (puritanic in its severity) to anything in the slightest indecorous' (Gunn 1964, 146) This prudishness, as we have seen, was shared by Eugene, who, as Lyon notes, 'could not read *Candide* because it was so revoltingly filthy, ... detested Swinburne, and ... thought Baudelaire a cad' (Lyon 1955, 185) yet both siblings produced work striking for its eroticism and violence.

Lee's tendency to play out in her creative work energies which she would not tolerate in her everyday persona is something she shared with her brother. Both writers also seem to have been inspired by what they claimed to loathe. Magnus in 'A Wicked Voice' is similarly repelled and attracted by the engraving of Zaffirino which reminds him of faces seen 'in my boyish romantic dreams, when I read Swinburne and Baudelaire, the faces of wicked, vindictive women' (1890, 206). Lee, in company with her brother, disapproved of Baudelaire and Swinburne,[17] yet as I have discussed elsewhere (Maxwell 1997, 253–9), her portraits of Zaffirino and other of her fatal women are clearly influenced by Swinburne's impressionistic descriptions; one obvious source being a lengthy passage in Swinburne's 1868 essay 'Notes on Designs of the Old Masters at Florence' where he describes Michelangelo's designs of a snake-like woman whom, in one instance, he calls 'the deadlier Venus incarnate'.[18] Part of this passage which describes in detail the woman's serpentine hair may well have had an impact on Eugene's 'The New Medusa'.

Vernon Lee's ambivalence about Swinburne is mirrored by her brother's sonnet on Baudelaire. Lee-Hamilton compares the poet to a Parisian gutter which holds effluvia and detritus, yet

> And everywhere, as glows the set of day,
> There floats upon the winding fetid mire
> The gorgeous iridescence of decay:

> A wavy film of colour, gold and fire,
> Trembles all through it as you pick your way,
> And streaks of purple that are straight from Tyre.
>
> (Lee-Hamilton 1894, 102; 2002, 179)

This description of squalor, then redemptively transformed into an impression of beauty, is classically Baudelairean, making its writer seem far more sympathetic to Baudelaire than one might at first have thought; indeed, throughout the sonnet, the speaker gives the impression he is fascinated by the composition (and decomposition) of the mire. In various of Lee's stories, such as 'Prince Alberic and the Snake Lady', 'A Wedding Chest' (1904, 1–111, 115–136), and 'Ravenna and her Ghosts' (1908, 157–203), we sense a pleasure in treating disconcerting detail in an aesthetic manner, so that, for example, brutal acts of violence are coolly and lucidly related as if they were simply elements of design in a larger artistic whole.

In the prefatory poem to his *The New Medusa, and Other Poems* ('Introduction'), Eugene showed that he was aware that his readers would find large portions of his material grotesque or macabre, but defended himself by claiming that this morbid material stems directly from the incarceration forced on him by his illness. His poems are 'prison work'; his tortured dramatis personae 'fantastic figures ... As with a rusty nail the captive scrapes/Upon his wall' (1882, 9). He announces defiantly

> But if some shape of horror makes you shrink,
> It is perchance some outline he has got
> From nightmare's magic lantern. Do you think
> He knows it not?

He concludes: 'The sentenced captive does not hide his mind;/He has no need' (Lee-Hamilton 1882, 9, 10). Such a public assertion did not stop John Addington Symonds from regretting that Eugene's subsequent verse collection *Apollo and Marsyas, and Other Poems* showed more of the darkness of Marsyas, the harrowed satyr-singer, than it did the brightness of Apollo, god of the sun and of song.[19] While Eugene Lee-Hamilton was canny enough to make his illness legitimate his poetic forays into the darker regions of human experience, Lee, who made it her business as a critic to find and celebrate 'healthy' forms of aestheticism, seemed far less able to recognize the 'morbid', sensational and decadent strain in her own writing. Aiming to expose vice 'and moralise the world' in her novel *Miss Brown* (1884), she was shocked to find herself attacked for writing an immoral book and wrote in her journal:

> I, who have written so many fine things about the complexity of our nature, the surprise at the deceptions to which these complexities subject us, the extreme difficulties of knowing one's self – am I not perhaps mistaking that call of the beast for the call of God; may there not, at the bottom of this seemingly scientific, philanthropic, idealizing, decidedly noble-looking nature of mine, lie something base, dangerous, disgraceful that is cozening me.
>
> (Colby 2003, 110)

Interestingly Lee's characterization of what she thinks are baser instincts or lower powers as 'the call of the beast' is the same characterization later employed by her narrator Magnus to describe the wicked voice 'begotten of the body, and which, instead of moving the soul, merely stirs up the dregs of our nature!' (1890, 198) In portraying Magnus's 'haunting', was Lee in some way half-acknowledging the inevitability of the shadow cast by her own unconscious? While as a critic she may have wanted to reject morbidity and decadence and embrace 'health', her own strong creative impulses appear not to have allowed her the easy separation of material such a categorization would imply. Indeed, it is clear that her work, like her brother's, depends on a powerfully mixed charge to achieve full expression. Her definition of 'health' is challenged by other elements in her writing which show that her unconscious refused such a hygienic and sanitized view of art. For her, as for her brother, her imaginative writing becomes a space wherein she can share with her readers the fantasies she found unspeakable in her ordinary life.

Notes

1   Where possible, I have given a second reference to *Selected Poems of Eugene Lee-Hamilton (1845–1907): A Victorian Craftsman Rediscovered*, ed. MacDonald P. Jackson, which, in some cases, uses other copy-texts for the poems I cite in this essay.

2   See Lee's letter to the novelist Mrs Jenkin of 6 April 1875: 'The name I have chosen as containing part of my brother's and my father's and my own initials is H. P. Vernon-Lee. It has the advantage of leaving it undecided

whether the writer be a man or a woman' (1937, 49). She would soon abandon her father's initials and use 'Vernon Lee' alone.

3 Now housed in the archive of Vernon Lee's Letters in the Miller Library, Colby College, Maine.

4 Maurice Baring, undated letter to Edmund Gosse (probably 1899 or 1900), in Letley, 1991, 49, cited in Colby 2003, 360, n. 10.

5 22 August 1886; 15 August 1887; 8 January 1889; 15 August 1887, in 1937, 235, 268, 304, 268.

6 VL to Kit Anstruther-Thomson, Letter of 6 August 1895, Colby College Archive.

7 Mary Robinson was widowed in 1894 and her second marriage to the scientist Emile Duclaux took place in 1901.

8 See Lee 1937, 292, 324, 345, 358.

9 See Gunn 163–4; Colby 149: 'Eugene never forgave his sister for her disapproval'.

10 ELH to VL, Letter of 7 October 1904, Colby College Archive.

11 For 'Dionea', see 1890, 61–103.

12 ELH to VL, Letter of 27 August 1893, Vernon Lee Archive, Colby College, Maine.

13 'Faustus and Helena: Notes on the Supernatural in Art', first published in *Cornhill Magazine* 42 (1880), 212–28, and then in *Belcaro: Being Essays on Sundry Aesthetical Questions* (1881), 70–105.

14 'A Culture-Ghost: or, Winthrop's Adventure', *Fraser's Magazine*, os 103, ns 23 (1881), 1–29, reprinted as 'Winthrop's Adventure', in *For Maurice: Five Unlikely Stories*, 141–205.

15 See 'The Song of the Plaster Cast' and 'Venus Unburied', in *Poems and Transcripts*, 87–98, 103–6.

16 For St Eudæmon and his Orange-Tree', see *Pope Jacynth and Other Fantastic Tales*, 171–91.

17 For Lee's disapproval of Baudelaire and Swinburne, see the views voiced by her Donna Maria in the dialogue 'Orpheus in Rome' in *Althea: A Second Book of Dialogues on Aspirations and Duties*, 84: 'take for instance Baudelaire's poems and many of Swinburne's: they are beautiful, but they appeal to things in us which are bad for our moral health.'

18 Algernon Charles Swinburne, 'Notes on Designs of the Old Masters at Florence', first published in the *Fortnightly Review* in July 1868 and then reprinted in *Essays and Studies*, 314–57; 320.

19 See John Addington Symonds's review in *The Academy* 27 (31 January 1885), 71, partly reprised in Symonds's introduction to a selection of Lee-Hamilton's poetry in *The Poets and the Poetry of the Nineteenth Century*, ed. Alfred H. Miles, 11 vols, 7: *Robert Bridges and Contemporary Poets*, 241–6.

2

Vernon Lee and the Pater Circle

Laurel Brake

Elle s'étendait à merveille avec Pater. Subtil et trenchant, son rare esprit avait de réelles affinitiés avec l'intelligence de votre célèbre voisin; ils étaient, l'un comme l'autre, speculatifs, dialecticiens, et pourtant épris du monde visible, artistes jusqu'au bout des ongles. Ils étaient devenus de véritables amis.

(Duclaux 1925, 344–5)

[She understood Pater completely. Subtle and sharp, her rare spirit had a genuine affinity with the intelligence of our celebrated neighbour: they were like one another, speculators, dialecticians, and nevertheless in love with the visible world, and artists to their fingertips. They became veritable friends.

(Seiler 1987, 67)]

When it appeared in June 1884, Vernon Lee's *Euphorion*, the first of her studies of the Renaissance, was dedicated to Walter Pater.[1] Preceding Henry James and following Mary Robinson, Pater is one of a succession of luminaries to whom Vernon Lee strategically dedicated her books in the 1880s, thereby anchoring and authenticating herself in English letters.[2] Her relationship with Pater and his circle is integral to an understanding of how she took her place in the English literary scene of her day. The present chapter has two parts: first, a trajectory of the biographical and literary relationship between Lee and Pater, and their London-based, shared 'set'. Located initially in Bloomsbury and then in Kensington at the Robinsons, it included her dedicatees Henry James and Mary Robinson while, with respect to the Lee-Pater nexus, its core comprised Walter Pater and his sisters Hester and Clara, the Humphry Wards, and Lee.[3] The second part of this study scrutinizes a moment in the history of this triangle when, remarkably, Mary Ward, Lee and Walter Pater all published first novels within four months of one another in 1884–5.

Lee's *Miss Brown*, Ward's *Miss Bretherton*, and Pater's *Marius the Epicurean* may be read as a cluster of novels on aspects of contemporary aestheticism and as a public dialogue among friends on issues that divided as well as united them. Each of these works provoked controversy at the time of its publication, and it is notable that each was deemed acceptable for bulk purchase by the circulating libraries. Moreover, the sensuality of two of them – *Miss Brown* and *Marius the Epicurean* – did not prevent highly respectable publishers such as Blackwood and Macmillan from including them on their lists.[4] I want to consider the novels as a group, and assess the effect of *Miss Brown's* harsh critique of aestheticism and marriage on her relationships with Ward and Pater. Lee regularly 'returns' to Pater in a series of written critiques largely of *Marius*, which grew increasingly hostile; Ward reviews *Marius* and Pater reviews Lee's *Juvenilia* (1887), and eventually Ward's edition of *Amiel's Journal* (1886) and her best-known novel *Robert Elsmere* (1888). None of these reviews is the anodyne 'puff' between friends that was common in the period.

Pater and Lee (i) Connection

Walter, Hester and Clara Pater seem to have been among Vernon Lee's earliest acquaintances on her first visit to Britain in the summer of 1881. The introduction was primarily through the Wards at whose Oxford house on Bradmore Road (on which the Paters also lived), Lee, Mary Robinson, the three Paters and the Wards dined together. By this point it is likely that Walter Pater already knew Mary Robinson, who had lodged with the Wards the previous summer when she attended a production of *Agammenon* early in June of 1880. By the autumn of that year Pater was reading Robinson's first volume of poems, *A Handful of Honeysuckle*, which he returned to Edmund Gosse in January 1881. Along with these men (Walter Pater, Humphry Ward, and Gosse), Mrs Humphry Ward, and others, Lee became part of a society that regularly gathered in Gower Street in London at the Robinsons, with whom Lee initially stayed as Mary Robinson's guest.

Vernon Lee's dialogue with Walter Pater began in her early work *Belcaro*,[5] written before she met him in 1881, and continues past his death in 1894, well into the twentieth century. In addition to the satirical pastiche of Pater and things Paterian in *Miss Brown*,

Lee comments explicitly on Pater's work on four further occasions: on *Marius* in *Juvenilia* (1887), in 'Valedictory' in *Renaissance Fancies and Studies* (1895), in 'Dionysus in the Euganean Hills: W. H. Pater in Memoriam' (1921), and lastly in the essay 'The Handling of Words: A Page of Walter Pater' (1933). Other quotations by Lee of Pater include her prominent and repeated usage of the word 'Studies' – in the title of her first book, *Studies of the Eighteenth Century in Italy* (1880), in the sub-title of *Euphorion* (*Studies of the Antique and Mediæval in the Renaissance*), and in the title of Lee's parallel collection of 'studies', the 1895 *Renaissance Fancies*. What is more, the binding of *Euphorion, Juvenilia*, and *Renaissance Fancies* closely resembles that of Pater's *Studies in the History of the Renaissance* and, as Vineta Colby argues, Lee also imitates the structure of Pater's 1873 *Studies* in *Euphorion* (Colby 2003, 67). Certainly for Lee, Pater's work remained a significant referent.

While Pater figures as one friend among many in Lee's long and well-documented life, her friendship with him and his sisters stands out in Pater's biography. In the very slender collection of Pater's extant letters, the Pater-Lee relationship remains among the best documented of his friendships, with six communications, some fulsome and descriptive, from Pater to Lee between March 1882 and December 1884. The unique loquaciousness of this correspondence is perhaps explained by his apology to her for his stylistic 'stiffness' in one of them, in comparison to her talent for the familiar style: 'I write so few letters! And this strikes me as a very stiff one, after yours' (Pater 1970, 52). These are supplemented by Lee's missives home, most of which can be found in the collection edited by Irene Cooper Willis (1937). This rare friendship of Pater with a woman is also singular in that it is documented at all. In the blurred map of Pater's personal relations, its suggestion of free intellectual exchange, of warmth, of acknowledged differences, and of parity between Pater and a woman scholar and writer, whose areas of research and writing were close to his own, is unique.

Although Walter Pater may have himself attended the Robinsons' salon before Lee arrived,[6] his link with the family and their circle was undoubtedly re-enforced by his friendship with Lee, who was Mary Robinson's close and romantic friend until the summer of 1887 when she learned of Mary's intentions to marry James Darmesteter. Lee eased Pater's passage into the wider circle at the Robinsons of which he and his sisters became part, first in Gower Street and after 1882 in Earl's Terrace.

In the 1880s, Mary's father and mother were renowned for their receptions or *tertullas*,[7] characterized by the poet William Sharp as 'a meeting-place for poets, novelists, dramatists, writers of all kinds, painters, sculptors, musicians, and all manner of folk, pilgrims from or to the only veritable Bohemia' (Sharp 1894, 801). Among the Robinsons' regulars in the early 1880s were Sharp, Philip Marston, the blind poet; Humphry and Mary Ward; Mary Robinson's sister Mabel, a novelist; Edmund Gosse, the critic; Edward Gurney, a journalist and psychical researcher, and Alma Tadema, the distinguished painter. Sharp met Pater there in 1881. Robinson's generous induction of Lee into English literary society in the summer of 1881 helpfully limns the parameters of Pater's acquaintances through this network.

The link between the Robinsons and Pater's introduction to Vernon Lee is the Wards. Humphry tutored at the same Oxford college as Pater, and Mary had worked with Clara Pater in the 1870s on the Association for Promoting the Higher Education of Women. Geography also facilitated the triangle of families (the Wards, Paters, and Robinsons) in which Lee moved in this early period in Britain. Until late 1881 the Wards lived opposite the Paters in Bradmore Road, in the new housing district of North Oxford for married Fellows. First, Mary Robinson lodged with the Wards in June 1880; then in July 1881 Mary and Mabel Robinson accompanied Lee to Oxford where they dined with the Wards, on which occasion Lee met the Paters, who duly invited the girls for dinner two days later. When the Wards moved to London in November 1881, it was to Russell Square, just around the corner from the Robinsons in Gower Street.

Lee's regular summer visits to Britain between 1881 and 1887, along with the Wards' friendship with the Robinsons reinforced the traffic among the three families, which was further increased in 1885 when the Paters moved to London. By 1883 the Robinson household had moved from Gower Street to Kensington, and when the Paters left Oxford for London in August 1885, it was to the same street as the Robinsons – Earl's Terrace, in Kensington – rather than to that of the Wards, their former Oxford neighbours.

In 1925 Mary Robinson, then known as Madame Duclaux, wrote a valuable memoir of Pater which is one of the fruits of the Pater-Lee friendship. It attests to cordial, and close neighbourly relations between the Robinsons and the Paters in Earl's Terrace, which included shared festivities at Christmas. In this memoir we find Pater's hair is ash blonde, his appearance that of ' "A military monk" ', his position that of a Platonist rather than an Epicurean and his famous ambivalence described as 'cette instabilité scrupuleuse' [scrupulous instability] (Duclaux 1925, 343, 344, 357, 354; Seiler 1987, 66, 67, 76, 74). These last two details in particular hint strongly at Pater's homosexuality.

While never as explicit about Pater's implication in homosexual culture as Duclaux, Lee's reiterated critique of Pater, from *Euphorion* onwards, also approvingly locates *Marius* as the launch of the better (but not perfect) turn from the aestheticism of *Studies*. It is part of her increasingly ideological reading of Pater, and her effort to disassociate him from the aestheticism she purports to despise by the time she publishes *Miss Brown*. In this respect, Lee's desire for the 'pure' Pater meshes with the efforts of those friends after his death who were most anxious to protect his reputation from the 'taint' of decadence and/or (homo)sexuality. Nevertheless, Lee's and Pater's joint investment in exploration of alternatives to heterosexuality, in life and literature, is probably what carried them through the rocky period of the publication of *Miss Brown*. If the Pater of the 1880s was dandified, then Lee exceeded the fashionable dress codes of the New Woman. Certainly, she was an exotic, with her short hair, and tailored, mannish clothes. Her undisguised distaste in the mid 1880s for the aesthetic dress of women is apparent to the point of disgust in *Miss Brown*.

Although Lee and Pater diverged in their decisions about how to negotiate the sexual prohibitions of their time, and their own sexual identities, they did share an interest in literary expression of the new sexualities. Dennis Denisoff draws a parallel between Lee's use of literary portraiture to represent same-sex friendship and love with Virginia Woolf's in *Orlando* (Denisoff 1999, 252), but one might equally cite the similarity in this respect of Lee and Pater. Lee's protagonist Anne Brown in her chaste sexlessness bears such a close resemblance to Pater's early portrait 'Diaphaneitè' (1864), unpublished during his lifetime but drawn on in 'Winckelmann' (1867), that Lee's heroine might be read in part as a female analogue to Diaphaneitè, Pater's idealized Hellenic type of the pure, transparent (and predominantly male) character.

By 1881 they also shared interest in Italian art and architecture, the Renaissance and aesthetics. Lee had published two papers on the Renaissance in 1879 in the *Contemporary Review*, and another in August 1880 on comparative aesthetics that Pater, as a reader of the reviews, was likely to have read. Given his interest in the art and architecture of Italy, both Renaissance and Antonine, it is unsurprising that Lee attests (1937, 78–9) on first meeting Pater that he had already read her *Studies of the Eighteenth Century in Italy* (1880), which had been published in

London and reviewed in the *Athenæum* and the *Spectator*. This catalogue of mutual interests goes some way to explain the shared intellectual ground between Pater and Lee and the longevity of the association, from 1881 until Pater's death. This personal match was reinforced by the common social circle – in Oxford and London – which shared a preoccupation with Italy.

From that July of 1881 a friendship between Lee and Pater formed, nurtured by regular summer visits, and letters and gifts in the intervals. Lee saw the Paters in the course of almost all of her trips to Britain, and stayed with them regularly in Oxford and London over a decade. These visits survived the publication on 22 November 1884 of *Miss Brown*, one of a steady stream of publications Lee sent Pater, after which extant letters from Pater to Lee cease. Yet, we know that she was with the Paters in London in June 1886 and August 1887 from *her* correspondence, that Pater obligingly reviewed *Juvenilia* in July 1887 for the *Pall Mall Gazette*, and that in August 1891 Lee writes to her mother of how 'exquisite' the Paters have been to her (Lee 1937, 338).

Pater and Lee (ii) Disruption?

The timing of the disappearance of the correspondence between Walter Pater and Lee after the appearance of *Miss Brown* does not seem accidental.[8] Lee's intemperate attack on the aestheticism with which – pre-*Marius* – Pater in 1884 was still clearly associated, combined with her voracious deployment of details of social and domestic aesthetic life culled from aesthetic paintings, poetry, and writing as well as the sitting rooms of her friends and acquaintances (including the Robinson tertullas), and the crude formal techniques of masking the originals of her *roman à clef* through transparent admixtures of names or initials, character traits, creative work, and physical features was guaranteed to offend almost everyone she knew in London.

In support of my contention that Pater took offence at *Miss Brown*, along with many of Lee's other London friends and acquaintances, I want to note the responses to the novel of others in the Robinson circle as well as outside it. We know from Lee herself that Mary Ward cold-shouldered her in June 1885 (Gunn 1964, 108 and Colby 2003, 107). We also have letters from a number of friends: Marie Stillman wrote reproaching her want of loyalty to her friends and lack of judgement, Henry James, the unfortunate dedicatee of the novel, wrote to friends immediately and Lee very belatedly expressing his alarm and distaste, and the Morrises were and remained incensed as did other members of the Pre-Raphaelite set, such as William Michael Rossetti and his wife (Colby 2003, 105–8; Gunn 1964, 102; Ormond 1970, 134–48).

We are also able to gauge Pater's reaction by the happy accident of two adjacent replies in the *Collected Letters* to his two friends, Lee and Ward, whose novels had appeared nearly simultaneously.[9] To Vernon Lee, Pater writes on 6 December 1884 a cool but evasive note in response to her prompting, and pads it out with an acknowledgement of receipt of her *brother's* book of poems: *Miss Brown* had 'arrived safely some days ago'; he has 'already read the greater part of it with much interest and amusement'; 'I send only brief thanks now in answer to your card of this morning.' He is far warmer about Eugene's poems: 'I lighted at once upon, and have read twice, a powerful ballad' (Pater 1970, 56). Pater's letter to Lee is in marked contrast to his enthusiastic responses in 1882 to receipt of *Belcaro*, sent in March and to a *Fraser's* offprint sent in November (Pater 1970, 42, 46–7). Moreover, when he publishes the review of *Juvenilia* in 1887, he omits *Miss Brown* from the list of Lee's achievements (Pater 1887, 5).

In comparison with Pater's appreciative letter to Ward nine days later, on receipt of a copy of *Miss Bretherton*, the letter to Lee appears tightlipped. He has promptly read Ward's novel 'with the greatest relish' 'for its literary finish, its dainty natural description, and the accomplished skill in the management of plot which seems to promise much for future work of a larger scope ... in quality it could scarcely be better.' It is 'a masterly sketch' and he 'hope[s] to read it over again soon' (Pater 1970, 57). Both in his willingness to engage in detailed comment on *Miss Bretherton* and to praise it with a succession of superlatives ending in his intention to reread it *soon*, Pater assures Mary Ward and ourselves of his pleasure in her 'sketch', while acknowledging its limitations. In his letter to Lee there is no such engagement with or pleasure in *Miss Brown*. Henry James also writes promptly to Ward at about this time, on 9 December, and in similar terms of engagement and pleasure (James 1980, III. 58–60). While Pater and James enact their approbation of Ward's book, by replying with promptitude, both men also act out their disapprobation of *Miss Brown* through belated acknowledgements to its author, Pater's delay being only a matter of weeks, but James' stretching into months.

Scholars such as Peter Gunn, Vineta Colby, and Christa Zorn have already noted and discussed adverse reactions by well-known figures such as Symonds and James to Lee's writing and judgment. I want to add another striking example to this catalogue, by way of arguing that, in concert with Lee's other friends, the dearth of extant correspondence between Pater and Lee after the publication of *Miss Brown* signals his and his sisters' similar disquiet. Walter Pater had been chary of his reputation since 1873, when the notoriety of *Studies*, published on 1 March, followed on closely after the fall of his friend and associate, the homosexual painter Simeon Solomon, arrested for 'buggery in a public place' on 11 February. Pater's own personal admonishment in the University in 1874 for his compromising love letters to the undergraduate William Money Hardinge (Inman 1991) may have made him feel particularly vulnerable at this time, in which he and his writing were again to be up for scrutiny in the public sphere. His first novel was in the press and due for publication just weeks after *Miss Brown*, while reviews of Lee's novel both linked his name with Lee's allegedly 'Paterian' views, *and* with the excesses of the aesthetes and Pre-Raphaelite Brotherhood whom she satirizes so recklessly. Pater and his sisters cannot have failed to notice that the name and initials of the principal male protagonist of Lee's *roman à clef*, Walter Hamlin, suggest Pater's own (W. H. Pater for Walter Horatio Pater), as does Lee's portrayal of Hamlin as a languid, distant, and dandified aesthete. That Hamlin is a painter/poet and heterosexual, and thus *unlike* Pater in other important characteristics, does not obliterate the damaging links, but rather resembles the hodgepodge of discordant elements Lee concocted for all her characters in *Miss Brown*, in order to confound alleged resemblances between them and real persons, most of them her acquaintances. Walter Hamlin, who is invariably named in the reviews, is described for example as 'such a wretched creature' in the *Athenæum* (6 December 1884, 730) and 'the wicked humanist ... who indulges not merely in aestheticism, improper speech [,] reading and writing, and Russian cousins but narcotics' in the *Pall Mall Gazette* (11 December 1884, 5).

Worst was the explicit link between Lee and Pater in the religiously-oriented, anti-aesthetic *Contemporary Review* piece in May 1885, which published in one article a signed review by Julia Wedgwood of all three novels.[10] Wedgwood effortlessly links an unfavourable notice of *Miss Brown* with a slightly less critical review of *Marius*: 'Vernon Lee and Mr Pater are kindred spirits, and their works follow without any change of key-note, while some of our remarks on the first novel [*Miss Brown*] apply to both.' Wedgwood's parallel transition to *Miss Bretherton* is by contrast a *juxtaposition* of Ward's novel to Lee's and Pater's. Wedgwood makes a clear attempt to distance Ward's novel from Lee's, and to identify *Miss Bretherton* as respectable, in tacit contrast to the other two: *Miss Bretherton* is a 'pleasant and popular novelette' which 'leads us to another region' (Wedgwood 1885, 751). ' "Miss Bretherton" is as free from the vigour as from the unpleasant qualities of "Miss Brown," and may be described as eminently a book to lie on the drawing-room table' (Wedgwood 1885, 751–2). This review flags up the unspoken charge against Lee's and Pater's novels, that they are precluded from the respectability denoted by the 'drawing-room table'.

The anonymous response of W. J. Stillman to *Miss Brown* in January 1885 is the angriest of the lot, its energetic vituperation of Lee's writing singling it out from its fellows.[11] It is perhaps the most naked testimony of the fury of the Pre-Raphaelite and Aesthetic sets at Vernon Lee's betrayal of the hospitality accorded her by these circles in the early 1880s. Based in London when Lee arrived, Mrs Stillman, a society hostess, welcomed Lee as a family friend of the Paget household in Italy. Her husband's sense of betrayal was profound, if disguised. His recourse appeared in the American weekly *Nation* in the guise of a review of the American edition of *Euphorion,* which distances it from other reviews of Lee's novel as well as from attribution by readers of the day, until 1888 when Stillman was outed in *Poole's Index to Periodical Literature*, the great nineteenth-century forerunner of all subsequent library indices and databases. Under these conditions, of anonymity and displacement onto another of Lee's titles, Stillman felt safe enough to vent his rage in the period in which the British reviews of the English edition of *Miss Brown* were appearing. As a sometime reviewer for the *Nation*, and as an art critic and journalist, he was in a position to request the review.[12]

Marie Stillman, née Marie Spartali (1844–1927), was a painter of repute closely implicated in Pre-Raphaelite circles, and a beauty who modelled for Burne-Jones and Ford Madox Brown. Greek by birth, she was widely understood to be one of the originals on whom Mrs. Argiropoulo, the ridiculed society hostess of Lee's novel, was based. By the date of her husband's review in January 1885, Marie, had already (on 27 December 1884) penned a robust letter to Lee about her tasteless ridicule of aesthetic friends in *Miss Brown*, promising Lee that 'you will one day regret this work' (Colby 2003, 106). Perhaps she already knew of her husband's piece on *Euphorion*, which begins with an ominous flourish: 'It is difficult to find any *raison d'être* for a book like "Euphorion," except the rashness of youth in rushing in to solve the most difficult problems of the philosophy of history and art, and of an opinionated and crudely informed youth at that' (Stillman 1885, 76).

Stillman's second paragraph continues at the same splenetic pitch, accusing Lee of 'enigmatical conclusions which she takes for profound truths, but of which the only remarkable quality generally is their utter absurdity'. Eventually the review is crowned with a bald charge of ignorance, 'especially in what is written of art'. This later expands into 'ignorance which is so complete that it is beyond instruction' and a propensity to 'to lay down rigorously the law of taste because it is absolutely devoid of the æsthetic sense' (Stillman 1885, 77).

But Stillman saves his harshest slur for last. He states that Vernon Lee's work is prurient and that as an author she breaches the limits of female modesty. He is perhaps the critic who most engages with the radicalism of her sexual exploration:

> The essay on "Mediæval Love" is one which can only excite wonder at the predilection of Vernon Lee, a woman and still young, for studies in a class of literature which is simply so filthy that most students of mediæval literature either leave it aside or do not admit that they have read it... . Vernon Lee knows little more about love, brave, healthy, and real passion, than she does of art (Stillman 1885, 77).

That this outstandingly aggressive review is provoked by the essays of *Euphorion* alone appears highly unlikely at this date, given the earlier letter of Marie Stillman to Lee, and the proximity of the review both to the publication date of the novel, and of its reviews, which were still appearing. That Stillman could vent his spleen on particular essays in the title under review helped disguise his identity, both as a family friend (whereby his attack on her is no worse than hers on his family) and as an outraged husband retaliating for an attack on his wife, neither of which postures would have improved his critical reputation. But Stillman's ire provides a glimpse of the emotion that Lee's novel elicited from those in her circle whose friendship had served the purposes of her pen.

Imaginary conversations: Lee, Pater, Ward

While these titles of the novels by Ward, Lee and Pater date from nearly a decade before the faltering of the three-volume system in 1894, their formats are already notably various, consisting of the one-volume Ward novel at 6s, the two-volume Pater at 21s, and the three-volume Lee at 25s/6d. This perception of these publications as a cluster was iterated in various forms in the press of the day. One journal noticed all three together, several treated Lee and Ward in tandem or comparatively, and others published individual reviews, with the weight, length or even inclusion of a review itself interpretable, as is illustrated by the *Athenæum*: on 6 December a prompt, serious, mixed review of *Miss Brown* appears, a fortnight after it was published. The featured novel in 'Novels of the Week' and an entire column long, the review occupied nearly a third of the whole. Now known to be written by editor Norman MacColl (Demoor 2000, 42), it aimed to be kind if critical to a young author, with whom the editor had recently dined. *Miss Bretherton*, fared notably worse: reviewed late, on 20 December, it had appeared only a week after *Miss Brown*. Dismissed briefly as hardly a novel, its celebrity tie-in with the American actress Mary Anderson[13] was deemed both vulgar and unoriginal. It also figured lower down in the column, fifth out of seven titles reviewed. When *Marius* appears in late February, it is fast-tracked by the *Athenæum* like *Miss Brown*: reviewed promptly (*on the day of its publication*), at length (over eight-columns), and relatively favourably, by an anonymous critic similarly acquainted with the author, who was in fact William Sharp (Sharp 1885). Moreover, the location of the review in 'Literature' is significantly more exalted than 'Novels of the Week', where Lee's and Ward's reviews appeared.

Each novel occupies a different market niche in its first edition: Lee's in three-volume format is expensive at 25*s*/6*d*, and likely to be read in a copy borrowed from a circulating library, as *Athenæum* adverts for it from Blackwood on 24 January and 7 March 1885 state: 'New Novels at all the Libraries.' *Miss Bretherton* is short and cheap by comparison, being published in a one-volume format, priced 6 shillings. As an affordable commodity, it is pushed hard by Macmillan before Christmas. In contrast, Blackwood's adverts for Lee's title in the *Athenæum* are infrequent in December, perhaps reflecting Blackwood's Scottish base. That Blackwood may routinely be advertising in Scotland is suggested by a quotation from a review of *Miss Brown* in the *Scotsman* included in the *Athenæum* advert for the novel on 10 January (*Athenæum* 10 January 85, 37). Miss Brown's Scottish parentage was finely calculated to appeal to the home market.[14]

Published in two volumes and having missed the Christmas market, *Marius* is cheaper than *Miss Brown,* and together with its greater gravitas, more likely to be purchased, but stocked by the libraries as well. It is prominently advertised by Macmillan in the *Athenæum* wrappers from 21 February when it is 'nearly ready', through 28 February, the date of its review when it receives second billing, until 4 and 11 April when, still with second billing, the listing is accompanied by quotations from reviews. So, of these three new novels, *Miss Brown* is by comparison least likely to be purchased because of its high price. But it may well have been read in the libraries. Unexpectedly, the cheapest of the three does not seem to have sold satisfactorily, and both Ward and her publisher did not deem *Miss Bretherton* a commercial success.[15]

Even if all three titles by Lee, Ward and Pater were safely in the libraries, the numbers of copies purchased by the libraries differed, in accordance with the estimated breadth of appeal to (and potential borrowing of) their readers and the respectability of the work. On these last two counts, the one-volume *roman à clef Miss Bretherton* scores highest, while both *Miss Brown* and *Marius* present potential problems: *Miss Brown* is full of dangers: its sensuality is so explicit that, to Vernon Lee's alarm, George Moore wished to quote passages from it in a polemical pamphlet to show the licence of extant Mudie stock,[16] while its attack on marriage and its portrait of an independent woman disgusted by heterosexual love might prove ideologically rather than morally objectionable to readers.

Reviewers also associated the 'disagreeable' elements of the novel with 'the realistic school' which 'depicts in true colours the ordinary forms of vice and sin, so as to intentionally disgust its readers' (Anon. *Graphic* 10 January 1885, 43).[17] The *Graphic*'s charge against *Miss Brown*, that the depiction of Sacha Elaguine, the cousin of the lead male character Walter Hamlin, and a sinister, apparently bisexual, seductress, is 'a study of morbid anatomy', had far more potential for damage with respect to a Library novel than to sales outside the libraries. However, even such a disapproving review of *Miss Brown* as the *Graphic*'s, which indicated its 'vice and sin', may have functioned similarly to the complaints in the unfavourable reviews of *The Mummer's Wife* advertised by the publisher Henry Vizetelly in the same pre-Christmas period (13 December 1884, 782), that is *to attract* readers who enjoy reading sexually charged material. (Vizetelly, a pioneer publisher of inexpensive books and magazines who was partly responsible for the demise of the costly three-decker novel, would be prosecuted for obscene libel in 1888–9. His publication of French naturalistic fiction and the associated realist and sexually explicit novels of the English writer George Moore gave his list a risqué allure.) It is altogether possible that *Miss Brown* was bought and/or read by prurient readers, who were *led* to the novel by the *Graphic*'s remarks on Sacha.

Marius raises different issues with respect to the violence in that novel, as well as similar ones. In a period when religion was taken very seriously, when believers included a high proportion of women, and when religious doubt and debate were largely appropriated to the male sphere, the address of *Marius the Epicurean* in fictional form to these questions might prove controversial in a reading audience that included high numbers of middle- and upper-class women. The classical setting of *Marius* made it equally alien to many women readers, even among the educated. Marius's (religious) quest involves extensive exposure to pagan alternatives, some of them violent and 'coarse', while the reiterated presence of male friendship and the absence of a convincing heterosexual courtship might occasion comment among those familiar with Pater's work, particularly those readers who viewed *Marius* as a 'reply' to the religious and sexual questions voiced when *Studies* was published. Mary Ward, in her review, writes from this position.

The three novels place quite different worlds at the centre of their narratives – *Miss Bretherton*, which is the most narrowly focussed, that of contemporary society drama; *Miss Brown*, contemporary Aesthetic and Decadent artistic circles, and *Marius*, Antonine, pre-Christian Rome, which serves to accommodate nineteenth-century religious debate. But the prominence of aesthetic questions unites them. In Ward's novel, Isobel Bretherton's exceptional physical beauty is juxtaposed with her allegedly modest talent as an actor. The debates around beauty dominate the first part of the novel, but dissipate markedly as the narrative rapidly shapes itself to a courtship-marriage denouement. The aesthetic elements in *Miss Brown* similarly present themselves most intensively in the first half of the novel, where the tenets of aesthetic painting and poetry, the morality of aesthetic artists, and the airs and fashions of aesthetic society are rendered preposterous, coarse, morally corrupt, and sexually explicit. If Ward and Lee both critique contemporary cultural life, then the most trenchant criticism of *Miss Bretherton* is directed at an undifferentiated group of philistines, the popular theatre-going audience, and the commercial theatre managers; the British social set at the heart of her novel – playwrights, journalists, and the stunner herself – are drawn with affection and tolerance, one of them constituting, along with the third person narrator, one of the two main narrative consciousnesses.

By contrast, a prominent consciousness of *Miss Brown* is Anne Brown, an *outsider*, who comes to aesthetic England from both a foreign country and a different social class. The vehemence of denunciation of aestheticism in *Miss Brown*, including aesthetic notions of beauty, distinguishes it sharply from the exploratory debate and limited action of *Miss Bretherton*, the shortness of which also serves to simplify the narrative. The larger canvas of *Miss Brown* results in the absorption of the social satire and intellectual critique of aestheticism that dominate the early part of the novel into an inner world, in which aesthetic issues are played out in the moralities of a Jamesian love triangle, with an important difference. While the enervated male aesthete and the decadent *femme fatale* echo James, making the second half of *Miss Brown* an alternative 'Portrait of a Lady', the female outsider is not 'American' in her morality. Rather, she is a new, independent woman with a Paterian take on 'the sex' debates. Anne Brown is not only implicated, like Isabel Archer in James's *Portrait of a Lady* (1881), in an unpalatable marriage with a corrupt, weak, aesthetic male, but Anne eventually re-endorses it in full knowledge of Hamlin's character and history.

At the same time, Lee provides a detailed account of an alternative to marriage, of what Anne envisages as 'that great bliss ... a life's solitude' (1884, III. 107). It is a radical, gendered vision outside (and precluding) marriage, for women who are not 'Masculine women' but 'true women ... but women without woman's instincts and wants, sexless – women made not for man but for humankind' (1884, II. 309).[18] Anne's version involves higher education (specifically anchored in contemporary Girton College, Cambridge, a byword for 'advanced' women), a career of learning and teaching, and a chaste, companionate life in political work, with her male cousin who is standing for Parliament.

Even in the actual ending of *Miss Brown*, the morally enforced marriage that appeared to many readers at the time as an unpalatable martyrdom, Lee produces a powerful critique of marriage through defamiliarizing it. This is truly a *grotesque* marriage. Many of the iterations of sensuality in the novel, which prompted reviewers to identify it with the realist school, are attached to (hetero)sexuality and/or marriage, among the poor as well as the aesthetes. Anne's renunciation of marriage as well as her eventual subjection to it both emanate from her position of austere chastity in contrast with an overdetermined sensuality.[19] *Miss Brown* is strikingly different from the romantic endorsement of marriage with which Mary Ward concludes *Miss Bretherton*.

Lee's identification of marriage and heterosexuality as elements of the novel she could not endorse in *Miss Brown* is unsurprisingly similar to Pater's deflection and extirpation of marriage in *Marius*, through his hero's early death, presaged by charged references to marriage throughout, such as the 'deadly bridal' of Psyche (Pater 1885, I. 68; 1910, II. 64). But in comparison to *Miss Brown,* the same-sex romantic friendship motif in Pater's novel figures far more prominently as a tacit alternative to marriage for its hero. Flavian and Cornelius are clearly among 'the [nameless] persons he had loved in life' (Pater 1885, II. 216; 1910, III. 223) whose memory Marius savours as he dies, and the 'fulsome' affection (Pater 1885, I. 223; 1910, II. 226) between tutor and pupil, Fronto and Marcus Aurelius, demonstrated in their correspondence, reminds the reader of the older Platonic model (Pater 1885, I. 221; 1910, II. 223–4). Pater habitually deploys circumstantial plot details to intimate homosocial readings of these relationships, such as that of Marius and Cornelius 'sleeping, for security, during the night, side by side with their keepers' (Pater 1885, II. 207; 1910, III. 212), and one of the most striking is the 'nuptial hymn' that Flavian dictates to Marius, a parting ceremony of mutual affection as Flavian is dying from the plague (Pater 1885, I. 114; 1910, II. 113). Pater's freedom and Lee's constraint are partly determined by setting, with the 'classical' world of *Marius* authorizing male friendship and the present of *Miss Brown* discouraging representation of analogous female relationships.

In a letter to Lee of July 1883, Pater explicitly links his aim in *Marius,* which he is writing at the time, to Lee's 'The Responsibilities of Unbelief' published in the *Contemporary* in May 1883, he will sketch 'a fourth sort of religious phase possible for the modern mind, over and above those presented in your late paper in the Contemporary' (Pater 1970, 52; cited Colby 2003, 65). Both *Miss Brown* and *Marius* are novels of education which conclude with glimpses of more perfect ways of life than their protagonists attain, and both novels offer description and analysis of a degree of 'corruption' in the 'present' of their respective periods which precedes a visionary future. The Aesthetic world in Lee's novel and the Pagan world in Pater's afford both writers an opportunity to air as well as judge corruption, which is doubly regretted in both novels for the betrayal of aesthetic form and beauty, by the particular corruptions alleged. Thus the purported beauty of nineteenth-century aestheticism and that of Flavian and the stoic world are betrayed by the corruption they harbour (Pater 1885, I. 57; 1910, II. 53). In its portrayal of corruption as well as art such as Lucian's *The Golden Ass, Marius* draws on the discourse of the supernatural like Lee, as well as on the sordid and macabre found in *Miss Brown* (Pater 1885, I. 62, 64; 1910, II. 58, 60).

Over and above Lee's reiterated criticism of Pater's style and position and her open acknowledgements of his talent and value is the palpable impact of Pater on her work. David Seed's assessment, that Pater was 'A crucial influence on the formation of Vernon Lee's thought' (Seed 1992, iii), is put in a different perspective by Gettmann ('Vernon Lee' 1968), who claims that Lee was the only disciple Pater ever acknowledged. Christa Zorn (1997) draws attention to another indebtedness or exchange between the two writers in 1886/7 with respect to a supernatural story Lee published in the January and February 1887 numbers of *Murray's Magazine*. Zorn reads 'Amour Dure: Passages from the Diary of Spiridion Trepka' as 'an animated version of Pater's portrayal of "la Gioconda" in *The Renaissance*' (Zorn 1997, 4).[20]

From a perusal of Lee's writing, it is fair comment to identify her work as under the influence of Pater's example, though 'disciple' may overstate Lee's active interrogation of Pater's positions and writing. Lee and Pater were friends and colleagues in the early 1880s, and in dialogue and contact long after that. Although they differed and even argued, as set out here, the number of their shared interests – in aesthetics, the Renaissance, Italy, (homo)sexuality, and the supernatural/unconscious – is persuasive in helping us believe that their relationship survived the rift of *Miss Brown* in some form. While Lee ceased to visit the Robinsons after Mary's marriage in 1888, the Paters, by then their neighbours, continued to enjoy the friendship begun at the *tertullas*, which Lee had facilitated. We know that Lee visited the Paters at that house in Earl's Terrace as late as 1891. It is a tribute to Lee's identity as a serious intellectual, engaged writer, formidable woman of letters, and impressive networker in the English literary world that she managed to maintain a longstanding relationship with Pater, as a fellow writer, in and beyond the Robinson circle.

Notes

1 *Euphorion* was the second book dedicated to Pater in 1884; William Sharp, the author of the first, *Earth's Voices, Transcriptions from Nature, Sospitra, and Other Poems*, was, like Lee, a member of the Robinson and Pater circles, and had met Pater at the Robinsons in 1881.

2 These pairings include *Belcaro* (1881) with Mary Robinson, *The Prince of the Hundred Soups* (1883) with the small daughters of W. J. Stillman, *Euphorion* (1884) with Pater, *Miss Brown* (1884) with Henry James, *Baldwin* (1886) with Eugene Lee-Hamilton, and *Juvenilia* (1887) with Carlo Placci.

3 From 1869 Walter Pater lived with his two sisters, Hester and Clara, first in Oxford and then from 1885 in London. In the 1870s Clara worked for higher education for women. One of the founders of Somerville College,

Oxford, she served there as tutor in classics and modern languages until 1894. See Online *DNB*.

4   Lee's firmness with Blackwood assured this, as four days after *Miss Brown* was accepted by Blackwood, a senior editor suggested that she change the ending, a request that she flatly refused, with the result that 'I have my hands free' (Letter 26 July 1884, cited in Colby 2003, 97). The raunchy element of *Miss Brown* is a useful reminder of how *unprudish* nineteenth-century publishers and circulating libraries could be, and the latitude in which discretion might be exercised. The other point here is the importance of commerce in the book trade: no doubt the racy nature of *Miss Brown* and the celebrity dimension of *Miss Bretherton* were part of Blackwood's, Macmillan's, and Harper and Bros's calculations for sales of these titles.

5   Lee was visiting Britain in the summer of 1881 to see *Belcaro* through the press. Its Introduction bears the date May 1881 and its Postscript that of 21 July 1881. Paterian elements of these 'Essays on Sundry Æsthetical Questions' are numerous. The structure of the work, like Pater's *Studies*, collects previously published pieces from the journals and adds a preface and a conclusion. One of the essays, 'The Child in the Vatican' seems explicitly to echo Pater's 'The Child in the House' which appeared in *Macmillan's Magazine* in August 1878, a view which Colby shares (2003, 10), while Lee's critique of Ruskin is from a Paterian position in Paterian cadences as its ending demonstrates: 'For though art has no moral meaning, it has a moral value; art is happiness, and to bestow happiness is to create good' (1881, 229).

6   Pater was appreciatively reading *A Handful of Honeysuckle* late in 1880 and returned it to Gosse (himself a guest at Gower Street) on 29 January 1881 (Pater 1970, 38), suggesting that Pater had visited the Robinsons before Vernon Lee's arrival in Britain.

7   As Colby explains (2003, 78), the Robinsons used this English adaptation of the Spanish word *tertulia* for their evening parties.

8   Colby disagrees. See Colby 2003, 65, 105.

9   According to adverts and listings in the *Athenæum*, they appeared on the 22 and 29 November 1884 respectively.

10 Wedgwood (1833–1913) was at this time the main reviewer for the Contemporary Records fiction slot for the *Contemporary*. She was a close friend of Emelia Gurney, a proponent of higher education for women, and an aunt of Edmund Gurney, a member of the Robinson set. A musician and psychic researcher, Edmund Gurney had, like Hamlin, educated a working class girl to be his wife. (See *ODNB* for Wedgwood and Edmund Gurney and Emelia Gurney; and Gunn 1964, 102.) As a result of this personal association with the Gurneys, Wedgwood may not have been well-disposed to *Miss Brown*.

11 William James Stillman (1828/9–1901), American artist, art critic, and foreign correspondent, was also part of the Robinson circle when in London, where he fed the London circle's involvement in Italian art, history and life. A frequent visitor to Italy, he served as the American Consul to Rome 1861–5, lived in Italy in 1877, and worked there as a journalist from 1878, becoming Special Correspondent to the *Times* for Italy

and Greece in 1886. Thanks to Dr Tom Tobin for help with locating Stillman sources.

12 Stillman reviewed Pater's *Studies in the History of the Renaissance* for the *Nation*, also anonymously, on 9 October 1873, 243–4. While intellectually robust, respectful, and selectively admiring, it is a disapproving and dissenting review.

13 Isabel Bretherton, Ward's heroine, is a foreign actress, read universally as based on an American newcomer to the contemporary English stage, Mary Anderson, whose beauty was said by some to excel her talent. A racy account of the fashionable London theatre world, and its philistine challenge to an intellectual aesthetic which occupies the first part of the novel gradually gives way to romance, enabled by a rapid education of the ignorant actress. Marriage results, from the added value of understanding of beauty. The germ of Henry James' *The Tragic Muse* (1889–90) is allegedly the same social occasion and performance as Ward's novel, which Ward and James attended together in 1884 (Horne 1995, xiv).

14 The *Scotsman* review of *Miss Brown* (26 December 1884) appears in the 'New Novels' rather than the 'Literature' department, but it receives top billing and is highly favourable (*Scotsman* 1884, 7).

15 According to John Sutherland the claim of a second edition in a 24 January advert (*Athenæum* 24 Jan 1885, 110) was a ploy by Macmillan to stimulate sales.

16 Lee indignantly refused Moore permission to include passages from *Miss Brown* in 'Literature at Nurse', privately published in 1885.

17 Thanks to Amanda Doran for information about this review.

18 *Miss Brown* here echoes ideas Pater developed between 1864 when he wrote 'Diaphaneitè' and 1867 when he published 'Winckelmann' anonymously in the *Westminster Review*, embedding portions of the unpublished 'Diaphaneitè' within it. 'Winckelmann' is singular in Pater's work for its explicit discussion of 'romantic fervent friendships with young men'. Its adaptation by Lee for purposes of re-thinking women's ineradicable link with marriage in fiction, at a time when she is socializing with Pater, is suggestive. 'Winckelmann' is suffused with notions that match the characterization of Lee's Anne Brown: Pater writes about a 'colourless, unclassified purity of life', 'indifference which lies beyond all that is relative or partial', 'characterless[ness], so far as character involves subjection to the accidental influences of life', 'sexless beauty', and 'moral sexlessness, a kind of impotence, an ineffectual wholeness of nature, yet with a divine beauty and significance of its own' (Pater 1873, 191, 192, 194; 1910, I. 218, 220–1).

19 Lee is not alone in this sexual purity position, which accommodated sexual radicals such as Lee (and ostensibly Pater) as well as sexual conservatives such as W. T. Stead. See Bland 1995.

20 There is also the possibility of Lee's influence on Pater in this instance. We know that Lee was working on this material as a novel from as early as 1882, and that Pater and Lee discussed it at the time. I note that the format of Lee's published story is a diary, a form which matches that of Pater's Imaginary Portrait, 'A Prince of Court Painters', published three years after their original discussion in *Macmillan's Magazine* in October 1885.

3

'Warming Me Like a Cordial': The Ethos of the Body in Vernon Lee's Aesthetics

Catherine Anne Wiley

Wyndham Lewis once made the startling observation that, 'To read [Vernon Lee's] pages is like watching a person of some intelligence administering electric shocks to herself' (Lewis 1927, 111). Some decades earlier, Virginia Woolf had given herself a warning in her diary that she must not 'let the pen write without guidance; for fear of becoming slack and untidy like Vernon Lee. Her ligaments are too loose for my taste' (Woolf 1977, 266). These comments invoke the body in contradistinction: one in terms of tension, the other of slackness. Woolf's reference to 'ligaments' is especially telling, suggesting as it does a physical body inadequately disciplined or regulated. This critical anxiety triggered by the somatic in Vernon Lee's writings is notable in the response of both her contemporary readers and her later critics, who have described her work in phrases including the following: 'unnatural, almost pathological, tension' (Gunn 1964, 95), 'unwholesome weirdness', 'perverse and brutal', 'unhealthy excess' (Gardner 1987, 21), and 'riotous verbiage' (Harriet Waters Preston quoted in Gardner 1987, 41),[1] – not to leave out Henry James, who, disturbed by what he called her 'ferocity', described her work as 'savage' and 'violent' (James 1980, III. 84–7). All of these comments similarly point to uncontainable or illegitimate sensations revealed in her prose, inappropriate extremes which tend to burst through her language, occasionally running counter to her seeming design, and producing a marked discomfort in her readers.

Ian Small describes the late-Victorian intellectual milieu as one in which the study of aesthetics was becoming a psychological rather than a philosophical field. Small notes that this shift caused 'aesthetics' to be defined more by effects on the perceiver's mind rather than by qualities inherent in the art object itself, granting almost anything the potential to count as art (Small 1991, 9). Despite Lee's scepticism towards the Aesthetic movement, she was sympathetic to these trends, becoming increasingly interested in the interactions between the mind and the body with regard to aesthetic experience. Writing in the introduction to her book *Euphorion* (1884) that, in viewing artefacts or reading descriptions of the distant past, we must 'lie passive and let it slowly circulate around us', she invites the reader to share what reads almost inescapably as a physical experience, something like lying in a whirlpool. In her essays, Lee frequently engenders a symbolic potential space between an internal, or bodily, and an external, or aesthetic, reality – a space in which a kind of radical empathy takes place.[2] By imperceptible degrees the reader's psyche is invaded, widened, and sensitized, made receptive to the presence of the other within the self, the self within the other, rooted in the inclusive sensuous experience of the body rather than in social structures imposed from without. In so doing she asks the reader to reject the classic cultural demand, described by the critic Henry Staten, to transcend the body in favour of the soul, the finite for the infinite, the individual for the universal.

Staten, in his *Eros in Mourning: Homer to Lacan* (1995), describes a theme underwriting aesthetic discourse throughout much of Western culture, a common desire to transcend the physical body's messy mortality for a cleaner, more spiritual realm, a realm in which one is no longer threatened with devastating loss. Staten argues that, from Plato onwards, 'for the religious-philosophical tradition in which Western literature is rooted, mourning is the horizon of all desire' (Staten 1995, xi), because the anticipation of loss haunts us even with regard to objects we desire but do not yet possess. In this tradition idealization and transcendence are posited as economizing strategies arising in response to the fear or anticipation of loss. Ultimately, Staten demonstrates, at the deepest level the fear is not of the loss of the other, but the *loss of the self* that either the unfulfilled craving for the other, *or* the other's unmediated *presence*, would necessarily entail. In the dynamic he describes, we also dread that which we desire: a complete, unmediated union with the other, a union that would render the intact, coherent 'self' no longer viable. Anxiety over these potential losses, Staten argues, has fuelled demands for the transcendence of the body throughout the history of Western culture.

Vernon Lee offers an alternative to this perhaps doomed project of transcendence; the intimacy of her use of the essay form breaks down barriers between writer and reader, paving the way for her to encourage a breakdown of the mind/body split, a merging of the internal and the external.³ In this informal, almost conversational genre, she offers an approach to art grounded in the fluid sensations of the body, moving toward an aesthetics that integrates the perceptions and ideas of the mind with these conventionally denigrated bodily sensations, attending to physical drives and currents on their own terms, and destabilizing, in the process, rigid social categories of sexuality and gender – in order to expand our sense of self to include or absorb elements of what might otherwise be viewed merely as 'foreign'. These moves take place, however, not on the level of philosophical argument but in the form and imagery of her own literary language. Over and over in Lee's essays we find the recurring presence of the body, aesthetic experience circling out from its source in the very fibres and sinews of the body's materiality. However, she carefully distinguishes the desire for *contact* with the external, from a longing for *possession*. She writes:

> When we are young – and most of us remain mere withered children, never attaining maturity, in similar matters – we are usually attracted by luxury and luxurious living. We are possessed by that youthful instinct of union, fusion, marriage, so to speak, with what our soul desires; we hanker after close contact and complete possession; and we fancy, in our inexperience, that luxury, the accumulation of valuables, the appropriation of opportunities, the fact of rejecting from our life all that is not costly, brilliant, and dainty, implies such fusion of our soul with beauty.
>
> (*Laurus Nobilis* 1909, 52)

In longing, we reach out and attempt to *fuse* ourselves with what we love or desire by 'owning' it. We want to destroy the boundary between ourselves and what we desire; we want, in a sense, to *become* ('union, fusion') what we desire. However, this turns out to be impossible: 'we find that this is all delusion' (*Laurus Nobilis* 1909, 52), and gradually realize that,

> The essential character of beauty is its being a *relation between* ourselves and certain objects. The emotion to which we attach its name is produced, motived by something outside us, pictures, music, landscape, or whatever it may be; but the *emotion resides in us*, and it is the emotion, and not merely its object, which we desire.
>
> (*Laurus Nobilis* 1909, 53, emphasis added)

Like Freud, Lee separates desire from its object. As I mentioned above, that with which we seek contact is ultimately found inside us, but only through *stimulation* from outside us.[4] In other words, we need to be touched by the *not-me* to feel the harmony and expansion of the me that we require. These longings often lead us to commit such errors in judgment as the collecting of artwork to display in our houses; Lee finds this impulse understandable, but fundamentally anti-aesthetic. This false 'possession' of objects is effective, *not* in giving us access to that which we desire and thus inspiring liberating emotions, but only in making sure that *no one else* has that access; like 'the idea of self' (*Laurus Nobilis* 1909, 56), possession has meaning only in the exclusion of others:

> I have spoken of *material, actual* possession. But if we look closer at it we shall see that, save with regard to the things which are actually consumed, destroyed, disintegrated, changed to something else in their enjoyment, the notion of ordinary possession is a mere delusion. It can be got only by a constant obtrusion of a mere idea, the *idea of self*, and of such unsatisfactory ideas as one's right, for instance, to exclude others. 'Tis like the tension of a muscle, this constant keeping the consciousness aware by repeating "Mine – mine – *mine* and not *theirs*; not *theirs*, but *mine*." And this wearisome act of self-assertion leaves little power for appreciation, for the appreciation which others can have quite equally, and without which there is no reality at all in ownership [Emphasis Lee's].
>
> (*Laurus Nobilis* 1909, 56–7)

She implies that the only thing we can truly, actually possess is food, which is broken down and becomes part of our bodies. If we cannot eat it, though, we do not really own it; the 'possession' we crave depends upon a falsely coherent entity (or 'mere idea') known as the 'self', which exists in our consciousness only as a *constriction*, 'like the tension of a muscle'. The analogy is potent, because one is only made conscious of a muscle by tensing it, but by doing so we also *limit* what it is capable of in its naturally relaxed or active states. Lee aims to persuade her readers – here explicitly, but elsewhere, as we shall see, by describing and discursively enacting the process – to loosen the bonds that limit the capacities of the imagination.

Engagement of the body: 'The Lake of Charlemagne: An Apology for Association'

Lee's essay entitled 'The Lake of Charlemagne, An Apology for Association' in *Juvenilia* (1887) does essentially what the title suggests it will: it makes a reasoned argument in favour of association as a basis for aesthetic appreciation. However, its theme is much deepened and complicated when one takes note of the forms of images presented in the interstices of the argument. She begins by recounting her arguments for and against the reliance on association as the basis for judging art, and seems quite clearly to have decided against it, saying finally, 'This I have thought and said, and indeed, at the moment of stating my position once more, it seems to me that I was perfectly right' (1887, I. 30). However, it soon emerges that she disagrees with herself, and the manner in which she describes this illustrates the limitations of her conscious and rational mind:

But now comes the mischief. Little by little, watching my own thoughts, my own living, moving, yet unstated thoughts, it appears to me that this very faculty of association is being highly honoured in my mind; that, in a sort of quiet, half-perceptible way, those thoughts of mine are attributing a great deal of good to it; indeed, are making for it quite a fine position. (1887, I. 30–1)

Lee splits herself in two; one, the rational and observing self; the other, her 'living, moving, yet unstated thoughts', which are, while out of her direct control, capable of attributing value. Her informal, self-revealing tone lends a sense of intimacy with the reader; her gentle self-mockery encourages the reader to listen to those voices or memories just beneath the surface of consciousness, in a widening circulation of sensual and conceptual experience.

In order to illustrate the workings and, almost incidentally, the value of association as an approach to aesthetics, she describes the experience of travelling up the Rhine River on a steamboat. At first, her rational self is comfortably in control, noting that the picturesque surroundings do not move her at all: 'I was neither surprised nor vexed at experiencing none of the delight which our fathers and mothers experienced on their first sight of the Rhineland ... I had clearly realized beforehand how completely the Rhine, with respect to its emotional and imaginative power, is a thing of the past' (1887, I. 32), she observes, placing the Rhine quite firmly within a historically-determined appreciation of the picturesque and applauding the current critical interest in 'realism'. However, at this point in the narrative, a change comes over her. She writes:

> But while such were my reasoned ideas, I gradually became aware of the presence within me of something different diffusing itself, and permeating my consciousness. Not exactly an idea, nor yet a set of impressions, something impossible to define ... first within myself, warming me like a cordial into vague pleasure, then afterwards surrounding me from outside, an all-encompassing medium in which the soul floated with languid enjoyment. (1887, I. 35–6)

This warmth unexpectedly coming over her as she sits detached, rejecting the aesthetic value of the scenery originates, she realizes, from her recognition that this was the place which had in her childhood been infused with mythology:

> this was the Rhineland. ... but not the Rhineland as a concrete reality, a sum total of present and actually perceived and analyzed impressions and ideas; not the Rhineland which was now before me, which I was now criticizing ... Not this Rhineland; quite another. A Rhineland of the past, ... which years ago I had constructed – or rather, which had constructed itself for me – from the random allusions, the incoherent descriptions of a servant-maid we had had while living in the neighbourhood of Frankfurt. (1887, I. 36–7).

Whatever 'it' is, at first she cannot name it except negatively (not an idea, nor a set of impressions); like syrup it oozes into her mind, 'permeating' her consciousness (1887, I. 36). Both foreign to her and part of her, it diffuses the boundary between 'inside' and 'outside' (1887, I. 36); starting inside, moving outward, it gives her a sensation of warmth, and then one of immersion, as if she suddenly found herself lounging in a warm bath. While she does not explicitly mention the body, the descriptions of her sensations inevitably allude to a sensual experience, suggestive of an erotic response.[5] It is notable that she thus responds, not to the imaginary Rhineland, nor to the 'real' Rhineland, but to the collision between the two, or the overlay of the imaginary Rhineland on the real one. Seemingly without agency in the process, she merely responds to the 'permeating' of her consciousness that sends her soul afloat; it is as if she has been pushed outside the parameters of her conscious identity for a moment – an experience she clearly presents as pleasurable, one which she even finds wryly humorous.

The memory for which she thus prepares us is one of an imaginary land, created for her child-mind by her servant maid, 'a buxom thing of eighteen or nineteen, romantic, poetic' (1887, I. 37). The maid and the child have created this imaginary Rhineland together, the one from memory and the other from stories; or rather, their emotional, perhaps sensuous bond brought about a potential space in which, as she says, this imaginary place 'constructed itself'. Both she and the servant maid feel an insatiable hunger for this imaginary place: 'Of this Rhineland of hers she was perpetually telling, and to me she could never tell enough' (1887, I. 38), their mutual desire engendering an offspring of sorts. The descriptive details of this place are not only marvellous but seem immediately to attach themselves to the child's already-present desires:

> it was the most marvellous region in the whole world; it never appeared to me as having anything in common with the rest of the earth. Everything was wonderful. Fruit trees, the like of which did not exist, covered it with miraculous blossom. Now fruit blossom, the transparent, easily shed pure white of the cherry; the solid creaminess, crowned with tiny pale green leaves, of the pear; the pink-tipped, woolly, unwillingly opening buds of the apple, the various foam-like flowering of all the various kinds of plums, fruit blossom of all kinds always had, I know not whether from the difficulty of obtaining it, its association with sweet taste, or with the excitement and surprise of spring, or merely from its own peculiar beauty, quite a particular fascination for my childhood. (1887, I. 38–9)

Importantly, the syntax of this passage does not permit the reader to separate the imaginary story land from the child's inner 'fascination' until the end of the quoted extract. In other words, the vividly sensual descriptions of specific fruit blossoms ('creamy', 'woolly', 'foam-like', not to mention the provocative 'unwillingly opening') seem at first to be part of the 'marvellous region', until the end of the long sentence reveals that she (also) refers to her own inner fascinations. The story-memory bleeds into her inner desires; the boundary separating them becomes permeable. In effect, Lee blurs this distinction for the reader as well, in order to reconstruct her experience in the reader's mind.

This very sensuous memory conflicts with the conclusions drawn earlier in the essay by her rational mind, and the reader cannot be certain where her ultimate loyalty lies:

> as the logical certainty of the insufficiency of all these sights and associations for us familiar with Italy, admirers of Whistler and readers of 'My Last Duchess,' came clearer and clearer before what ought to be called, I suppose, the more intelligent portion of my mind; the rest of my mind, nay, somehow my whole nature, was invaded by the consciousness of that imaginary Rhineland of my childhood. (1887, I. 42)

Lee gently mocks the aesthetic principles of her own day, the attachment to Whistler and Browning, at the same time that she acknowledges their prominence in her own mind. Earlier in the essay she hints at her own lack of agency in the process of remembering the imaginary Rhineland; here she refers to it as an 'invasion', intimating the somewhat unwelcome nature of the memory, its disruption of her complacent self-knowledge, even though her lack of agency constitutes part of her pleasure. In a sense, the normal structure of her identity has been violated and dissolved by her own memory of desire, by the mad power of bodily memory in confrontation with the 'real'. Her excited emotional response continues to disrupt the 'intelligent portion of her mind', for she becomes somewhat disoriented: 'I felt excited, pleased, scarce knowing at what' (1887, I. 42).

However 'superior' her rational mind to the 'rest' of her mind and body, the former can neither 'place' the latter satisfactorily nor simply ignore them. Not only do these memories overtake her conscious mind; ultimately they alter her views on the question of association. For, although she continues to present all the good arguments against association as an approach to art, seeming still to believe them, she finally concedes her 'superior' intellect to the power of emotional experience and bodily memory, and finally, significantly, locates the value of art specifically in its ability to commit this kind of destruction upon the 'real', aiding in the formation of identity's particularity:

> I am of opinion that without association there would be no relations to art; nay, no art at all … . [Association is] an allusion of all manner of chaotic thoughts and impressions washing over the definite artistic forms which are settling in our mind; it is evident that the definite artistic forms run the risk of being completely

obliterated ... . [But] had there not been that wave tossing the past to the present, no solid wisdom or beauty, nay, no individuality of ourselves would have existed at all (1887, I. 54, 56).

Association, here described as a wave constantly beating upon the shore of the more objective world, 'brings to the nucleus of solid earth all the floating things which can make soil' (1887, I. 61) and leads Lee to speculate about how the mind itself works. What is at stake here is, in a sense, the freedom to be our own ever-changing selves, as defined against, for example, the aesthetic principles of our historically-bound society – in other words, she pits the particularity of erotic memory against hegemonic expectations.

Interestingly, as with Freud (for surely she is writing about a kind of unconscious function, a nascent return-of-the-repressed), for Lee, that force which invades our consciousness (as we have seen in the Rhineland scenario) has a familiar form:

Do you think that we perceive, much less remember, the totally unknown? Not a bit of it; we merely constantly recognize the already familiar; what we catch hold of with our mind is not that which is new, which belongs to to-day; but that which is old, and belongs to yesterday: the different, the new, we take in, tolerate, enjoy, only later. We wander, as it were, through a vast and populous city; those that we notice and speak to are our old acquaintance; but the old acquaintance introduce new ones, whom we admit for their sake. (1887, I. 61)

Nothing unfamiliar makes it into our minds without an association with something familiar. She posits here a continuous relation, dialogue, with our past selves. Again like Freud, she suggests that libidinal memory grounds the very structure of thought.[6] The Rhineland would have remained as meaningless to Lee as her exposition of historical taste made it, if her love for the nursemaid, her passion for fruit-trees, her nursemaid's longing for her homeland had not imbued it with emotional attachment, causing her to take a freshly individual look at the Rhineland (that is, one based on her individual emotional history, rather than on a more general, socially-sanctioned viewpoint), as well as the very structure of association itself. This kind of attachment, Lee asserts, is not only how art works; it is how the *mind* works. Eros drenches the world with significance, creating internal images or melodies; subsequent stimuli from the external world triggers those images, invading our rationality with waves of feeling, enriching the more logical dynamic by which we understand the world and ourselves.

However, these deceptively gentle musings cannot fully account for the intense anxiety expressed by many of Lee's readers. It is not only her ideas, but the strange periodic excesses in her use of language that cause such discomfort. Or, rather, it is the teetering imbalance she occasionally permits between her ideas and the passionate language with which she pummels them into the reader's mind – a tendency I call 'unbridled writing'. Not only does she explicitly advocate giving control of one's thoughts over to unconscious forces; she sometimes enacts this abdication by letting her pen run riderless, as it were, across the page, producing prose which, however graceless or awkward in places, strikes a note of unusual power and depth, lending her ideas a kind of illegitimate force with which to wreak havoc on the reader's sensibilities.

Unbridled writing: 'The Italy of the Elizabethan Dramatists'

The essay which perhaps most vividly displays Lee's tendency toward what I call 'unbridled writing' is the one entitled 'The Italy of the Elizabethan Dramatists', which narrates the influence of Italian travel on sixteenth-century English playwrights. Contrasting the English approach with that of earlier travellers to Italy such as the Spaniards or Germans, who, Lee writes, 'came as mere greedy and ... savage mercenaries' (1884, I. 60), she describes with vivid relish the English traveller's weird fascination with Italy's culture, fashion, music, and, particularly, with the Italians' seeming lack of morality. In Lee's view, the English were so appalled and shaken by the immoral behaviours they saw and the crimes of which they heard, that they could not forget them and eventually wrote about them in the form of drama. The explosion of English plays with Italian settings and telling of Italian villainy is given, here, a fairly reasonable source narrative.

However, the manner in which this narrative is performed throughout this essay is startling, to say the least. In this essay especially, the excesses in Lee's prose – the endless examples, images, details, breathless additions and supplements to every thought – frequently seem to drown or consume the ideas she ostensibly wants to express. It is as if, in order to make the reader understand what she means and see what she sees, she must articulate every *conceivable* possibility and veritably *assault* the reader with her own vision. In deceptively calm fashion, the

essay begins with a description of the fifteenth-century French occu-
pation of Rome, and of the Spaniards and Germans who came to Italy
merely for mercenary purposes and were relatively unaffected by their
stay. An early sentence which begins to startle the reader is that
describing the first wave of English travellers to Italy:

> To Italy they flocked and through Italy they rambled, prying greed-
> ily into each cranny and mound of the half-broken civilization,
> upturning with avid curiosity all the rubbish and filth; seeking with
> aching eyes and itching fingers for the precious fragments of intel-
> lectual splendour; lingering with fascinated glance over the broken
> remnants and deep, mysterious gulfs of a crumbling and devastated
> civilization. (1884, I. 63)

The disturbing intensity of sensuality and desire emanating from this
description lends a new significance to a previous characterization of
the collective mind of England as a freshly nubile young man, flush
with life after the long 'sleep' of puberty – particularly to its suggestion
of a sexual awakening, swollen and stimulated by the touch of the
'other':

> For, in the sixteenth century, on awakening from its long evil sleep,
> haunted by civil war nightmares of the fifteenth century, the
> English mind had started up in *the vigour of well-nigh mature youth*,
> nourished and rested by the long inactivity in which it had slept
> through its period of assimilation and growth. It had *awakened at the
> first touch* of foreign influence, and had *grown with every fresh contact
> with the outer world*: with the first glance at Plato and Xenophon sud-
> denly opened by Erasmus and Colet, at the Bible suddenly opened
> by Cranmer; it had grown with its sob of indignation at the sight of
> the burning faggots surrounding the martyrs, with its joyous heart-
> throbs at the sight of the seas and islands of the New World; it had
> *grown with the sudden passionate strain of every nerve and every muscle*
> when the galleys of Philip had been sighted in the Channel. And
> when it had paused, taken breath, and looked calmly around it,
> after the tumult of all these sights and sounds and actions, the
> English mind, in the time of Elizabeth, had *found itself of a sudden
> full-grown and blossomed out into superb manhood*, with burning
> activities and indefatigable powers.
>
> (1884, I. 61–2, emphasis added)

Read in this way, what Lee describes could be a traditional, straightforward scenario of heterosexual seduction: pure-minded boy wakes into manhood, from the 'sleep' of childhood and puberty, through stimulation by exotic other; boy goes to enticingly glorious but ruined harlot, excitedly violates her to experience sensual delight. (He does so because, as Lee mentions, once awakened as described above, and despite bursting with youthful energy and passion, the English mind 'had found itself without materials for work. ... All the intellectual wealth of England remained to be created; but it could not be created out of nothing' (1884, I. 62). Masturbation, after all, is not a reproductive act.) An appreciation of this essay's narrative calls for an implicit faith in an orderly set of differences: between sixteenth-century Italy and England; between the Middle Ages and the Renaissance; between morality and immorality.

This tidy set of binaries, however, quickly breaks down. While Italy's treasures are hidden, in stereotypically 'female' imagery, among filth, decay, and chthonic chaos, having to be penetrated and excavated by the young, rational, pure-minded but excitable male 'English mind' (which, rather suddenly and inexplicably, becomes embodied in a multiplicity of 'Englishmen of thought and fancy' (1884, I. 63), thus referred to in the plural, and gender-nonspecific 'they'), it is in fact *Italy* which ultimately seems to ejaculate, and it is England which experiences something like a contracting female orgasm and goes home containing, and covered with, what might suggest semen:

> And then, impatient of their intoxicating and tantalizing search, *suddenly grown desperate, they clutched and stored away everything,* and returned home *tattered, soiled, bedecked with gold and with tinsel, laden with an immense uncouth burden of jewels, and broken wealth, and refuse and ordure,* with pseudo-antique philosophy, with half-mediæval Petrarchesque poetry, with Renaissance science, with humanistic pedantry and obscenity, with euphuistic conceits and casuistic quibble, with art, politics, metaphysics – civilization *embedded in all manner of rubbish and abomination, soiled with all manner of ominous stains.*
>
> (1884, I. 63–4, emphasis added)

It is interesting in this context to note that, according to the OED, the word 'ordure' which means 'dung, filth, manure, excrement' (Webster's) was used figuratively in the nineteenth-century to describe an object or exclamation, perhaps morally questionable, *thrown* at a person, evocative of the Latin root of 'ejaculate'. Lee's veritably percolating scenario, in which multiple bits of civilization, a plural potentiality awash in a soup of refuse, leads ultimately to the birth of Elizabethan tragedy – in which, Lee writes, one can see 'the deep impression, the indelible picture in the memory, of Italy itself' (1884, I. 65) – more than suggests the procreative function of semen, and the reflection of the father in the face of the child.

The speaker, in other words, unravels the necessary binary distinctions by focusing most of her attention, and drawing the reader's attention, neither to the conscience-laden purity of the nubile English mind, nor to the fascinating degeneracy of Italy, but rather on the violently sexual and (re-)productive *rape* of the former on the latter. One is left, after reading this essay, *not* with a renewed appreciation of the Elizabethan tragic sense stemming from the exposure of pure England to the immorality of the Italian Renaissance. Rather, one is left with (among other things) a chaotic beehive of images in which a newly-grown and multi-gendered youth of clear mind plummets the depths of a dark and already-violated treasure-trove which, after a gradual increase of tension and excitement, explodes all over him/her, sending him/her home covered and dripping with a stew of treasure and filth, which s/he ultimately cultivates into the variegated 'product' of Elizabethan drama.

The multigenderedness of both the youth/English mind and the older, plundered Italy in this scenario, as well as the uncontrolled excesses of the prose, equally point to an uneasy urge in Vernon Lee's work to access a polymorphous perversity. The suggestion of polymorphous sexuality in this scene is almost unbearably intense; the power of the language is in conflict with Lee's failed attempt to control it. The perverse depictions of sexuality are reflected in the excesses of words, in the repetitions and endlessly long lists of examples. Many of her descriptions of the 'goods' the English brought back to include in their plays are breathlessly long, such as this one, in which Lee goes beyond the typical verbosity of Victorian writing to produce an unending current of visual detail:

> They filled their works with Italian things: from the whole plot of a play borrowed from an Italian novel, to the mere passing allusion to an Italian habit, or the mere quotation of an Italian word; from the full-length picture of the actions of Italian men and women, down to the mere sketch, in two or three words, of a bit of Italian garden

or a group of Italian figures; nay, to the innumerable scraps of tiny detail, grotesque, graceful, or richly coloured, which they stuffed into all their works: allusions to the buffoons of the mask comedy, to the high-voiced singers, to the dress of the Venetian merchants, to the step of a dance; to the pomegranate in the garden or the cypress on the hillside; often mere names of Italian things: the *lavolta* and *corranto* dances, the *Traghetto* ferry, the Rialto bridge; countless little touches, trifling to us, but which brought home to the audience at the Globe or at Blackfriars that wonderful Italy which every man of the day had travelled through at least in spirit, and had loved at least in imagination. (1884, I. 66–7)

The doglike infatuation of the young English leads them to fill their plays with a multiplicity of possibly unnecessary, certainly unimportant details of Italian life; so, too, does Lee feel compelled to make long lists of details, even to support relatively minor points. For she has not yet come to what will be her main focus: how the English responded to Italian vice.

Finally, it is not only the young sixteenth-century mind of England, but also, clearly, Lee herself who is so irresistibly seduced by these details.[7] When she finally does come to characterize the root of English travellers' fascination for Italy, her description revs up to a fever pitch:

We can imagine the innumerable English travellers who went to Italy greedy for life and knowledge ... possessed by the *morbid passion for the stories of abominable and unpunished crime* ... with which the Italy of the deeply corrupted sixteenth century was permeated. We can imagine how the prosaic merchants' clerks from London; the perfumed dandies, trying on Italian clothes, rehearsing Italian steps and collecting Italian oaths, ... how all these privileged creatures *ferreted about for monstrous crimes* with which to horrify their stay-at-home countrymen; how the rich young lords, returning home with mincing steps and high-pitched lisp, surrounded by a train of parti-coloured, dialect-jabbering Venetian clowns, deft and sinister Neapolitan fencing masters, silver-voiced singing boys decoyed from some church, and cynical humanists escaped from the faggot or the gallows, were expected to bring home ... *stories of hideous wickedness, of the murders and rapes and poisonings* committed by the dukes and duchesses, the nobles and senators, in whose palaces they had so lately supped and danced. The crimes of Italy fascinated Englishmen of genius with a fascination even more potent than that exerted over the vulgar imagination of mere foppish and swash-buckler lovers of the scandalous and the sensational. ... To these men – ardent and serious even in their profligacy, imaginative and passionate even in their Puritanism – all *sucking avidly* at this newly found Italian civilization, the wickedness of Italy was more than morbidly attractive or morbidly appalling: it was imaginatively and psychologically fascinating. (1884, I. 68–9, emphasis added)

We are never to learn in any detail *what* crimes are being committed by these horrifying Italians; the reader however is placed in a position strangely akin to that of the English. As Lee illustrates her own fascination with the strangely perverse sucking of the English at the fount of Italian vice, the reader gradually develops a kindred fascination with Lee's own excesses of description. She hints at the psychological disturbance that results from this tantalizing encounter:

Nothing which the English stage could display seemed to the minds of English playwrights and the public to give an adequate picture of the abominations of Italy; much as they heaped up horrors and combined them with artistic skill, much as they forced into sight, there yet remained an abyss of evil which the English tongue refused to mention, but which weighed upon the English mind; and which, unspoken, nay ... unhinted, yet remained as an incubus in the consciousness of the playwrights and the public, was in their thoughts when they wrote and heard such savage misanthropic outbursts as those of Tourneur and of Marston. The sense of the rottenness of the country whence they were obtaining their intellectual nourishment, haunted with a sort of sickening fascination the imaginative and psychological minds of the late sixteenth century (1884, I. 73).

Doomed to repeat their futile attempts to plumb the depths of evil they had witnessed, it is that same evil (to which they cannot adequately do justice), which works in their creative minds like yeast in the making of bread. England's very sense of self is annihilated, exploded, shattered into pieces. And yet Lee's explosively violent narrative culminates, surprisingly, simply, in superior art. England, it turns out, was far from destroyed by its contact with the degenerate and multi-gendered hag that was sixteenth-century Italy; rather, its (perhaps priggish) immature character was broken down and rebuilt, recreated, in stronger, richer form.

In the 'Valedictory' to *Renaissance Fancies and Studies* (1895) which she wrote many years later, Lee proposes that the widespread late-nineteenth-century passion for Italy was not unlike that of the sixteenth-century English travellers she describes in 'Elizabethan Dramatists'.[8] Aestheticians, herself included, developed a passion for Italy which, in her own case, she tried to cure, or as she writes, 'to vent the intense discomfort of spirit', by writing 'Elizabethan Dramatists' (1895, 247). In this essay, the structures of identity and national culture and even gender are not only loosened or melted but shattered, with an unquestionably good aesthetic result. Perhaps with the flood of imagery, the excesses of her prose, she was attempting a similar violation upon the innocence of her readers. If art is a playground, if, as she writes in an essay entitled 'Beauty and Sanity', 'art can make our souls more resisting and flexible' (*Laurus Nobilis* 1909, 157), then it is possible that her own aesthetic assault on the reader's imagination aims to work likewise as a playground, teaching us by example to listen to the multiplicities of ourselves. For the aesthetic project she finally describes is the creating of an identity, the strengthening and deepening of character. Therefore, in purging her own 'discomfort' – her own anxiety (like that of her critics) over the excesses of sensation her prose reveals, Vernon Lee ultimately proves a point similar to the one implicit in 'Association' – that, by transcending discomfort or anxiety and paying attention to the excesses of sensation, we allow for the possibility of a richer, more deeply authentic identity.

Notes

1 The Waters Preston quotation is taken from the *Atlantic Monthly* 55 (February 1885), 219–27.

2 Empathy was an increasingly important part of Lee's work; she has been credited with bringing this concept to British aesthetics (see Small 1977, 1991).

3 As she writes in an essay called 'Higher Harmonies' in *Laurus Nobilis: Chapters on Art and Life*, 'To a large extent man feels himself tortured by discordant impressions coming from the world outside and the world inside him; and he seeks comfort and medicine in harmonious impressions of his own making, in his own strange inward-outward world of art' (1909, 88).

4 In 'The Sexual Aberrations', in *Three Essays on Sexuality* Freud writes, 'Experience of the cases that are considered abnormal has shown us that in them the sexual instinct and the sexual object are merely soldered together – a fact which we have been in danger of overlooking in consequence of the uniformity of the normal picture, where the object appears to form part and parcel of the instinct. We are thus warned to loosen the bond that exists in our thoughts between instinct and object. It seems probable that the sexual

instinct is in the first instance independent of its object; nor is its origin likely to be due to its object's attractions' (Freud, 1953, 14).

5   A similar bodily response to art is briefly described in her essay 'The Use of Beauty' which appears in *Laurus Nobilis*: 'I was seated working by my window, depressed by the London outlook of narrow grey sky, endless grey roofs, and rusty elm tops, when I became conscious of a certain increase of vitality, almost as if I had drunk a glass of wine, because a band somewhere outside had begun to play. ... And, noticing my feelings, I seemed to be conscious that those notes were being played on me, my fibres becoming the strings; so that as the notes moved and soared and swelled and radiated like stars and suns, I also, being identified with the sound, having become apparently the sound itself, must needs move and soar with them' (1909, 14–15).

6   This is evocative of Freud's notion of 're-finding' a familiar object of desire; see 'The Transformations of Puberty' in *Three Essays on Sexuality* (Freud 1953, 88 and see also 94–5).

7   Fifteen years later, in her tribute to Walter Pater entitled 'Valedictory' which appears in *Renaissance Fancies and Studies*, Lee compares the sixteenth-century English response to Renaissance Italy to the later Victorian one, including her own, and notes that she wrote 'The Italy of the Elizabethan Dramatists' expressly 'to vent the intense discomfort of spirit which I shared assuredly with students older and more competent than myself' (1895, 247–8).

8   In some corners, this passion for Italy was used as a code for homosexuality. For example, in his book *Closet Writing/Gay Reading: The Case of Melville's Pierre*, James Creech quotes from the 'one surviving letter [from Henry James] to [John Addington] Symonds'. James writes, referring to his essay on Venice which he had sent to Symonds: I sent it to you because it was a constructive way of expressing the good will I felt for you in consequence of what you had written about the land of Italy – and of intimating to you, somewhat dumbly, that I am an attentive and sympathetic reader. I nourish for the said Italy an unspeakably tender passion, and your pages always seemed to say to me that you were one of the small number of people who love it as much as I do – in addition to your knowing it immeasurably better, I want to recognize this ... for it seemed to me that the victims of a common passion should exchange a look. Creech continues, 'Almost every word has homosexual resonance if not outright reference but reveals absolutely nothing compromising to an unaware reader. James even points out that he is resorting to a coded wink when, employing an oxymoron, he admits to speaking "somewhat dumbly" of the passion the two share' (Creech 1993, 96–7).

4
Vernon Lee, Decadent Contamination and the Productivist Ethos

Dennis Denisoff

One of the first dandy-aesthete-bashers in history! The accusation is cast at Vernon Lee far less often now but it remains, unfortunately, one of the most enduring characterizations of her work and of the novel *Miss Brown* (1884) in particular. The label has misleadingly positioned her closer in values to men who had little appreciation for the Decadent aesthetics that held an attraction for her – writers such as W. H. Mallock, author of the novelistic satire *The New Republic* (1877) and the journalist and critic Max Nordau, author of *Degeneration* (1892), that scourging analysis of the degenerate *fin de siècle*. In reality, she used no more ink in criticizing the dandy-aesthetes than she did in challenging the more central social order of the era, that of the productivity-minded bourgeoisie. In Lee's time, the term 'Decadent' generally referred to either a society's fall into a state of ruin marked by the debauchery and excess of the wealthy elite, or to an individual who supported such a condition. While such societies were usually located in the ancient past, Lee recognised parallels between these characteristics and the economic tenets supporting the middle class and gentry of her day. Indeed, she saw the markings of Decadent excess, waste, and contamination more boldly emblazoned on the latter group. In accord with other participants in the Decadent Movement, Lee's work reflects an appreciation for the more traditional manifestation of Decadence, which she genders feminine and characterizes by historical sensitivity and empathy. Lee is unique, however, in negatively delineating a particularly aggressive, masculine Decadence marked by an obsession with a productivist ethos.

I. The Decadence of modern England's productivity

Although Lee mocked Max Nordau for his 'generalising genius' (1909, 265),[1] his 1892 *Degeneration* takes on the same small group of educated, financially secure dandy-aesthetes whom Lee attacks in *Miss Brown*. According to Nordau, when 'an Oscar Wilde goes about in "æsthetic costume" among gazing Philistines, exciting either their ridicule or their wrath, it is no indication of independence of character, but rather from a purely anti-socialistic, ego-maniacal recklessness and hysterical longing to make a sensation' (Nordau 1993, 319).[2] The strategy of sensationalism becomes dangerous, in Nordau's view, when the individual's performance of exclusive taste results in a wave of copy-cats sidling forward from among what he describes as the 'weak', 'dependent', 'nervous' masses (Nordau 1993, 7). The swarm of consumers afflicted with the 'buying craze' (Nordau 1993, 27) is no less than an infection marked by the commodification of taste itself.[3] Nordau's argument suggests that the threat of Decadence lay not in its sterility or abject status. Rather, it is found in its ease of proliferation, and in its depiction of the productivist promise of satiated desire as leading to punishment for gluttony and egotism. This anxiety of excess output parallels a growing realization that productivity for the sake of productivity eventually results in diminishing returns.[4]

Notably, Nordau is joined by writers who were associated with Decadence, such as Charles Baudelaire, Joris-Karl Huysmans, Rachilde, and Wilde, in depicting a lack of control in contemporary production and acquisition. But if Decadence is as pervasive a phenomenon as these writers suggest, it begs one to re-examine recent theorizations of Decadence as a strategy of dissidence or even liberation operating from the margins.[5] If Decadence is so thorough in its influence, if it can be readily conjoined to both lethargy and industry, illness and vigour, economy and sloth, then one should be able to locate it not only in those usual suspects such as the authors who self-defined as Decadent and the social groups commonly characterized as marginal and dissident, but also in the ethics and economic motivations of the dominant order. With regard to Lee's works, this in fact proves to be the case. Indeed, I would argue that it proves to be the point.

Concerns regarding industry and ethics were surfacing frequently in Lee's time. The closing decades of the century saw a shift towards critiques of capitalism, an entrenchment of a poor working class, and a growing grumbling against the oppression of the masses. As Sally Ledger and Scott McCracken have noted, 'the poverty wrought by the depression years of the 1880s weakened the ideological dominance of *economic* liberalism and individualism. ... From the 1880s onwards a growing number of middle-class intellectuals found themselves more attracted to socialist than to liberal ideas' (Ledger and McCracken 1995, 7). This is the era of the New Unionism, the Fabian Society (formed in 1884), the Match Girls' Strike (1888), the London Dock Strike (1889), and the formation of the Labour Representation Committee that would eventually lead to the Labour Party (1900).

Notably, it had been commonplace to argue that the signs of social upheaval among the working class were reflected in the actions that Decadent authors and artists took against the bourgeoisie. In 1895, Hugh E. M. Stutfield argued that 'the aesthetic sensualist and the communist are, in a sense, nearly related. Both have ... a common parentage in exaggerated emotionalism.' For Stutfield, there is a direct connection between 'the unbridled licentiousness of your literary decadent' and 'the violence of the political anarchist' (Stutfield 1895, 841). With the established bourgeois male individualist as the key target of these two groups, commodity culture became both the site of contestation and an instrument of attack.

Lee was no stranger to these debates. She attended various socialist meetings, made herself known to the Fabians, and made the acquaintance of reformers such as Cunninghame Graham and Bernard Shaw (Gunn 1964, 123). She also read extensively on issues of economics and socialism, including Charles Booth's *Life and Labour of the People in London* (1902), Margaret L. Davies's *The Women's Co-operative Guild, 1883–1904* (1904), Henry Fawcett's *Manual of Political Economy* (1888), and Karl Marx's *Das Kapital* (1887) (Colby 2003, 273). Finding Marxism too 'mechanical' in its economic determinism (1909, 268), she searched for a more flexible, empathic model. According to Vineta Colby, the one thing in which Lee was consistent all her adult life was in being 'a liberal with socialist leanings' (Colby 2003, 272). Lee's combination of Decadent aesthetics and socialist sympathies resulted in her articulation of two models of Decadence – a beautiful, feminine Decadence of an Italian past and an unsympathetic, masculine Decadence of contemporary England.

Issues of economics, empathy, and ethical responsibility permeate Lee's aesthetic views. In Diana Maltz's words, Lee's aesthetics 'intensified art's ethical imperative' (Maltz 1999, 218). In *Juvenilia*, Lee compliments Walter Pater's *Marius the Epicurean* (1885) because it recreates a Roman era in which 'the good and the beautiful seemed as the concave and the convex of all things' (1887, 7). Italy in general, she argues, 'makes one think of the past' while hiding its 'evils ... thanks to climate, beauty, and a certain dignified stagnation' (1887, 13). Although Lee associates Italy with torpor and age, traits commonly associated with Decadence, the result is a dignity and beauty permeated by a sense of good.[6] England, conversely, 'leads one to speculate on the future' and yet 'shows its evils grimly' (1887, 13).

In *Juvenilia*'s opening dedication to her friend Carlo Placci, Lee formulates this grim, sad quality as a contemporary, English Decadence. Despite her association of the country with the future, it fails to evoke any sort of inspiration. Instead, she sees the prime symbol of the nation to be the sluggish Tyne River:

> A vast mass of leaden water, polluted with every foulness, flowing heavily, or scarce seeming to flow at all, between lines of docks and factories, their innumerable masts and innumerable chimneys faint upon the thick brown sky, faintly reddened with an invisible sun, and streaked in various intensities of brown and grey and black, with ever rising curls of smoke. This river flows, most often as deep as in a gorge, between banks of blackish cinders, of white poisonous chemical refuse, or worst of all, of what was once pure live soil, now stained and deadened into something unnatural, whereon the very weeds refuse to grow. Down these banks trickle, from black blast furnaces, and rotting greenish docks, and white leprous chemical works, crumbling with caries, foul little streams, vague nameless oozes, choking with their blackness, staining with their deadly purple and copper colour and green and white (1887, 13–14).

Here, then, is a Decadence arising from the industrial revolution and carried on by England's obsession with progress. The flow of Lee's sentences seems to echo that of the Tyne while the mish-mashed colours – rotting green, leprous white, choking black, deadly purple – bob and mingle like refuse through the passage. One's imagination is overwhelmed by the blur of stained, deadened, crumbling, trickling, oozing elements that ultimately become a single immense over-load of imagery. Indeed, the river's progress is often blocked by its own waste, with industrial output eventually fostering its own state of stagnation.

This 'great river of hell' is presented as an extension of the 'black, red-faced, and blistered' workers 'who are yet human beings, intelligent and sensitive, who get treatises on political economy from the free library, in order to see why things should be so very queer and uncomfortable down here' (1887, 14–15, 16). These she compares to men and women 'clean, well-dressed, appreciative of art and music and literature, with whom we can sympathize vastly about Wagner, and Swinburne, and Whistler, and Venetian sunsets' (1887, 16–17). Despite the hellishness of the workers' lives, the wealthier people demonstrate that 'there are things more polluted and blacker still, and more noisome and sterilizing' (1887, 17). The description's richest Decadent imagery does not distinguish between classes, but demonstrates the mutual reliance of the industrial waste, the wounded workers, and those people with the means of improving everybody's quality of life but who choose not to do so.[7]

In *Hortus Vitae* (1903), Lee proposes that humans 'cannot be thoroughly alive except as a result of such exercises as come under the headings: Work and Duty. That seems to be the law of Life – of Life which does not care a button about being æsthetic or wisely epicurean' (1904, 8).[8] The proposition chastises not only the fashionable aestheticism that Lee had already heavily criticized in *Miss Brown*, but also the amorality that had been recently popularized as part of Pater's aesthetic values. In the passage, she goes on to celebrate a pastoral ideal that can include 'even the solemn Juggernaut traction-engines' running along the village high-roads (1904, 9), and she situates her values within a more socialist trajectory of aesthetics that she sees running through Carlyle, Ruskin, and Morris. Meanwhile, she associates the 'black, oozy factory yards and mangy grass-plots heaped with brickbat and refuse' with the routine of 'useless work and wasteful play' (1904, 10). Such worthlessness, Lee proposes, is connected to everyday commerce, because 'being busy and idle and mercantile' are all 'compatible qualities' that foster a hyper-materialism (1904, 47). The end result is diminishing returns: 'we usually have far too many pleasant things about us, to be able to extract much pleasure from any of them; while, of course, somebody else, at the other end of the world let us say, or merely in the mews to the back, has so very much too little as to have none at all, which is another way of diminishing possible enjoyment' (1904, 87–8). Decadence, here, is the result of a self-defeating culture of capitalism.

In 'The Economic Parasitism of Women' (1908), Lee reinforces the association of this decadence with men, blaming the gender disparity on 'the insufficient production, the wasteful expenditure, the degrading mal-distribution of wealth' (1908, 268). The central problem of the modern economic system, she says, is the invention of the patriarch, the man who provides food for the child, and food for the woman who rears it; the man who procures, by industry, or violence, a home (cave, cabin, tent, or house) in which the woman remains with the children, while he himself goes forth to hunt, to tend flocks, to make captives, to till the ground, to buy and sell; and in modern times to do those hundred curious things which, producing no tangible product, come under the heading of "making money" (1908, 269–70).

The implication is that the curious things men do behind closed doors have little real value. Rather they fulfil the image of productivity that maintains their authority within the economic system.

For Lee, the duplicity of this economy is apparent in biased cultural developments that rely on an ungrounded assumption of privilege. This form of false essentialism was a central issue of Decadent literature at the time. As Françoise Galliard has noted in an analysis of *A Rebours*, for example, Joris-Karl Huysmans uses the artifice of Decadence to bring attention to the illusion of realism. While realism attempts to obscure its own falsity as a means of asserting a faith in an essential reality, the Decadent celebration of artifice and imitation is a more honest reflection of the commodified sphere in which we exist.[9] It offers a 'true fake' that proposes a new morality through its lack of guilt for being a copy (Galliard 1980, 131). And yet, Galliard concludes, the pleasure that Huysmans's hero receives from artifice belies his belief in a fixed reality and truth. If there were no such fixity, the argument goes, there would be no pleasure to be found in challenging it. Transgression, however, does not require one to actually maintain an essentialist faith oneself; it is only necessary to recognize that such ideologies dominate one's society.

Decadent art does not aim to replace a fixed notion of reality with some other model. It is rather a dissident strategy of proliferation. Barbara Spackman has described this as a process of contamination 'whereby the logic of diversity functions to contaminate and introduce an asymmetry into the logic of absolute difference' (Spackman 1999, 41). This is done, most notably, through an emphasis on the honesty of artifice. Rather than positioning itself against some sort of indescribable ideal or reality, the Decadent object maintains its position as one link in a tangled chain of representations. Spackman proposes that the proliferation that characterizes Decadence perpetually dissolves polarizing conceptions of society. Lee's image of the Tyne is an accurate symbol for this simultaneous industry, proliferation, contamination, and dissolution. But her writings return again and again to empathy, emotion, and feeling. She would probably have felt that situating the social crises represented by Decadence within a bloodless concern with the conceptual structure of western epistemology risked erasing the abuse suffered by the environment, and especially by the working poor.

Lee's conception of Decadence arises from a vision of England's economy as a materialist value system run by a myopic elite. In works such as *Miss Brown* (1884), *Baldwin* (1886), and *Althea* (1894), these privileged members of society are chastised for leading lives of pleasure and excess that depend on the labour of others who are not themselves given any opportunity for cultural growth or refined aesthetic knowledge. Notably, Lee discourages a simple contrast of an abusive select few and an altruistic working poor by having reformist characters prove less than perfect as well. In *Miss Brown*, for example, the heroine cannot bring herself to encourage the advances of the social reformer Richard, despite his 'positivist philanthropy' (1884 and 1978, III. 76) and his sensitivity to the plight of his workers. The key to the heroine's difficulties lies in her growing awareness that the man's motivations are based on both a desire to possess and control and an admiration for material progress that is as disreputable as the inaction of dandy-aesthetes. Such destabilizations of binary models in *Miss Brown* and elsewhere reflect what Spackman describes as the asymmetry of Decadence, its contamination of the logic of absolute difference (Spackman 1999, 41). In works such as the 1892 story 'Oke of Okehurst', however, Lee's conceptualization of Decadence shows its uniqueness. Offering little of the garish material excess, innovative sexual proclivities, and baroque stylistics commonly associated with the movement and the art itself, she uses Decadence instead to destabilize the claims of moral superiority on which productivist masculinity is based.

II. Addictions of excess

'Oke of Okehurst' depicts not only a Decadent masculinity caused by recent shifts in society's economic emphasis, but also what for Lee was the crucial empathy found in an imperfect but historically sensitive Decadence that her society was ignoring. This empathic tendency is presented as part of the conventional image of Decadence – ancient, artificial, and exotic – and is made manifest in the home in which the landed gentleman William and his wife Alice live. An English manor-house, it does not reflect contemporary British values; rather its identity derives from its admirable preservation of distinctly Italian qualities from the past. Lee's description of the manor's glory pours on for pages with walls of family portraits, suits of armour, sixteenth-century Persian rugs, and an old clock whose chimes sound like an Italian fountain (1890, 118). We are told of an 'overhanging mantel-piece of inlaid Italian stonework, a vague scent of rose-leaves and spices, put into the china bowls by the hands of ladies long since dead', and a clock that plays a 'faint silvery tune of forgotten days' (1890, 119). When describing the room in which Alice finds herself most comfortable, the narrator – a portrait painter – notes its seventeenth-century, Tuscan furniture, pictures by a Bolognese master, Italian harpsichord, and collections of English and Italian poetry of the Elizabethan era. 'It reminded me,' he sums up, 'more of an Italian room than an English one' (1890, 144). And it is in this room that the eccentric heroine keeps the records – locked securely in an ancient Italian cabinet – of an adulterous ancestor whom she utterly admires.

In these passages, Lee associates the conventional image of Decadence with a clock symbolizing both time passing and time everlasting. The object itself is ancient and yet seems to keep alive the very history whose passage it marks. It is a Decadence gendered feminine, with the same evanescent quality of the house permeating the character of Alice Oke herself.[10] With perfectly Decadent logic, she argues that nothing can be established as more permanent or more real than anything else. One only knows something to be true, she argues, 'because one feels it to be true' (1890, 141). The situating of truth within individual perception leads her to attend to historical individuals as if they were as important as those of the present day. She even dresses in clothes of her seventeenth-century ancestor, also named Alice, and fancies that she herself has had encounters with the ancestor's illicit lover Lovelock. Fully sensitive to the transhistorical beauty of her home, Alice has centred her attention and emotions on her namesake and the lover, an absorption that she correlates with the spiritual love that the narrator of Dante's *La vita nuova* feels for Beatrice (1890, 187).

Lee herself so appreciated the beauty of past eras that she spent many years articulating a theory of empathy that maintains that a person can feel the presence of people from history.[11] The argument is enlivened by the aged, feminine Decadence that permeates Okehurst Manor, just as it defines Alice herself. To the male characters, however, her obsession with the past comes across as dangerously eccentric. Within the first paragraph of the story, the narrator describes the heroine as 'exotic, far-fetched,' and 'artifical[ly] perverse' (1890, 109). But his own words are stylistically Decadent, the excess of adjectives tumbling over themselves. The verbal proliferation is reinforced by the fact that the narrator, hired to paint portraits of Alice and her husband, ultimately fills an entire sketchbook with her image. In fact, he mentions that he had to draw 101 sketches of the woman 'before even determining in what attitude to paint her' (1890, 129). It is as if the heroine stimulates a proliferation of her image through the artist's mass production. And yet it is not the woman, but this hard-working man who is giving birth to all these Alices, with the excess of images only emphasizing the impossibility of his intention of capturing the original.

The portraitist might find the woman eccentric, but he also admits that his own unfinished likeness of her is 'quite mad' and 'rather insane' (1890, 110). In accord with the contamination model of Decadence, efforts at segregation prove impossible. His difficulties arise in part from the fact that he is struggling to attain financial stability. The commission with the Okes has the potential of putting his career back on track, but he finds himself over-powered by Alice's magnetism. Although she is unable to have children, the painter finds himself instilled with a reproductive energy beyond his control. Meanwhile, the Decadently feminine atemporality that the heroine shares with the manor-house undermines the man's efforts to create the item that will result in payment. His mass production of inadequate copies stymies the exchange of labour for money and clogs economic flow. The individual who should embody bourgeois manliness is instead stuck in the rut of creating more and more copies that glut the market with valueless wares. The male privilege that Lee questions in 'The Economic Parasitism of Women' results here in a failure marked as the flawed product of a masculine Decadence.

Not surprisingly, the portraitist tries to blame the woman for his misspent efforts. He describes her as suffering from a 'psychological peculiarity.' Her 'morbid' imagination, he warns, is 'all turned inwards, and with no outer characteristic save a certain restlessness, a perverse desire to surprise and shock, to surprise and shock more particularly her husband, and thus be revenged for the intense boredom which his want of appreciation inflicted upon her' (1890, 127). The language of narcissism, self-centeredness and morbidity is the same rhetoric that Nordau used at the same time to criticize the dandy-aesthetes. The claim that she enjoys shocking her husband likewise repeats the common criticism of Decadence and aestheticism as being rooted in the immature pleasure of taunting the bourgeoisie. But the painter also unwittingly exposes an inadequacy within the image of masculinity that he and Alice's husband William are struggling to affirm.

According to the portraitist, Alice is reacting against the boredom caused by a lack of appreciation, but it is not a lack of appreciation for her that is being referenced, for we are given numerous examples of William doting on his wife. The heroine is reacting against the men's disregard for that which she finds all absorbing – the transhistorical empathy triggered by the experience of beauty. Meanwhile, the ancestors that William describes as 'honourable and upright', Alice finds 'flat, stale, and unprofitable' (1890, 132). Profit, for Mrs Oke, is measured at the point of an individual's experience of pleasure and not, as her husband and the painter would see it, at the site of production. This distinction reflects a major shift in perspective at the *fin de siècle*. Britain's economy was being met with growing scepticism regarding the viability and benefit of industrialist and imperialist methods. Victorian society itself had been moving for some time toward a consumerist ethos that looked to taste, pleasure, and conspicuous consumption as the markers of success.

Lee genders her two models of Decadence here, in accord with the common conception of production as energized and masculine and consumption as passive and feminine. While Alice and the house embody the feminine, emotional, 'Italian' Decadence with which Lee sympathized, the Decadence of high-performance, 'British' masculinity is captured in her depictions of the lands and the patriarch of Okehurst. The portraitist describes the surrounding countryside from which the Okes continue to reap their wealth as desolate: 'nothing but the undulation of sere grass, sopped brown beneath the huge blackish oak-trees, and whence arose, from all sides, a vague disconsolate bleating' (1890, 115). There is no lawn or garden, only 'on the other side of the sandy dip, which suggested a filled-up moat, a huge oak, short, hollow, with wreathing, blasted, black branches, upon which only a handful of leaves shook in the rain' (1890, 115). The land has become isolating and barren. Meanwhile, hints of familial glory such as the abandoned moat and wasted oak signify the decayed state of the family.

The landscape may seem to accord with the supernatural experiences of the mistress of the house, but the narrator more than once suggests a distinction between the two. In one instance, he describes a pleasant reverie as he rests in an arm-chair, 'letting all these impressions of the past – which seemed faded like the figures in the arras, but still warm like the embers in the fireplace, still sweet and subtle like the perfume of the dead rose-leaves and broken spices in the china bowls – permeate [him] and go to [his] head'. But as the embers in the fireplace fade, his eyes wander out the window to a distinctly separate vision, 'a greyish-brown expanse of sere and sodden park grass, dotted with big oaks; while far off, behind a jagged ring of dark Scotch firs, the wet sky was suffused with the blood-red of the sunset.' And just in case the image is not sufficiently disturbing, he also hears 'the recurring bleating of the lambs separated from their mothers' (1890, 120). The depressing, vivid images culminate in the heavy-handed description of a bloody sunset, a twilight image of modern civilization marked by the image of lost lambs, symbolizing the uncertain capitalists as much as the sacrificed workers.

Throughout the century, an increasing number of men were self-defining as white-collar workers or individuals whose purpose in life involved 'those hundred curious things which, producing no tangible product, come under the heading of "making money" ' (*Gospels* 1908, 270). The bourgeois population, meanwhile, was becoming more and more concerned about men who did not accept their responsibilities as breadwinners and familial patriarchs. 'In its relaxation of community controls,' Peter Stearns writes, 'the nineteenth century in fact provided more outlets for diverse male behavior than had been possible for the general run of men in preindustrial society. But this only increased the rigor with which most men, in working class and middle class alike, held to basic notions of what a real man should be' (Stearns 1990, 67).

During the nineteenth century, the bourgeoisie, more than any other class of men, faced a new challenge in establishing signifiers of their masculinity. According to James Eli Adams, they increasingly 'legitimated their masculinity by identifying it with that of the gentleman [who was rendered] compatible with a masculinity understood as a strenuous psychic regimen, which could be affirmed outside the economic arena, but nonetheless would be embodied as a charismatic self-mastery akin to that of the daring yet disciplined entrepreneur' (Adams 1995, 6–7). The performance of restraint, rigour, and professionalism had begun to evoke the character of the gentlemanly capitalist. Meanwhile, as the centrality of the middle-class grew, the image of the aristocratic male became less appealing, making the image of the businessman more attractive to members of the landed gentry such as William Oke. For Lee, the responsibility for the plight of the poor lay on the shoulders of all those with economic agency. As 'Oke of Okehurst' demonstrates by situating the image of the gentlemanly capitalist within a consumerist context, the notion of capitalist exploitation as a manly ideal is fabricated through the same artifice and elitism that defines the Decadent.

Although a member of the landed gentry and invested in the affairs of his property, the master of Okehurst Manor struggles to create an image of himself as virile, sensible, and stable. Actually, the narrator asserts that William does fulfil this system of signification: 'He was a very tall, very well-made, very good-looking young man, with a beautiful fair complexion, beautiful fair moustache, and beautifully fitting clothes; absolutely like a hundred other young men' (1890, 111). Later, William is described as a 'perfectly conscientious young Englishman' and a 'serious, conscientious, slow-brained representative of English simplicity and honesty and thoroughness' (1890, 128, 168). The phrases appear to credit the man for his responsibility and stability but eventually such descriptions function to cover the persona in a sort of waxiness that fosters an image of him as isolationist and brittle. The repetition of bland words like 'very', 'beautiful' and 'fair' drain the words of any potency. Like the sketches of Alice, William is himself a copy of an image, identical to the hundreds of others who wish to be seen as responsible, hard-working men. One gets the sense that, should anything in William's life ever alter, he would lack the malleability to react.

Much of the image of William as incapable of action arises from the struggling commercial painter's descriptions of this landed gentleman turned businessman. When the artist follows up his description of William by concluding that the patriarch is 'absolutely uninteresting from the crown of his head to the tip of his boots' (1890, 112), one is reminded of the intense boredom defined as the catalyst for Alice's desire for revenge. Elsewhere, the narrator comments that William depresses him because 'he had a listless, puzzled look, very much out of keeping with his evident admirable health and strength' (1890, 116). The ambivalence that the painter feels reflects an admiration for an image of masculine performance complicated by jealousy for Oke's success – a success reliant extensively on his inheritance. Pierre Bourdieu refers to this mixed response as a 'dialectic of resentment' (Bourdieu 1996, 17). It reflects the petit-bourgeoisie's pretension and its attempt to claim possession of what it sees the bourgeois controlling. According to Bourdieu, 'the unhappy passion for inaccessible possessions and the extorted admiration that goes along with it are fated to end in hatred of the other, the only way of escaping hatred of oneself when envy attaches itself to properties – notably corporal or *incorporated*, such as manners – that one cannot appropriate' (Bourdieu 1996, 17). The issue is not one of productivity but of conspicuous consumption – of ownership and the display of ownership.

In Lee's story, the working artist attempts to straddle the economic and aesthetic spheres but, recognizing the advantages of his male privilege, is drawn most strongly to the former. The language of the time reinforced this direction. Arthur Waugh offers an example of this rhetoric in his attack on Decadent works as a signal of gender deviancy: 'It is unmanly, it is effeminate, it is inartistic to gloat over pleasure, to revel in immoderation, to become passion's slave; and literature demands as much calmness of judgment, as much reticence, as life itself' (Waugh 1894, 355). Lee's portraitist, however, is also forced to recognize that William's masculine persona is quickly crumbling under the pressure of a new value system. The painter reveals a sense of injustice in William's assumed superiority over less established men such as himself. He notes, for example, that Oke is 'nervously anxious' of treating the painter like a tradesman (1890, 112). Elsewhere, he points out that William, due to his family lineage, 'in his heart, thoroughly looked down upon all his neighbours' (1890, 134). Oke is described as going into a paroxysm of anxiety when his wife mentions any peculiarities in the family line in front of the servants (1890, 141). And despite presenting himself as the embodiment of a self-defining manliness, he is described as notably lacking in action or decisiveness. The walls of his study display a collection of sporting equipment that he no longer actually uses (1890, 116). The man also lacks political dynamism and the best that the painter can say on this account is that 'Oke, although always slow and timid, had a certain amount of ideas, and very defined political and social views, and a certain childlike earnestness and desire to attain certainty and truth which was rather touching' (1890, 125). The patriarch, to put it succinctly, is 'a little intellectually dense' (1890, 128).

The painter does note, however, that William 'spent hours every day in his study, doing the work of a land agent and a political whip, reading piles of reports and newspapers and agricultural treatises; and emerging for lunch with piles of letters in his hand, and that odd puzzled look in his good healthy face, that deep gash between his eyebrows, which my friend the mad-doctor calls the *maniac-frown*' (1890, 128–9). Later, he is again described as 'engrossed in his accounts, his reports, and electioneering papers' (1890, 148). But the narrator adds: 'As I sat and watched him, with his florid, honest, manly beauty, working away conscientiously, with that little perplexed frown of his,

I felt sorry for this man' (1890, 148). Financially secure yet eager to perform prosperity, William should embody the ideal masculinity of an industrialized nation. Indeed, it seems to be what the man hopes his pile of reports will symbolize. But instead he comes across as timid, isolated, and cowering within a garrison of papers and bureaucracy. The disrespect and boredom that Alice feels – and a notable portion of late-Victorian society had also felt – when faced with this model of masculinity disempowers males such as William. We see the master of Okehurst Manor, in an effort to reaffirm his position, snatching at his aristocratic heritage, his military uniform, his performance of business responsibilities, and such like so many straws. It is not only that none of these associations suffices any longer to confirm his authority that brings attention to the artifice of them all, but the fact that William has such a Decadent proliferation of inadequate significatory tools.

III. The last straw

William is especially eager to avoid becoming reliant on the consumerist ethos that has enveloped his society. The flaneurism, passivity, and self-display that characterize this model of economic value would appear to a traditionally productivist individual as unbecomingly feminine. To such a person, to accept the rising star of commodity culture involves either seeing one's social position fall or adopting a new persona. The latter act of identity fashioning, however, would undermine the essentialist rhetoric on which these men had in the past been able to maintain hegemonic privilege. This crisis of gendered identity is captured most succinctly in Lee's depiction of the patriarch succumbing to his own objectification. As the painter notes, William is intensely embarrassed even to discuss his likeness being recreated. In raising the possibility, he blushes 'perfectly crimson ... , as if he had come with the most improper proposal' (1890, 112). For William to ask another man to construct him as an object of admiration – that is, to commodify him – is to request his own subordination to the painter and the eventual viewers of the artwork. The productivist masculinity that William wishes to see glorified through art is challenged by the very need for idealization because it turns the man of energy into a passive object consumed by others. William had invested his sense of self-worth in an industrial model that had begun to wane. But as the economic system shifted to a model defined by a consumerism culturally coded as passive and feminine, he found himself, like so many men of the era, forced to acknowledge his own obsolescence.

The Decadence of late-Victorian productivism generates so much of this waste that, like the River Tyne, it eventually contaminates and chokes off not only those with differing ethics and aesthetics, but its own champions as well. William's loss of authority leads him, at the story's end, to take his gun and kill not only Alice, but himself too. With this grim conclusion, it would seem that Lee is suggesting that vulgar masculine Decadence rooted in modern economic exploitation, if left unchecked, will ultimately destroy feminine Decadence marked by aesthetic, emotional, and historical sensitivity. And yet, Lee does not construct this latter Decadence as devoid of agency. After all, the heroine's disregard for her husband is the key catalyst for his fatal actions. Moreover, the shooting occurs only after William has yielded to commodification. Meanwhile, the story 'Oke of Okehurst' itself continues to this day to generate support for Alice's model of Decadence. Through the admiration that readers have for Lee's work, the author and her audience maintain a transhistorical appreciation for beauty and an empathy for unique, sensitive individuals of the past.

Notes

1　This essay first appeared as 'Economic Dependence of Women', in *North American* 175 (July 1902), 71–90, and was subsequently reprinted as 'The Economic Parasitism of Women' in *Gospels of Anarchy*, first published in 1908.

2　This 1993 edition reproduces the 1895 English translation of the second edition of the German work. *Degeneration* was first published in German in 1892.

3　Such a devaluation of the masses also appears in the image of modern society articulated by the French writer Paul Bourget in his 'Essai de psychologie contemporaine: Charles Baudelaire' (1881). For him, a Decadent era was marked not only by the exemplary art of a few geniuses such as Baudelaire; it was also characterized by a general anarchy that arises when members of a society stop subordinating their energy to the mechanics of the social organism as a whole.

4　This process is even enacted on the level of reading, with consumers of Decadent literature often feeling overwhelmed by its excessive imagery and verbiage. The narrative drive and aim of the text become lost, affecting a sense of boredom with a work that seems self-indulgent. This impatience echoes an appreciation for economic efficiency, while the boredom reflects the satiation arising from excessive consumption. Jeff Nunokawa addresses this issue in *Tame Passions of Wilde* (2003).

5　Recent scholarship exploring the dissident potential of Decadence includes Dowling 1989, Felski 1995, Hannoosh 1989, Spackman 1989, and the collection *Perennial Decay*, eds. Constable, et al 1999.

6 Pater, it would seem, was not entirely satisfied with Lee's reading of his
work. In a review of her *Juvenilia*, he questions the ethical weight Lee placed
on works such as his own, arguing that she 'brings now and again into her
exposition of what is perhaps decadent art a touch of something like
Puritanism' (Pater 1887), 5.

7 See also *Althea* (1894) in which she proposes that those in charge of
society's material and spiritual capital have been wasting it rather than
working to increase and distribute it.

8 The edition used is that of 1904.

9 Pierre Bourdieu discusses the points of convergence between the prac-
titioners of art for art's sake and realism, both movements articulating
their position in distinction to the bourgeoisie and its art (Bourdieu
1996, 73–7).

10 For an analysis of Lee's heroines as feminine forces, see Maxwell 1997,
253–269.

11 Lee's theory of transhistorical empathy and affection is discussed in
Denisoff 2004, 99–106.

5
Vernon Lee and the Gender of Aestheticism

Stefano Evangelista

In recent years critics have eloquently documented the connection between aestheticism and an emergent male homosexual subculture.[1] The central figures in the aesthetic canon – Walter Pater, John Addington Symonds, Oscar Wilde, Henry James – are now seen to have explored the ways in which the desire of men for other men influenced the artistic and literary production of the past, and to have tried to create cultural spaces in which the discussion and practice of male homosexuality might be made acceptable in their own time. Today the aesthetes are retrospectively seen as having made a shaping contribution to the formation of a twentieth-century 'gay' identity, and their received critical reputation has subsequently shifted from that of art historians and moralists to sexual radicals. Liberal critics see this highly sexualized version of aestheticism as a positive energy; problematizing current notions of masculinity, aestheticism emerges as a counter-cultural movement that defines itself in opposition to the values of Victorian patriarchy. Inasmuch as these values are questioned or downright rejected, gender roles become more fluid and so, it is implied, women as much as homosexual, effeminate or simply progressive men enjoy the benefits of aestheticism's sexual dissidence.

In this chapter I explore Vernon Lee's troubled relation with the gender of aestheticism in the period between the publication of *Belcaro* (1881) and *Renaissance Fancies and Studies* (1895). These are the years in which Lee's engagement with aestheticism was at its most intense. As a woman and as a lesbian, Lee occupied a doubly marginalized position in the cultural life of her times. At a very early stage in her career, at the age of twenty-two, her motivations for adopting a male pseudonym show a precocious awareness of moving within a strongly male-gendered field: 'I am sure no one reads a woman's writing on art,

91

history or æsthetics with anything but mitigated contempt.'[2] Lee was eager to be taken seriously as an aesthete, and the mixture of ambition and hostility contained in the previous passage is characteristic of her engagement with aesthetic writing. Aestheticism gave her a language to explore gender difference and play with ideas of androgyny and sexual perversion; but at the same time it constrained her within a masculine discourse created by male homosexual authors such as Pater and Symonds, in which the aesthetic ideal was created through a process of cultural-erotic negotiation between men. In the years between 1881 and 1895, Lee consistently uses the works and careers of Pater and Symonds as models to define her own practice as aesthetic writer. Lee's writings share the gender complexity of the male aesthetes, who strive to forge a new relationship between art, criticism and sexual desire; but they also show the limits of her sympathy with the homoerotic models of cultural history advanced by her male predecessors.

The aesthetic education

> The union of extensive knowledge and imaginative power, which [*Belcaro*] presents, is certainly a very rare one, and of course could hardly exist without an unusual power of expression, in which, if I might make one exception, there is perhaps at times a little crowding.
>   Walter Pater, writing to Vernon Lee (Pater 1970, 42).

Belcaro (1881) marks Lee's transition from historian of the eighteenth century to aesthetic critic. In order to rid herself of the historical method and the 'desire to teach' of her earlier work (*Studies of the Eighteenth Century in Italy*, 1880), Lee decides to go 'to school as a student of aesthetics': 'mainly to art itself, to pictures and statues and music and poetry, to my own feelings and my own thoughts' (1881, 5). Although she claims to have gained 'but small profit' (1881, 5) from other writers in this process, it is clear that the 'school' Lee talks about here is the school of aesthetic criticism defined by Pater in the 'Preface' to *Studies in the History of the Renaissance* (1873): 'What is this song or picture, this engaging personality presented in life or in a book, to *me*? What effect does it really produce on me? Does it give me pleasure? and if so, what sort or degree of pleasure? How is my nature modified by its presence, and under its influence? The answers to these questions are the original facts with which the æsthetic critic has to do' (Pater 1910, I. viii). Pater's impressionistic criticism, with its rejection of didacticism, its insistence on personal experience and its emphasis on pleasure is the critical method that Lee applies to her studies of art in *Belcaro*. Pater's injunction to regard all works of art 'as powers or forces producing pleasurable sensations' (Pater 1910, I. ix) is accepted by Lee without qualification. In her own introductory essay she follows Pater, connecting the 'value' of a work of art with 'the amount of pleasure' which it can afford (1881, 12). Lee defends the need for a sensual rather than intellectual appreciation of art, attacking those critics who substitute 'psychological or mystic or poetic enjoyment, due to their own literary activities, for the simple artistic enjoyment which was alone and solely afforded by art itself' (1881, 11–12).

Pater's legacy pervades *Belcaro*. Lee's essay 'The Child in the Vatican', for instance, clearly recalls, both in its title and content, Pater's early imaginary portrait 'The Child in the House' (1878). Lee examines the effects of art on the formation of a child's consciousness, introducing discussions on the question of materiality in art and on the relationship between form and matter which are clearly influenced by Pater's essays on Winckelmann and Giorgione.[3] The 'lesson' of the essay is also recognizably Paterian: the only intrinsic perfection of art is the perfection of form, and that such perfection is obtainable only by boldly altering, or even casting aside, the subject with which this form is only imaginatively, most often arbitrarily, connected' (1881, 48). In spite of her overt rejection of didacticism, Lee insists on offering clearly spelt-out morals to her readers. Her next essay, 'Orpheus and Eurydice: The Lesson of a Bas-Relief', argues that the art object does not tell a 'story' (the mythic tale of Orpheus and Eurydice in this case), but 'it tells us the fact of its beauty, and that fact is vital, eternal, and indissolubly connected with it. To appreciate a work of art means, therefore, to appreciate that work of art itself, as distinguished from appreciating something outside it, something accidentally or arbitrarily connected with it' (1881, 61–2). The extreme privileging of form over content brings Lee to formulate her own version of art for art's sake.

It is however the essay on Ruskinism which most clearly shows Lee's allegiance to Pater's theories. Here Lee picks up the oblique revision of Ruskin made by Pater in *The Renaissance* and voices it with characteristic boldness. Ruskin is criticized for looking for an unobtainable and ultimately irrelevant union of moral and physical perfection. The aesthetic and ethical are discrete spheres for Lee: 'the qualities of right and wrong, and of beautiful and ugly, and our perceptions of them, belong to different parts of our being' (1881, 207). In the 'Preface' to *The Renaissance*, Pater had expressed the need to define beauty 'not in the most abstract but in the most concrete terms possible' (Pater 1910,

I. vii). It is because the beauty of art is an essentially physical quality that sensation or appreciation through the senses is the only valid form of epistemology. Following Pater again, Lee writes that 'whatever abstract instinct of beauty we may possess, it is only through physical sensations that this instinct is reached' (1881, 209). This enables her to refute the influence of moral concerns in the appreciation of art: 'beauty is a physical quality' and there is 'no justice, no charity, no moral excellence in physical beauty' (1881, 210). In this physical world, as in the ever-evolving universe of Pater's 'Conclusion' to *The Renaissance*, the aesthetic critic is freed from moral imperatives.

Paterian aestheticism is still a dominant influence in *Euphorion* (1884), Lee's study of the Italian Renaissance, which is tellingly dedicated to Pater. After the publication of Pater's and Symonds's acclaimed books on the subject, the study of Renaissance art had become a canonical subgenre of aesthetic criticism. Lee's contribution to the field signifies her ambition to belong to the high cultural tradition of aestheticism. But, possessing neither the imaginative force of Pater's book nor the scholarly rigour of Symonds's, *Euphorion* rapidly fell into neglect.

Euphorion bears the mark of both Pater and Symonds. Like her male predecessors Lee sees the Renaissance as a period of intense artistic achievement and like her fellow aesthetes, and in direct opposition to Ruskin, she insists on continuity rather than breach between medieval and Renaissance traditions. Lee's continued use of the impressionistic method forms the strongest link between *Belcaro* and *Euphorion*. In the 'Introduction', comparing her art to the landscape painter's, she defends her choice of method in a language which is thick with allusions to Pater's *Renaissance*:

> The art which deals with impressions, which tries to seize the real relative values of colours and tints at a given moment, is what you call new-fangled: its doctrines and works are still subject to the reproach of charlatanry. Yet it is the only true realistic art, and it only, by giving you a thing as it appears at a given moment, gives it you as it really ever is; all the rest is the result of cunning abstraction, and representing the scene as it is always, represents it (by striking an average) as it never is at all. (1884, I. 10)

Lee combines Pater's polemic inversion of Matthew Arnold's precept to 'see the object as in itself it really is' ('to know one's own impression as it really is') in the 'Preface' (Pater 1910, I. viii) with his advocacy of relativity in the 'Conclusion'. As in *Belcaro*, Lee's emphasis here is on sensation, conveyed to the reader in the form of a sustained metaphor from the visual arts. Paterian impressionism gives Lee an anti-positivist historiographical model that substitutes emotion for science. To the question of whether the past is 'to be treated only scientifically' (1884, I. 12), Lee's answer is unfaltering:

> Surely not so. The past can give us, and should give us, not merely ideas, but emotions: healthy pleasure which may make us more light of spirit, and pain which may make us more earnest of mind; the one, it seems to me, as necessary for our individual worthiness as is the other. (1884, I. 12)

It is worth digressing here to establish how crucial the notion of pleasure is to the method of aesthetic criticism. In the 'Preface' to *The Renaissance* Pater comes back to it insistently: his aesthetic critic treats the objects of his criticism as 'powers or forces producing pleasurable sensations' (Pater 1910, I. ix); the business of criticism is to analyze and discriminate between different pleasures. The critic for Pater is not the bearer of a specialized scientific knowledge but of a special sensibility: 'What is important, then, is not that the critic should possess a correct abstract definition of beauty for the intellect, but a certain kind of temperament, the power of being deeply moved by the presence of beautiful objects' (Pater 1910, I. x). The 'beautiful objects' mentioned here not only include, as we might expect, music, poetry, pictures and works of art, but also 'artistic and accomplished forms of human life', 'the fairer forms of nature and human life', the 'engaging personality *in life* or in a book' [my emphasis] or, in the suggestive words of the 'Conclusion', 'the face of one's friend' (Pater 1910, I. viii, ix, 237). The beauty of the human body, both in art and in life, is also the object of the aesthetic critic, who treats it as a legitimate site for the enjoyment of pleasure. When Pater talks of the 'certain kind of temperament' that marks out his ideal critic he deliberately confuses cultural and sexual categories, enabled by the discourse of sensation. Pater's aesthetic critic is therefore also distinctly a sexual persona who applies the rules for the enjoyment of art to the erotic sphere. And just as there are to be no moral restrictions in the appreciation of art, there is no normativity in this model of sexual desire: 'He will remember always that beauty exists in many forms' (Pater 1910, I. x). Indeed, sexual experimentation contributes to the aesthetic *Bildung*, for 'Our education becomes complete in proportion as our susceptibility to these impressions [of pleasure] increases in depth and variety' (Pater

1910, I. ix). Departure from normativity, in artistic as in sexual matters, widens the understanding. Pater's model of aesthetic criticism not only opens a space in which sexual pleasure is allied with cultural refinement, but turns perversion into what, after Bourdieu, we would call cultural capital.[4] The Renaissance became central to aesthetic criticism precisely because it was seen as a culture which, like aestheticism itself, opened up the gap between aesthetics and ethics in which aesthetic critics like Pater and Symonds locate the value of the sexually perverse.

In Pater's transformation of sexual perversion into epistemology, male homosexuality takes a privileged role. In the essay on Winckelmann, Pater argues that the appreciation of 'beauty of living form' (Pater 1910, I. 193) is a constitutive element of the art historian's revolutionary understanding of the plastic arts of antiquity: sexual desire for the male body and the aesthetic pleasure afforded to the critic by ancient Greek sculpture become one, as in Pater's famous image of Winckelmann 'fingering' the pagan marbles in Rome. The historical Winckelmann emerges as the ideal aesthetic critic just as Pater writes himself at the end of a long line of male critics in whom homoerotic desire is part of the special 'temperament' described in the 'Preface'. Symonds does something similar in his *Studies of the Greek Poets* (1873), where he visualizes the 'Genius of the Greeks' as a 'young man newly come from the wrestling-ground, anointed, chapleted, and very calm' (Symonds 1873, 399). Presenting this sexually-charged image to his readers, Symonds alerts them to the fact that to understand Greek culture is also to desire this young male body. The ancient Greek context, here as in 'Winckelmann', severely limits the likelihood that the implied desiring subject might be a woman. It should moreover be remembered that *Studies of the Greek Poets*, like *The Renaissance*, was written by an Oxford don from within a culture that generally discouraged women's interest in the study of the classics or of aesthetics. Elevating men's desire for other men to the status of a privileged critical sensibility, Symonds and Pater therefore redeploy the structures of homosociality onto the study of culture.

To return to *Euphorion*, the passage quoted above about the use of emotion in the study of the past shows Lee experimenting with the link between pleasure and perversion forged by aesthetic criticism. Like Pater's aesthetic critic, Lee's historian is not so much a scholar as the possessor of a special sensibility, who is capable of reacting to his/her object of study emotionally but also very physically, through sensations of pleasure and pain. Lee values the past (which is her collective name for Pater's lists of art objects) because it operates a fusion of cultural and sensual discourses. But while Pater's model is based on the radical refusal to exclude ('He will remember always that beauty exists in many forms'), Lee is keen to qualify and therefore limit the aesthetic paradigm of sexual/cultural experimentation by making a neat distinction between 'healthy pleasure' and 'pain', that is, perversion. For Pater pain is an acceptable category or form of the pleasure that the aesthetic critic seeks in art and life, and its enjoyment takes place within the morally neutral field of the aesthetic – as his own explorations of morbidity demonstrate. Lee, in direct opposition to Pater, values pain inasmuch as it 'makes our moral fibre more sensitive' (1884, I. 13). By introducing this moral element into the practice of aesthetic criticism, Lee revises her unqualified acceptance of art for art's sake in *Belcaro*. The link between art and pleasure is still upheld, but Lee's problematic distinction between healthy and unhealthy pleasures, as well as her recourse to ethics, seek to overthrow Pater's aesthetic model while still operating within it. Eager to find her own voice as a woman writer in a canon that had turned sexual desire between men into a motor for understanding culture, in *Euphorion* Lee starts to question the basic validity of perversion as a critical category.

Disillusionment and distance

> I was rather predisposed in her favour but [*Euphorion*] made me hate her. She is thoroughly disgusting, narrow, conventional, superficial, sickly.
> Havelock Ellis, writing to Olive Schreiner (Grosskurth 1981, 78)

As Laurel Brake points out in the present volume, Lee met both Pater and Symonds during some of her frequent visits to Britain in the early 1880s, and corresponded with both.[5] Pater's letters to Lee reveal a relationship based on respect of each other's work and a friendship developed through Lee's several stays with the Paters both in Oxford and London. Vineta Colby talks of their 'bond of mutual recognition of their sexual ambiguity' and Burdett Gardner claims that 'Their co-operation in literary enterprises was just short of collaboration' (Colby 2003, 63; Gardner 1987, 541). Affinity, whether between fellow aesthetes, fellow inverts or both, is the sentiment that dominates their exchange. In June 1884, in a characteristic letter written on receiving a copy of *Euphorion*, Pater mentions 'three things which especially impress' him in the book: its 'Very remarkable learning'; its 'Very remarkable power of style'; and the fact that 'that admirable power of writing is evidenced ... in the treatment of very difficult matter. It is not *easy* to do what you have done in the essay on 'Portrait Art', ... – to make, viz. *intellectual theorems* seem like the life's essence of the concrete, sensuous objects, from which they have been abstracted' (Pater 1970, 53–4). Adding to his praise of Lee's aestheticism he writes that 'this evidence of intellectual structure in a poetic or imaginative piece of criticism ... is also an effect I have myself endeavoured after' (Pater 1970, 54). The challenges of fusing critical and imaginative writing and of experimenting with a historiographical model that foregrounds the sensuous element of culture will lead Pater and Lee to their parallel development of the hybrid genre of the imaginary portrait in the 1880s.

By contrast, Lee's correspondence with Symonds is pervaded by estrangement and competition. Symonds shows himself anxious to establish a clear master-pupil relationship with Lee from his very first extant letter (23 May 1880), where he speaks to her as 'an older craftsman' to 'a younger craftsman' and adopts the critical and patronizing tone that he would never relinquish (Symonds 1967–9, II. 635). What makes Symonds's hostility to Lee particularly striking is the fact that it is often expressed in a heavily gendered language. In a letter to Lee of April 1884, commenting on her writing, he observes that she gets 'the charm of printing a clever woman's aperçus, recording in the press her passing thoughts, stereotyping her table talk, by your method. But you miss, according to my notion, the supreme grace of dignity & sweetness & nobility' (Symonds 1967–9, II. 898). Her impressionistic method, in other words, places Lee's writings in a gap between the feminine and the masculine, in which feminine notions of charm and amateurism are defamiliarized by the masculine traits of bluntness and ambition. Commenting on this letter, Christa Zorn rightly sees in Symonds's words an 'anxiety over prominent female intellectuals' (Zorn 2003, 12). Criticizing Lee's alleged literary shortcomings in terms that imply the usurpation of a masculine persona, he accuses her of being 'cocksure' and 'to have posed as an oracle' (Symonds 1967–9, II. 898). Indeed Symonds consistently represents Lee's experiments in the male-defined field of aesthetic criticism as acts of gender transgression. In another letter written later that month, for instance, he accuses her of following 'some crude notion that the prizes of our art are to [be] scrimmaged after by a struggle & a self assertion wh are neither feminine nor masculine' (Symonds, 1967–9, II. 906).

Symonds's critiques of Lee concentrate around the two key notions of 'cleverness' and 'vulgarity', which come up repeatedly in their correspondence. These terms, like his coinage 'stylistic perversities', which he also uses when discussing Lee, have both a literary and a sexual resonance: if cleverness is the trick of the woman writer masquerading as male intellectual, then vulgarity is inevitably the result.[6]

Sometimes Lee's acts of authorial gender transgression are interpreted as personal affronts by Symonds, who, in letters to other correspondents, represents Lee as an intellectual vulture feeding on his ideas.[7] Writing to T. S. Perry in July 1883 he indignantly describes how 'she pitchforks immediately the slightest hint into the robust & original but rather hasty & coarsely-grinding mill of her brain' (Symonds, 1967–9, II. 833). And after the publication of *Euphorion* he complains of being 'just a little sore at her bagging the metaphor of her book (Euphorion) from me, & for wholesale reproductions of my opinions ... . I don't think there is any conscious plagiarism; & Miss Paget's originality is indubitable. But there is a certain carelessness & arrogance about her, wh makes her think that she has thought out a great deal wh she has really absorbed from other writers & remembered' (Symonds 1967–9, II. 935). This anxiety of ownership is entirely absent from Pater's recorded responses to Lee, even though Pater had also used the 'metaphor' of Euphorion in *The Renaissance* and Lee, as we have seen, had borrowed very freely from him in her writings of the early 1880s.[8] Undoubtedly Symonds's resentment was also grounded in another type of sexual jealousy of a very personal nature, for in those years Lee had formed a strong emotional attachment with Mary Robinson, who was Symonds's protégée and to whom he appears to have been sexually attracted.[9] This ulterior act of sexual transgression must have further helped to cement the sexual and intellectual elements in Symonds's characterization of Lee as male-gendered predator, 'robust', but 'coarsely-grinding'; filching his intellectual and sexual property, the female aesthete debases and vulgarizes them through her improper use.

Symonds's letters, however, also contain several expressions of genuine praise. He was impressed, for instance, by Lee's essay 'Mediæval Love' in *Euphorion*, in which she examines the importance of adultery in the development of chivalric poetry. Writing to her in June 1884 he remarks that her treatment 'of the more repulsive side of the subject is pretty much the same as that of a man who, dealing with the real Greek Platonic Love, should insist upon the patent fact that it had more or less of an indissoluble connection with a vice wh bears an uglier name than Adultery' (Symonds 1967–9, II. 923). Symonds's parallel between Lee's exploration of medieval adultery and his own insistent preoccupation with male homosexuality reveals that, like Pater, although less ready to admit it, he too recognized areas of similarity and the potential for collaboration in their work. Symonds and Lee shared a fascination in the imaginative force of sexuality and in tracing a history of the relation between sexual desire and aesthetic experience. Lee's defence of the aesthetic function of adultery in 'Mediæval Love' will indeed be used (and clearly acknowledged) by Symonds to support his defence of homosexuality in his essay 'The Dantesque and Platonic Ideals of Love'.[10] The fact that a lesbian writer's study of medieval heterosexual adultery could provide the basis for a bisexual man's apology of modern male homosexuality shows not only how complex but also how fluid the networks of aestheticism's sexual politics could be.

The sexual politics of aestheticism are the subject of Lee's novel *Miss Brown* (1884), which came out only a few months after *Euphorion*. In *Miss Brown*, Lee radicalizes her use of the moral imperative as a discourse of dissent against the homosocial and misogynist milieux of the male aesthetes. As Zorn has noted, the novel dramatizes 'Lee's own ambivalence over her role as an aesthetic critic' and can therefore be read as an aesthetic Bildungsroman (Zorn 2003, 115). Anne Brown, the Italian servant girl of Scottish parentage turned Pre-Raphaelite beauty, with her split identity between English and Italian culture and her constant, virtuous self-learning, is certainly a figure of Lee's authorial ambition. The basic plot of the novel, which follows the aesthete Walter Hamlin's *Pygmalion*-like experiment to turn Anne into a lady, mirrors the progress of Lee's problematic integration as a female author within the aesthetic circles in England in the 1880s.

In May 1885 Henry James remarked to Lee that there is perhaps 'too great an implication of sexual motives' in *Miss Brown* (James 1980, 86). It is in any case certain that issues of gender are treated with a noticeable lack of discretion, the more so since *Miss Brown* is a *roman à clef* based on fairly transparent fictional transpositions of prominent members of the Pre-Raphaelite circles of the 1860s and 70s.[11] The male characters in the novel are essentially a set of languid heterosexual artists and poetasters who are all, in differing degrees, effeminate and sexually predatory, fleshly, hysterical, amoral, vain and narcissistic. In *Miss Brown*, Lee continues her attack on perversion which she had formulated in the introduction to *Euphorion*, exposing 'the mistake of thinking indecent things interesting and dramatic' (1884, II. 67), the doctrine, in other words, that sexual perversion is connected to a higher artistic understanding. Anne stands as a living antidote to 'the worn-out aphorism' that 'Everything is legitimate for the sake of an artistic effect' (1884, II. 94). Her healthy and beautiful female body, her virginal purity and her desire to sympathize and help stand in clear didactic contrast to the aesthetic set's moral debauchery and morbid taste. Whilst Anne's morality might appear far-fetched and unnecessarily provocative, it is also, importantly, the essence of her sexual radicalism. Lee wants to show that Anne is in fact the only sexual radical among the aesthetes, refashioning their sensational use of perversion into an effective language of social criticism.

Miss Brown contains some of Lee's most radical pronouncements on gender: 'Some few women seem to be born to have been men, or at least not to have been women.' Such are not 'Masculine women, mere men in disguise', but 'women without woman's instincts and wants, sexless – women made not for man but for humankind' (1884, II. 307–9). Anne Brown embodies a deviant model of femininity which stands defiantly not only outside the marriage market ('they are not intended to be ... either wives or mothers', 1884, II. 308), but also outside the patterns of sexual deviance of the aesthetic set. For all their encouragement of sexual experimentation and radicalism, the aesthetes in the novel are just as repressive of Anne's own deviant sexuality as the patriarchal society whose moral narrowness they mock. Just as the male aesthetes had created a space in which male homosexuality is the symbol and manifestation of cultural refinement, in Lee's novel this type of sexually deviant woman is considered 'superior to the ordinary run of her sex' (1884, II. 309). But Lee's idealized woman radical, predicated on a negative model ('women *without* woman's instincts and wants, sex*less*', my italics), based on an awkward model of androgyny ('born to have been men, or at least not to have been women') and visualized through Anne's embarrassing masquerade as an aesthetic woman, unfortunately recalls Symonds's image of Lee as neither man nor woman, but vulgarly posing as a man – showing perhaps just how much Symonds's offensive characterization influenced Lee's own perception of her position as woman aesthete.

Kathy Alexis Psomiades has noted the correspondence between Anne's description as 'sexless' in the passage above and Pater's use of the word in 'Winckelmann'. Reflecting on Anne's role as artistic subject, Psomiades argues that, as in Pater's essay, 'sexless' here 'signifies both the ideal nature of the artwork and the specificity of same-sex desire. Anne's sexlessness is both a feminist critique of aestheticism's eroticized images of femininity and a simultaneous demonstration of the radical power of these images to put into question the entire apparatus of heterosexual desire on which they are supposedly based' (Psomiades 1997, 171). Anne's paradoxical status as sexless object of male desire thus exposes the potentially homosocial matrix of the aesthetes' collective erotic interest in her – the aesthetes, in other words, are actually interested in each other and use Anne as a convenient object to displace their self-obsession. This reading gains particular poignancy if, like Psomiades and Martha Vicinus among others, we see Anne as a lesbian heroine (Psomiades 1997 and 1999, Vicinus 2004, 154–7). In this context Anne is 'sexless' only in the eyes of male aestheticism and, more generally, of nineteenth-century society, which cannot see her sexual desire because it is directed towards other women and therefore is outside the realm of the 'visible'.

To me what is most interesting in Lee's use of the term 'sexless' is the fact that it illustrates her ambiguous practice of simultaneously following and questioning the male aesthetes' sexual politics. Pater uses the word in his discussion of Winckelmann's Hellenism: 'The beauty of the Greek statues was a sexless beauty: the statues of the gods had the least traces of sex. Here there is a moral sexlessness, a kind of ineffectual wholeness of nature, yet with a true beauty and significance of its own' (Pater 1910, I. 220–1). This type of 'moral sexlessness', defined as the absence of 'want, or corruption, or shame', is for Pater the attitude that characterizes Winckelmann's 'friendships' with young men in Rome, and is essentially a type of sexual freedom. Pater's 'sexlessness' is therefore a highly sexually-charged concept: through it he simultaneously looks back to pagan times when male homosexuality was tolerated by society, argues for its naturalness even in modern times and shows that Winckelmann's own homosexuality gave him the special 'temperament' (Pater 1910, I. 220) that coloured his achievement as a scholar. Lee's borrowing of the term ambiguously evokes the discourses of Hellenism and male homosociality introduced by Pater.

In a disturbing scene earlier in the novel Anne is forced to model a Greek dress especially designed by Hamlin that he wants her to wear in a forthcoming aesthetic soirée. Lee shows Anne being subjected to Hamlin's invasive gaze, objectified into a cheap art-object and turned into erotic spectacle, lingering on the alienation produced in Anne by this enforced cross-dressing (1884, I. 305–9). On one level, Anne Brown dressed as a Greek goddess is a striking visualization of just how uncomfortably women fit in aestheticism's neo-Greek and homosocial models. And yet it is her act of masquerading as a Greek statue or, more generally, it is her experience of aestheticism that gives Anne, the uneducated Italian servant girl, the means to understand her sexual difference – just as it is the work of Pater that lends Lee the terms to formulate her feminism and to come up with her own feminine ideal of sexual radicalism.

The plot of *Miss Brown* enacts Lee's practice of writing simultaneously *within* and *against* aestheticism, or what Zorn calls the 'split voice' of Lee's intervention into the aesthetic male discourse (Zorn 2003, 126). Despite all her radicalism and moral commitment, Anne, when she is given the final choice, *does not leave* the aesthetic set, preferring the effeminate Hamlin over the hypermasculine and morally upright Richard and giving up her chance to go to Girton and become an independent woman. When she makes up her mind to marry Hamlin after all, she imagines her married life as that 'of a woman who devoted herself to nurse a person sick of an incurable disease' (1884, III. 278), and approaches marriage as a doomed redemptive mission and form of 'pollution' and 'prostitution' (1884, III. 280). Anne's perplexing decision to marry Hamlin on these premises represents Lee's own troubled identification with the male writers of the aesthetic movement, with whom, in 1884, despite everything, she had decided, metaphorically, to stay. If, with Psomiades, we see Anne's self-immolation at the end of the novel as a refusal of 'heterosexual romance' and an opening toward a 'realm of perverse desire' (Psomiades 1997, 176), then we recognize with Lee that male aestheticism, despite its exclusive homosocial networks and its masculine bias, still offered an attractive network of intellectual support for a woman writer who was interested in the relationship between the study of culture and sexual desire.

The aesthetic mistake

> [*Miss Brown*] is violently satirical, but the satire is strangely without delicacy or fineness, and the whole thing without form as art. It is in short a rather deplorable mistake – to be repented of. But I am afraid she won't repent – it's not her line.
>
> Henry James, writing to T. S. Perry (James 1980, 61)

In the years that followed the professional and personal disaster caused by *Miss Brown*, Lee's engagement with aestheticism becomes even more openly polemical. In her introduction to *Juvenilia* (1887) she reviews and reassesses but effectively reclaims her position within the aesthetic movement. Pater is again the figure against which she formulates her ideas and, implicitly, measures her achievements. Revising her condemnation of Ruskin in her early work, she accuses Pater's *Marius the Epicurean* (1885) of having established a delusive correspondence between the beautiful and the good. She describes Paterian aestheticism as a naïve and essentially childish doctrine and compares its exclusive preoccupation with beauty to the egotistic morality of the young child. The 'juvenilia' of the title are therefore Pater's aesthetic works and her own youthful imitation of them. Cleverly inverting the common use of the term, Lee offers her readers the essays in this collection as the products of artistic maturity. She presents her departure from Pater's aestheticism in terms of natural growth. In the healthy course of things 'we discover that to be good means, unluckily, to deal with evil ... . Of course we may still go and live with the daisies and the statues, seeing only them with the eyes of body and soul; unfortunately to live with the daisies and statues means no longer to be like unto them, but like rather to the dust-heap and the scarecrow, not much more beautiful in soul, certainly' (1887, I. 10–11) The mistake of aestheticism consists in its reluctance to grow up and accept the ethical imperative, in preserving a self-caused pathological condition of arrested development.

In the introduction to *Juvenilia*, Lee revises Pater's doctrines in the 'Conclusion' to *The Renaissance*. Pater had described a universe in continuous change in which the individual, given the impossibility of affecting the natural world's course of events, resorts to live a life of contemplation of its ever-changing beauty. In Pater's vision each individual lives in 'isolation', enveloped in 'that thick wall of personality' that mediates our exchanges with external reality (Pater 1910, I. 235). In *Juvenilia* the image of a world in which 'the whole of all things is ever moving' suggests to Lee the need to 'take part in the movement that alters the world' (1887, I. 18). Lee sees the world 'no longer as a mere storehouse of beautiful inanimate things, but as a great living mass, travailing and suffering in its onward path; and it makes one feel less isolated, in a way, to recognize all round ... the companionship of the desire for good' (1887, I. 20). Picking up on his use of the idea of 'isolation', Lee turns Pater's aesthetics of contemplation and passivity into an imperative to act, presenting this imperative as an anti-Decadent force for social cohesion. Lee's introduction aspires to the status of a new aesthetic manifesto. Its prominent place in the opening of her collection stands in deliberate counterpoint to Pater's

'Conclusion': Lee substitutes Pater's sense of ending and belatedness with a new aestheticism that, laying the stress on activity and intervention, looks to the future rather than the past.

In an anonymous review of *Juvenilia*, Pater expresses his anxieties over the 'increasing "ethical" tone' in Lee's work, retrospectively seeing 'a touch of something like Puritanism' in her oeuvre (Pater 1887, 5). The charge of Puritanism, although apparently mentioned *en passant*, is a serious one. Aestheticism, from its embryonic formulations in Arnold, had defined itself in reaction to the puritan, philistine and prosaic forces that dominated Victorian middle-class culture. Insisting that art matters precisely because it is disengaged from the ethical realm, the aesthetes had created a culture in which the study of art constitutes *in itself* a criticism of Victorian values. This is why art for art's sake appeared such a radical doctrine. The notion of a 'puritan aesthete' is intriguing because it is oxymoronic; indeed, it was under this paradoxical label that Lee came back to wider visibility in the twentieth century, as one of the case studies in Vineta Colby's volume on nineteenth-century women novelists (Colby 1970, 235–304). Accusing Lee of Puritanism, Pater rightly charges her with abandoning one of the most fundamental principles of the aesthetic movement. As Pater suspected, the '"ethical" tone' of Lee's more recent writings was destined to increase in the later years of her engagement with aestheticism. Following *Miss Brown*, Lee uses aesthetic writing to expose the mistakes of aestheticism and the fact that these mistakes are inextricably bound with its treatment of gender and sexuality.

Lee's 1890 collection of supernatural tales, *Hauntings*, marks the culmination of her exploration of the gender of aestheticism. The stories in *Hauntings* have been at the centre of the recent revival of interest in Lee's work, probably due to their exceptional fusion of symbolic, mythic and psychological elements. Several critics have concentrated on their intertextual links with Pater. Angela Leighton, for instance, has claimed that in *Hauntings* Lee attempts 'an experiment in psychology which is the logical conclusion of Pater's aestheticist manifesto' (Leighton 2003, 235). Catherine Maxwell and Christa Zorn have read Lee's supernatural tales as feminist reworkings of Pater. Relating 'A Wicked Voice' and 'Dionea' to Pater's explorations of the Dionysian, Maxwell sees Lee's ghosts as embodiments of 'the transcendent force of female power' (Maxwell 1997, 265). Zorn interprets 'Amour Dure' as a deconstruction of the myth of the femme fatale promulgated by Pater's Mona Lisa: for Zorn, Lee's story 'exposes the limitations of the male point of view from which traditional historiography is written and discovers behind the glory of "great" men in history immense fears and anxieties' (Zorn 1997, 7).

Hauntings can be located, chronologically and culturally, between Pater's *Imaginary Portraits* (1887) and Wilde's *Picture of Dorian Gray* (1890, revised 1891).[12] The four short stories that make up the collection all play on instances of abnormal interaction between artefacts and human consciousness. Like Pater's *Portraits*, Lee's tales fall across the boundary that divides criticism from fiction and therefore build an element of indeterminacy into their very form. Their use of the fantastic is both a device to articulate the culturally unacceptable (in this instance perverse sexuality) and to achieve a sense of irresolution that represents a self-conscious departure from nineteenth-century realism. As in Pater's tales, the past *physically* comes back to life to question and disrupt the patterns of modern society. Lee's tales also show the influence of Symonds, which can be seen especially in Lee's fusion of impressionistic travel narrative and historical writing, and in her use of the evocative power of the *genius loci* with which Symonds had experimented in collections such as *Sketches in Italy and Greece* (1874), *Sketches and Studies in Italy* (1879) and *Italian Byways* (1883).

Lee had explored the concept of 'haunting' ever since her first experiments with aestheticism in *Belcaro* (1881, 2). In that collection 'haunting' as metaphor for the physical connection between the individual and the cultural tradition is the theme of 'The Child in the Vatican', in which the spirits of the pagan gods trapped in ancient statues come back to take possession of a young child. The connection between 'haunting' and the methodology of aesthetic writing is spelt out in the 'Preface' to Lee's historical novella *Ottilie* (1883), another imaginary portrait set in eighteenth-century Germany. Here Lee reflects on the art of negotiating the balance between historical and imaginative writing: 'In studying any historical epoch, in trying to understand its temper and ways, there rise up before the unlucky Essayist vague forms of men and women whose names he does not know, whose parentage is obscure; in short, who have never existed, and who yet present him with a more complete notion of the reality of the men and women of those times than any real, contradictory, imperfectly seen creatures for whose existence history will vouch' (1883, 13). Here it is the author, who is 'haunted' (1883, 14) by her imaginary characters, who are a ghostly materialization of the truth of imaginative writing, suppressed by the demands of positivist historiography. Lee's reflections here point forwards to Pater's definition of the 'imaginative sense of fact' in the essay on 'Style' (1888) as the quality that makes the writer of prose into an artist (Pater 1910, V. 8, 9–10). The same polemic against the restrictions of historiography appears in Lee's preface to her 1907 reprint of *Studies of the Eighteenth Century in Italy*. Here Lee, looking back on the historical inaccuracies of her first book, defends the 'sins of the imagination' of her youth, declaring to be 'quite satisfied to have endowed my eighteenth-century people with virtues and graces of my own making; it was more satisfactory and perhaps more *just* than insisting on them from poor living creatures' (1907, xx, xlvii, my italics).

In the 'Preface' to *Hauntings*, Lee returns to using the figure of the ghost as an anti-positivist force in the study of the past. Hers are not 'ghosts in the scientific sense', but 'things of the imagination, born there, bred there, sprung from the strange confused heaps, half-rubbish, half-treasure, which lie in our fancy, heaps of half-faded recollections, of fragmentary vivid impressions' (1890, xi, ix). Her ghosts emanate from the impressionistic method which grounds the study of culture in individual sensation and therefore they embody the seductive power of aestheticism itself (cf. Leighton 2000, 2). Ghosts, writes Lee, have their origin in 'our fancy': they are also figures of individual psychology, located in the *personal* past, that is, in the terrain where the nascent science of psychoanalysis locates the origin of sexuality.[13] Lee's ghosts are also, importantly, sexual ghosts. 'Haunting' provides Lee with an evocative metaphor with which to explore the relationship between art, scholarship and sexuality on which aestheticism is founded. Identifying sexual desire with the supernatural, Lee implicitly exposes the inadequacy of science as a medium to analyze sexual behaviour. She presents desire as a fluid cultural category that cannot be made to fit in the narrow scientific and sexological studies current at the time. Sexually as well as intellectually desiring the embodied ghosts of the past, the male modern subjects of Lee's stories experience epistemological and sexual crises (inasmuch as sexuality is part and parcel of epistemology in aesthetic writing) that result in illness and death. The revenges of the past narrated in *Hauntings* are Lee's revenges on the male aesthetes' treatment of gender in their writings.

Epilogue

In 1895 Lee published *Renaissance Fancies and Studies*, a collection of aesthetic criticism which she intended as a sequel to *Euphorion*. The book closes with a 'Valedictory' in which Lee reflects on her career so far and bids 'farewell to some of the ambitions and most of the plans of [her] youth' (1895, 235). 'Valedictory' is the culmination of the process of self-scrutiny that Lee had started with *Euphorion*. It repeats a familiar autobiographical narrative in which she represents herself as a voice of ethical dissent within aestheticism. In 1895 Lee traces once again her evolution from being 'an historian and a philosopher' (1895, 235) to realizing the need to apply her knowledge to the improvement of the present. This shift from abstract aestheticism to an ethics of sympathy and usefulness is the same as the one described in *Miss Brown* and *Juvenilia*. But in *Renaissance Fancies and Studies*, Lee uses it to formulate a retrospective assessment of the importance of the study of the Renaissance in aesthetic writing. Clearly hinting at Pater and Symonds, Lee attacks the 'morbid pre-occupation' and the 'exaggerated repulsion' (1895, 247) that for her characterized the treatment of the Renaissance in the 1870s. She compares the aesthetes to those italianized Englishmen of the sixteenth century whose 'conscience was sickened, their imagination hag-ridden, by the discovery of so much beauty united to so much corruption' (1895, 247). She denounces the 'spiritual consequences' (1895, 248) of the aesthetes' attraction to the perverse. Her mission as author and scholar, as performed in this volume, is to correct her male predecessors' ethical mistake. Lee wants to deliver 'other readers from this perhaps inevitable but false and unprofitable view' which has made the study of the Renaissance 'distasteful' to the majority and 'too congenial to an unsound minority' (1895, 248).

In 'Valedictory', Lee still defends the uses of pleasure in the appreciation of art and in the study of the past. But she identifies the pleasure of art with the 'satisfaction which it can bring to every individual soul' (1895, 240), stripping the idea of artistic pleasure from its physical associations, increasing its moral charge and therefore distancing it even further from the realm of perversion explored by the male aesthetes. As in *Juvenilia*, Lee measures her distance from the aestheticism of the 1870s in terms of growth into maturity. Art for art's sake is a mistake of the past. Art and the study of the past are to be appreciated as 'a holiday' from the concrete moral and material needs of the present (1895, 238): the value of art is no longer intrinsic, but is determined in relation to what is outside it. Lee goes to great pains to identify art with sanity and wholesomeness, offering a somewhat bland definition of art as 'the expression of the harmonies of nature, conceived and incubated by the harmonious instincts of man' (1895, 254).

'Valedictory' concludes with an assessment of Pater, who had died the previous year. For Lee, Pater 'began as an æsthete, and ended as a moralist', rising from 'the perception of visible beauty to the know-ledge of beauty of the spiritual kind' (1895, 255–6). Responding to his criticism of her 'increasing "ethical" tone' in the review of *Juvenilia* quoted above, Lee effectively rewrites Pater's career to match her own idea of aestheticism's natural progression into ethics. She dismisses *The Renaissance* as the product of the amoral sensationalism that characterized the 'narrow' aestheticism of the '70s: Pater's early work is presented as an aberration in a career that is otherwise pervaded by spiritual health and congruity. Lee follows her own definition of art as harmony formulated in the previous pages and argues that Pater's conception of art is 'not for art's sake, but of art for the sake of life – art as one of the harmonious functions of existence' (1895, 259). 'Valedictory' is, like the introduction to *Juvenilia*, a rewriting of Pater's 'Conclusion' to *The Renaissance*, the most important aesthetic mani-festo, and a text that Lee repeatedly uses to define her ethical position-ing within the aesthetic movement. Lee had placed her earlier rewriting in the opening of a collection, signalling the belief that, in 1887, aestheticism was still intrinsically viable, and presenting her reformed version of it as a fresh start. In 1895 Lees sees no future for aesthetic writing. Her 'Valedictory' carries the full force of definitive closure: it represents the conclusion of Lee's personal engagement with aestheticism but also, more generally, it argues that aesthetic culture has reached the end of its course. *Renaissance Fancies and Studies* closes with an ambiguous tribute to Pater, which, together with her dedica-tion of *Euphorion* to him, is meant to frame her relationship with her declared 'master':

> Many years ago, in the fullness of youth and ambition, I was allowed, by him whom I already reverenced as a master, to write the name of Walter Pater on the flyleaf of a book which embodied my beliefs and hopes as a writer. And now, seeing books from the point of view of the reader, I can find no fitter ending to this present volume than to express what all we readers have gained, and lost, alas! in this great master. (1895, 260)

In 1895 Pater and Symonds were both dead. In that same year the trials of Oscar Wilde would bring aesthetic culture to a scandalous end. Freed from the constraining influence of her male predecessors, in 'Valedictory' Lee reclaims her own role in the aesthetic movement, rewriting the history of aestheticism and asking posterity to look back on it through the modifying influence of her own writings. Lee's rhetorical shift from writer to reader, used in the previous passage and all through 'Valedictory', makes it clear that for her, in 1895, the aesthetic critic has nothing left to write. Aestheticism, its theories of art and its sexual politics, are no longer a field of *writing* but of *reading*. The image of Lee rereading aestheticism provides a fitting ending to her ambiguous relationship with aesthetic writing: her final injunction to reread aestheticism expresses the need to reinterpret it, but it also contains a plea not to forget – an invitation to keep going back to its defining works.

Notes

1 See for example Adams 1995, Dellamora 1990, Dowling 1994, Sinfield 1994.
2 Lee's letter to the novelist Mrs Jenkin, 18 December 1878 (1937, 59).
3 Although 'The School of Giorgione' was only included in the third edition of *The Renaissance* (1888), it had at that point already appeared in the *Fortnightly Review* in October 1877.
4 For Pierre Bourdieu (1984) cultural capital is constituted by the non-economic forces that contribute to academic and social success.
5 Lee's first meeting with Pater took place in Oxford, in July 1881. In her letter to her mother detailing the event she describes him as 'a heavy, shy, dull looking brown moustachiod creature over forty, much like Velasquez' Philip IV, lymphatic, dull, humourless.' She also seems to hint at the open secret of Pater's homosexuality, reporting with characteristic glee her landlady's cheeky remark that 'Mr. Pater don't seem to be getting married, do 'ee, Miss?' (1937, 78) Lee met Symonds only once, in London, in June 1882. She described him to her mother as 'very ill' and 'dreadfully depressed' (1937, 91). They had corresponded since 1880.
6 For 'Vernon's stylistic perversities' see Symonds's letter to Mary Robinson of 3 May 1883 (Symonds 1967–9, II. 814).
7 This was also the reaction of Bernard Berenson, whose relationship with Lee is treated in Jo Briggs's chapter in this collection.
8 Cf. Pater 1910, I. 226–7.
9 See Grosskurth 1964, 223. Grosskurth also writes that Havelock Ellis proposed to use Lee and Mary Robinson as a 'possible case-history for the section on Lesbianism in *Sexual Inversion*' (ibid.). The two women became estranged after Robinson's sudden engagement to James Darmesteter in 1887. Robinson dedicated her *The End of the Middle Ages* (1889) to Symonds, her 'dear Master'.
10 The essay was originally published in the *Contemporary Review* in September 1890 and later reprinted in *In The Key of Blue and Other Prose Essays* (Symonds 1893).
11 Anne Brown can be identified with Jane Morris, the wife of William Morris, and Walter Hamlin with Dante Gabriel Rossetti. Hamlin's first name and his description as 'gemlike' (1884, 1. 5) suggest that Lee might have wanted to give him some elements of Pater. For a detailed identification of the characters in *Miss Brown* see Ormond 1970.

12 Of the stories in *Hauntings*, 'Oke of Okehurst' had appeared as 'A Phantom Lover' in 1886 and 'Amour Dure' had previously been published in 1887. 'A Wicked Voice' is a substantial rewriting of an 1881 tale, 'A Culture Ghost: or, Winthrop's Adventure'. 'Dionea' had not been published before.

13 For a study of Lee's exploration of sexuality in 'A Wicked Voice' with reference to psychoanalytic criticism, see Pulham 2002.

6

The Snake Lady and the Bruised Bodley Head: Vernon Lee and Oscar Wilde in the *Yellow Book*

Margaret Stetz

As Vineta Colby says in *Vernon Lee: A Literary Biography* (2003), with 'Prince Alberic and the Snake Lady' the reader is 'in as rich and exotic a realm of fantasy as Vernon Lee ever created' (Colby 2003, 227). Surely that is an accurate pronouncement, for Lee's 1896 short story takes place in a parallel aesthetic universe, in which certain imaginary works of art did exist once and still supposedly live on at the end of the nineteenth century. In that other world, there is a tapestry 'of old and Gothic taste, extremely worn ... [which] represented Alberic the Blond and the Snake Lady Oriana' (1896, 290). By the end of the narrative, we are told that the tapestry enjoys a second, ongoing life as upholstery, for 'certain chairs and curtains in the porter's lodge of the now long deserted Red Palace are made of the various pieces' (1896, 344). The narrator says drily, 'These things the traveller can confirm' (1896, 344), yet only a tourist venturing into Lee's own fancy can do so, for the chairs decorate a room that never was. Similarly, the narrator invites the reader to visit this magnificent Italian castle, originally the residence of Duke Balthasar Maria, and to examine its murals: 'Now Balthasar Maria had assembled at Luna ... a galaxy of beauty which was duly represented by the skill of celebrated painters on all the walls of the Red Palace, where you may still see their fading charms' (1896, 332). But again, the invitation opens no doors except those into the author's psyche. The fantastic events in Lee's story occur in a sphere subject to time, change, and decay, but one that is also self-contained and that has no direct link to the actual world – or so it might seem.

I would like to suggest that the opposite is true. 'Prince Alberic and the Snake Lady' may appear to be a tale set in an imaginary Italian landscape at the end of the seventeenth century, but its framing serves as an elaborate blind, concealing a narrative that refers to late-nineteenth-century British matters. The fate of Alberic, the art-worshipping dreamer who is persecuted and imprisoned for refusing to renounce an outlaw love in favour of a socially approved one, is as much a political allegory as a fairy tale. It alludes throughout to the contemporary circumstances of Oscar Wilde, who was halfway through his sentence of two years at hard labour when Lee's story was published in the *Yellow Book* of July 1896. Written to express Vernon Lee's sympathy for a fellow aesthete, disciple of Walter Pater, and sexual dissident, 'Prince Alberic' also uses readily identifiable Wildean literary tropes throughout. Thus, at a time when Wilde's own works were regarded as dangerous or seen as taboo, Vernon Lee kept the memory of them clearly, though covertly, before the public, even as she argued for a mitigation of Wilde's unjust punishment. She did so through the medium of the *Yellow Book*, the art-and-literature quarterly issued by the Bodley Head, the very firm which had also published Wilde and then removed his name from its lists. Lee joined a surprisingly large assembly of Bodley Head authors who produced texts in solidarity with Wilde, while he was locked away and unable to speak for himself. That stories such as Vernon Lee's – or Ella D'Arcy's equally Wilde-friendly 'The Death Mask', which appeared in the same volume of the magazine as 'Prince Alberic' – were allowed to hide in plain sight says much about the ambivalence of John Lane, owner of the Bodley Head firm, who had reason to identify with Wilde, as well as to abhor and shun him.

Before the catastrophe of 1895, Vernon Lee's relations with Wilde had been of a mixed character. Their acquaintance began promisingly in 1881, on Lee's visit to England as guest of the poet Mary Robinson. Writing to her mother on 22 June 1881, Lee described how

> the wonderful Oscar Wilde was brought up [i.e., into the Gower Street drawing-room] – the Posthlethwaite [*sic*] of Punch. I must send you a caricature of him. He talked a sort of lyrico-sarcastic maudlin cultschah [sic] for half an hour. But I think the creature is clever, & that a good half of his absurdities are mere laughing at people. The English don't see that. (1937, 64–5)

Vineta Colby suggests that Lee felt a 'special affinity' for Wilde based on their shared laughter at the absurdities of radical art movements: 'In his unabashed flaunting aestheticism she quickly detected the satire he was directing at the humorless aesthetes of Pre-Raphaelitism' (Colby,

2003, 80). I would add, however, that Lee's words to her mother hint at something else: a connection rooted instead in a shared sense of foreignness, of un-Englishness or even anti-Englishness. Lee's own cultural identity was pan-European, growing out of her greater experience in her youth with countries other than Britain. Although her executor, Irene Cooper Willis, would claim later that she 'was at home in England, France, Germany and Italy' (Preface, in Lee 1937, xiv), her performance as an English lady would always be a slightly alien role. What she responded to, in this early encounter with Wilde, was his undercurrent of Irish irony and his mockery of the English in general – a joke, as Lee implies, that his comic targets did not get, but that she, with her own sense of difference and distance from the English, could appreciate.

Lee's falling out with Wilde (and with most of the British avant-garde art and literary world) was of her own making, due to her novel *Miss Brown* (1884). Less than a month after meeting Wilde in 1881, she attended a performance of Gilbert and Sullivan's *Patience* in London and reacted with delight to the actor George Grossmith's lampooning of Wilde, telling her mother that this was 'far the best comic acting' she had seen, 'really delicately excellent', and quoting (or rather, misquoting) in a letter home as many of the lyrics ridiculing that 'greeny & yellary [sic], Grosvenor Gallery' poet based on Wilde as she could recall (1937, 78). Clearly influenced by that performance, she created in 1884 her own Wildean figure of fun in *Miss Brown*, with the character of 'Mr. Posthlethwaite', to whom she wickedly assigned a 'mellifluous fat voice' (1884, II, 16) and a body described as both 'unwieldy' and 'elephantine' (1884, II, 8). Wilde blithely and shrewdly had made literary capital out of *Patience*'s Bunthorne, as well as of George Du Maurier's visual caricatures of him as the poet 'Maudle' (a friend of the painter 'Jellaby Postlethwaite', who was drawn as a take-off on J. M. Whistler), and used these potentially offensive images to enhance his public recognition. Did Vernon Lee imagine that he would, therefore, take her satirical portrait in stride? If so, she was wrong. It was one thing to be laughed at by other gentlemen and another to be the butt of a woman's joke. Vineta Colby notes that Wilde 'avoided meeting her again until about ten years later' (Colby 2003, 106). To do so would have required considerable effort, for the social circles in which they moved overlapped at many points.

Among their common acquaintances was Margaret de Windt (1849–1936), Lady Brooke, who became the Ranee of Saràwak. A figure of distinction in her own right, she was, in the parlance of the day, also a lion-hunter, who gathered artists and writers around her. With a social position that was virtually unassailable, she enjoyed the luxury of associating with controversial figures, of flouting conventional judgments, and of having her name linked to radical works. Thus, when Oscar Wilde produced *A House of Pomegranates* in 1891, he dedicated 'The Young King', the most politically charged of the four stories in that volume, 'To Margaret, Lady Brooke'.

Set in an imaginary Germanic royal court, 'The Young King' uses the narrative structure of a fairy tale for its account of a lovely, golden youth, a 'dreamer of dreams' (Wilde 1891, 25; 1994, 95), who, as heir to the throne, learns to value social justice above his attraction to the decorative arts. Wilde's story echoes British socialist doctrine of the 1880s in general and the influence of William Morris in particular, as it reveals the terrible price of aristocratic vanity; every trapping associated with kingship is a selfish pleasure that comes at the price of suffering and exploitation. As one weaver of royal garments laments to the eponymous hero in a dream-vision, 'We have chains, though no eye beholds them; and are slaves, though men call us free' (Wilde 1891, 10; 1994, 87). The story itself, however, revels paradoxically in its descriptions of the very ornaments that it condemns on moral grounds, lingering over the chamber of the 'boyish' King, where

> The walls were hung with rich tapestries representing the Triumph of Beauty. A large press, inlaid with agate and lapis-lazuli, filled one corner, and facing the window stood a curiously wrought cabinet with lacquer panels of powdered and mosaiced gold, on which were placed some delicate goblets of Venetian glass, and a cup of dark-veined onyx. Pale poppies were broidered on the silk coverlet of the bed, as though they had fallen from the tired hands of sleep (Wilde 1891, 7; 1994, 86).

Despite his initial appreciation of such luxuries, the Young King readily gives them up, for he is both of the Court and alien to it, having been raised by peasants and having lived for sixteen years 'like a brown woodland Faun, or some young animal of the forest newly snared by the hunters' (Wilde 1891, 2; 1994, 83). But Wilde's story has its aesthetic cake and eats it too. The narrative of 'The Young King' extols simplicity and goodness as divine, while crafting elaborate, fanciful objects out of words and making its audience feel their divinity as well. This practice of speaking in praise of asceticism while revelling in aestheticism would, in fact, also serve as the guiding principle for the narrative voice of Vernon Lee's 'Prince Alberic and the Snake Lady', published five years afterward.

Vernon Lee's biographer, Vineta Colby, dubs Lee's story 'pure fairy tale' (Colby 2003, 230). It is certainly a fairy tale, though not 'pure' at all, in the sense of existing wholly in the realm of the fantastic or in relation solely to folk traditions. Instead, it is a tale rich with borrowings from contemporary, late-nineteenth-century sources, constructed purposefully to be in dialogue with Wilde's *A House of Pomegranates*, and brimming with allusions throughout to two stories in particular: 'The Young King' and 'The Birthday of the Infanta'. Like these, it invents historical settings in fictional European courts, where murderous and duplicitous hangers-on cater to selfish monarchs ('The Birthday of the Infanta' takes place in a Renaissance Spanish world that never was) and where love and loyalty are perpetually frustrated, rewarded only with death. At the same time, Lee's 'Prince Alberic' reaches back self-consciously to other well-known texts by Wilde. It features such recognizable tropes as birds singing ecstatically in gardens (from 'The Nightingale and the Rose', in the 1888 *The Happy Prince and Other Tales*); a conspicuously dominant moon (from the 1893 play *Salomé*); doomed attachments between a living being and a work of art that comes to life and performs altruistic service (from 'The Happy Prince'); a man ruthlessly determined to look young forever, even at the price of harming others (from *The Picture of Dorian Gray*, 1890, revised 1891); and many others. Wilde's *Salomé* had ended with the body of the princess crushed under the shields of soldiers, on the order of Herod; Lee's narrative concludes with 'the body of a woman, naked, and miserably disfigured with blows and sabre cuts' – the snake lady killed on the order of Duke Balthasar (1896, 343).

Along with these borrowed themes, images, and devices come unmistakable Wildean rhetorical flourishes, such as this lengthy passage, which performs no narrative function other than to evoke similar descriptions in Wilde's prose:

> Prince Alberic was awakened by the loud trill of a nightingale. The room was bathed in moonlight, in which the tapers, left burning round the bed to ward off evil spirits, flickered yellow and ineffectual. Through the open casement came ... the silvery vibration of the cricket, the reedlike quavering notes of the leaf frogs, and, every now and then, the soft note of an owlet, seeming to stroke the silence as the downy wings growing out of the temples of the Sleep god might stroke the air. The nightingale had paused; and Alberic

listened breathless for its next burst of song. At last, and when he expected it least, it came, liquid, loud and triumphant; so near that it filled the room and thrilled through his marrow like an unison of Cremona viols. He was singing in the pomegranate close outside, whose first buds must be opening into flame-coloured petals. (1896, 326)

It is insufficient to note, as Christa Zorn does, that 'The aesthetic symbolism in "Prince Alberic and the Snake Lady" makes it very much a story of the *Yellow Book* days in the same vein as Oscar Wilde's precious fairy tales' (Zorn 2003, 152). The resemblances are not accidental ones or mere reflections of the shared *Zeitgeist*; rather, they are Lee's artistic and political gestures of homage to a fallen, disgraced master of this form.

Why, we might ask, would Vernon Lee bother to preserve and celebrate both the style and substance of Wilde's prose – especially of his fantasies – in 1896, while he was in the depths of shame, a social outcast? Some ten years earlier, she had mocked him; for a decade afterward he had kept clear of her. What had he come to represent for her, to make her want to rise to his defence in the mid-Nineties by bringing back into sight his banished name through a *Yellow Book* tale redolent of his texts? Why, too, would she wish to create a story about a beautiful, aristocratic, blond youth who falls afoul of his tyrannical guardian by clinging disobediently to a forbidden love – a situation that drew so clearly upon the well-known conflict between Lord Alfred Douglas and his father, the Marquess of Queensberry, and revealed the latter as a monster of heartlessness? And why would she make Prince Alberic's fate demonstrate so plainly the cruelty and injustice of imprisonment, especially for one whose only crime was loyalty to his beloved?

As was true for many of the publisher John Lane's authors, ranging from 'George Egerton' (Mary Chavelita Dunne), to Richard Le Gallienne, to Max Beerbohm – all of whom produced work for the Bodley Head, in the years 1895 to 1897, that alluded to Oscar Wilde's case subtextually and that was designed to move the public to reconsider its verdict upon him – Vernon Lee quite rightly identified with Wilde's plight. The stones cast at him were directed at anyone who violated bourgeois sexual norms or who, moreover, dared to place artistic ideals above conventional moral sentiments. Wilde's antagonists were hers (and most certainly his enemies would have pursued her, had they known how far from respectable were her own secret passions for women).

Yet there were more concrete factors behind her attempt to intervene on Wilde's behalf. On 19 May 1894, a year before the trials, Wilde had visited her brother, Eugene Lee-Hamilton, in Florence. Richard Ellmann's 1987 biography of Wilde records that occasion in the words of Mary Smith Costelloe: 'It was a great success. Oscar talked like an angel, and they all fell in love with him, even Vernon Lee, who had hated him almost as much as he had hated her. He, for his part, was charmed with her' (Ellmann 1987, 395; see also Colby 2003, 106). Two months later, Vernon Lee wrote in a letter, 'Did I tell you I met Oscar W. the other day in Piccadilly, & he stopped me & asked very much after Eugene, & took down his address to send him a book. I think he is quite kind, whatever else he may be' (1937, 376). If loyalty was the dominant characteristic of her fictional hero, Prince Alberic, it was present, too, in Lee herself. In her eyes, Wilde's kindness to her beloved brother had earned him an answering gesture of her own.

But Lee's allegiance to her women friends was even greater. In 1895 to 1896, while Lee was writing 'Prince Alberic', Margaret, Lady Brooke, the Ranee of Saràwak, was involved actively in Wilde's situation, trying to alleviate both his sufferings and those of his wife, Constance. More Adey wrote to Wilde in prison on 23 September 1896, reassuring him that Constance was being looked after, for 'Lady Brooke has been with your wife during the last nine months' (Holland and Hart-Davis 2000, 663). Meanwhile, as Barbara Belford, Wilde's recent biographer, reports, the Ranee 'urged her friend – Richard Burdon Haldane – to visit Wilde in prison' (Belford 2000, 269). Haldane, a Member of Parliament who was part of a government committee investigating prison conditions, then used his influence on Wilde's behalf, first to have books sent to him in Pentonville and later to have him transferred twice (to Wandsworth and finally to Reading Gaol), in hopes of obtaining better conditions for him. Lee could hardly have failed to know of her friend's efforts to aid and support the Wildes. In response, she not only created a story that affirmed her appreciation of Wilde as an artist and denounced imprisonment for the so-called crime of loving in secret, but she made her support anything but covert through the dedication line on the first page of the printed text. It read, '[To H. H. the Ranee Brooke of Saràwak]' (1896, 289), thereby linking 'Prince Alberic' explicitly both to Wilde's 'The Young King', which had also been dedicated to Brooke, and to the Ranee's humanitarian campaign. Lee's gesture, in such a context, called attention to itself boldly and invited decoding by the audience, for dedications were uncommon among the contributions to the *Yellow Book*. Hers was indeed the only work of either prose or verse in Volume 10 of the quarterly to bear any dedication whatsoever.

Vernon Lee's 'Prince Alberic' may have been unique in carrying a dedication that linked it to Wilde and to efforts by friends to aid him, but it was only one among numerous short stories, essays, and poems by *Yellow Book* authors to address Wilde's plight sympathetically, if obliquely, while he was in prison. Somewhat surprisingly, Wilde had been shut out of participation in the magazine at the time of its debut in 1894, thanks to a joint decision by Henry Harland (its literary editor), Aubrey Beardsley (its art editor), and John Lane (its publisher and the co-founder of the Bodley Head firm which issued many of Wilde's books), all of whom knew Wilde well as a Bodley Head author and found that his egotism made him difficult and undesirable as a collaborator (Stetz and Samuels Lasner 1994, 19–20). Nonetheless, Wilde was acknowledged by all the avant-garde writers and visual artists of the *Yellow Book* circle as central to their movement and to their own artistic and political projects. Whatever attacks were levelled against him either directly or indirectly threatened them.

When catastrophe struck and Wilde was arrested on charges of gross indecency in the spring of 1895, Henry Harland, the American-born fiction writer responsible for the *Yellow Book*'s literary contents, spoke plainly – if privately – of the distress that both he and his wife Aline, a *Yellow Book* poet (under the pseudonym Renée de Coutans), felt on Wilde's behalf. In a 5 May 1895 letter to the critic Edmund Gosse, Harland wrote,

> Oh, poor Oscar, indeed! We have followed the story of his ruin with the keenest pain. ... It seems to us a pity that the law should take cognizance of a man's private morals, his vices, his bad tastes. ... But, dear me, if all the men of Oscar's sort in England were suddenly to be clapped into gaol, what miles of new prison-houses Her Majesty would have to build, and what gaps would be left in the ranks of artists, statesmen, and men o' letters! (Mattheisen and Millgate 1965, 231).

Three years later, as Karl Beckson records in his biography of Harland, both Henry and Aline would dine with Wilde in Paris and, by doing so, would distinguish themselves from so many members of the literary world who shunned Wilde upon his release from prison in 1897 (Beckson 1978, 148, n. 62). Harland was thus understandably receptive to showcasing a story such as Vernon Lee's 'Prince Alberic', which wore its high regard for Wilde on its embroidered velvet sleeve. It is even tempting to see Harland's editorial hand at work in the placement of 'Prince Alberic' as the final selection in Volume 10, immediately following Charles Conder's drawing of two elegant ladies, titled *Windermere*. Was there a *Yellow Book* buyer in 1896 who could read the word 'Windermere' and not think first of Wilde's hit play of four years earlier and then of its incarcerated author?

If anyone might have taken umbrage at Lee's pro-Wilde tale, it would have been John Lane, owner of the Bodley Head publishing firm which produced the *Yellow Book*. Yet Lane clearly did not bear a grudge against Lee for her support of Wilde; he later issued twelve of her books, beginning in 1903. The question we might ask is why, in 1896, Lane agreed to print her story. Why, after withdrawing all of Wilde's titles, publicly expunging Wilde's name from his list of books, and even firing Aubrey Beardsley, because some of his prize authors wrongly associated the latter with Wilde's 'bad tastes', would he reverse himself so far the following year?

Lane's dislike of Wilde was well known, even before the disaster of April 1895. The trials themselves, he asserted, gravely harmed and nearly ruined his business, especially after a young man named Edward Shelley came to the stand to testify about a sexual relationship with Wilde, presenting 'a sad picture', as Thomas Mallon writes, 'of victim-ization' (Mallon 2001, 214–15). Shelley had been a clerk in Lane's establishment and had met the much older Wilde there, in the Heady world of the Bodley. But Shelley's correspondence from 1891 (now in the Humanities Research Center at the University of Texas) with the ostensibly heterosexual Lane offers a startling glimpse of the question-able, perhaps not-so-innocent relations between Lane and his clerk. These are enough to suggest that Lane's wish to dissociate himself from Wilde in 1895 was more than merely sound business sense. Lane cast out Wilde in a panic, for he had reason to fear that his own ambiguous attachments to younger men like Shelley might come under scrutiny. Yet he must have retained some identification with one whose fate could have been his own and, therefore, permitted – or perhaps even welcomed – such covert and discreet expressions of support as 'Prince Alberic'. If nothing else, the presence of Lee's story in the *Yellow Book* helps us to understand more clearly that there was more than one snake or one secret love, hidden and coiled at the heart of the Bodley Head.

Indeed, Lane would have been particularly well placed to appreciate some of the ways in which Lee evoked and paid tribute to Wilde. In their invaluable research into the historical – often, the pseudo-historical – underpinnings of 'Prince Alberic' for their edition of Vernon Lee's *Hauntings and Other Fantastic Tales* (Broadview Press), Catherine Maxwell and Patricia Pulham have made it clear that the story's setting was both actual and imaginary. Based though it was on Massa Carrara in Italy, a province in Tuscany, the 'Duchy of Luna', where the beautiful young prince experiences his forbidden attachment to a 'snake lady', was Lee's own invention. Reading this heavily aestheticized tale, *Yellow Book* audiences could not have failed to hear in the name 'Luna' Lee's allusion to the lunar imagery which had dominated an earlier and more notorious Bodley Head publication, the 1894 English edition of Oscar Wilde's *Salomé*. There, the Princess Salomé is repeatedly associated with the moon, which looms perpetually over her fatal actions. More important, Lee's invented setting would have recalled – no doubt to John Lane himself – the controversies, both inside and outside his publishing firm, over Beardsley's illustrations, including the image titled *The Woman in the Moon*. Stephen Calloway reminds us that, 'as a final point of contention' between Beardsley and Wilde

> there was the matter of how amusingly Beardsley had chosen to caricature the author in his designs. In fact, Wilde's distinctive cast of features appears, quite recognizably and, as most observers thought, somewhat unflatteringly portrayed in a number of drawings, most notably as the pale, bloated face of the *Woman in the Moon*. (Calloway 1998, 80)

To place her Wildean story in 'Luna' was to underline the connection that Vernon Lee wished to draw between this fictional narrative of an idealist's persecution for a forbidden attachment and the 'moon'-faced author whose prosecution shook London's literary world.

When read as a story inspired by and responding to contemporary events, 'Prince Alberic' helps us to appreciate how deeply Lee's imagination was informed by historical research, but also by the figures, events, and movements around her. An earlier tale, such as 'Lady Tal' (from the 1892 *Vanitas: Polite Stories*), with its direct references to her friend Henry James and to fiction of the 1890s, thus becomes not an aberration in her oeuvre, but merely another example of Lee's interest in commenting upon modern life – a further outgrowth of the critical impulse which, in the preceding decade, had produced *Miss Brown*. In 'Lady Tal', moreover, we can find the seed of the Wildean homage that blossomed in 'Prince Alberic'. Although Lee's response to James dominates the narrative, her dialogue occasionally falls into rhythms borrowed from Wilde. In the voice of the much-maligned Lady Tal, for instance, there are unmistakable resemblances to the voice of another socially outcast figure, Mrs Erlynne. Lady Tal's speech – ' "One thinks one has a soul sometimes," she mused. "It isn't true. It would prevent one's clothes fitting, wouldn't it? One really acts in this way or that because *it's better form*" ' (1892, 83; 1993, 239) – recreates the brittleness, the self-mockery, and the deliberate rejection of sentimentality of Wilde's anti-heroine, who proclaims, ' "I lost one illusion last night. I thought I had no heart. I find I have, and a heart doesn't suit me, Windermere. Somehow it doesn't go with modern dress. It makes one look old" ' (Wilde 1982, 253). Wilde's play opened in February 1892, while the volume *Vanitas* was not listed in the *Bookman* as among the 'New Books of the Month' until December of the same year – time enough to enable Lee to incorporate echoes of a comedy that was widely quoted in the press and seen by many of her friends ('New Books' in *Bookman*, 95).

Encountered through a modern reprint, decontextualized, and stripped of its political import, 'Prince Alberic and the Snake Lady' seems merely a highly wrought tale of the fantastic inspired by research into a distant past. But when restored to its place in the *Yellow Book* milieu where it first appeared, Lee's 1896 story becomes something quite different: a passionate defence of over-the-top Wildean aesthetic writing of the sort that the Bodley Head once had championed, as well as an equally passionate declaration of the importance of Wilde himself and of the right of artists to choose their own love-objects, however unconventional. It stands then as a work of great immediacy, both engaging with and attempting to influence the British literary and social worlds of the 1890s, even as it takes on the wrongheaded decisions of a publishing firm that had blamed and punished the victim. And it reminds us that Vernon Lee was, like Wilde himself, a writer who took pleasure in contradiction – a conjurer of pictures of the far-away whose deepest interest was in the near-at-hand.

7
Duality and Desire in *Louis Norbert*

Patricia Pulham

Vernon Lee's novel, *Louis Norbert: A Two-Fold Romance* (1914) was to be her last. Despite her accomplishments in other genres and the comparative popularity of her short stories, success in the novel form eluded her. Vineta Colby, somewhat unfairly perhaps, appears to agree with the general opinion of these works. In her literary biography of her, Colby writes: 'Vernon Lee's novels – those, that is, that were written in the popular modes of social realism (*Miss Brown*) and the neo-gothic thriller (*Penelope Brandling*) – deserve the neglect they have received' (Colby 2003, 92). However, of *Louis Norbert* she makes an exception, seeing it as 'a charming romance, blending history with mystery' (Colby 2003, 92). While agreeing in principle with Colby's assessment, I would argue that Lee's novel is far more interesting than this simple description suggests, concealing a sexual subtext within the complexity of its narrative form.

The novel's subtitle, 'A Two-Fold Romance', hints at both its content, the development of parallel love stories, and at its hidden concerns which imply other forms of duality. The plot concerns itself with the efforts of Lady Venetia Hammond and a young archaeologist (bearing only the name 'Schmidt') to search for the true identity of Louis Norbert de Caritan whose memorial tablet they encounter while visiting the Campo Santo at Pisa. Intrigued by the discovery that a portrait of the same Louis Norbert hangs in the Hammond ancestral home, Lady Venetia and the archaeologist exchange a series of letters and it is through this correspondence that the narrative is developed. Within these letters we are also provided with the narratives of their seventeenth-century counterparts: Louis Norbert and his love, Artemisia del Valore, an acclaimed woman poet, who, after Norbert's death, devotes herself to God and becomes the abbess of a convent.[1] By an intricate process of detection including the breaking of codes, the amateur sleuths discover that Norbert, the legitimate son of Cardinal Mazarin's niece, Maria Mancini, and Louis XIV of France, was secretly taken from his mother at birth, raised by Lady Venetia's ancestors, and later poisoned and murdered at Pisa by friends of the French court.

The dual love stories of Lady Venetia and the archaeologist (in the present), and of Louis Norbert and Artemisia (in the past), that unfold through a process of intellectual endeavour, foreshadow the parallel love plots in A. S. Byatt's *Possession* (1990) in which the romance between twentieth-century literary scholars, Roland Michell and Maud Bailey, develops through their research into the lives and letters of Victorian poets, Randolph Henry Ash and Christabel LaMotte, and one might easily speculate on the influence of Lee's work on Byatt's novel.[2] Similarly, it is possible that the star-crossed love between Norbert and Artemisia del Valore, may have been inspired by the true-life romance between a Venetian nobleman, Andrea Memmo (1729–93), descendant of a long line of Doges, and Giustiniana Wynne (1737–91), a celebrated essayist and intellectual writing in the latter half of the eighteenth century. Wynne's illegitimacy made her an unsuitable match, but the lovers maintained a clandestine relationship, developing a code in which to express their love in passionate letters that form the subject of Andrea di Robilant's recent book, *A Venetian Affair* (2004). Naturally, it is difficult to determine whether Lee knew about Memmo and Wynne, and there appears to be no direct mention of them in her work. However, as di Robilant observes, knowledge of their longstanding liaison was more widespread than at first appeared:

> When my father began to dig around Andrea and Guistiniana's story, he soon found traces of their romance in the public archives in Venice, Padua, and even Paris and London. It turned out that students of eighteenth-century Venice had first become acquainted with the relationship through the writings of Giacomo Casanova, who had been a close friend of both Andrea and Guistiniana. In the first years of the last century Gustav Gugitz, the great Casanova scholar, identified Mademoiselle XCV who figures prominently in Casanova's memoirs as Guistiniana. (di Robilant 2004, 5)[3]

Given that Lee's first book, *Studies of the Eighteenth Century in Italy* (1880), is 'fortified with diligent research in documents of the past' (Colby 2003, 30), and demonstrates an engagement with Venetian life and culture,[4] she may well have been among those 'students of eighteenth-century Venice' who knew about the love affair. In addition, it is possible that Gugitz's identification, made in 1910, four years before the publication of *Louis Norbert*, may have stimulated her interest. Whatever the truth may be, what concerns me here is primarily Lee's focus on the doubling of past and present loves which offers her a covert way in which to play with the performance of gender and sexuality.

Double identities

In the closing pages of the novel, it is evident that neither of the two romances achieves a happy resolution. In her final letter to the archaeologist, Lady Venetia announces her coming marriage, which she enters into for practical rather than romantic reasons, and expresses the hope that the archaeologist himself might acquire a partner with whom he may 'in years long hence ... discuss the strange story which happened at Pisa in 1684. Or was it rather ... in 1908?' (1914, 302). The uncertainty voiced by Lady Venetia highlights the doubling of time, as well as the intrusion of the past on the present that is so familiar to readers of Lee's fantastic tales.[5] In *Louis Norbert*, however, I would argue that the doubling of time is also reflected in the doubling of identity to be found within its pages. This process of replication offers us clues that seem to reveal a sexual subtext. While much has been written about the underlying homosexual anxieties of her first novel, *Miss Brown* (1884),[6] Lee's other longer works are seldom examined for further evidence. In this chapter, I look at the way in which these tensions also manifest themselves in *Louis Norbert*, and suggest that covert expressions of desire are mediated primarily through the portrait – the central art object in the text – a medium Lee uses to similar effect in short stories such as 'A Culture Ghost: Winthrop's Adventure' (1881), 'A Wicked Voice', 'Amour Dure: Passages from the Diary of Spiridion Trepka' and 'Oke of Okehurst'.[7] In her study, *Spurious Ghosts: The Fantastic Tales of Vernon Lee*, Mary Patricia Kane notes how, in Lee's stories, 'portraits act as passageways into a liminal space where conventional notions of individual identity are destabilised and the delimitations of the past and present are collapsed' (Kane 2004, 24). What I want to do here is to examine the implications of this destabilization of identity in *Louis Norbert* in order to show how it permits expressions of homoerotic desire in the context of the protagonists' seemingly heterosexual couplings.

The portrait in question hangs, as Lady Venetia informs the archaeologist, in a space known as the 'Ghost's room' (1914, 27), a room in
which she enjoyed a delicious sense of childhood fear and that is
imprinted on her memory for she sees it quite clearly in her mind's
eye. She offers Schmidt a detailed description of the painting:

> The portrait of Louis Norbert is the only one in the room. ... he has
> black clothes which you can't see quite plainly, and long black hair;
> and his face and hands and collar stand out from all that black.
> I don't know whether the picture is any good as a picture. I haven't
> seen it since I got married, and that's more than twenty years ago.
> But I see it quite clearly in my mind; I mean, I see *him*, for it never
> struck me to think of him as a portrait! (1914, 28–9)

Recalling her youth, she remembers that the painting of Norbert
became the subject of her romantic fancies, and the room in which
it hung, her '*secret place*' which she visited with a sense of contrived
formality (1914, 31). She describes the experience as 'something like
going to church ... and also like being in love' (1914, 33).

Seeing the portrait for the first time, the archaeologist is, it appears,
equally smitten, perhaps because the occasion replicates Lady Venetia's
initial encounter with the same painting, for as she tells him: 'I have a
fancy for your seeing Louis Norbert for the first time at the hour that I
first did, all those endless years ago' (1914, 197). At this moment
Schmidt experiences a sense of déjà vu which suggests a doubling
between Lady Venetia and himself that manifests itself in his own
romantic response to the image of Louis Norbert:

> The Archæologist stepped close and looked carefully. It was a fairly
> good picture; or rather a fairly bad one of a very good school, some
> belated disciple of Van Dyke's at a time already given over to Lely;
> and well preserved. All *that* the Archæologist made a note of in
> order to remark upon to Lady Venetia. For he knew at once that he
> could not, somehow, remark to her on what was his instant and
> growing impression, namely, how astonishingly handsome and fas-
> cinating this painted young man was, with his white, eagle face
> between long brown hair, and eyes like deep pools drawing one in.
> ... It is almost impossible to put to paper the utterly foolish things
> which the Archæologist was aware of thinking and feeling. It was
> intolerable that men of past centuries should have been so romantic
> and good-looking; only women were allowed that nowadays. And,

at the same time, this lovely, languishing youth was manly – that was the worst of it! (1914, 199–201)

Superficially, the archaeologist's response might be attributed to a love of historical, and beautiful, things, but a sense of fascinated homosexual attraction is implied in his reluctance to share his thoughts with Lady Venetia, and is perhaps most evident in the fact that it is Louis Norbert's 'manly' beauty which attracts him, for, after all, that is 'the worst of it' in his mind. But, one might argue, the love story which is unfolding is ostensibly that which concerns the archaeologist's love for a woman – Lady Venetia. However, if one looks closely at Schmidt's representation of Lady Venetia in the narrative, then one discovers that, in his opinion, she shares Louis Norbert's androgynous beauty. To his ear, her voice is 'dusky, a little veiled, decidedly contralto and Duse-like' (1914, 189), reminiscent of Zaffirino's castrato tones in Lee's short story 'A Wicked Voice' where the latter's voice is described as 'full, passionate, but veiled, as it were, in a subtle, downy wrapper' (1890, 214), while Lady Venetia's hands are 'strong ... almost like very exquisite man's hands' (1914, 198). Moreover, in the novel Lady Venetia is 'twinned' with Louis Norbert's seventeenth-century lover, the poetess Artemisia, whose own portrait also kindles the archaeologist's desire. Soon after their first meeting, the archaeologist shows a likeness of the abbess to Lady Venetia who notes that he seems 'rather in love' with her, a love he appears to transfer to Lady Venetia herself (1914, 25). It is also later revealed that Lady Venetia's middle name is 'Artemisia' and that, due to a request made by Louis Norbert on his deathbed, she and all the females of her line bear this in honour of his lover, the renowned improvisatrice.

This link between the two women is especially intriguing because Artemisia, despite her female charms, also displays androgynous qualities. On first seeing her, Norbert states that she displays a 'maidenly decorum and manly gravity' (1914, 225). She is an intellectual woman: her father, lacking a son, teaches her things that only men should know. In her autobiography, a portion of which is reproduced in the novel, we learn that until she met Louis Norbert, she thought of the other sex 'with such disdain ... as is fabled of the virgin amazons' (1914, 275). Interestingly, viewed through Artemisia's eyes, Louis Norbert himself once more becomes androgynous, for she tells us that his face was such a one as 'painters have given to the youthful martyrs Stephen and Sebastian, or indeed [to] that angel who carried the lily to the living Lily of Carmel and spake the words – "Hail Mary"'

(1914, 272–3). Angels are usually considered asexual, and it is worth noting that the beautiful boys, Stephen, and St. Sebastian in particular, bearing the androgynous features of adolescence, are associated with what Camille Paglia calls 'homoerotic iconicism' (Paglia 1991, 112).

The past and the present love stories, and even those that exist across time, therefore contain homoerotic implications within their seemingly heterosexual frameworks. It is especially curious that the archaeologist, who responds erotically to all three of the other protagonists – Lady Venetia, Artemisia, and Louis Norbert – arguably appears trapped in an infantile, undifferentiated, sexuality: he loves Lady Venetia, a maternal substitute who is, as he himself admits, 'old enough to be his mother' (1914, 183); who reminds him of Demeter (1914, 12); and who, seen across the waxlights and flowers of the dinner table, once more recalls the mother goddess herself (1914, 191). I will return to the significance of his seemingly pre-Oedipal desire later in this essay.

Examined in detail, Lee's *Louis Norbert* seemingly encodes homosexual desires that are expressed via a doubled and interlinked model of heterosexual love. Yet, why should this desire express itself via the portrait? Perhaps it is because 'A portrait in a novel or a story may be a portrait of invisible things – thought processes, attractions, [and] repulsions' (Byatt 2002, 1). In other words, portraits can express, and simultaneously hide, the seemingly inexpressible.

Blaming portraits

In her short essay 'The Blame of Portraits' published in *Hortus Vitae: Essays on the Gardening of Life* in 1904, Lee writes eloquently of the futility of the portrait form as a means of capturing the 'most fleeting, intangible, and uncommunicable of all mysterious essences, a human personality' (1904, 140). She centres on the medium's inability to produce a 'pure' reflection and argues that the 'imperfect likeness[es]' that appear on canvas are always filtered through the artist's consciousness:

> For the image of the sitter on the artist's retina is passed on its way to the canvas through a mind chock full of other images; and is transferred – heaven knows how changed already – by processes of line and curve, of blots of colour, and juxtaposition of light and shade, belonging not merely to the artist himself, but to the artist's whole school. ... The difference due to the individual artist is even

greater; and, in truth, a portrait gives the sitter's temperament merged in the temperament of the painter. (1904, 141–2)

Not only is the purity of the reflection contaminated by the artist's own consciousness, but the portrait's stillness can itself contaminate the memory of the original. Lee warns that 'During the *period of activity* of a portrait' while it is still looked at, 'we must beware lest it take, in our memory, the place of the original' and she fears that those 'unchanging features' which have 'the insistence of their definiteness and permanence, ... may insidiously extrude, exclude, the fleeting, vacillating outlines of the remembered reality' (1904, 146).

Byatt seems to share Lee's conception of the portrait form. Like Lee, she sees it as merely 'an artist's record, construction, of a physical presence, with a skin of colour, a layer of strokes of the brush, or the point, or the pencil, on a flat surface' which is in 'an important sense arrested and superficial' (2002, 1). Yet Lee's model, in which the artist's image is present in that of the sitter appears to permit an interesting dynamic to exist: instead of representing a 'life in death', Lee's portrait, despite its fixity, is, arguably, always 'alive', shifting between the image of the artist and of the sitter. This model is suggested earlier in Oscar Wilde's novel, *The Picture of Dorian Gray* (1890, revised 1891), in which Basil Hallward claims that 'every portrait that is painted with feeling is a portrait of the artist, not of the sitter' (Wilde 1988, 10), sentiments that are echoed obliquely in *Louis Norbert*. When the archaeologist accuses Lady Venetia of inventing 'facts', she states that she does not recognize herself in his portrait of her, exclaiming, 'it is *you*, my poor young, learned friend, who have been inventing, *inventing a me* utterly unlike the reality' (1914, 169).

Later, visiting Lady Venetia at her ancestral home, the archaeologist, using the language of painting, acknowledges that there is truth in this. The narrator tells us:

He did not want to see Lady Venetia. Not only not now, but, if possible, never again in all his life. He became aware that he had made her up during the past seven or eight months; he could have told you how and when he had added each touch to her wholly imaginary image; he could have recited (indeed did recite to himself) every item in her various letters which now brought home the willfully disregarded certainty that the reality of this lady was utterly unlike his portrait of her. (1914, 182)

The archaeologist's realization resonates interestingly with a diary entry made by Lee in 1883. Writing of Annie Meyer, an early love who died in 1883 and whose photograph would hang over Lee's bed until her own death in 1935, Lee acknowledges that in the death of her friend, she 'lost nothing or but little; of the real Mme Meyer', for, she argues 'does not there remain, unchanged and unchangeable, the imagined one?' (quoted in Gardner 1987, 312). According to Lee, the advantage of the 'imagined' beloved lies in the fact that one cannot lose 'the creature born of one's fancy and one's desires, the unreal' (quoted in Gardner 1987, 312).

While Byatt argues that 'Portraits in words and portraits in paint are opposites, rather than metaphors for each other' (Byatt 2002, 1), she acknowledges that the portrait in fiction can be used as a kind of mirror. She suggests that novelists usually use the portrait form 'to play in different ways with characters who use portraits from other times and places as temporary mirrors of themselves with a difference' (Byatt 2002, 5). Kane observes Lee's use of this motif in her own fiction, arguing that the 'empathetic relations that her characters have with the subjects of portraits ultimately reveal more about the characters themselves than about the illusive objects of their gaze' (Kane 2004, 23), and claims that 'the narrative of haunted portraiture, like a hall of mirrors, tells the story of the constitution of the self through the other' (Kane 2004, 23).

It is possible to go further and to imply that in Lee's works, the portrait seems to tell us as much about the author as about the characters in the texts thus constituting the author's 'self ' through the 'other' and the reason for this is suggested in the writings of Pierre Nicole, the seventeenth-century logician and moralist.[8] For Nicole, the language of painting and portraiture offers a powerful metaphor for the under-standing and construction of the self. In his essay, *Traité de la connais-sance de soi-même* (1725), he argues:

> One must act more or less in this life as if one had a life-long undertak-ing to paint one's portrait, that is to say that one must add everyday a few strokes of the brush without blotting out what has already been painted ... By this means [by this continuous portraiture] we will form little by little a portrait so resembling that we will be able to see at any moment everything which we are. (Quoted in Marin 1991, 286)

As Louis Marin observes in his discussion of Nicole's metaphor, accord-ing to this method, 'The true portrait is not under layers of paint; it is made up of these strokes, these marks and these remarks' (1991, 286). The true portrait is [therefore] 'the *figure of an excess* formed by repeated strokes' (Marin 1991, 286–7). However, as Marin points out, this excess can be problematic for 'at each moment, by the addition of a new stroke, this resemblance becomes unlike itself ... by "amassing" and by "excess"' the 'spectator – painter of his own portrait' runs up 'against the defacement of his own face': the self becomes a 'formless mass' (Marin 1991, 287).

While Nicole is concerned with the moral development of man, his metaphor provides an interesting model to apply to Vernon Lee's relationship with portraiture in her life and in her work. In a letter to her publisher John Lane at The Bodley Head dated the 13 January 1908, Lee makes her position regarding her own image particularly clear. In reply to Lane's request for the use of her photograph on one of her publications, Lee writes:

> As I have refused two other publishers, and everyone else the right to use any portrait of mine, Sargent's included, I have to be consistent [and] say no. I hate this hawking about of people's faces. I took a *nom de plume* in order to keep my private personality separate from my literary one.[9]

It is apparent from this passage that Lee is intent on constructing her own literary identity and, on the surface, her reluctance in agreeing to Lane's request appears perfectly reasonable. However, the fact remains that, by 1908, it was no longer a secret that 'Vernon Lee' was a woman. While she equates her 'nom de plume' with anonymity, functioning as a form of 'mask', she perceives the portrait to act as a revelation.

However, Lee's androgynous pen-name, or literary 'self-portrait', is equally revealing in that it is in itself a reflection of her own sexual ambiguity which is also evident in John Singer Sargent's 1889 sketch in which she wears mannish clothes and an air of youthful masculine arrogance.[10] Lee was equally reluctant to accede to a public unveiling of another form of literary portrait after her death. In her will she wrote: 'I absolutely prohibit any biography of me. My life is my own and I leave that to nobody' (quoted in Gunn 1964, ix). Here, Byatt's claim that 'Portraits in words and portraits in paint are opposites, rather than metaphors for each other' (Byatt 2002, 1) appears to be undermined because Lee seems reluctant to expose herself to either type of representation, however revealing or concealing its effects. One cannot help but wonder whether this division between public and private images – a division that Lee seemed so eager to maintain – was prompted by a fear of their coalescence and possible exposure of her own homosexuality.

Reading portraits

While refusing to allow herself to be defined by her portraits or her biography, I would suggest that Lee has left masked portraits of herself in her own literature. If the portrait tells us as much, and perhaps more, about the artist than the subject of his or her art, then it is worth looking at what the portrait, and the language of portraiture in *Louis Norbert* tells us about Lee. Images of Lee have certainly been recognized in other works by her. Writing of the characters in *Miss Brown*, Mabel Robinson remarked:

> Miss Brown never to my eyes has that Etheopian [sic] type you so much admire but in all her sudden impulses and tricks of expression reminds me of a certain animal (not without piquancy and charm) familiarly known as the 'little vermin flea [Vernon Lee].' Mary [Robinson] tells me that Hamlin is the true portrait of that said flea as seen by itself but if that be so I should advise that lively animal to buy a new mirror and if it be a true one it will see a much more noble looking personage. (Quoted in Gardner 1987, 366–7)

Similarly, Gardner suggests that in Lee's works we see the recurrence of what he calls 'the semivir idol' and describes as 'the feminine counterpart of Miss Paget's own idealized image.' He explains:

> The exalted 'Vernon,' Violet's compulsive masculine super-ego, adopted from Eugene in her childhood, required an opposite number – a person 'fit' for 'Vernon' to love. As a derivative of Miss Paget's own mask, the idol shares all of the qualities which she, in her more confident moments, took pride in, and, like the 'Vernon image,' embodies the opposites of all her weaknesses ... The idol is static and dead. It is a pure, abstract essence – the essence of female superiority – and can be more satisfactorily superimposed upon an inanimate substratum than a living one. (Gardner 1987, 316)

Gardner goes on to argue that Lee attempted to make 'the actual women of her acquaintance' into 'bearers of the semivir idol' (Gardner 1987, 316).[11] While he acknowledges her failure to do so, he suggests that more successful examples of this effort can be found in 'her identification of the idol with churches, dolls, images, statues, pictures, puppets and the dead' (Gardner 1987, 316). According to Gardner, an interesting version of this idol appears in Artemisia's 'auto-biography' in *Louis Norbert* in which she gives an account of her unusual education and achievements:

> Almost the earliest of my recollections is being stood by my father on a table and made to recite, with puerile voice, the death of Dido and the lament of Hecuba to an audience of learned men. At five years old I was carried to Florence, there to extemporise verses before the Grand Duke Cosimo dei Medici ... Soon after, being but seven years old, I was elected a member of the Philharmonic Academy of Bologna and of the Alphean of Pisa ... And by the age when other maids still play with dolls, I had been carried from one end of Italy to the other, receiving on all hands universal flattery ... until, in the twenty-first year of my age, it pleased the Senate and the people of Rome, in the reign of Pope Innocent XI, that I should receive publicly at the Capitol the Crown of Poetry. (1914, 270–1; quoted in Gardner 1987, 443–4)

Artemisia describes how, at this moment, she becomes aware of what she calls 'the vanity of the world' and experiences a strange paralysis as the Senator of Rome places the laurel wreath on her head:

> My heart, which had been beating violently, stood still, freezing my limbs and checking my breath ... I was aware that I had, in some manner, died, and was looking on ... at a simulacrum or *eidolon* of myself moving and speaking with a semblance of life. ... I had died and left but this ghost behind me. (1914, 271–2; quoted in Gardner 1987, 444).

Gardner's interpretation of this scene forges a connection between Artemisa del Valore's spirit and Vernon Lee: 'Just such a dead self, not, as here, rejected, but idealized, and later curiously merged with her image of Anne Meyer's death mask [photograph], became the sacred original of all the semivir idols' (Gardner 1987, 444). In fact, it is not too difficult to make a more direct link between Artemisia and Vernon Lee. Recounting memories of her mother and of her own education, Lee observes: 'While my father thought poorly of writing ... my mother had made up her mind that I was to become, at the very least, another de Staël' (1923, 301).[12] In a sense, perhaps, in her depiction of Artemisia, Lee does indeed become 'another de Staël' for Lee's abbess bears more than a passing resemblance to Mme de Staël's Corinne (eponymous heroine of *Corinne or, Italy* (1807)) who, like Artemisia, is crowned at the Capitol in Rome and who, sharing de Staël's literary renown, is conceivably, like Artemisia, a fictional version of the author.

However, since he is intent on a vulgar Freudian reading of Artemisia's dead alter ego, Gardner fails to notice that the poetess is brought back to life. Having described her uncanny metamorphosis, Artemisia continues:

> the eyes of my spirit ... were led into the crowd before me, and without seeing a single one of the hundreds of spectators I had seen hitherto all too vividly applauding me, they, *id est*, my spiritual eyes, rested on the face of an unknown youth ... which met them with a look that transpierced my soul and restored it to life, though to a changed one. (1914, 272)

That face belongs, of course, to Louis Norbert. Norbert's face, whether living or dead, painted, or real, appears to have a transformative power.

Given Lee's assertion in 'The Blame of Portraits' that all such works are images of the artist as well as of the subject, the importance of the portrait in *Louis Norbert* takes on an added significance. The portraits of Norbert and Artemisia del Valore are effectively 'painted' by Lee and must therefore reveal, by her own suggestion, aspects of herself. Therefore, the doubles in the text, framed in, and by the portraits, arguably function as figures of '*an excess* formed by repeated strokes' (Marin 1991, 286–7) that deface, or perhaps efface, Lee's homosexual desires even as they express them. Interestingly, portraits of Lee herself seem to lack a distinct form. Sargent's sketch has an unfinished quality, and his 1881 painting of Lee[13] lacks the clarity of line that generally marks his portraiture. Portraits of Lee, then, appear to retain that 'formlessness' that Marin identifies as a feature of Pierre Nicole's subject in process: a 'formlessness' which is due to an 'excess' which both 'defaces' and 'effaces' the original. However, this 'formlessness' also allows a living fluidity of representation and perhaps even the gender slippage that is evident in the portraits of Lee, of Louis Norbert and of Artemisia which, in the latter two, appear to elicit seemingly both heterosexual and homosexual attraction. The portrait of Norbert, as we have seen, is the object of Lady Venetia's heterosexual, and Schmidt's homoerotic desire, and Artemisia, the original object of the archaeologist's desire, is reminiscent not only of de Staël's Corinne but also of Sappho, and thus implicitly representative of lesbian love.[14]

Decoding desire

Yet the novel provides us with other clues which mirror those suggested by the portrait form. Marin claims that the true portrait is to be found, 'not under layers of paint' but made up of the brushstrokes, those 'marks' and 'remarks' (Marin 1991, 286) which build up the image and contribute to the portrait's potential formlessness. In *Louis Norbert*, the 'marks' and 'remarks' which build up the portraits of both its eponymous protagonist, of Artemisia, and, arguably, of the author, also contribute to the construction of another work of art – the text itself. It is therefore worth looking more closely at exactly what kind of text it is. *Louis Norbert* is clearly a novel, a tale of detection employing secrets, codes, and discoveries, a scholarly search, and a 'ghost' story: but it is also presented to the reader as a form of play. Lee gives us a list of 'Dramatis Personae' divided into 'Personages of the Twentieth Century' whose 'scene' is 'Pisa and Arthington Manor, 1908–9', and 'Personages of the Seventeenth Century' whose scene is 'Rome and Pisa, 1683–4' (1914, 7). *Louis Norbert* is therefore not only a novel, but a drama, and as such, its characters are roles to be performed. The characters, then, are 'masks' to be worn by real-life actors, who presumably can play more than one role, be more than one person, thus legitimizing the doublings which so clearly occur in the narrative.

Yet, this dramatic backdrop, that implies 'masking' and 'make-up', also leads us to re-read the conflict between discovery and invention that informs the novel and becomes the subject of a debate between Lady Venetia and the archaeologist. In one of his letters to Lady Venetia, he says: 'Do you remember writing to me that if I could find out nothing I was to "make it up"? Well, I venture to say the same to you – *invent*! it is but another form of the Latin word which means *to discover*! ... Invent your *Louis Norbert*' (1914, 101–2). Lady Venetia's reply admonishes him for his suggestion, telling him that she has '*discovered*' two letters in Norbert's own handwriting, and that she assumes that his interest in invention is 'some new-fangled *pose* of you *jeunes*!' (1914, 104–5). The tension between the words 'invention' and 'discovery', bound together by their Latin roots, undermines the 'truthfulness' of Lady Venetia's 'discovery' and obscures textual meaning – is the story of Louis Norbert real or not? Is it Lady Venetia's invention? Are Artemisia's memoirs the archaeologist's invention?

Moreover, both texts are presented to the reader in 'translation'. Of the transcribed Louis Norbert's letters she sends to the archaeologist, Lady Venetia writes: 'I have not copied the misspellings. And there aren't more of them, very likely than in my own letters' (1914, 105), and of the copy of Artemisia's memoirs sent to Lady Venetia, the archaeologist says:

> These memoirs of the Abbess of St. Veridiana, previously known in the world as Artemisia del Valore, were composed in a language you are not quite familiar with, though (for reasons which I will later explain)[15] I am unable to inform you whether that language is Latin, Greek ... or mere Italian; so what I send you is a translation made to the best of my slight powers. (1914, 266)

Our 'trust' in the validity of their 'discoveries' is destabilized: can either of these texts be taken at face value? or are they an elaborate code in which each writer reveals, and yet conceals, his/her love for the other? A similar textual codification takes place between Louis Norbert and his lover, Artemisia, in the seventeenth century. The archaeologist informs Lady Venetia that he is unable to decipher certain documents found in Artemisia's library, which may have a bearing on Norbert's history, because 'they are, if they exist at all and are not mere imagination ... in cypher, or rather *cryptogram* ... That is to say, that, *if they exist*, they exist in single words and phrases which must be picked out of books according to a clue which has in each case to be discovered' (1914, 123).

The exact method of this secret correspondence is finally revealed in Artemisia's 'autobiography'. Unable to see Louis Norbert freely due to her father's jealousy, and concerned for Norbert's safety, Artemisia contrives a means of covert communication:

> I devised the plan of sending that sick Cavalier [Norbert] a book wherewithal to beguile his idleness, wherein I placed a slip, stating he would find information of interest to his studies on certain pages, and on these pages I faintly wrote in the margin numbers of other pages, in which I had underlined separate words, which, added together, made this phrase: 'Beware false friends. You are being poisoned.' (1914, 281–2)

Norbert returns her book, and by the same means, replies: 'Greetings and gratitude. Love makes life worth keeping' (1914, 283). Artemisia goes on to describe how this form of communication allows them to express their desire for one another, how they found 'great sweetness in discoursing freely of our love, which we had meanwhile confessed to each other in this fashion' and how they derived a 'marvellous joy' from 'this strange courtship, wherein never came a kiss nor barely a handclasp ... but only riddles and symbols concerted together in those letters made up of a few words underlined in books that passed from hand to hand' (1914, 284–5).

Beautiful 'Boys'

Such encodings of desire in language and art are familiar to scholars of late-Victorian literature. In his 1986 essay 'Pater's *Renaissance*, Andrew Lang, and Anthropological Romanticism', Robert Crawford identifies a range of meanings relating to 'the Greek term "poikilos"' used 'to refer to homosexual love in Plato's *Symposium*', including ' "pied," "dappled," "flashing," "intricate," "ambiguous" ' (Crawford 1986, 854) and in her study, *Sappho and the Virgin Mary: Same-Sex Love and the English Literary Imagination*, Ruth Vanita suggests that particular words such as 'strange', 'exquisite', 'mysterious' can connote homoeroticism (Vanita 1997, 66).[16] In the 'ambiguity' and the 'pied beauty' of the Louis Norbert portrait, showing his white face and hands set against dark hair, clothes and background, we see, perhaps, an instance of the Greek term 'poikilos' and its implications. Similarly, Lee's choice of the word 'strange', used to describe the courtship between Artemisia and Norbert, a courtship which in its apparent platonic purity resembles Lee's own romantic friendships with other women, seems suggestive. Alone, these allusions would signify little, but if we look at the fact that at the heart of novel lies the portrait of a handsome youth – Louis Norbert – it is worth considering Martha Vicinus's assertion that 'Even though ... most lesbians did not look like boys, the boy was the defining, free agent who best expressed who they were' and that it is therefore important to 'look – and then look again – to see the hidden meaning of the beautiful boy' (Vicinus 1994, 92).

According to Vicinus, many lesbians, 'rather than fully embracing an impossible adult masculinity, identified with the adolescent boy' for 'the androgynous boy had a long history in the arts as a symbol of a rare and delicate erotic potentiality' (Vicinus 2004, 163).[17] In *Louis Norbert*, there is, arguably, more than one 'beautiful boy', for the archaeologist is also presented to us as a young man. Moreover, desire seems to operate through these similar figures: the archaeologist desires all of the protagonists and Norbert himself is the focus of all the pro-tagonists' desires. If, indeed, the 'boys' in *Louis Norbert* are covert repres-entations of the lesbian woman and, by implication, Lee, then they appear to suggest a need to be both the desiring and the desired figure: active and passive simultaneously.

Interestingly, both the archaeologist's relationship with Lady Venetia and Norbert's with Artemisia appear to follow, to a greater or lesser extent, the 'rituals of friendship' or adopted patterns of same-sex liaisons posited by Vicinus:

> Romantic friendships began as a series of steps leading to emotional intimacy. As in heterosexual love, these included gifts, letters, and long private conversations ... The written word, whether one's own or that of a current favourite author, became an emissary, a means of indirectly declaring one's love and then of explaining a whole range of new, tumultuous feelings. Intellectual curiosity stood in for sexual curiosity: 'we two' want to learn more about a favourite author or artist, and in the process of doing so, we will learn more about our feelings for each other. A love of learning strengthened a friendship, drawing two women into a world marked by serious spiritual and intellectual concerns, rather than the frivolity of heterosexual court-ship or the dull routine of family duties. (Vicinus, 2004, 7–8)

Such rituals and interests characterize two of Lee's intense romantic friendships: first, her intimate relationship with Mary Robinson with whom she shared a love of European history and literature, and secondly, her personal and professional closeness to Clementina Anstruther-Thomson with whom she produced treatises on psycho-logical aesthetics, culminating in a collection of essays in art ap-preciation, *Art and Man: Essays and Fragments* (1924), written by Anstruther-Thomson (with Lee's guidance) which Lee introduced. While such same-sex relationships seem based on mutual concerns, respect and supposed parity, Vicinus argues that a more common model of lesbian desire resides in the inequalities of the mother-child dynamic. She acknowledges that such a model cannot be applied indiscriminately and takes many forms. She writes:

> Judith Roof has argued that lesbians create a successful path to sexual maturity not through a return to the pre-Oedipal stage of unity with a nurturing mother, but rather through the construction of an absent, fantasy mother. They learn to desire desire itself, which

remains always unfulfilled and therefore always open to negotiation. But her formula may be too schematic to fit the many different configurations mother-love could take. (Vicinus 2004, 163–4)

Earlier, I suggested that, for the archaeologist, Lady Venetia functions as a form of mother substitute and that she is associated with the goddess Demeter. If the archaeologist does indeed function as a version of the lesbian 'boy' then he encodes homoerotic desire within the mother-child framework, mirroring Lee's own early attraction to Annie Meyer. Vicinus argues that, in this friendship, Lee, 'imagined herself as an adolescent boy in love with an older woman in order to explore a perfect love relationship' (Vicinus 2004, 164). According to Vicinus, this fantasy 'helped to normalize a forbidden and impossible love that was fundamentally different from and yet better than all other love' (Vicinus 2004, 164). Such a relationship fits into the model of pre-Oedipal unity. Yet, if we recall Lee's assertion that in the death of her friend, she 'lost nothing or but little; of the real Mme Meyer' (quoted in Gardner 1987, 312), because one cannot lose 'the creature born of one's fancy and one's desires, the unreal' (quoted in Gardner 1987, 312), Roof's model of the 'absent, fantasy mother' (quoted in Vicinus 2004, 163) seems equally valid.

It is worth noting that the love explored in *Louis Norbert* is often 'forbidden', generally 'impossible', and focussed on an 'absent' and often 'fantasy' love-object. The protagonists' love for Norbert is particularly so, for he is dead, a 'ghost' whose presence is defined by his seemingly disembodied parts for, in the portrait, 'he has black clothes which you can't see quite plainly, and long black hair' and only his face and hands 'stand out from all that black' (1914, 29). Catherine Maxwell writes that 'the portrait has always had a special relationship with death', it is 'an absent presence, a shadow that lingers after the sitter is gone' (Maxwell 1997, 253) and this comment on the portrait form resonates interestingly with Norbert's liminal status. Now himself a portrait that hangs in the 'ghost's room', Norbert is both ghostly and yet not a ghost. His image seemingly acts as a meeting-point for a nexus of encoded desires that mirror the portrait's 'tangible' intangibility and remain spectral, hovering above, and beyond the text.

Hauntings and homoeroticism

In *The Apparitional Lesbian: Female Homosexuality and Modern Culture* (1993), Terry Castle suggests that the figure of the lesbian has been

' "ghosted" – or made to seem invisible' and that 'the work of ghosting [has] been carried on more intensely ... in the realm of literature and popular fantasy' than anywhere else (1993, 4, 6). In Vernon Lee's works, particularly in her stories of the fantastic – *Hauntings: Fantastic Stories* (1890); *Pope Jacynth and Other Fantastic Tales* (1904); and *For Maurice: Five Unlikely Stories* (1927) – it is easy to find suggestions of such 'ghosting' in the sexually ambiguous protagonists and spectres that people her writings. While the negative aspects of such 'ghosting' are self-evident, Castle makes a convincing case for a positive reading of the spectral metaphor in lesbian writing:

> A ghost, according to *Webster's Ninth*, is a spirit believed to appear in a 'bodily likeness.' To haunt, we find, is 'to visit often,' 'to recur constantly and spontaneously,' 'to stay around or persist,' or 'to reappear continually.' The ghost, in other words, is a paradox. Though nonexistent, it nonetheless *appears*. Indeed, so vividly does it appear – if only in the 'mind's eye' – one feels unable to get away from it. (Castle 1993, 46)

For the lesbian writer, she argues, ' "seeing ghosts" may be a ... rhapsodical embodiment: a ritual calling up, or *apophrades*, in the old mystical sense ... Used imaginatively ... the very trope that evaporates can also solidify' (Castle 1993, 46–7).

Such vacillation between solidity and spectrality also suggests an inability to affirm one's sexuality. In such circumstances, the portrait, which functions as a 'ghostly' presence, and simultaneously expresses and conceals the self, is a fitting medium for Lee, the literary artist who, Irene Cooper Willis remarked, 'was homosexual, but ... never faced up to sexual facts' (Gardner 1987, 85). Yet those 'marks' and 'remarks' that make up its surface and are mirrored in the language and form of *Louis Norbert* should also reflect the ambiguity of any reading of the novel as a revelation of Lee's lesbian desire. In her 1989 essay, 'Ruskin's Pied Beauty and the Constitution of a "Homosexual" Code', Linda Dowling warns of the dangers of 'reductionism' and 'anachronism' in such readings (Dowling 1989, 1), of a tendency to construe 'surface episodes ... as evidence of a massive ... effort of repression designed to keep the real subject – sex – safely out of sight'; and of reading 'nineteenth-century phenomena in terms of twentieth-century categories' (Dowling 1989, 1). Dowling, of course, is right, but the tantalizing possibility of 'hidden' potentialities that enrich our analyses of Lee's works need not be avoided altogether, providing that our research, like that of Lee's protagonists in *Louis Norbert*, remains poised on the cusp of 'discovery' and 'invention'.

Notes

1 Artemisia del Valore is perhaps based on Maria Maddalena Morelli, a famous musician and poet, who was honoured with the name 'Corilla Olimpica' by the Academy of the Arcadians, a literary society founded by Queen Christina of Sweden, and crowned by its members as poet laureate at the Capitol in Rome in 1776, a fate she shares with Lee's Artemisia del Valore (1914, 271). The Arcadian Academy was housed in what became known in 1883 as the Corsini Palace and, interestingly, *Louis Norbert: A Two-Fold Romance* is dedicated to 'Elisabetha, Lucresia, and Filippo Corsini'. Fillipo Corsini (1873–1926) was a relation of Prince Tommaso Corsini (1835–1919) who presented the Corsinian library to the Lincei Academy, now also housed in the Corsini Palace. *In Studies of the Eighteenth Century in Italy* (1880), Lee dedicates a chapter to the Arcadian Academy.

2 As an acknowledged user and supporter of The London Library where many of Lee's works are held, it is feasible that Byatt may have read *Louis Norbert*.

3 Gustav Gugitz wrote about the affair in both 'Eine Gelibte Casanovas', *Zeitschrift fur Bucherfreunde* (1910), and in *Giacamo Casanova und sein Lebensroman* (1921).

4 *Studies of the Eighteenth Century in Italy* contains a chapter dedicated to Count Carlo Gozzi (1722–1806) and the Venetian Fairy Comedy.

5 See for example Vernon Lee, *Hauntings: Fantastic Stories* (1890); *Pope Jacynth and Other Fantastic Tales* (1904); and *For Maurice: Five Unlikely Stories* (1927).

6 See Kathy Alexis Psomiades, 1999, 21–41, and Psomiades 1997.

7 'A Culture Ghost; or Winthrop's Adventure' was first published in *Fraser's Magazine* (1881) and later reprinted in the collection *For Maurice: Five Unlikely Stories*.

8 Pierre Nicole (1625–95), a distinguished writer, theologian, and controversialist who defended Jansenist philosophies, taught in the schools of Port-Royal where Racine was one of his pupils. Together with Pascal, he contributed much to the formation of French prose. The quotations used in this essay are taken from Nicole's *Traité de la connaissance de soi-même* which appeared in *Essais de Morale* (1725), vol. III, quoted in Marin, 1991.

9 John Lane Company Records, Series A: Correspondence 1856–1933, Harry Ransom Humanities Research Centre at the University of Texas at Austin, USA.

10 See cover and frontispiece of Peter Gunn's 1964 biography of Lee for reproductions of this image.

11 Among these is Clementina Anstruther-Thomson, Lee's close friend and companion for many years who, according to Peter Gunn, is the model for Althea who appears in *Althea: A Second Book of Dialogues on Aspirations and Duties* (1894), (1964, 112). A 'pupil' of Lee's earlier alter ego, the philosopher, Baldwin who features in *Baldwin: Being Dialogues on Views and Aspirations* (1886), Althea becomes 'the precursor of many of Baldwin's thoughts, the perfecter of most of them' (Lee, 1894, xviii).

12 Anne-Louise Germaine Necker, Baroness de Staël-Holstein (1766–1817), French-Swiss woman of letters and early advocate of women's rights. Openly critical of Napoleon, de Staël spent much of her life in exile. *Corinne: ou L'Italie* (1807) is her most famous novel and tells the story of a celebrated female poet.

13 See Gunn 1964, 165, and the frontispiece of Colby's biography of Lee (2003) for reproductions of this image.

14 Angela Leighton argues that *Corinne, or Italy* (1807) functions as 'a Sappho story brought a little up to date' (Leighton 2003, 222).

15 No such explanation is provided.

16 See also Linda Dowling 1994.

17 Such 'beautiful boys' appear in other works by Lee such as 'A Culture Ghost or Winthrop's Adventure' and 'A Wicked Voice', 'A Wedding Chest', published in *Pope Jacynth and Other Fantastic Tales* (1904) and 'Prince Alberic and the Snake Lady', published originally in the *Yellow Book* (July 1896) and reprinted in *Pope Jacynth and Other Fantastic Tales*. A cross-dressed version of the 'boy' appears in 'Oke of Okehurst' in which Alice Oke wears the costume of a page.

8
Performing Pacifism: The Battle between Artist and Author in *The Ballet of the Nations*[1]

Grace Brockington

1. The battle scene

In autumn 1915, Vernon Lee published an allegorical satire against war entitled *The Ballet of the Nations*. Subtitled 'A Present-Day Morality', it imagines Satan and his ballet-master Death staging a diabolical *danse macabre* in the Theatre of the West.[2] Accompanied by a motley band of human passions, jumbling together Sin, Adventure and Idealism, Heroism, Hatred and Self-Righteousness, the nations perform a choreographed massacre. Having pounded the smallest into a dancing-mat, they attack one another, lopping off limbs and blinding each other 'with spirts of blood and pellets of human flesh' (*Ballet* 1915, 14). When the orchestra begins to flag, and the dancers confused, curtsey to their adversaries, Satan summons his prima donnas, Pity and Indignation, whose song revives the company to a new lease of slaughter (*Ballet* 1915, 18–20). The story ends inconclusively with the nations 'still a-dancing' and Satan plotting its perpetual run (*Ballet* 1915, 20). Its indeterminacy lifts it out of its historical moment, encouraging us to trace the pattern of its dance in all conflicts. Yet it is also entirely *of* its moment, written during the first twelve months of World War I, when the battle seemed interminable.

As an illustrated volume inspired by recent events and appealing to a particular readership, the book carries the trace of a specific episode in time. Yet even before it reached the press, Lee was planning a longer, unillustrated edition to appear after the war. The *Ballet*, never actually staged,[3] was from the outset an instalment toward her definitive argument against violence which appeared as *Satan the Waster* (1920). Although largely written before the Armistice, *Satan*'s late publication augments its authority: twelve times its length, it embeds the *Ballet* in an elaborate apparatus of prologue, epilogue and notes, reducing the 1915 publication to a sketch.

The recent resurgence of interest in Lee's pacifism has therefore focused on *Satan*, mentioning the *Ballet* only as a colourful first draft.[4] However, the *Ballet*'s very lack of hindsight gives it a resonance lost in the postwar revisionist mood. Its publication captures the writer in crisis, putting her political and artistic convictions in the firing line. The history of the book's production, essential to its interpretation but never before told, is bound up in the history of wartime peace activism. Moreover its rich illustrations, advertised on the title page as 'a pictorial commentary by Maxwell Armfield', but expelled from the austerely textual *Satan*, transform our response to Lee's narrative. The *Ballet* in effect contains not one, but two books, two conflicting interpretations of art's role in defending international peace. Yet among critics only Gillian Beer has paused to describe the images (Beer 1997, 120). Discussion of the *Ballet* has been frustratingly one-dimensional, favouring only the narrative itself, and isolating it from the complex meanings conveyed by the complete book on its publication. In this chapter, I argue that the problems inherent in the *Ballet* deserve greater scrutiny because they bring to the fore an aesthetic controversy about the function of art in a belligerent society.

A naked Atlas and Caryatid frame the title-page, supporting the graven capitals of **THE BALLET OF THE NATIONS** to form a proscenium arch around the publication details. The visual patterning of the typography and calligraphic delineation of the nudes merge word and image, creating a formal synthesis. Within the body of the book, the page design reinforces the effect of cooperation, even role-reversal, between text and illustration (Figure 8.1). An ornate band frames each episode, echoing the proscenium design of the frontispiece. Lee's narrative literally performs within the theatre it evokes, the text hanging like a figured stage-curtain over the passage of gesticulating characters beneath. The circuitous phrase 'pictorial commentary', however, warns of disagreement rather than faithful translation, and the coherence implied by the design grows ragged on close reading. Only about half the pictures correspond to Lee's narrative. When Widow Fear appears (*Ballet* 1915, 2), Armfield's dancers cower and disperse, hair and limbs streaming horizontally in the delineation of flight. When baby Belgium is told to stand quietly while the others dance around it, the picture shows it chubby and irresolute, enveloped in an ominous vacuum, with towering adults menacing from the wings (*Ballet* 1915, 10).

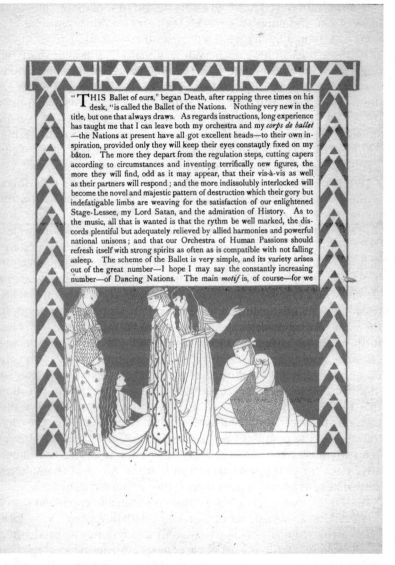

" THIS Ballet of ours," began Death, after rapping three times on his desk, "is called the Ballet of the Nations. Nothing very new in the title, but one that always draws. As regards instructions, long experience has taught me that I can leave both my orchestra and my *corps de ballet* —the Nations at present have all got excellent heads—to their own inspiration, provided only they will keep their eyes constantly fixed on my bâton. The more they depart from the regulation steps, cutting capers according to circumstances and inventing terrifically new figures, the more they will find, odd as it may appear, that their vis-à-vis as well as their partners will respond ; and the more indissolubly interlocked will become the novel and majestic pattern of destruction which their gory but indefatigable limbs are weaving for the satisfaction of our enlightened Stage-Lessee, my Lord Satan, and the admiration of History. As to the music, all that is wanted is that the rythm be well marked, the discords plentiful but adequately relieved by allied harmonies and powerful national unisons ; and that our Orchestra of Human Passions should refresh itself with strong spirits as often as is compatible with not falling asleep. The scheme of the Ballet is very simple, and its variety arises out of the great number—I hope I may say the constantly increasing number—of Dancing Nations. The main *motif* is, of course—for we

Vernon Lee, *The Ballet of the Nations*, pictorial commentary by Maxwell Armfield, London: Chatto & Windus, 1915, p. 7.

Elsewhere, however, Armfield elaborates his own narrative, imposing ideas of fate and puppetry on Lee's text, and introducing sexual frictions unexplored by her neutered personifications. He refuses to disguise the artifice of his theatre. While, visually, his designs share the stage with Lee's gory fable, the tension pervading his illustrations always stops short of her explicit violence. Contemporary reviewers disliked those inconsistencies, criticising his 'exaggerated avoidance of the brutal' (*Manchester Guardian*, 27 November 1915, 4). *The Evening Standard* delivered a particularly scathing attack on his 'unforgivable' commentary, claiming that its irrelevance to Lee's text reduced the whole volume to a ' "book of nonsense" ' (29 November 1915, 9).[5]

Letters filed in the archives of Chatto & Windus, Lee's publishers, reinforce the effect of schism. Shortly after accepting her script, the publishers wrote alluding to her disapproval of Armfield's designs, and suggesting another, more sympathetic artist.[6] Lee backed down, but their relationship clearly remained precarious, for Armfield declares that he avoided showing her the images until the point of publication 'for fear', he writes, 'she would be too dismayed'. In the event, he claims, she reconciled herself to the final result. Yet however much Lee resigned herself to a compromised *Ballet*, she still made provision, in the same letter in which she finally accepted Armfield's services, for a further edition, salvaging her text and framing it herself with *Satan's* elaborate apparatus. She even offered to forfeit her royalties on condition that production of the illustrated version should cease after six months.[7] Critics seem subsequently to have accepted the implication that the 1915 edition is provisional, even inconsequential. The disharmony between author and artist resulted from their respective commitment to the politics of realism, and of art for art's sake. Whereas Lee surrendered the privilege of aesthetic autonomy to the imperative need for propaganda against militarism, Armfield championed aestheticism as a form of pacifist resistance in its own right.

Few critics, then or now, have either recognized or condoned such a strategy.[8] In an article about war and art dating from 1915, John Galsworthy repudiated 'the extravagant dandyism of aestheticism'.[9] More recently, Martin Caedel has accused pacifist aesthetes of the First World War of cowardice (Caedel 1987, 140; Caedel 1980, 44–6), while David Peters-Corbett has argued that aestheticism precluded wartime 'engagement and opposition' (Corbett 1997, 25). Yet the antagonism between lived experience and the autonomous stage that fragments the *Ballet* also divided artists politically during the war. The book stands out as the archaeological remnant of a dispute that, though long buried, complicates the map of British modernism (see Brockington 2003).

2. 'The Heart of a Neutral': Vernon Lee as pacifist activist

Despite the transparency of the *Ballet*'s fable, with Belgium the 'Smallest-of-all-the-Corps-de-Ballet', and Germany the tall dancer who leap-frogs over it (*Ballet* 1915, 11), its enduring impact arises from the openness of its moral censure. All nations, whether combatant or neutral, share responsibility for the destruction. Each, as Death directs, should look as innocent as possible, while inflicting maximum damage on their opponent (*Ballet* 1915, 8). The villain is not Germany, but war and a shared predilection for conflict; the victim is not Belgium alone, but international harmony, each nation's probity, and the integrity of art itself.

Lee's refusal to vilify Germany lost her friends, but she persistently challenged the stereotype of Prussian barbarism. She complained about the censorship of German liberal opinion in Britain, and made a point of reading the German press even when it became hard to obtain.[10] The parties of aggression, she warned, were everywhere on the increase, as was a civilian market for 'clichés of obscene bloodthirstiness'.[11] The British attempt to demonize Germany merely betrayed its own militarism, which she defined as the failure to accept any portion of blame.[12]

Her indictment of all parties highlights the ambiguity of Lee's own national identity. Though nominally English, she was born in 1856 in Boulogne-sur-Mer. Her family belonged to a circle of well-to-do expatriates, who moved with the seasons between France, Italy, Germany and England. In 'The Heart of a Neutral', a brief allegory published shortly after the *Ballet*, she explores the mixed blessing of a cosmopolitan upbringing. Her parents, she imagines, invited all the fairies of Europe to her christening, each of whom brought her the gift of understanding their country's beauty. But the fairy they forgot cursed her, and predicted that she would be alien to each, understanding their weaknesses, but with no power to help them ('Heart' 1915, 687). Lee may sometimes have felt like a Cassandra, prophesying the fall of European civilization. Nevertheless, she used her anomalous status to referee between the two sides, cajoling and condemning them both.

At the outbreak of war, she found herself stranded in England, where she felt exiled from her domicile in Florence, and alien to the fervour of British self-affirmation. Yet her sense of being *'out of it'* here in

England',[13] and even herself at fault,[14] did not prevent her from conducting a vociferous campaign for peace through writing and membership of the Union of Democratic Control (UDC), a pacifist pressure group which campaigned for open diplomacy, democratic control of foreign policy and a fair peace settlement (Caedel 2000, 198–203). Her pamphlet *Peace with Honour* (1915), published by the UDC, challenged conventional understanding of both honour and peace.

Her wartime protest was consistent with long-held pacifist convictions sustained throughout the Boer War and subsequent European skirmishes (Colby 2003, 172). In the decade preceding 1914, she regularly published articles warning against war and stressing Britain's obligation to prevent it. From 1911, she became involved in collective peace action, cooperating with a group of English and European intellectuals who opposed Britain's intervention in Agadir, and who eventually contributed to the founding of the UDC (Colby 2003, 288, 296). The *Ballet* was the culmination of many years' pacifist agitation, and its fictional performance rehearses the ideas expounded in Lee's journalistic polemics.

The *Ballet's* cast of masochistic dancers gives flesh to the liberal nightmare of a centralised government that disregards, or even counteracts, the interests of individual citizens. In Lee's iconoclastic analysis, the nation disintegrates into a confusion of disparate interests subsumed by a tyrant state. Like the Scandinavian gods who 'slash each other to ribbons after breakfast and resurrect for dinner', the body of a dancing nation can suffer infinite mutilation, yet still grow fresh limbs (*Ballet* 1915, 13–14). However, its head (known to itself as its government, but mistaken by others for the whole country) is well protected, and always escapes unscathed (*Ballet* 1915, 14). The dancer becomes a travesty of the human form, in which the head punishes its own frame.

The image of society as a body corrupted by Satanic possession recurs in Lee's non-fictional writing about the war. Nation-making, she argues, is 'Devil's surgery' which violates the integrity of the international corpus ('Bismarck Towers' 1915, 483). She rejects as arbitrary the existing concept of nation, preferring a society structured around local communities and trans-national organisations. However, she does not deny the value of nations altogether. Rather, she redefines nationalism as sensitivity to national difference, an unaggressive pride in diversity that enriches the larger community.[15] Thus, the fairies in 'The Heart of a Neutral' greet baby Lee each in their own special way: England and Italy with poetry, humour and common sense; France with humane and rational wit; and Germany with music and philosophy, 'and the children's tales roosting in her Christmas tree' ('Heart' 1915).

In June 1915, about the time she was composing the *Ballet*, Lee published a critique of collectivism that draws a connection between militarism and the desire for unanimity ('The Wish' 1915, 482, 484). War, fear and hatred generate far stronger feelings of solidarity than admiration or compassion, she explains, which is what makes the thought of war universally attractive. On close inspection, however, she discerns that the 'imposing monumental lump of rigid One-ness' that constitutes the united nation is still compacted of individuals, 'merged like composite photographs', but displaying a disparity of motivation ('The Wish' 1915, 484). Dissolve the national collective, she argues in 'Enmity' (October 1915), and there will be peace ('Enmity' 1915, 12).[16] Society, she declares in *Peace with Honour*, must become decentralized and democratic to avoid conflict (*Peace* 1915, 30, 35–6, 58).

The melting together of meaningful distinctions in the *Ballet* demonstrates the damage caused by redundant national conglomerates. It is satire in the literal sense of medley, juxtaposing different emotions and historical periods to create an effect of chaos, not abundance. Widow Fear and her family carry a motley rag-bag of musical instruments, including 'a cracked storm-and-massacre bell, genuine mediæval but wrapped in yesterday's *Daily Mail* and *Globe*', whose anachronisms demonstrate the failure of progress (*Ballet* 1915, 3). The orchestra, dressed in a mixture of classical, medieval, biblical and tribal costumes, shows how war disrupts a sense of historical decorum. Science and Organisation abandon their affiliation with Life and Progress, striking an odd alliance with Death (*Ballet* 1915, 5–6). The music is deliberately discordant, and the dancing becomes more effective the more it abandons the rules of choreography. Death loves Heroism for his blind inability to discriminate, his willingness to sit among evil-doers. As the dance becomes more frenzied and the atmosphere increasingly murky, the audience's view also begins to blur, and the dancers lose their distinct humanity, becoming 'mere unspeakable hybrids between man and beast' (*Ballet* 1915, 15). The *Ballet*, observes Beer, 'is a work that raises the question: who is licensed to write, and especially to write satire in wartime?' A soldier can satirise with authority but, she queries rhetorically, 'a non-combatant woman, a writer on aesthetics, what does she here?' (Beer 1997, 108). She draws a forceful riposte from Lee's writing on social theory and psychology and, as I demonstrate below, Lee's use of an audience in the *Ballet* further answers Beer's question.

The *Ballet's dramatis personae* include an audience of neutrals, Sleepy Virtues, and Ages-to-Come, who enact our responses to the imagined show, forcing us to recognize that, as readers, we too are implicated. Lee's casting of the audience as an active player, accountable for its response – or failure to respond – to the performance, demonstrates how non-combatants, whether individuals or neutral nations, have an obligation to publicize their opposition to the bellicose spectacle.

At first, Lee gives the spectators a minor role, introducing them casually, but she keeps returning to them until, at the climax, they become the centre of attention, and key to the dance's infinite perpetuation. Some among the audience, like Wisdom, Equanimity, Temperance and Truthfulness, are culpable for their passivity (*Ballet* 1915, 18). Others participate with too much alacrity. Pity and Indignation, summoned by Satan, rally the diabolical orchestra (*Ballet* 1915, 18–19). Although they carry no instruments – no weapons of war – their voices are enough to rouse the troupe to the last and everlasting step, '*Revenge*' (*Ballet* 1915, 20). Lee's contemporary statement in *Peace with Honour*, that the neutral nations have a duty to preside over any peace negotiations shows up their failure in the *Ballet* to engineer such a settlement (*Peace* 1915, 20). Long before the outbreak of war, Lee had been challenging British liberals to take steps to prevent it. The English radical, she complained, was guilty of insularity and isolationism ('The Lines' 1910). Denying them the refuge of the helpless onlooker, she declared that in the event of battle 'absent-minded English liberals' would be largely responsible. It is the apathy of reasonable people, she pointed out, that cedes fanatics the field: 'fools would not rush in ... if the angels were not so abominably afraid of treading' ('Angels Fear' 1912, 829).

In *Peace with Honour*, Lee answers Beer's challenge almost prophetically, advocating discussion as an active measure against war. Lethal conflict, she points out, also kills desire for and freedom of discussion. She admits that, in the face of carnage, debate seems indecent. It seems appropriate 'either to bind up wounds or stand aside in silence'. But, she counters, the seemingly heartless habit of discussion is in fact 'a respectful standing aside from personal sorrow, an attempt to bind up the wounds of European civilisation' (*Peace* 1915, 61–2).[17] The suspension of open debate, she warns, would surrender the floor to the politics of coercion, ensuring the victory of militarism everywhere ('The Policy' 1915). She herself kept the discussion alive through an onslaught of pacifist propaganda that sought constantly to provoke a return. The *Ballet* was one statement in a campaign that made little distinction between literature and polemic.

3. 'Art for *life's* sake': Lee's wartime aesthetics

Lee's long-standing belief in 'art, not for art's sake, but … for the sake of life' underpinned her pacifist propaganda, and her disagreement with Armfield's aestheticist strategy ('Valedictory' 1895, 259).[18] The *Ballet*'s jarring juxtapositions of life and art – the shockingly incongruous description of a child pounded into a dancing-mat (*Ballet* 1915, 11), the jumbling together of mutilated bodies and stage properties, and the 'majestic pattern' of destruction devised by Death (*Ballet* 1915, 7) – illustrate her conviction that autonomous art is fundamentally immoral, because it fails to acknowledge suffering. The disintegration of the allegorical dance into real-life battle exposes the flimsiness, even fraudulence, of its fabrication. In 'The Wish for Unanimity' (1915), she even goes so far as to suggest that the dearth of good art is directly responsible for modernity's battle-lust, because it compels people to seek stimulation in war ('The Wish' 1915, 484).

Allegory, notes Jay Winter, became important after 1914 as 'a device of indirection, of the interposition of a narrative form between artists and audience' (Winter 1995, 132). In the *Ballet*, Lee evokes this oblique approach only to repudiate it. The realism of her battle scenes undoes her own symbolism, as the dancers mutilate one another in earnest, littering the stage with blood and guts. Vineta Colby's description of the *Ballet* as 'generalizing about the horrors of war', and Beer's contention that it 'avoids individual scenes of horror in close-up' fail to take account of its graphic depictions of violence (Colby 2003, 293; Beer 1997, 108). Scenes in which a nation continues to 'dance upon stumps, or trail itself along, a living jelly of blood and trampled flesh' (*Ballet* 1915, 13) do not generalize, but rather scrutinize in repulsive detail the trauma of war, unmasking the allegorical figure, and threatening to dismantle the stage itself.

An early statement of Lee's positive philosophy of art for *life's* sake appears in her paean to Pater in *Renaissance Fancies and Studies* (1895) ('Valedictory' 1895, 235–60).[19] Life engenders art, she asserts, and therefore only art which responds to life is truly 'vital'. Art's secession from that union undermines the integrity of our existence, creating a futile, superficial delusion which puts the cart of expression before the horse of emotion ('Valedictory' 1895, 258–60). In *Laurus Nobilis* (1908) she continues her attack, asserting that aestheticism has no practical purpose, resulting merely in an illogical, immoral and commercialized culture (1908, 260). Art, she declares, should be functional, like 'furniture and utensils' (1908, 208–9). Beauty is not an end in itself but a means to a life that is fuller, more intense, and 'at the same time more peaceful' (1908, 239).

That pacifying influence only works when the attention is externalized, the pleasure applied to the business of living. Otherwise, art has a dangerous capacity to aestheticize suffering, enticing us to enjoy the spectacle of other people's pain. Language seduces. The delusions of war may resemble a 'Maya's veil thrown over the intelligible universe', but, asks Lee, 'what is prettier than a face seen through a veil, and what more like a girl's name than this *Maya*?' ('Après' 1915, 251). In the *Ballet*, she cunningly employs the seductions of art, clothing gruesome events in lyrical phrases that tempt her audience to enjoy the horrors it should condemn. The 'Roman-candles and Catherine-wheels' of explosions blot out the sky (*Ballet* 1915, 13). Heroism, Death's favourite, is 'a star-like youth, with eyes which laughed and saw not' (*Ballet* 1915, 9). Pity and Indignation, who incite more battle, appear 'wan like waters under moonlight' and 'golden and vivid as flame' (*Ballet* 1915, 18). Our pleasure in these metaphors induces an emotional ambivalence, compelling the reader to join the ranks of Lee's complicit audience.

One's complicity in the aestheticization of suffering is underlined by Lee's indictment of what she calls 'tragic rapture' in her article 'Vicarious Tragedy' (1912), ('Vicarious' 1912, 466) that anticipates the *Ballet's* satire on war as a 'higher form of tragic art' (*Ballet* 1915, 1). She examines pain's paradoxical potential to wound and titillate through an analysis of her own mixed emotions at the death of a friend. 'I was enjoying the romantic savor of tragedy', she confesses, 'like a drink of excellent wine', and observes how the sound of her friend's laboured breathing mingled artistically in her imagination with the bawdy chatter of medical students and nurses. She experiences a 'Zola-ish allegoric vision' whose combination of horror and levity, *joie-de-vivre* and mortality, looks forward to the discordant couplings in the Zola-esque allegory of the *Ballet*. Yet her humanitarian instincts baulk at the taste of tragic pleasure. She prefers sobering morality to the sort of 'acquiescent ecstasy' that makes no attempt to alleviate the evils it contemplates ('Vicarious' 1912, 467). Instead, she celebrates the aesthetic pleasures of life itself, and the methods of commenting on our condition, so as to improve it.

Lee insisted on the possibility of progress, but stressed its incompatibility with war and the (to her mind) associated values of aestheticism. In the *Ballet* she implies an antithesis between battle and the reforming zeal of doctors, economists and trade unions, while *Peace with Honour* states explicitly that 'peace is not only the result of every kind of progress, but its *sine qua non*' (*Peace* 1915, 39.) Furthermore, she argues that art for art's sake is symptomatic of the anti-progressive turmoil of modernity, an 'aesthetic maladjustment', caused by sudden and superficial change. Once the social crisis resolves itself, she predicts optimistically, there will come an artistic revival, a reconciliation of art and life, and an age of peaceful stability (1908, 265–6).

Yet the *Ballet*'s evocation of ultra-modern music and avant-garde dance indicate that the war frustrated Lee's expectation of cultural renaissance. Ironically, it also thwarted the pacifist expectations of aestheticists such as Maxwell Armfield who, in her eyes, should have thrived on conflict. The antagonism between their concepts of renaissance becomes apparent in the *Ballet* when Armfield chooses to illustrate, and vindicate, the aestheticism which Lee's text lampoons, rather than to visualize the battlefield which is the real subject of her polemic. In its own terms, however, Armfield's oblique commentary makes as powerful a pacifist statement as Lee's overt propaganda. An analysis of those terms, taking into account his motivations and milieu, can transform our understanding of the relationship between art and pacifism, and hence our estimation of the 1915 *Ballet*.

4. Maxwell Armfield and the pacifist politics of art for *art's* sake

Armfield (1881–1972) and his wife, Constance Smedley (1876–1941), describe the making of the *Ballet* in memoirs that allow us to trace the book's inconsistencies to the circumstances of its production. They write about the pacifist beliefs which gave them common ground with Lee, but show how they used art for *art's* sake to promote peace.

In early 1915, they arrived in London, intent on developing the techniques of symbolist performance that they had begun to explore after their marriage in 1909. Settling in Chelsea, they fell in with a circle of performers, artists and writers, whose subversive loyalty to art for art's sake reinforced the Armfields' commitment to political, pacifist dissent. World War I was famously bad for British theatre. Historians dismiss it as a stagnant episode, dominated by propaganda and escapist comedy.[20] However, the survival of the Chelsea community challenges this verdict, calling attention to a forgotten culture of experimental drama that, in the context of local peace campaigning, amounted to a protest against war and wartime reaction.[21]

In their studio in Glebe Place, Armfield and Smedley worked out a system of theatre that, through formal and narrative symbolism, celebrated peace, and art's capacity to transcend national boundaries. In the same studio, they hosted meetings of the UDC, the pacifist organisation to which Lee belonged, and which provided a focus for their anger about the war. It was at this meeting-place of the disaffected that Lee's *Ballet* had its first reading, although the conditions of that reading also generated the rival conception of theatre that divides the book. The Armfields had met Lee in Florence before the war. In July 1915, they arranged for her to recite her *Ballet* for the UDC, first in their studio, and then at the neighbouring Margaret Morris theatre, the focal point of Chelsea's avant-garde community. After this second reading, Chatto & Windus made an offer for the book, duly commissioning Armfield to illustrate it.

I contend that Armfield's own theatrical experiments, rather than Lee's script, inspired his commentary. Contemporary photographs of his performances, and his written defences of his work, expose the direct visual and ideological link between his illustrations and the symbolist stage. His play *The Minstrel* (1915) is particularly resonant. Like Lee's recital of the *Ballet*, it was performed in 1915 both in the Armfields' studio, and at the Margaret Morris Theatre. Their circumstantial proximity only serves to highlight the aesthetic opposition between the two events, and their competing claims to mediate the meaning of the *Ballet*.

Records of the studio production of *The Minstrel* correspond strikingly with the appearance of the *Ballet*, in the use of costumes, pose and gesture. Note, for instance, how the final scene (Figure 8.2) evokes Armfield's imagining of a conversation among female nations (Figure 8.1). As they idle before the show, the women's self-conscious elegance suggests a dance-troupe, limbered-up and ready. In both images, the outstretched arm of the upright figure traces a suspended contour around the crouching woman to its right. Kneeling and standing characters face one another in an unequal parley, while a third looks on, askance and slightly withdrawing.

The Minstrel is the first of a trilogy examining 'the Artist in his relation to life' (Armfield 1915, 7).[22] This relationship, central to the doctrine of art for art's sake and to its pacifist implications, is also key to its misrepresentation. The story tells of a Persian king whose subjects

Maxwell Armfield, Phyllis Holt and Joyce Holt as the King, the Minstrel and the Maid in Armfield's play *The Minstrel*, here performed London, 1915. Photograph, artist unknown. Maxwell Armfield papers, Tate Archive. © Courtesy of Kate Ballard/Photo: Tate Archive, 2005

are starving after years of war. He offers them spiritual relief in the form of music, and sends his minstrel to administer among them. After a year the minstrel returns, convinced that he has achieved nothing. He discovers, however, that his listeners have been flocking to the palace to give thanks for his ministry. Its very indirectness has cured the trauma of war. Art helps not by reflecting reality, but through its uplifting vision of a better world.

The Minstrel's dedicatory inscription to 'all the Artists of the New Renaissance' makes a defiant declaration of fidelity to the European avant-garde at a time of increasing cultural conservatism. In particular, it signals Armfield's commitment to the symbolist practice of Edward Gordon Craig, the stage-designer whose pioneering practice instigated what Craig called a 'renaissance of the Art of the Theatre' (Craig 1905, 51). His concept of 'synthetic' theatre, which correlates all the arts in an aesthetic unity, was particularly important to Armfield's pacifist interpretation of the symbolist stage. It linked what Smedley called 'the essential brotherhood' of the arts with an ideal brotherhood of nations (Smedley 1929, 133). Their otherwise detached art of the theatre became a metaphor for global harmony, affiliating the other-worldly doctrine of aestheticism with worldly demands for peace.

Smedley's defence of experimental wartime theatre as 'a language of communication for all peoples', mitigating the chaos of war, reinforces the association between the Armfields' version of symbolism and their internationalist politics (Smedley 1929, 222). The idea of art as a universal language, encoding an abstract essence of meaning, was key to the symbolist aspiration toward a higher reality. For the Armfields, the promise of global understanding put the linguistic model at the centre of their formal innovations. It underpinned their attempts to create synthetic theatre, extending beyond mere words to a stylized system of movement that intensified the play's symbolic eloquence.

The text of *The Minstrel* incorporates a so-called 'body-movement script', a cartoon of stick-people dictating the gestural plan for the entire play (Armfield 1915, 15). Body-language becomes precisely that: a system of symbols loaded with significance, coordinating the visual and aural dimensions of the performance into a linguistic whole. Like a film-reel, the pictograph conveys movement through a series of adjacent stills. Armfield's instruction above the script that 'each posture should be held till the next is indicated' ensures that in performance the play preserves that staccato quality, dissolving any fast distinction between his dramatic and pictorial art.

The merging of stage and page in Armfield's oeuvre encourages us to read the *Ballet*'s illustrations as an elaborate body-movement script, drawing on what Smedley termed their 'universal vocabulary' (Smedley 1922, 58) of symbolic movement, and communicating to an international audience the priorities of peace. Armfield's concept of art as language strengthens the pacifist implications of his contribution to the *Ballet*, but also distances him from Lee's realism. His assertion that 'art is only valuable as a symbolic language', and that the more it seeks to imitate life, the less effective it becomes, threatens to muffle her eloquence (M. and C. Armfield 1920, 1). It propels their commentary into the limelight, refuting accusations of arbitrariness, and putting art for art's sake centre-stage in wartime political debate.

5. Conclusion: 'a beautiful offering on the altar of peace'?

In March 1916, Lee wrote to the Armfields thanking them for their help in producing her *Ballet*. 'Without your energy and resourcefulness', she told them, it 'would still be unpublished for many a month'.[23] Her tribute tactfully side-steps their disagreement about the book, while acknowledging their common need to broadcast its pacifist message. In retrospect, Armfield is likewise magnanimous, agreeing that, as propaganda, the merits of Lee's text outweighed its problems of form.[24] Momentarily, the competing aesthetics of art for art's sake, and art for *life's* sake, were made to cohabit, although their display of solidarity before the 'altar of peace' (to quote Armfield) convinced nobody.[25]

The 1915 *Ballet* is remarkable because it raises the curtain on a neglected world of wartime cultural debate. It lifts the profile of pacifist literature written controversially *during* the war, not in the relative safety of the Armistice. It articulates the pacifist motivation behind Lee's realist technique, encouraging us to make the link between her political polemics and better-known treatises on aesthetics. Most dramatically, it brings to the fore a forgotten battle between realism and art for art's sake which, gathering momentum after 1914, disrupts the history of British modernism. Aesthetic controversy was unavoidable during the war, and unavoidably political. Played out in the pages of the *Ballet*, it gave rise to a book rich in artistic and political meanings, as well as contradictions.

Notes

1 For their help and advice, I would like to thank Christopher Green, Jon Stallworthy, Douglas Newton, Jo Briggs, Carol Peaker, Alex Harris, Linda Goddard and staff at the Tate Gallery Archive Centre.

2 Lee added to a pervasive image of war as theatre. See Fussell 1975, 191–230.

3 Although never staged, *The Ballet of the Nations* was recited by Lee for the pacifist group, the Union of Democratic Control at the Glebe Place studio run by the artist Maxwell Armfield and his wife, and at the Margaret Morris theatre, both in Chelsea.

4 Gill Plain bases her discussion of Lee's modernism on *Satan* rather than the *Ballet*. See Plain 2000, 6. I am very grateful to Dr Plain for sending me a copy of her essay. Gillian Beer vividly conveys the experience of reading the illustrated *Ballet*, but her analysis of Lee's ideology likewise draws more on *Satan* (Beer 1997, 107–31).

5 *The Athenæum* similarly wished that Armfield's illustrations had 'kept more closely to the text' ('Our Library Table', 4 December 1915, 417), while *The Times Literary Supplement* remarked that 'as the reader will not always readily discern their exact relation to the text he must make what he can of them' ('New Books and Reprints', 25 November 1915, 431).

6 Chatto & Windus to Violet Paget, 29 July 1915, University of Reading Modern Publishing Archive: Chatto & Windus, vol. 86, 1034. They proposed Norman Wilkinson ('of Four Oaks').

7 See correspondence between Chatto & Windus and Violet Paget, 27, 29 and 30 July, 2 and 4 August, 1915, Reading: Chatto & Windus, vol. 86, 1016, 1051, 1069 and General Publishing Correspondence File CW 17/7.

8 Exceptions include Christopher Reed 2004, who argues that the aestheticism practised by members of the Bloomsbury Group reinforced their pacifism and Modris Eksteins, who asserts that art for art's sake was subversively political, though he does not make the connection with pacifism (Eksteins 1989, 42).

9 John Galsworthy, 'Art and War', *The Atlantic Monthly* CXVI (5 November 1915), 625. See also: W. K. Colton, 'The Effect of War on Art', *The Architect* XLV (17 March 1916), 200; and anon., 'Current Art Notes', *Connoisseur* XLII (1915), 52.

10 See the following by Lee: Letter to the Editor, *The Nation* XV (22 August 1914), 767; 'The Lines of Anglo-German Agreement', *The Nation* VII (10 September 1910), supplement between pp. 838 and 839; and 'War the Grave of All Good', *Labour Leader* XII, no. 43 (28 October 1915), 3.

11 Vernon Lee, 'The Policy of the Allies', *The Nation* XVI (2 February 1915), 649; Vernon Lee, *Peace with Honour: Controversial Notes on the Settlement* (London, 1915), 21.

12 Vernon Lee, Letter to the Editor; Lee, *Peace with Honour*, p. 39; Lee, 'Militarists against Militarism', *Labour Leader* XII, no. 13 (1 April 1915), 3.

13 Vernon Lee to Irene Cooper Willis, Ash Wednesday 1915, Colby College Manuscript Collections. I am extremely grateful to Dr Douglas Newton for sending me copies of his notes from the Colby archives.

14 The war-fever sapped Lee's confidence. She felt 'an overwhelming sense, through all [her] antagonism, of the extraordinary *naturalness* and inevit-

ableness of it all'. 'Myself', 5 September 1916, unpublished, quoted in Gunn 1964, 206.

15 Vernon Lee, 'The Sense of Nationality', *The Nation* XII (12 October 1912), 97; Vernon Lee to Maurice Baring, January 1906, quoted in Gunn, 1964, 201; Vernon Lee, 'Après la Mêlée', *The New Statesman* V (19 June 1915), 251.

16 Vernon Lee, 'Enmity', *War and Peace* III, no. 25 (October 1915), 12. See also Lee, 'May Day Messages from British Women', *Labour Leader* XII, no. 17 (29 April 1915), 5.

17 See also Vernon Lee, 'War the Grave of All Good', *Labour Leader* XII, no. 43 (28 October 1915) 3.

18 See the discussion of Lee's equivocal attitude to aestheticism in Colby 1970, 235–304.

19 For a discussion of Lee and Pater, see Bizzotto 2004, 62–3.

20 Chotia 1996, 85; Collins 1998, 2. Williams 2002.

21 Much more could be said about wartime avant-garde theatre. For further discussion, see Brockington 2003, 204–27.

22 The others were *The Grassblade* and *Lost Silver.*

23 Vernon Lee to Constance Smedley, 29 March 1916. The original letter is enclosed in the Tate Archive copy of the *Ballet.*

24 M. Armfield, 'Section 6 – My World and I – the Cotswolds and London in War' (c. 1970), 49, Tate Gallery Archives: Armfield, Manuscripts Box 3.I reference the catalogue I compiled in 2001.

25 Ibid., 51. See note 4.

9

Plural Anomalies: Gender and Sexuality in Bio-Critical Readings of Vernon Lee

Jo Briggs

Since the publication of Vineta Colby's *The Singular Anomaly: Women Novelists of the Nineteenth Century* (1970), Vernon Lee's work on aesthetics has received most attention from feminist literary critics (Colby 2003, 235–304). Gillian Beer has written that 'Vernon Lee does not "fit"' (Beer 1997, 109) and this statement seems to hold especially true for Lee's numerous writings on the perception of form, beauty and ugliness, as well as on psychological and physiological aesthetics. In this chapter I take a new angle on these works and their reception, beginning with a survey of the secondary literature on Lee's treatises on aesthetics and comparing this to existing and potential readings of similar writings by the connoisseur and art historian, Bernard Berenson, Lee's acquaintance and neighbour in Florence who famously accused Lee of plagiarism in 1897.

In comparing the works at the centre of the plagiarism claim – Berenson's *The Florentine Painters of the Renaissance* (1896) and Lee's article 'Beauty and Ugliness' published in the *Contemporary Review* (1897), and subsequently reprinted in *Beauty and Ugliness and Other Studies in Psychological Aesthetics* (1912) – I highlight posterity's divergent treatment of these two intellectuals and their respective current positions within the academy. What becomes particularly clear from this comparison is that Vernon Lee's writings are often read as examples of sexual dissidence, while Berenson's works remain 'unsullied' by similar observations. Such readings of Lee have their origins in Burdett Gardner's doctoral dissertation of 1954, published in 1987 under the title *The Lesbian Imagination (Victorian Style): A Psychological and Critical Study of 'Vernon Lee'*. Gardner examines the impact of Lee's lesbianism, which he defines as a 'neurosis' (Gardner 1987, 28), on her literary output, and his theories have been particularly important for more

160

recent feminist studies. Given that the aims of each are entirely different, it is ironic that Gardner's pathologized references to Lee's sexuality have made her a key figure in feminist criticism and fuelled subsequent academic interest. In the following pages, I argue that sexualized readings of Lee's work on aesthetics are also informed by other discourses with alternative agendas that have significant implications for the ways in which gender is addressed in the academy and in literary criticism. As Christa Zorn has observed, and as I hope to demonstrate: 'Reading Vernon Lee today reveals as much about her critics as it does about herself' (Zorn 2003, 19).

Critical continuities

Lee's approach to art criticism is usually referred to as 'psychological aesthetics', a technical term widely used in the theoretical literature of the period in which she was writing, and which I will expand on later in this chapter. However, in the literary critical accounts of Lee's writing on aesthetics, from the 1950s onwards, a range of sexually dissident practices associated with the female body and Lee's lesbian sexuality have become linked with the term, so that 'psychological aesthetics' has become a convenient shorthand for a variety of associated meanings. In fact these uses of the term are symptomatic of the way in which the recent secondary literature on Lee's writing on aesthetics could be said to function as an ever more elaborate and complex 'outing' of Lee's lesbian sexuality which is read into this part of her work. This tendency to 'out' Lee holds so true that even when critics detect a lack of sexual expression in Lee's writing, this absence is interpreted as 'less a denial of sexuality than it is a sexual style' (Psomiades 1999, 30).

Taking a survey of the criticism which chooses to approach Vernon Lee's writings on aesthetics in this way we can see that certain themes are consistently emphasized, namely, that these writings are part of Lee's relationship with Clementina Anstruther-Thomson, and additionally that the ideas that Lee expresses in them contradict other aspects of her work. In her study of Anstruther-Thomson's letters to Vernon Lee, Diana Maltz identifies a subversive language that she interprets as coded forms of sexual expression. Like Phyllis F. Mannocchi, Maltz suggests that the romance between Lee and Anstruther-Thomson is central to their writing on aesthetics (Mannocchi 1986, 129–48). Maltz subtitles one section of her essay 'The growth of a romance and a theory' and she argues that 'To tell the story of psychological aesthetics is to tell a love story' (Maltz 1999, 212). For Mannocchi, the friendship between Lee and Anstruther-Thomson is an example of the 'romantic friendships' that existed between women up to and during the nineteenth century which were, she writes, 'idealistic' and 'blissfully free' (Mannocchi 1986, 131; 145 n. 6).[1]

Accounts which foreground the relationship between Lee and Anstruther-Thomson when discussing their writings on aesthetics also focus on this work's role in its breakdown. Mannocchi sees their friends and society as at fault, since they were unwilling to accept the intellectual partnership of two women, while Vineta Colby has commented that Lee was 'unable to separate her personal need for love from her intellectual work' (Mannocchi 1986, 139; Colby 2003, 168). Notably, the sources drawn on in these cases are primarily letters between Lee and Anstruther-Thomson, and in the case of Maltz, the gallery tours Anstruther-Thomson led in the late 1890s.

Other critics of Lee's studies on aesthetics, as well of her broader oeuvre, have used her writings as a counterpoint to more well-established readings of the aesthetic movement in Britain. Talia Schaffer and Kathy Psomiades have emphasized how Lee's work 'broadens our notion of aestheticism and our sense of the possibilities it offered both women and men' (Schaffer 2000, 1–33; Psomiades 1999, 22). However, these readings have been at the expense of a coherent picture of Lee's literary output. Psomiades also observes that Lee's work 'reminds us that sexual dissidence takes many, sometimes contradictory, forms' (Psomiades 1999, 22). This account highlights the disjunction in Lee's writings between the puritan aesthete who authored *Miss Brown* (1884), and the body-centred Decadent who authored 'Beauty and Ugliness'.[2] Most significantly, perhaps, this survey of the literary criticism of Lee's writings on aesthetics shows that as a result of this sexualized focus, to date, the intellectual merits of Lee's work have often been neglected. Lee and Anstruther-Thomson's collaborative work has been described as the 'stuff of decadent high comedy', reporting aesthetic observations 'in detail so minute that at times it borders on the ludicrous' (Maltz 1999, 213; Colby 2003, 157). The hyperbolic nature of these readings also plays into the idea that women's writings are only ever a form of confession or autobiography. In other words, women prove through their writings that they are forever unable to escape from the self.

The provenance of the words, sources and references used in Lee criticism goes some way to explaining this situation – in particular, as indicated at the beginning of this chapter, those originating with

Burdett Gardner. Gardner was unable to refer to the private papers deposited at the Colby College Library since Lee had stipulated in her will that prior to the 1980s they be available only for private study. For personal details he therefore relied predominantly on the testimony (both written and oral) of Lee's friends and acquaintances including Ethel Smyth, Irene Cooper Willis (the executor of Vernon Lee's will whose typewritten manuscript on Lee is also deposited at Colby College) and Bernard Berenson. These friends were, with the exception of Berenson, not well informed about the complexities of contemporary thinking about aesthetics: Smyth admitted as much herself, stating 'aesthetics are absolutely beyond me' (Mannocchi 1986, 139).[3] Despite this, Gardner used their comments to read pathological sexual repression into Lee's approach to and writings on the subject.

Gardner's style of thinking about Lee and his presentation of the source material set up a surprisingly enduring framework for subsequent readings. For example, Gardner selects two quotations from primary sources that he did have access to, and he reproduces them as particularly significant in relation to the lesbian subtext in Lee's writing on aesthetics. From Anstruther-Thomson's correspondence with Lee he highlights the phrases 'delicate brains' and 'little gasp' (Gardner 1987, 215), phrases which Maltz later reads as 'code word[s] for lesbianism' and 'sign[s] of sexual passion projected onto the art object', that help form the basis of her argument (Maltz 1999, 224, 222).

Likewise, Psomiades, despite being critical of Gardner's study, presents a thesis which derives from Gardner's view (originally voiced by Cooper Willis) that Lee's work on aesthetics was a form of repression, reading Lee's puritan aestheticism, her denial of sexuality, as the 'sexual style that governs the conflicted and interesting relation of Vernon Lee's aesthetics to the female body' (Psomiades 1999, 30). Hence, even when Lee is not talking about sex she is nonetheless talking about sex. At a key moment in her essay Psomiades cites Gardner and, building on his argument with precisely the same extract from Lee's introduction to *Art and Man* (1924) (Gardner 1987, 224–5; Psomiades 1999, 30–1), moves on to observe that 'This is less a passage about two women looking at art, than it is about a woman watching another woman experience art', before concluding that 'Aesthetic experience is thus based in lesbian desire' (Psomiades 1999, 31). It seems clear that Gardner's psycho-pathological approach to Vernon Lee's work in this area has set a remarkable precedent in the critical literature that has followed.

So, why should it matter that Lee's aesthetics have primarily been read as an expression of her lesbian sexuality? Although the readings of Lee put forward by feminist critics are groundbreaking and significant, in basing them in Gardner's reductive theories they omit equally important factors operating in Lee's work. As Richard Dellamora has observed, it is the case that 'antihomophobic inquiry tends to ignore other aspects of dissidence; for example, the connections between sexual and cultural dissidence in cultural production by women' (Dellamora 1999, 5). Arguably, such considerations are absent in readings of Lee's writings on aesthetics to date. Crucially, Lee's gender seems to have made it easier for critics to talk about her sexual inclinations rather than her scholarship. Focusing on Lee's sexuality, these readings often fail to evaluate the real intellectual achievement of her work on aesthetics, work which is all the more noteworthy when we consider the period in which she was writing. The broader-reaching and, I believe, more urgent implications of Lee's gender on the criticism of her aesthetics become evident when one considers, as I go on to demonstrate, that Bernard Berenson wrote in a very similar way on the same subject, yet his reputation has fared very differently. It is important to remember that, in the 1890s, the discipline of art history took a psychological turn, and that Lee's and Berenson's respective writings need to be read in this context. This theoretical framework has led many critics to look for emotional or psychological reasons for what seem to be peculiarities and contradictions in Lee's writings at the expense of the intellectual content.[4]

Lee and Berenson: a comparison

Psychological aesthetics has its origins in the work of William James, Carl Lange, Theodor Lipps and Karl Groos. Lipps and Groos (two German psychologists) studied the concept of 'empathy'. Groos connected the observation of form and movement to physiological changes in the viewer that he labelled 'inner mimicry', while Lipps called empathy 'the inward side of imitation' (quoted in Mannocchi 1986, 137). James and Lange (independently) formulated a theory of emotion that focused on the mind's response to its perception of physiological changes prompted by an external stimulus. James put forward the idea that emotions were the result, rather than the cause, of physical changes in the body. In *The Principles of Psychology* (1890), James observed that the emotions are 'made up of those bodily changes which we ordinarily call their expression or consequence' (James 1890,

452). Such a theory seemingly offered a way to ground aesthetics in empirical fact since the emotions produced by viewing art would, if we accept the James-Lange theory, stem from observable bodily changes, hence Lee's and Anstruther-Thomson's interest in observing physical responses in order to explain aesthetic emotion. As Francis Edward Sparshott notes, this was an approach that flourished in late-Victorian aesthetics (Sparshott 1963, 243), and it is therefore unsurprising that the body should have been the focus of their work, as it was in many of their contemporaries' writings on the same subject, including Berenson's.[5]

Given the prominence of the body in contemporaneous thinking on aesthetics and the body's centrality in the secondary literature on Lee, we might be surprised at the precise emphasis it receives in 'Beauty and Ugliness'. Psomiades's claim that Lee 'produced a theory of the aesthetic grounded in the congress between female bodies' (Psomiades 1999, 21) finds little support when we consider the language of the essay in question and the objects Lee and Anstruther-Thomson selected for analysis: a chair, a jar, an abstract Greek honeysuckle pattern, the façade of Santa Maria Novella in Florence, and the pointed Gothic arch, among others. The way in which Lee writes about these objects does not suggest a foregrounding of, or revelling in, the bodily: she observes that 'the æsthetic pleasure in art is due to the production of highly vitalizing, agreeable, adjustments of breathing and balance as factors of the perception of form' (Lee and Anstruther-Thomson 1912, 224–5). The ideas expressed in 'Beauty and Ugliness' are therefore in agreement with Colby's characterization of Lee as a 'Puritan Aesthete' (Colby 1970, 235–304) rather than the result of a Decadent, or even diseased, eroticism.

It is in this emphasis on health that Lee's work is most similar to Berenson's in *Florentine Painters of the Renaissance*. It was probably these similarities that led Berenson to claim that Lee had appropriated his ideas via his conversations with Anstruther-Thomson. Lee wrote that when experiencing an aesthetic object 'we seem to be living at twice our normal rate, and life, for no definable reason seems to be twice as much worth living' (Lee and Anstruther-Thomson 1912, 201), while Berenson claimed that we grasp objects represented through art more quickly and easily than if we had encountered them in reality and are therefore overwhelmed by the 'sense of having twice the capacity' with which we had credited ourselves (Berenson 1896, 10). However, their arguments are not identical as Lee herself states in a footnote to 'Beauty and Ugliness' where she points out that Berenson offers a

'different and more intellectual reason' for the increased vitality produced by viewing art (Lee and Anstruther-Thomson 1912, 225). As Lee
emphasizes the difference between them, she expands on Berenson's
ideas, arguing for a more controlled and balanced experience from
viewing art, stating that 'the function of art is not merely to increase
vitality, but to regulate it in a harmonious manner' (Lee and
Anstruther-Thomson 1912, 225).[6] Lee is clearly on more familiar terms
with the theories of Lange and James which are central to her engagement with aesthetics, whereas Berenson is interested in aesthetics only
in so far as they enable him to answer an art-historical question. Both
writers set themselves very different agendas: where Lee sets out to
answer the problems of aesthetics – Why do we enjoy art? What is the
purpose of this enjoyment? – Berenson remains interested primarily in
explaining the specific characteristics of Florentine painting in the
Renaissance, from Giotto to Michelangelo.

As a consequence perhaps, Lee's idea of aesthetic empathy, according
to which the viewer responds emotionally and physically to the art
object, is ironically much more abstract and, in fact, less focused on
the body and bodily pleasure than Berenson's. Lee is primarily concerned with the changes in breathing and balance triggered by a range
of objects which do not necessarily depict the human form. Berenson
on the other hand is only interested in figural art: in the stimulation of
our sense of touch by, and also a more straightforward miming of, the
actions of the depicted human form. Thus, Berenson's theories on art's
effectiveness ask us to consider the content and narrative of the art
work, what we observe the figures doing and how those figures are rendered by the artist, whereas Lee's idea of the enjoyment we derive from
art is not connected to content or narrative but is formal – it may as
well be a chair we choose to focus on as a statue.

A useful case study of divergent responses to Lee's and Berenson's
respective works on aesthetics can be found in a comparison of the arguments each author makes about nude statues, in particular the Venus de
Milo, and in an examination of the ways in which such arguments have
been read and analysed in recent criticism. Lee and Anstruther-Thomson
read the Venus de Milo in terms of form. The draperies and its incom-
pleteness (the statue is missing its arms) are seen as adding to the beauty
and harmony of the art object. Lee quotes the following observations
made by Anstruther-Thomson in *Art and Man*:

> *My connexion with her is through my motor impulses, and so I feel just as
> much connected with her drapery as with her body; both of them*

balance and have movement. ... *She does not look like an alive woman wearing inanimate drapery; but she and her drapery are one.* (Anstruther-Thomson 1924, 94, 95).

In 'Beauty and Ugliness', they argue: 'indeed, it is possible that the persistent belief in the Venus of Milo as an original masterpiece of the greatest epoch may be due to the fact that the absence of arms makes her compose in the very happiest equilibrium when seen from the front' (Lee and Anstruther-Thomson 1912, 220). These quotations show that for Lee and Anstruther-Thomson, the draperies and missing arms are useful as they produce a more satisfactory form.

By contrast, since he is not interested in pure form, Berenson complains that the draperies hinder the appreciation of the nude. He writes:

If draperies are a hindrance to the conveyance of tactile values, they make the perfect rendering of movement next to impossible. To realize the play of muscle everywhere, to get the full sense of the various pressures and resistances, to receive the direct inspiration of the energy expended, we must have the nude. (Berenson 1896, 86)

When we turn to the secondary literature, we see that, despite Berenson's insistence that the absence of draperies is required to reveal the nude as a highly physical representation of the human body which is to be understood and enjoyed by the viewer as just such a physical presence, critics have gone to great lengths to show that it is Lee and Anstruther-Thomson's reading of the nude as abstract form which is sexualized, in fact far more sexualized than Berenson's. Gardner writes: 'In ironic contrast to Bernard Berenson's more normal feeling about the relation of draperies and the nude ... Kit's anthropomorphizing of the draperies in order to render abstract her appreciation of the Venus has upon it the strain of a compulsive sublimation' (Gardner 1987, 232). This analysis paved the way for Psomiades's more recent reading.

Psomiades reproduces a section taken from *Art and Man*, part of which I quoted above. The quotation ends: '*These movements I may be said to imitate, but I should find them and imitate them equally in a Renaissance monument or a mediæval chalice. They are the basis of all Art'* (Anstruther-Thomson 1924, 94). Rather than reading this passage as an indication of Lee and Anstruther-Thomson's argument that the Venus de Milo affects us as form rather than content, Psomiades suggests that

Anstruther-Thomson's 'physical activity before art turns all art, whether it be statue, monument, or chalice, of all periods, into a feminine body with which she has congress and all aesthetic experience for a moment becomes a bodily exchange between women' (Psomiades 1999, 35). Once again Lee's work on aesthetics is seen as sexual dissidence: 'physiological aesthetics is located in the congress between two feminine bodies, one made of marble (she) and one of flesh (I)' (Psomiades 1999, 35).

Alternative readings which could reveal Lee and Anstruther-Thomson's thinking as strikingly modern, paving the way to an appreciation of abstract art as expounded in the works of Clive Bell and Roger Fry more than a decade later, are bypassed. For instance, Lee and Anstruther-Thomson use the example of how we react to a blank white wall, which they refer to as a 'white void' and contrast this with the effects produced by looking at a wall coloured terracotta before going on to discuss the effects of viewing abstract patterns of dots, lines and triangles in that void (Lee and Anstruther-Thomson 1912, 173–4). Thus, unlike Berenson's work, which is preoccupied with canonizing the art of the past, Lee's work with Anstruther-Thomson radically calls into question what art is and what it can be. Berenson's idea is that art is effective precisely because it condenses reality: in his words it lends 'a higher coefficient of reality' (Berenson 1896, 10). That is to say, art has impact only in so far as it imitates and condenses the qualities of some other actual object we can recognize and compare it to. Unlike the modernity of Vernon Lee and Anstruther-Thomson's understanding of what may constitute art, this way of thinking seems firmly rooted in the nineteenth century.

This comparison between Bernard Berenson and Vernon Lee highlights the latter's position as an innovative female critic in the field of aesthetics whose publications demonstrate her considerably advanced thinking on form and art. Yet her writings on aesthetics, unlike those of Berenson, have been read predominantly through the lens of sexuality. In contrast to those works of art discussed by Lee, those referred to by Berenson in *The Florentine Painters of the Renaissance* are mostly figural and indeed those singled out for special note feature mainly male subjects: *The Battle of the Nudes, Hercules Strangling Antaeus,* and *David* all by Pollaiuolo, various paintings of religious figures by Andrea del Sarto, the 'Boy Angel' and Adam by Michelangelo from the Sistine Chapel (Berenson 1896, 54–6, 78, 79, 89). Berenson, taking the imagined example of an art work depicting two men wrestling, writes: 'unless my retinal impressions are immediately translated into images of strain and pressure in my muscles, of resistance to my weight, of touch all over my body, it means nothing to me in terms of vivid experience', and making an argument for the supremacy of the nude as an aesthetic type: 'here alone can we watch those tautnesses of muscle and those stretchings and relaxings and ripplings of skin' (Berenson 1896, 50, 86–7). Berenson praises the nude bodies depicted in unabstracted terms; referring to Pollaiuolo's *David* as 'this wonderful youth', and exclaiming at Andrea del Sarto's work 'what a back St. Sebastian's!' (Berenson 1896, 56, 79).

Having pointed out that Berenson's *Florentine Painters of the Renaissance* is equally open, if not more so, to the type of readings which have been applied readily to 'Beauty and Ugliness', I want to consider whether Berenson's life, like that of Lee's is open to homo-erotic re-reading and, if so, to explore the reasons behind the divergent development of their reputations as art critics in the twentieth century. As Zorn has commented, Lee was writing at 'a time when public discourses were being reshaped by an ongoing process of institutional restructuring that also reflected the way social and intellectual authority interlocked with the aspects of sex and gender' (Zorn 2003, 21), and it is important to take these changes into account when assessing their relative positions within the academy.

Gender and reputation

Berenson's working life, like Lee's, was characterized by close collaborations: first, with his wife Mary Berenson (née Costelloe) and secondly, and more significantly for my argument, with his male pupils or 'disciples'.[7] Berenson had close, even intimate, friendships with the young men who came to spend time working with him at I Tatti, his villa outside Florence. Berenson nicknamed one pupil, John Walker, 'cherubino' (Samuels 1987, 384),[8] while he found Kenneth Clark 'genial and lovable and always consumed with intellectual passion' (Samuels 1987, 348).[9] After Kenneth Clark left his post at I Tatti, affectionate letters passed between him and Berenson. On one occasion, Clark wrote to his mentor: 'it is with a real pang of emotion that I have unpacked and opened the volumes of the Florentine Drawings [the book Clark had helped Berenson to update]. They are intimately connected with the whole of my life ... I needn't tell you how touched I am by your reference to me in the introduction' (Samuels 1987, 449).[10] Another research assistant Arthur Kingsley Porter wrote: 'I am very fond of you. I wonder if you realize how much so, and how deeply you have influenced my way of looking at things' (Samuels 1987, 406).[11]

I have reproduced these quotations in order to show that Berenson's life could be read in terms of his homosocial, and possibly homoerotic, relationships, yet has not been. Drawing on the work of Eve Kosofsky Sedgwick, one might ask, how it is that Lee's working relationship with Anstruther-Thomson 'counts as sexuality', colouring almost all recent readings of Lee's writings on aesthetics, whereas Berenson's working relationships with his pupils are not read in this manner? (Sedgwick 1985, 2).[12]

While Lee's works on aesthetics fell into relative obscurity after her death, Berenson's close relationships with a younger generation of art historians allowed for the preservation of his intellectual reputation. Berenson, like Lee, had slim claims to qualification on art, art history or aesthetics. His reputation rested on his training with the famous connoisseur Giovanni Morelli and his own writings and lists of attributions rather than on institutional backing and qualifications.[13] Thus, rather like Lee, his reputation was still dependent on the Victorian model of the man or woman of letters. However, in the late nineteenth and early twentieth century a new intellectual class of professionalized academics began to emerge. Art history as a discipline followed this trend: the first international association of art historians was formed in Vienna in 1873 and the early twentieth century saw the culmination of the institutionalization of art history as a serious academic discipline, the College Art Association of America being founded in 1911. Crucially, unlike Lee, Berenson was able to link himself, through his pupils, with this increasingly professionalized world.

Berenson's pupils became museum curators, academics or had careers combining the two: John Walker became director of the National Gallery of Art in Washington D. C.; Kenneth Clark became director of the National Gallery in London; Arthur Kingsley Porter became a professor at Yale, and was the first William Dorr Boardman Professor at Harvard; John Pope-Hennessy worked at the National Gallery, the Victoria and Albert Museum, the British Museum in London, and the Metropolitan Museum in New York, as well as being the Slade Professor at Oxford and Cambridge. The articles and reminiscences published by Berenson's pupils ensured the preservation of his reputation, especially post-World War II at almost exactly the same time as Lee was being re-read by Gardner for insights into the 'Lesbian Imagination'.[14] Berenson's alignment with and legitimation by the academy was sealed through the gifting of I Tatti to Harvard in 1935 to serve as their centre for Renaissance Studies (although it was fourteen years until the villa was passed to the university at Berenson's death in

1959). This gift also ensured that his papers, unlike Lee's, would remain intact and accessible in one location.

It is also crucial to realize that the professionalization of art history, with which Berenson's name became associated, excluded women. Women became the amateurs against whom male professionals defined themselves. Indeed, it could be said that the gender of art history in the late nineteenth and early twentieth century became masculine. Here, a comparison of Lee and Berenson, their writings and their lives, forces us to recognize that the reputations of male writers included in the canon are constructed and, therefore, are as open to reassessment and re-reading as those of female writers who have been excluded. Thus, I want to argue that there is a counterpart to the process which allowed Berenson to gain his place as a founding father of art history and cement his reputation: the process which confined Lee to the category of non-serious, un-intellectual women, and exposed her to modes of interpretation that foreground her sexuality and her emotional life.

The problems affecting Lee criticism are those that often accompany the reinstatement of female writers into the canon. As Pamela Gilbert observes:

> One of the most serious failures of feminist criticism as a corpus is its tendency, even today, to focus principally on authorial biography, a practice which unintentionally replicates the traditional sexist tendency to read canonical male-authored texts as self-contained 'art' and female-authored texts as simple extensions or reflections of personal experience. (Gilbert 1997, 7)

Likewise, Talia Schaffer has commented: 'Any literary critic knows how enormously tempting it is to call a neglected women writer "subversive," since that is the accepted way to demonstrate her worth' (Schaffer 2000, 11). Perhaps we need to ask ourselves whether reading Lee as the author of subversive writings in which she played out her lesbian sexuality must necessarily exclude readings of Lee as a groundbreaking intellectual able to compete with male writers at the forefront of her chosen field. The latter is surely as subversive as the former.

It is revealing that Lee's writings on aesthetics have never been wholly neglected: on the contrary, the bibliographical essays published in *English Literature in Transition* show that her work on aesthetics has received almost constant attention.[15] If Lee has been excluded from the canon becoming a forgotten female aesthete, as the title of Talia

Schaffer's book might suggest, then the marginalization of Lee has been an active, and consistent, process. In the shaping of Lee's reputation the question is not whether she is written about, but how she is written about. The fact that the marginalization of Lee forms a corollary to the discourse surrounding the institutionalization of art history is the most important point to be gleaned from a comparative approach to her writings on aesthetics. There is an important alternative to the representation of Vernon Lee as a romantic friend of interest for her lesbian imagination, mixing of aesthetics and desire, sexual dissidence and puritan aestheticism – the reclamation of her intellectual contribution to the discipline of art history.

Notes

1 Mannocchi takes the term 'romantic friendship' from Lillian Faderman (Faderman, 1971).

2 In her introduction to '"Still Burning from this Strangling Embrace": Vernon Lee on Desire and Aesthetics', Psomiades writes: 'in this essay I will show how the work of Vernon Lee ... complicates any easy opposition between liberatory and conservative aestheticisms and complicates too our ideas about Victorian sexual dissidence' (Psomiades 1999, 21).

3 Mannocchi quotes Smyth's comment that 'aesthetics are absolutely beyond me' from Smyth's autobiography, *What Happened Next* (1940) (Mannocchi 1986, 139).

4 For example Gardner saw the discrepancies between Lee's early writings on aesthetics and her later book *Art and Man* (1924) as due to her 'embarrassment at the gross somatic quality of Kit's original theory of muscular participation' rather than as in line with developments in the field of aesthetics (Gardner 1987, 233).

5 See Vischer in Mallgrave 1994.

6 This footnote reads in full 'In his remarkable volume on Tuscan painters (1896) Mr. B. Berenson has had the very great merit, not only of drawing attention to muscular sensations (according to him in the limbs) accompanying the sight of works of art, but also of claiming for art the power of *vitalising*, or as he calls it, *enhancing life*. Mr. Berenson offers a different and more intellectual reason for this fact than is contained in the present notes. In a series of lectures on Art and Life, delivered at South Kensington in 1895, and printed the following year in the *Contemporary Review*, one of the joint authors of the present notes had attempted to establish that the function of art is not merely to increase vitality, but to regulate it in a harmonious manner' (Lee and Anstruther Thomson 1912, 225).

7 Mary Berenson played a vital but now hidden role in creating the list of attributions which were to cement Berenson's reputation as a connoisseur. As Ernest Samuels comments, 'she brought to their work a capacity for painstaking record keeping which he lacked. The ledgers identify the paintings and drawings which she began to keep that winter 1891–2, in which she listed in alphabetical order hundreds of artists with concise descriptions

of their works' (Samuels 1987, 148). *The Venetian Painters of the Renaissance* (1894) was also expanded from an essay by Mary Berenson. It appeared under Berenson's name only because at the time Mary was married to another man and her family feared scandal. Mary Berenson referred to John Walker, in a letter to Berenson's mother dated 7 December 1930, as a 'nice new "disciple" ' (quoted in Samuels 1987, 384).

8 Samuels is here quoting from *Forty Years with Berenson* (1966) by Nicky Mariano.

9 Samuels, quoting from a letter from Mary Berenson to Alys Smith Russell, 18 November 1926.

10 Samuels, quoting from a letter to Bernard Berenson from Kenneth Clark, 3 December 1938.

11 Samuels, quoting a letter from Arthur Kingsley Porter to Bernard Berenson, 23 December 1929.

12 Sedgwick wrote that what counts as sexuality depends on and affects historical power relationships adding: 'A corollary is that in a society where men and women differ in their access to power, there will be important gender differences, as well, in the structure and constitution of sexuality' (Sedgwick 1985, 2).

13 Berenson took two art history classes in his final year as an undergraduate at Harvard, both with Charles Eliot Norton. However, at Harvard, Berenson had specialized in languages: Greek, Latin, Sanskrit, Hebrew and German, graduating with an Honorable Mention in Semitic languages and English composition. It was Berenson's exposure to Pater's writings, *Studies in the History of the Renaissance* (1873) and *Marius the Epicurean* (1885), which was to prove to be most significant for his later writing on aesthetics. Interestingly, according to Berenson, neither Charles Eliot Norton (who discovered Berenson reading Pater's *Studies in the History of Renaissance* in Harvard Yard) nor William James (to whom Berenson lent the same volume) liked the book (Samuels 1979, 28–40, esp. 36–9).

14 See, for example, 'Thoughts of a Great Humanist', Kenneth Clark's review of *Aesthetics and History in the Visual Arts* in Clark 1949, 144–5; Benedict Nicolson's editorial, 'In honour of Bernard Berenson' in Nicolson 1955, 195–6, and Kenneth Clark's 'Bernard Berenson', in Clark 1960, 381–6.

15 See Markgraf 1983, 268–312 and Mannocchi 1983, 231–67.

10

The Handling of Words: Reader Response Victorian Style

Christa Zorn

In recent years, as literary scholars have tried to develop theories explaining the kinship between the Victorian and the modernist eras, interesting new connections have been forged, not only between these two periods, but also between the Victorians and ourselves. The beginnings of postmodern critical theories have been traced back to the aesthetically and psychologically charged cultural transformations of the late nineteenth and early twentieth centuries. It was during that time period that most academic disciplines, as we know them today, began to be established. Literature and language studies were re-fashioned by the changing relationship between art and science and the newly emerging empirical disciplines; psychology was separating itself from philosophy, while aesthetics and literary scholarship found practical application in criticism and teaching.[1]

It was during this formative period in linguistic studies and practical criticism that Vernon Lee published *The Handling of Words* (1923), a collection of essays written over a time span of over 30 years (1891–1923). These 'notes', as she calls them, were 'jotted down in the course of reading ... not yet arranged to suit any theory' (1923 and 1992, 136). They include loosely connected thoughts on writing as a craft, the aesthetics of the novel, and psychological speculations on reader and writer, all accompanied by case studies of nineteenth-century works, 500 words randomly selected from each. The book gains its importance in being one of the first attempts of a literary critic to address seriously questions of literary value from a scientific angle, and Lee, aware of her own innovative approach, writes, 'I seem to have been pursuing for the first time and in solitude the minutest elements to which literary style can be reduced, namely, single words and their simplest combinations' (1923 and 1992, 187). The contemporary reviews were mixed. Most reviewers, obviously not yet sure where to place her study, merely described the method: 'concrete studies in the psychology of literary effectiveness' (*Nation* 22 August 1923, 201) or 'a useful system of stylistic analysis in quantifiable terms' (*TLS* 22 March 1923, 185). Some saw the practical value of her work realizing that *The Handling of Words* answered 'the questions that editors don't on their rejection slips' (*Bookman* September 1923, 90). But critical comments were never far off, either directed towards the author, 'sometimes she totally misses effects of colour and personality in the writing' (*Bookman* September 1923, 90), or towards the approach, 'this is enough to warn us of the limitations of the method' (*Spectator* 21 April 1923, 671).

Modern critics, such as the editors of two later editions – Royal A. Gettman and David Seed – have honoured Lee as one of the first to 'grasp firmly the elusive problem of prose style' (Gettmann 1968, vii). David Lodge even pronounced her an 'unacknowledged prophet of modern criticism' (Lodge 1986, 275). Vineta Colby describes *The Handling of Words* as an extension of Lee's earlier studies in psychological aesthetics in which she depicts her own reaction to art in pseudo-scientific terms: 'But instead of noting pulse rates, heartbeats, and muscle tension, she analyzes the effects that writers achieve with language' (Colby 2003, 201). David Seed dismisses these empirical studies before World War I as 'a phase in her career' (Seed 1992, v), but not as an integral part of her larger work. Similarly, even though praising her anticipation of postmodern theories, he sees *The Handling of Words* in the same league as 'the manuals of composition which appeared at the turn of the century' (Seed 1992, vi).[2]

It is tempting to imagine a direct line between *The Handling of Words* and Lee's experimental studies in psychological aesthetics, such as *Beauty and Ugliness* (1912) and *The Beautiful* (1913) but this proves to be a more complex issue. In the heterogeneity of her diction, one senses Lee's struggle to configure her own literary experience in the new, empirical modes of thought and to respond creatively to their challenges for reader and writer. She aligns herself broadly with the field of psychology that was far from homogenous then (Ryan 1991, 10). So her judgments are informed by both philosophy and psychology and are not always in step with her empirical data. In fact, her statistics are often pushed so far to the extreme that they undermine themselves – vide her analysis of Hardy's *Tess of the D'Urbervilles* (1891) – as a useful tool for literary criticism. To make matters worse, her opinions are heavily burdened by the Victorian heritage of normative evaluations. And yet, Lee's stylistic 'handbook' is a valid attempt to bring to the study of literature a new language of precision without closing the open process of interpretation. In this respect, she offers us a glimpse back into the disciplinary transformation of literary criticism, just before it became the province of modernist and postmodernist theories. Returning literary criticism into its historical possibilities, then, should provide the context for evaluating *The Handling of Words* today.

In the notoriously contentious arena of nineteenth-century language studies, the years between 1860 and 1916 witnessed a transition from historical philology (focusing on the etymological roots of words) to the 'new' synchronic linguistic approaches, which split the form of language from its content and, eventually, from the human subject. Notions of progress and decline, pervasive in the cultural climate of the fin de siècle, also shaped the linguistic debates. The loss of inflection, the dropping of parts of speech, or the collapse of grammatical distinction were seen as symptoms of general cultural decay. Mid-Victorian etymologists, deploring degeneration and entropic decline in contemporary language, believed that their 'excavations' could lead to a clearer understanding and employment of words in the present language. Extreme defenders of this philological school, such as William B. Hodgson (*Errors in the Use of English* (1881)), would argue that by retrieving the roots of words one could put an end to misuse and false application (Taylor 1993, 225–6). And Richard Chevenix Trench, a respected Victorian philologist, not only connected the degeneration (or bastardization) of English with the laws of evolution, but also with the expansion of the British Empire (Trench 1905, 11).[3]

Such culturally and nationally motivated historicism was outmoded by the end of the nineteenth century, especially, during 'the radical 1890s' (Taylor 1993, 369), the time when languages began to be studied synchronically and comparatively. From then until the era of Saussure, historic philology was considered an impediment to the linguist's work so that the investigation of 'roots' was replaced by systematic studies of current practices in living speech. In 1881, Alexander Ellis had told the Philosophical Society, 'if we really wish to penetrate into the meaning and growth of languages, we must look behind the conventional written form in the penetralia of living speech' (quoted in Dowling 1982, 169). The linguist Henry Sweet, a model for Shaw's Professor Higgins in *Pygmalion* (1914), proposed that the new key to understanding language had to be a synchronic one, since the presence of language suggested by its phonetic immediacy, was more 'real' than the written word from the past.[4] Under the influence of philosophical and psychological scholarship from the continent – such as Bopp's or Schleicher's comparative Indo-European studies – the 'new' philologists dismissed the history of words in favour of exposing the inner workings of verbal patterns 'an order of meaning completely detached from the representational order' (Dowling 1982, 167).[5] The controversial philologist, Max Müller, made language itself the sole object of scientific inquiry utilizing the study of literature only for the purpose of knowing language. Eventually, language was no longer seen as a mythic whole in its meaning, but treated as an autonomous system detached from its aesthetic and practical end, including the speaker – a disturbing thought for Victorians. Thomas Hardy, who took a close interest in these epistemic shifts, feared that language might be turned into something dead if treated as a thing 'crystallized' at an arbitrarily selected stage and denied both its past and future (Taylor 1993, 221).

But if linguistics was to be a science, what would its character be? Was language an organism obeying fixed natural laws or was it an 'institution'? Was the science of language to be historical or physical? Questions like these dominated the discipline in its phase of consolidation. Although Hardy blamed linguistics for taking the life out of language, the 'new' philologists still treated speech systems as living organisms, an assumption not so much based on Romantic ideas of organic growth as on Victorian theories of evolution. Linguists around 1900, then, assumed that there was a special dynamic between past and present meanings in language which became visible in the continuous phonological and semantic changes. Unlike their predecessors, they no longer saw these changes as signs of a 'diseased' language and culture, but as a trace of the *living* meaning of words.

Returning to *The Handling of Words*, we notice that many of these linguistic debates are echoed in Lee's essays. The aesthetic problems she presents here are those of her period, and her ways of dealing with them appear familiar to us. Her diction reflects not only contemporary trends in linguistic and psychological sciences but also her own exploration of aesthetic psychology dating from the early 1890s when she continued her experiments with empathy (*Einfühlung*), a concept mainly developed in Germany at the time.[6] To be sure, *The Handling of Words* moves beyond the questions raised by the psychological schools from Robert Vischer, to Theodor Lipps or Karl Groos, and even beyond the theories of William James who was equally influential on her.[7] Lee's argument in the 1920s absorbed more of the body-centered theories of Carl Stumpf and August Schmarsow, Théodule-Armand Ribot's *images motrices,* and especially, Richard Semon's *Mnemic Psychology* (1923), for which she wrote the introduction.[8] But Pater still looms large as well. A key figure in aesthetic criticism, he had shifted emphasis from the abstract to the particular; and from the art object 'as it really was', to a concern with the movement of consciousness in aesthetic response: 'What is important, then, is not that the critic should possess a correct abstract definition of beauty for the intellect, but a certain kind of temperament, the power of being deeply moved by the presence of beautiful objects' (Pater 1910, I. x). His aesthetic impressionism was steeped in the Heraclitean philosophy of life in flux and of consciousness as an encounter of vital forces in body, mind, and soul: 'Was not the very essence of thought itself also such perpetual motion?' (Pater 1910, VI. 15).

Pater's notion of beauty as something to be found in and through the senses (and thus in our consciousness) influenced the debates on perception theories in physical sciences, philosophy, and language studies. Ironically, the interest in the life of the mind was cast in the non-sensual clinical language of empirical and physical sciences. But the shift towards empiricism also made language and art studies more descriptive than prescriptive. Normative concepts of style, for instance, became increasingly behavioural, 'placed between social conventions and personal preferences, on the one hand, and perceptual motor habits, on the other' (Davis 1996, 13). Whitney Davis's summary here describes accurately Vernon Lee's approach to literary style in *The Handling of Words*. Although she emphasizes the singularity of the aesthetic experience *sui generis,* as I. A. Richards does, Lee shows equal interest in what is habitual (and thus ubiquitous) in an author's style and, therefore, an integral part of his – Lee uses the masculine pronoun – literary persona. It follows that style is replicated whenever a literary work is produced.

The extension of Lee's study from mere rules of form and simple fact to matters of more general behaviour may be interesting for the modern reader. Yet it is still difficult to see where exactly *The Handling of Words* fits in the development of modern literary and cultural theories, since the curious mixture of unblushing Victorian judgmentalism grafted on to lengthy exercises in pedantic word-counting strikes us as antiquated and, at times, rather annoying: Hardy's style is reduced to 'lack of coherence, of sense of direction' (1923 and 1992, 234); De Quincey accused of 'mismanagement' (1923 and 1992, 145); and Kipling of 'lack of logical connection' (1923 and 1992, 210). But if we ignore her Victorian smugness, we find that she also offers a good dose of aesthetic intuition paired with shrewd and accurate observations on the underlying mechanisms of literary narrative and, especially, their 'physical' effects on the reader in scientific terms.

Few critics have addressed Lee's serious commitment to behavioural sciences in *The Handling of Words*. Much more has been said about her role as precursor in formal and structural literary criticism and reader response theories.[9] She has regularly been credited for anticipating Richards's 'empirical method of close verbal scrutiny by as much as thirty years' (Seed 1996, i), first made popular in *Principles of Literary Criticism* (1926) and *Practical Criticism* (1929). Lee's *The Handling of Words* resembles Richards's only tangentially, even though they share some common ground. Both Richards and Lee have their roots in Paterian aestheticism that stressed the 'concrete', not the 'abstract' in art and had a deep distrust of a 'universal formula' (Pater 1910, I. vii). Both abandoned the totalizing humanist discourses of the nineteenth century in favour of empirical case studies. Although Richards and Lee pursue similar goals, that is the demystification of the reading process, they differ in their assumptions about the relationship between reader and writer. Since Lee is interested in the subjectivity of the reading process, she acknowledges that misreadings cannot be avoided; indeed, that they constitute a necessary and productive experience in interpretive processes. Richards, however, attributes misreadings to bad training or lack of competence in the reader. In general, Lee sees the responsibility for successful reading in the writer, a claim she had already made in her *Belcaro* essay, 'A Dialogue on Poetic Morality' – albeit from a Victorian stance against moral evil: the writer must carry 'the soul of his reader – of each of his thousands of readers ... souls in many cases weak' (1881, 273).

Two central essays in *The Handling of Words* – 'Studies in Literary Psychology', and 'The Handling of Words' – best illustrate Lee's behavioural study of reading. Less interested in establishing theoretical rules than in finding out why readers can be affected positively or negatively by certain literary works, she investigates the sensory aspect of the reading process, tracing a writer's style and linguistic patterns as symptoms of mental habits which may or may not harmonize with those of the reader. Although coming from separate histories, reader and writer are brought together in a communicative and communal exercise that can only be realized mutually. This collaboration, she claims, occurs in the invisible part of literature where emotions and attitudes take shape because writing to her 'is nothing but the handling of the associations and habits, especially the emotional ones, existing potentially in the mind of the Reader' (1923 and 1992, 303). By treating the subjectivity of reader and writer as two sides of the same process mediated by the text, she challenges an important concept in contemporary philological studies, which construed the text as an object artificially separated from its content or the reader. Whether in defence of her approach or as a genuine gesture toward the open process of research, she proclaims her awareness of her methodological limitations (in 'On Literary Construction'), but also her hope that one day we may 'be able to explain the phenomenon of a creature being apparently invaded from within by the personality of another creature' (1923 and 1992, 22).

Lee's main concern in *The Handling of Words* is to find a precise language which can describe the volatile moment where reading and writing merge, a moment not actually existing before, but momentarily enacted in individual readers: 'there arises in the Reader another succession, or more properly, a simultaneous *continuum* in which it all takes place. Thus the Reader's own experience, moving beneath the pressure of the word, brings into consciousness how many sights, how many feelings of which the author of that word can have no notion' (1923 and 1992, 79–80). Since she claims to have less knowledge of the writer than of the reader, she focuses on the reading process, described as mental movement along 'a series of *planes of action*' to the '*intellectual space*' established by grammatical forms 'obedient to the Writer's behest' (1923 and 1992, 235).[10]

In the 1880s, Lee had feared for the soul of the Victorian reader at the hand of a morally irresponsible writer, but in *The Handling of Words*, she looks at a 'lazy' modern consumer of books who might be bored by an indifferent or incapable writer. If a literary work does not motivate the reader, it will be rejected and no benefit can be gathered. Thus, modern readers require special treatment. She illustrates her point by posing as a model reader with certain likes and dislikes. To find out why one text may be more pleasing than another, she selects passages from well-known nineteenth-century novels, from Meredith to Kipling to James. Her statistical evaluation – pedantic, tedious, but also brilliantly ironic – is not meant to arrive at a coherent theory, but rather to account for literary taste by objective empirical means. Lee figures out how the author positions the reader and moves him around – the masculine pronoun is hers – at a pace depending on the former's individual style. She then invites us to observe her own mental movements elicited by textual motion, in other words, how the reader is coerced into participation by the way the text 'thinks' or 'feels':

So much for the items of experience and the words ... which the Writer groups into patterns of almost magical power within the mind of the Reader. The magic is not merely inherent in those nouns and adjectives, due to the community of experience of Reader and of Writer. Even more, in my opinion, its very mysterious essence requires to be sought in what I have alluded to as movement, as *pace and weight, impact and rhythm*. (1923 and 1992, 131–2)

Derived partly from Pater[11] and partly from her studies of the German physio-psychologists, Schmarsow and Stumpf, Lee's notion of 'movement' is an equivalent to aesthetic contemplation which involves the process of 'feeling oneself into' an object of art (*Einfühlung*).

Throughout her book, Lee describes and traces textual patterns by paying attention to the smallest linguistic elements, but with little regard for the work's larger meaning. Since her analysis follows behavioural rather than philosophical models of thinking, she has to stick to a language that deals with the description of the senses, not with metaphysical questions of meaning. In order to avoid a hermeneutic dilemma, she can only work with what she gathers from the text experientially, through the senses of a virtual reader. Thus the linear, sequential movements of literary writings are first described behaviourally, that is in terms of the reader's performance.[12]

For the reading process, Lee introduces two related notions of movement: on the one hand, the movement of language keeps the reader interested and thus functions as 'motivation'. Henry James had equated movement and motivation before, but without the behaviourist implication (James 1984, 922). Lee probably found the elements for her study in the mnemic laws of bodily responses that build our preferences and aversion in Semon's *Mnemic Psychology*.[13] Textual movement for Lee also translates for the reader the writer's emotional energy that entered a text in the act of composition so that 'the degree of life in a Writer's style depends upon the amount of activity he imposes upon his Reader' (1923 and 1992, 199). Therefore, 'A page of literature ... gives us the impression of movement in proportion as it makes *us* move' (1923 and 1992, 232).

It follows that the writer's attention (or lack thereof) works directly on that of the reader's with positive or negative effects. While she praises Meredith's 'swiftness' of language, 'his wonderful vividness' because it forces us 'to spot and to conjecture', she is sceptical of the shifting viewpoints in Kipling or Hardy (1923 and 1992, 196, 197). After feeling 'jerk[ed]' back by Kipling's perspectival ambiguities – her judgment of his free indirect style – she admires Stevenson's orderly pace as a model of harmonious movement (1923 and 1992, 207). Her analysis of an excerpt from *Kim* (1901) is particularly negative: the reader is confused by Kipling's constant changes of tense and perspective, which she blames on his 'lack of attention' or 'causal clearness' (1923 and 1992, 206, 210). Similarly, she is confused by Hardy's directionless and repetitious writing in *Tess* which supposedly shows his indifference toward the reader: 'This page is so constructed, or rather not constructed, that if you skip one sentence, you are pretty sure to receive the same information in the next; ... This makes lazy reading; and it is lazy writing' (1923 and 1992, 230). Hardy's 'slovenliness' and 'slackened interest' (1923 and 1992, 240, 228), then, is traced minutely in every seemingly unmotivated turn of the narrative until its content is reduced to his lack in energy, his inability to stimulate the reader's mind. What Lee demands for the reader instead is that 'Our attention, when we really give it, wants to be made to move briskly, rhythmically, nay, as Nietzsche puts it, *to dance*' (1923 and 1992, 231). Her extract from Meredith's *Harry Richmond* (1871), although described in equally critical terms as Hardy's or Kipling's, fares surprisingly well. Whereas Hardy appears to encourage laziness in the reader, Meredith is 'perpetually forcing us to spot and to conjecture' so that he remains 'a sealed book to careless or unintelligent Readers' (1923 and 1992, 196). She praises Meredith's 'wonderful vividness' because it is an intellectual challenge: 'we are never allowed to sit still and wait to be told' (1923 and 1992, 196). In sum, her value judgements do not follow a consistent pattern and often miss the point of the writer's intention. But if we are annoyed by her quirky and reductive criticism, we need to be reminded that it refers exclusively to the skeletal part of the text, its patterns and rhythms, merely leading us to the meaning of form. And that meaning she describes accurately as the positioning of the reader through the movement of the literary work.

Such movement can also stand still, if the text requires it. De Quincey's relative infrequency of verbs and insertion of a great number of pronouns, stops textual movement, suggesting 'his indifference to action' (1923 and 1992, 141), here seen as positive since 'One seems to feel the infirmity of the opium-eater's will' (1923 and 1992, 145). Likewise, Henry James's style in *The Ambassadors* (1903) has to contain 'the most elusive of psychological abstractions', because the novel is not about anything tangible. His 'circling of pronouns' constantly reassembled in new combinations, thus makes heavy demands on the reader's intellectual ability. And yet, his writing shows 'movement, of the finest sort', since what the people '*do*' and any amount of 'vivid feeling' is meant to feed into metaphor, 'illustrating purely subjective relations' or what she calls 'storms in teacups' (1923 and 1992, 250, 249, 250). Abstraction, which she often criticizes in other writers, is considered appropriate in James because it positions the reader rightly in the realm of contemplation.

What, then, is the value of Lee's empirical studies, accurate in their descriptions but warped by uneven judgments that tell us little about a literary work's larger literary value? Does she 'run the matter aground' (1923 and 1992, 163) because she is mocking the 'new' philological methods even as she applies them slavishly? It does seem odd, for instance, that after a detailed dissection of Hardy's 'slovenliness', she dismisses the whole study in one sweeping gesture, concluding that 'the very faults of Hardy are probably an expression of his solitary and matchless grandeur of attitude' (1923 and 1992, 241). This is maybe an indication of Lee's belief that the quality of Hardy's art cannot be made visible nor explained beyond the reader's preference. 'He belongs to a universe transcending such trifles as Writers and Readers and their little logical ways' (1923 and 1992, 241). What *can* be explained, however, is the performative part of speech that appears when we cut a window into the text to see what it does, in other words, how the writer's word patterns determine the reader's mental moves.

As we have seen, what is stored as energy in the text and replicated as movement in the act of reading, comes from the writer's original interest, thought, and creative process.[14] Lee recreates this process with all its searches, errors, and preliminary certainties that seem to have disappeared from the mere surface of the text. If the reader manages to 'feel' this process, he or she can connect with the writer. The forces at work here originate in the writer's and reader's multi-dimensional lives but, although now compressed in the one-dimensional surface of the text, they are still active underneath: 'Each Reader, while receiving from the Writer, is in reality reabsorbing into his life, where it refreshes or poisons him, a residue of own living; but melted into an absorbable subtleness, combined and stirred into a new kind of efficacy by the choice of the Writer' (1923 and 1992, 79). There is embedded in language 'a halo of *something else*' which she identifies as 'the Reader's own experience, moving beneath the pressure of the word' (1923 and 1992, 79).[15] The literary work is returned to life by the reader's re-experiencing the writer's creative process, in 'the community of experience of Reader and of Writer' (1923 and 1992, 131). In this sense, Lee uses 'objective' linguistic analysis to re-translate the text into the writing process and, therefore, the writer's subjectivity that cannot be made visible as such. What can be shown, though, is 'the peculiar organism called the Writer' with his unconscious *habits*, manifested in morphology and grammar.

Based on her studies of Semon and Ribot, she argues that the writer's habits of style, like all motor skills, are located in the bodily memory and, therefore, applied without the conscious mind. Style, then, is part of the informal memory of the individual, 'a kind of gesture or gait, revealing with the faithfulness of an unconscious habit, the essential peculiarities of the Writer's temperament and modes of being' (1923 and 1992, 136); it is performed through 'the Writer's *constitutional tradition*, of the habits and standards which operate in re-reading and revision' (1923 and 1992, 212). As such, style has an individual and a communal component, and since it is located in the unconscious memory of the body, we become aware of it only through its enactment.

Lee's notion of 'habit' located in our behavioural memory finds much attention in recent social and cultural studies. Paul Connerton, for instance, defines 'habitual memory' as a way of knowing that structures our lives through the informal memory in individual and collective bodies: 'Habit is a knowledge and a remembering in the hands and in the body; and in the cultivation of habit it is our body which "understands"' (Connerton 1989, 95). Lee similarly understands style as 'a remembering in the hands and in the body', which traces the text back to the moment of production, and to the writer's behavioural 'self', which is an effect of his habits. Since habits are owned by the body, and their reactivation can only occur in performative acts, she focuses on writing and reading as concrete acts assumed to be present in any production. Hence Lee's random selection of 500 words from each writer. The habitual 'handling of words', then, would reveal the writerly personality close up so that at the end, she can exclaim (albeit ironically), 'I have watched Landor at work!' (1923 and 1992, 170). Similarly, the reader's collaboration takes place on the pre- or unconscious level of habit that creates expectation. We are only impressed by what is close to our own expectation or understanding, that is the awakening of latent 'echoes, images, feelings' occurs only when these are 'connected with our habits and interest' (1923 and 1992, 74, 77). Obviously, reading is most successful when both writer and reader come together in the same rhythm of habits. Thus the act of reading activates spontaneously what is habitual, the stored-up thoughts and emotions that then direct *how* we read.[16]

By returning the one-dimensionality of the text into its multi-dimensional origin in life, Lee stresses its materiality: 'For art and thought arise from life; and to life, as principle of harmony they must return' (1895, 260). If we are brought into the presence of the writer (albeit his habitual side) we can partake in the moment of writing, which is still contained in the text and can be uncovered by a method that describes this aspect of intersubjectivity between reader and writer. Lee's notion of reading as connection between different experiential dimensions finds some confirmation in recent theories of psychological aesthetics and art history. For instance, as Whitney Davis has argued, the sequencing of images or phenomenological forms in text, does preserve something of the mobility originally provoked by the material threat of the 'inaugural terror' (Davis 1996, 252). The optical figure – as figure of speech, he reminds us, is 'a two-dimensional "reduction" of three-dimensional materiality' (Davis 1996, 247). Using the example of the French Egyptologist Claude Etienne Savary, Davis illustrates how the experience of size in the material world enters our language after it is first absorbed sensually: 'The human language of judgment changes the very "size" of the pyramids for the observer. And no measurement captures the subjective or "phenomenal" dimension' (Davis 1996, 234). In other words, to convey a sense of his impression, his human apprehension of the Pyramids, Savary has to create an affective dimension of the concrete experience which is rendered in a language that reflects the actual process of bodily measuring (by walking on and around it). From an idealist vantage point, Davis explains, we can suppose that the mind *intends* to move optical figures – to inspect the world by moving through it – and to arrest rhetorical ones, to select its labels and descriptions. The 'necessary conversion – from material form/optical figure to phenomenal form/linguistic figure – then, transpires when *motion* occurs' (Davis 1996, 247).

What does this mean for our study of Vernon Lee? Davis's conclusion that the domains of materiality and language are actually the same but in different dimensions closely resembles Lee's thinking about aesthetics in the 1920s: '*Language* not only employs all manner of motor images, it actually calls them by the names derived from movement in space, even when they refer to movements ... of THOUGHT' (Lee, Introduction to Semon 1923, 37). What she describes in her introduction to Semon's study is directly applied in *The Handling of Words*, especially, the idea of translating the movements of the mind into motivation, or as Whitney Davis puts it: 'Cognitive movement, then, is *motivation'* (Davis 1996, 249). By tracing the behavioural aspect of reading and returning literary writings to the physical and material world, Lee gives a new spin to contemporary aesthetics. Of course, Lee cannot fully restore the original three-dimensionality of the work, but her exploration of movement points to the tensions between the concrete experiential world and the metaphorical reduction of figures of speech. We may even go further to argue that her unravelling of a text through a virtual reader, undermines the conception of eighteenth- and nineteenth-century aesthetics since Kant which had been determined by its distance from real life, providing a contemplative space for a viewer not called into action. Aesthetic *Entrücktheit* (removal *and* rapt absorption)[17] from life and from the material self had originally created the objects of art that could then be studied in themselves.

One problem remains. The process of reading occurs in the elusive encounter between two subjectivities, for which language can only provide objective terms. To refer once more to Whitney Davis we can assume that the paradox in writing about another's subjectivity is still that it can become at best the 'subjective object' of the one writing it. And since we can only speak about our own subjectivity as representation, that is, as an object, we cannot reveal our subjectivity in the reading process. That, he argues, can only be done by another historian who writes us as we are writing another subject and so on. Representing subjectivity becomes almost impossible when we are dealing with historical texts, since their makers cannot talk back to us. Did Lee recognize this impasse? Does, then, her exaggerated empiricism alert us to the discrepancy between objective language and subjective – or rather, intersubjective – processes? Wolfgang Iser, who equates the reading process to 'virtual reality', has pointed to this problem in his *PMLA* essay, 'Do I Write for an Audience?'

> If the study of literature arises out of concern with texts, there can be no doubting the importance of what happens to us as readers of those texts. A literary work is not a documentary record of something that exists or has existed; it brings into the world something that hitherto did not exist and that at best can be qualified as a virtual reality. Consequently, my theory of aesthetic response found itself confronted with the problem of how such emerging virtual realities, which have no equivalent in our empirical world, can be processed and, indeed, understood. (Iser 2000, 311)

In *The Handling of Words*, Lee is struggling with a similar challenge. Her study of Carlyle, in particular, reveals a certain scepticism as to whether empirical methods can bring the reader into the 'virtual' presence of the writer. While her essay on his work shows her profound insight into Carlyle's historical style, it is also – as Vineta Colby has pointed out – the most subjective and the 'least supported by word counts' (Colby 2003, 203). Lee's explication of Carlyle's historical present is sharp and plausible, but it does not quite reveal the 'material' connections with the reader, such as she has meticulously traced in Landor or Hardy. Obviously aware of her limitations, she refers to Carlyle's use of tense as 'only one of the inevitable literary expressions' of his personal attitude towards past ideas (1923 and 1992, 184). Still, she enters his *The French Revolution* through linguistic form. She identifies the historical present in this work not simply as grammatical tense, but as a morphology of presence which creates 'lyrical illusions' (rather than causal connections as made by the past tense) and as such, the present tense 'answers to Carlyle's very personal attitude in what is really the world of contemplation' (1923 and 1992, 181, 184).[18]

To prove her point, she translates a passage into the past tense demonstrating by doing so that 'all cohesion, all coordination will disappear' (1923 and 1992, 182). Indeed, she asks, 'what connection will there be among those historical affairs, stranded in bits, if we no longer feel their connection in the ... spirit of the Seer?' (1923 and 1992, 183). Carlyle's view of the French Revolution thus cannot be separated from his narrative about it. It is so 'organically personal' and 'so intimately interwoven with individual habits of thought and feeling' (1923 and 1992, 184) that we are constantly forced into his presence. Once the reading is over, the historical figures cease to exist, but what remains is the prophet's voice, since the present tense dispenses with explanations and gives continuity not to things but to what he says about them.

Is it really linguistic analysis that has made visible the intersubjective exchange between Carlyle and his reader so that 'what we are witnessing is not the drama down below in the streets and fields, nor even the drama in human hearts ... but is the drama up here in the soul of this strange, marvellous prophet' (1923 and 1992, 181–2)? 'Strange' and 'marvellous' indicate that something in Carlyle's text is left unaccounted for. But we should also pay attention to the way she speaks of his style as an expression of habit: 'no man's style was ever so organically personal as his, so intimately interwoven with individual habits of thought and feeling' (1923 and 1992, 184). The empirical method can reveal Carlyle's habit of style, his positioning of the reader through tense and other verbal gestures; but it cannot offer a language that wholly displays subjectivity in its full bodily and psychic constitution. And so she merely confirms what she has stated all along: the text *is* the writer.

Lee's reading of Carlyle shows most saliently her motivation as reader to come face to face with a writer through a 'construction answering not to the necessity of outward things but to the needs of the inner nature, the microcosm, the soul' (1923 and 1992, 78). Despite her empirical grid, she has retained a deeply romantic longing for retrieving an almost mythical process that connects writer and reader, humans and human history over time. She finds the continuous power of this process in our habitual, unconscious memory that is only accessible to the senses. Behind the quasi-objective study, there is a search for an encounter with human feeling and thought, tied up in communal and individual practices of style. These 'unseens' of the text occupy a space similar to the ghosts of her nineteenth-century tales: psychological phenomena no more to be documented than other forms of historical (un)consciousness.

In *The Handling of Words* she comes closest to describing these 'ghosts', now empirically, as recollections through our senses, and therefore our bodies, ever present in the writer, the text, and the reader, but incompatible with reality: 'Like ghosts, recollections can enter by closed doors, occupy seats already filled ... but like ghosts they can only be seen and not touched, only heard and not seen ...' (1923 and 1992, 76). Since her early historical essays in the 1880s, she had been looking for the 'right' entrance into the past and a more immediate experience of it. For the historian, as I have shown elsewhere, she saw a possible connection, not in the great lines of abstraction and theory, but in the less spectacular habitual memory of the people at large. Habits of style, how things are seen and done, including the way they are passed on – informally and unconsciously – those are to her the historical forces which create continuity and, therefore, our connection with the past.[19] *The Handling of Words* tries to tap into literary texts as the informal memory of minds long gone, as the reality of past cultures and societies brought back to life in the energy of a text. Such endeavour reminds us of Stephen Greenblatt's 'desire to speak with the dead' in *Shakespearean Negotiations*, where he sees the reactivation of the 'intensity' and the 'social energy' stored in literature as the motivation for critics to get in touch with the 'literary traces of the dead' (Greenblatt 1988, 1, 3).

The Handling of Words is an important step in the history of reception theories that conceive literature as a form of interaction; in Lee's view, an interaction of the life of the present with the life of the past. We are linked with a literary text, not so much through our intellect, but rather through our unconscious linguistic habits that constitute styles of writing and reading. By tracking textual movement as a trace of the multi-dimensional origins of writing, Lee offers a method to link reader and writer at a point before the consolidation of the text. This moment is not to be found in the final form of the text, nor in its ideally perceived content, but only available through the study of dimensional shifts in language. Although aware of the impossibility of documenting something as elusive as the intersubjective exchange between writer and reader, something that has no real existence, Lee yet makes it visible in the virtual handling of words.

Notes

1 John Bowen makes this point in connection with the standardization and professionalization of the disciplines (Bowen 1987).

2 David Seed finds her book less 'a late contribution to aesthetics' than of the same genre as P. Goyen's *Principles of English Compositon* (1894) or George Saintsbury's *History of English Prose Rhythm* (1910). However, he rightly observes that Lee's position probably comes closer to Hardress O'Grady's *Matter, Form, and Style* (1912) which avoids the 'two of the main pitfalls in the discussion of prose at this time: prescription and pseudo-classical terminology' (Seed 1996, vi–vii).

3 By the middle of the nineteenth century, language studies intersected with an interest in national languages and a growing sense of nationalism, of which Trench's *English Past and Present* is a prime example. According to Trench, the English language should be purified as part of a larger national project: 'the love of our own language, what is it in fact, but the love of our country expressing itself in one particular direction?' (Trench, 1905, 3).

4 Professor Higgins in Shaw's *Pygmalion* (1912) is a combination of the famous phonetic linguists, Henry Sweet, and Shaw himself. Like the character, Higgins, who transcribes language in phonetic systems, Shaw had tried to transcribe accurately interesting dialects in his plays. Higgins – by dissecting and categorizing language scientifically – believes that he makes it available as an instrument with which to intervene into social structure. In his character, Shaw exposes the limitations of a mere scientific approach to language that fails to take into consideration its human dimension that is beyond Higgins's control.

5 Franz Bopp (1791–1867) was a famous German professor of linguistics. He was one of the first to show the connections between all Indo-European and Sanskrit languages in a comparative grammar. August Schleicher (1821–1868) engaged in similar comparative philological studies, but his were decidedly influenced by Darwinian evolution theory. His *Comparative Grammar of the Indo-European Sanskrit, Greek and Latin Languages* was

published in Germany in 1861 and appeared as an English translation between 1874 and 1877.

6 The concept of *Einfühlung* (empathy) became a major concept in nineteenth-century German aesthetics. The term, 'empathy' has been attributed to Theodor Lipps (1851–1914), a prominent German philosopher and psychologist who developed aesthetics as the 'psychology' or 'science' of beauty. His notion of empathy implies that pleasure in the contemplation of beautiful objects elicits mental activities in the observer. Vernon Lee became a proponent of his work but then created her own version of empathy since she was critical of his metaphysical approach.

7 Robert Vischer (1847–1933) was the son of the famed aesthetician Friedrich Theodor Vischer. His 1873 essay 'On The Optical Sense of Form' (collected in Mallgrave 1994, 89–123) marked the first appearance of the term *Einfühlung*. Vischer did little to follow up on his own lead, but he set in train a psychological approach to aesthetics that dominated discussions for decades. Karl Groos (1861–1946) was the German philosopher and psychologist who has been credited with the discovery of the psychological and biological significance of playing. His aesthetic theories were based on the notion of 'inner mimicry' of aesthetic objects conducted by the human senses and respiratory activity. Between 1902 and 1908 Lee and Groos carried on an extensive correspondence in which they discussed their individual aesthetic experiments. William James (1842–1910), like his brother Henry James, corresponded with Vernon Lee and was a major influence on her psychological aesthetics. William James had emphasized the experiential quality of aesthetics that he saw as an effect of physical sensation.

8 Carl Stumpf (1848–1936) was a German philosopher and psychologist. His major contributions to aesthetics were in the realm of psychological acoustics, on which he published in two volumes between 1883 and 1890 under the title *Tonpsychologie* (psychology of sound). Yet it was his earlier work on spatial perception that arguably had the greater influence on Schmarsow and other aesthetic theorists. Stumpf rejected the 'false empiricism' of contemporary perception theories and argued that spatial perception is originally three-dimensional in its formation.

The French psychologist Théodule-Armand Ribot (1823–1891) is best known for his theory of memory loss as a symptom of progressive brain disease. Ribot was influenced by the German experimental psychologist, Wundt, in tying psychology to biology and rejecting its 'spiritualist' or philosophical aspect.

August Schmarsow (1853–1936) was a German art historian whose 'science of art' proposed an aesthetics 'from within' which implies that the aesthetic experience takes place not only in the mind, but in the entire human being, i.e. the physical and mental organization. Different from other aesthetic theorists at the time, Schmarsow attributed to the perceiving subject the freedom of movement which he considered necessary for humans to grasp the corporeality of objects.

9 Lee's approach has often been compared to reader response theories, such as Rosenblatt's removal of boundaries between reader and text; Booth's concept of the reader created by text; Fish's focus on what the text *does* (rather than what it means); and Iser's imaginative reader animating the

outlines of the text. In her seminal book, *Literature as Exploration* (1938; repr. 1968), Louise Rosenblatt first proposed a theory of reading that blurs the boundaries between reader and text, subject and object. She further developed this position in *The Reader, The Text, The Poem: The Transactional Theory of the Literary Work* (1978; repr. 1994). Wayne Booth's *The Rhetoric of Fiction* (1961) has become a classic in Reader Response Theory. Booth recognized that a writer controls a reader through rhetorical strategies but did not go so far as to give readers the principal responsibility for making the meaning. Like Iser, Booth employs the term 'implied reader'. Stanley Fish, following Rosenblatt, contrasted reader-response criticism with formalism and, more specifically, New Criticism. In the late 1970s Fish shifted his focus and argued that shared 'interpretive strategies' which exist prior to the act of reading are held in common by 'interpretive communities'. See, for instance, Stanley Fish (1980).

10 Lee's description of the reading process here owes a lot to Richard Semon's *Mnemic Psychology* for which she wrote an introduction parallel to assembling the essays of *The Handling of Words*. Lee defines 'mneme' as the partial return of a 'matrix of images, of *engrams*, left by previous sensations', in other words, the transformation of sensation into perception (Lee, Introduction to Semon 1923, 20). The chief characteristics of 'mneme' to her is that it is 'merely *potential*' (Lee, Introduction to Semon 1923, 51).

11 Pater described Heraclitean flux as the essence of thought; he believed that mental perspective could be affected by the physical movement of the text: 'It might seem that movement, after all, and any habit that promoted movement, promoted the power, the successes, the fortunate parturition, of the mind' (Pater 1910, VI. 179).

12 She borrows her terms from physical sciences and from aesthetic psychology, which first introduced the concept of movement as 'empathy' into aesthetics. In *Beauty and Ugliness* (1912), she uses 'empathy' as a 'revival of past experience' reenacted in ourselves through a perceived form. Satisfaction or dissatisfaction with that form occurs according to the degree of vividness of that experience (1912, 21). Empathy is not limited to art, but accompanies all spatial contemplation; we feel animated 'because our own activity, our own life have been brought into play' (1912, 22). While agreeing with Lipps's notion of empathy (*Einfühlung*), she accuses him of using a metaphysical 'I' which makes it difficult 'to follow the real process which is hidden under this phraseology' (1912, 57). Instead, she suggests the ego is 'a group of subjective phenomena ... made up in part of the experience of movements of our own body' (1912, 59).

13 See especially, Semon 1923, 40–2.

14 Stumpf had argued that our notion of unified space arises out of a synthesis of successive visual fields. 'What we perceive originally and directly is the visual field, the whole visual field ... If this continually changes through movement, we retain the disappearing parts in our minds and unite them with the newly perceived spaces into a whole' (quoted in Mallgrave 1994, 60). In other words, out of many spaces rises one space, which means that our spatial perception is three-dimensional in its formation.

15   In an earlier historical study, *Renaissance Fancies and Studies* (1895), Lee had
     already suggested that the reading process involves more than meets the
     eye, here, in reference to Walter Pater: 'The completion, the rounding
     of his doctrine, can take place only in the grateful appreciation of his
     readers. We have been left with unfinished systems, fragmentary, some-
     times enigmatic utterances. ... For art and thought arise from life; and to
     life, as principle of harmony, they must return' (1895, 259–60).

16   We find the germ for this idea in *Belcaro* (1881), whereas aesthetic pleasure
     'means merely the pleasing activity of your visual and æsthetic, or acoustic
     and æsthetic organism, you instinctively wish to increase the activity in
     order to increase the pleasure; the increase of activity is obtained by approx-
     imating as much as possible to the creative activity of the original artist, by
     going over every step that he has gone over, by creating the work of art
     over again in the intensity of appreciation' (1881, 62).

17   The German word collapses two aspects of the aesthetic here: its removal
     from direct material experience and the more spiritual meaning of rapture
     or rapt absorption. The twofold meaning is reminiscent of William
     Wordsworth's Romantic concept 'emotion recollected in tranquility'.

18   The theoretical groundwork for this function of the present tense can be
     found in the introduction to *Mnemic Psychology*, where she lists aspects of
     language which position speaker and listener: 'there are the tenses of verbs,
     by whose correlation we express, not, indeed, the (often visible or tangible)
     nature of an action, which is given in the infinitive or root of a verb, but
     the relation of various actions towards each other, ... everything which a
     writer conveys by the concordance or inhibition of the various forms of
     past, and concordance between past, present, and future: these apparently
     empty words express our attitudes, our acquiescence' (Lee, Introduction to
     Semon 1923, 38).

19   Much earlier, in her Renaissance study, *Euphorion* (1884), she had described
     these unconscious habits as our most crucial connections with history:
     'We see only very little at a time, and that little is not what it appeared to
     the men of the past; but we see at last, if not the same things, yet in the
     same manner in which they saw, as we see from the standpoints of personal
     interest and in the light of personal temper. ... The past can give us and
     should give us, not merely ideas, but emotions' (1884, 12).

Bibliography

Archives

Chatto & Windus papers, University of Reading Modern Publishing Archive.
John Lane Company Records, Harry Ransom Humanities Research Center, University of Texas, Austin, Texas.
Maxwell Armfield papers, Tate Gallery Archives, London.
Vernon Lee papers, Colby College, Maine, Manuscript Collections.

Primary Texts

Lee, Vernon. *Studies of the Eighteenth Century in Italy*. London: W. Satchell, 1880.
Lee, Vernon. *Belcaro: Being Essays on Sundry Æsthetical Questions*. London: W. Satchell & Co., 1881.
Lee, Vernon. 'The Responsibilities of Unbelief: A Conversation Between Three Rationalists'. *Contemporary Review* 43 (May 1883): 685–710.
Lee, Vernon. *Ottilie: An Eighteenth Century Idyl*. London: Fisher Unwin, 1883.
Lee, Vernon. *The Prince of a Hundred Soups: A Puppet-Show in Narrative*. Illustrated by Sarah Birch. London: T. Fisher Unwin, 1883.
Lee, Vernon. *Euphorion: Being Studies of the Antique and Mediæval in the Renaissance*. 2 vols. London: T. Fisher Unwin, 1884.
Lee, Vernon. *Miss Brown: A Novel*. 3 vols. Edinburgh and London: William Blackwood and Sons, 1884. Rpt. *Miss Brown*, 3 vols. New York: Garland, 1978.
Lee, Vernon. *Baldwin: Being Dialogues on Views and Aspirations*. London: T. Fisher Unwin, 1886.
Lee, Vernon. *Juvenilia: Essays on Sundry Æsthetical Questions*. 2 vols. London: T. Fisher Unwin, 1887.
Lee, Vernon. *Hauntings: Fantastic Stories*. London: William Heinemann, 1890.
Lee, Vernon. 'Lady Tal'. In *Vanitas: Polite Stories*. London: William Heinemann, 1892. 7–19. Rpt. in *Daughters of Decadence: Women Writers of the Fin-de-Siècle*. ed. Elaine Showalter. London: Virago, 1993. 192–261.
Lee, Vernon. *Althea: A Second Book of Dialogues on Aspirations and Duties*. London: Osgood, McIlvaine, 1894.
Lee, Vernon. *Renaissance Fancies and Studies*. London: Smith, Elder, & Co., 1895.
Lee, Vernon. 'Valedictory'. *Renaissance Fancies and Studies*. London: Smith, Elder, & Co., 1895. 255–60.
Lee, Vernon. 'Prince Alberic and the Snake Lady'. *Yellow Book* X (1896): 289–344.
Lee, Vernon and Clementina Anstruther-Thomson. 'Beauty and Ugliness' (Part I) *Contemporary Review* 72 (October 1897): 544–69; (Part II), *Contemporary Review* 72 (November 1897): 669–88. Rpt. in *Beauty and Ugliness and Other Studies in Psychological Aesthetics*. London and New York: John Lane, The Bodley Head, 1912. 156–239.
Lee, Vernon. *Ariadne in Mantua: A Romance in Five Acts*. Oxford: B. H. Blackwell, 1903.

Lee, Vernon. *Hortus Vitae: Essays on the Gardening of Life*. London: John Lane, 1904.

Lee, Vernon. *Pope Jacynth and Other Fantastic Tales*. London: John Lane, The Bodley Head, 1904.

Lee, Vernon. *Studies of the Eighteenth Century in Italy*. 2nd edition. London: T. Fisher Unwin, 1907.

Lee, Vernon. *Limbo and Other Essays to which is now added 'Ariadne in Mantua'*. London: John Lane, The Bodley Head, 1908.

Lee, Vernon. *Gospels of Anarchy and Other Contemporary Studies*. London and Leipzig: T. Fisher Unwin, 1908.

Lee, Vernon. *Laurus Nobilis: Chapters on Art and Life*. London and New York: John Lane, The Bodley Head, 1909.

Lee, Vernon. 'The Lines of Anglo-German Agreement'. *The Nation* VII (10 September 1910), supplement between pp. 838 and 839.

Lee, Vernon and Clementina Anstruther-Thomson. *Beauty and Ugliness and Other Studies in Psychological Aesthetics*. London and New York: John Lane, The Bodley Head, 1912. 156–239.

Lee, Vernon. 'Vicarious Tragedy'. *The Nation* XI (29 June 1912): 466–7.

Lee, Vernon. 'Angels Fear to Tread'. *The Nation* XI (7 September 1912): 828–9.

Lee, Vernon. 'The Sense of Nationality'. *The Nation* XII (12 October 1912): 96–8.

Lee, Vernon. *The Beautiful: An Introduction to Psychological Aesthetics*. Cambridge: Cambridge University Press, 1913.

Lee, Vernon. Letter to the Editor, *The Nation* XV (22 August 1914): 766–7.

Lee, Vernon. *Louis Norbert: A Two-Fold Romance*. London: John Lane, The Bodley Head, 1914.

Lee, Vernon. *The Ballet of the Nations. A Present-Day Morality*. Illustr. Maxwell Armfield. London: Chatto & Windus, 1915. (Unpaginated.)

Lee, Vernon. *Peace with Honour: Controversial Notes on the Settlement*. London: Union of Democratic Control, 1915.

Lee, Vernon. 'The Policy of the Allies'. *The Nation* XVI (2 February 1915): 649–50.

Lee, Vernon. 'Bismarck Towers'. *The New Statesman* IV (20 February 1915): 481–3.

Lee, Vernon. 'Militarists against Militarism'. *Labour Leader* XII, no. 13 (1 April 1915): 3.

Lee, Vernon. 'May Day Messages from British Women'. *Labour Leader* XII, no. 17 (29 April 1915): 5.

Lee, Vernon. 'Après la Mêlée'. *The New Statesman* V (19 June 1915): 249–51.

Lee, Vernon. 'The Wish for Unanimity and the Willingness for War, France-Italy, 1911–13'. [Written before August 1914.] *The Cambridge Magazine* IV (12 June 1915): 482, 484.

Lee, Vernon. 'War the Grave of All Good'. *Labour Leader* XII, no. 43 (28 October 1915): 3.

Lee, Vernon. 'Enmity'. *War and Peace* III, no. 25 (October 1915): 11–12.

Lee, Vernon. 'The Heart of a Neutral'. *The Atlantic Monthly* CXVI (November 1915): 687.

Lee, Vernon. *Satan the Waster. A Philosophic War Trilogy with Notes and Introduction*. New York: John Lane, 1920.

Lee, Vernon. 'Dionysus in the Euganean Hills. W. H. Pater In Memoriam'. *Contemporary Review* 120 (September 1921): 346–53.

Lee, Vernon. *The Handling of Words*. London: John Lane, The Bodley Head, 1923.

Lee, Vernon. Introduction. *Mnemic Psychology*. By Richard Semon. Trans. B. Duffy. New York: Macmillan, 1923. 11–53.

Lee, Vernon. Introduction. *Art and Man: Essays and Fragments*. By Clementina Anstruther-Thomson. With Twenty Illustrations. London: John Lane, The Bodley Head, 1924.

Lee, Vernon. *For Maurice: Five Unlikely Stories*. London: John Lane, The Bodley Head, 1927.

Lee, Vernon. *Music and Its Lovers: An Empirical Study of Emotional and Imaginative Responses to Music*. London: G. Allen and Unwin, 1932.

Lee, Vernon. 'The Handling of Words: A Page of Walter Pater'. *Life and Letters* 9: 50 (Sept–Nov 1933): 287–310.

Lee, Vernon. *Vernon Lee's Letters*, with a preface by her executor Irene Cooper Willis. Privately printed, 1937.

Lee, Vernon. *The Handling of Words*. Introduction by Royal A. Gettmann. Lincoln: University of Nebraska Press, 1968.

Lee, Vernon. *The Handling of Words*. ed. and intr. D. Seed. Lewistown: Edward Mellen Press, 1992.

Secondary Texts

Adams, James Eli. *Dandies and Desert Saints*. Ithaca and London: Cornell University Press, 1995.

Agnew, Lois. 'Vernon Lee and the Victorian Aesthetic Movement: "Feminine Souls" and Shifting Sites of Contest'. *Nineteenth-Century Prose* 26: 2 (1999): 127–42.

Anon. 'Review of Miss Brown'. *Athenæum* (6 December 1884): 730

Anon. 'Review of Miss Brown'. *Pall Mall Gazette* (11 December 1884): 5.

Anon. Review of *Miss Brown* and *Miss Bretherton*, 'New Novels'. *Graphic* (10 January 1885): 43.

Anon. [*Miss Brown*] 'Editor's Literary Record'. *Harper's New Monthly Magazine* 70 (May 1885): 977–8.

Anon. Review of *Miss Brown* and *Miss Bretherton*, 'New Novels'. *Scotsman* (26 December 1884): 7.

Anon. 'New Books of the Month.' *Bookman* III (October 1892–March 1893): 95.

Anon. 'Current Art Notes'. *Connoisseur* XLII (1915): 52.

Anon. 'New Books and Reprints'. *The Times Literary Supplement* (25 November 1915): 431.

Anon. 'Various War Books'. *Manchester Guardian* (27 November 1915): 4.

Anon. 'Print versus Pictures'. *Evening Standard* (29 November 1915): 9.

Anon. 'Our Library Table'. *Athenæum* (4 December 1915): 417.

Anon. 'The Handling of Words'. *TLS* (22 March 1923): 185–6.

Anon. 'Words, Words, Words'. *Spectator* (London) 130 (21 April 1923): 671.

Anon. 'Books in Brief'. *Nation* 117 (22 August 1923): 201.

Anon. 'Recent Books in Brief Review'. *Bookman* 58 (September 1923): 90.

Anstruther-Thomson, Clementina. *Art and Man: Essays and Fragments*. With Twenty Illustrations and an Introduction by Vernon Lee. London: John Lane, The Bodley Head, 1924.

Armfield, Maxwell. *The Grassblade, Lost Silver, The Minstrel* [1915]. Greenleaf Theatre Plays (Greenleaf Rhythmic Plays). London: Duckworth & Co., 1922–5.

Armfield, Maxwell and Constance. 'The Importance of Gesture'. *The Little Theatre Review: A Fortnightly Survey*, I, no. 2 (4 November 1920): 1.

Armstrong, Isobel. 'Textual Harassment: The Ideology of Close Reading, Or How Close Is Close?' *Textual Practice* 9 (1995): 401–20.

Beckson, Karl. *Henry Harland: His Life and Work*. London: Eighteen Nineties Society, 1978.

Beer, Gillian. 'The Dissidence of Vernon Lee: *Satan the Waster* and the Will to Believe'. In Suzanne Raitt and Trudi Tate, eds. *Women's Fiction and the Great War*. Oxford: Clarendon, 1997. 107–31.

Belford, Barbara. *Oscar Wilde: A Certain Genius*. New York: Random House, 2000.

Berenson, Bernard. *The Venetian Painters of the Renaissance: With an Index to their Works*. New York: G. Putnam's Sons, 1894.

Berenson, Bernard. *The Florentine Painters of the Renaissance, with an Index to their Works*. New York and London: G. P. Putnam's Sons, The Knickerbocker Press, 1896.

Bizzotto, Elisa. 'Pater's Reception in Italy: A General View'. In Stephen Bann ed., *The Reception of Walter Pater in Europe*. London: Athlone, 2004. 62–80.

Bland, Lucy. *Banishing the Beast: Feminism, Sex and Morality*. Harmondsworth: Penguin, 1995.

Booth, Wayne. *The Rhetoric of Fiction*. Chicago and London: University of Chicago Press, 1961.

Bourdieu, Pierre. *Distinction*. London: Routledge, 1984.

Bourdieu, Pierre. *The Rules of Art: Genesis and Structure of the Literary Field*, trans. Susan Emanuel. Stanford: Stanford University Press, 1996.

Bourget, Paul. 'Essai de psychologie contemporaine: Charles Baudelaire'. *La Nouvelle Revue* 13 (1881): 398–417.

Bowen, John. 'Practical Criticism, Critical Practice: I. A. Richards and the Discipline of "English"'. *Literature and History* 13: 1 (1987): 77–94.

Brockington, Grace. '"Above the Battlefield": Art for Art's Sake and Pacifism in the First World War'. D. Phil. Oxford, 2003.

Byatt, A. S. *Portraits in Fiction*. London: Vintage, 2002.

Byatt, A. S. *Possession* (1990). London: Vintage, 1991.

Caballero, Carlo. '"A Wicked Voice": On Vernon Lee, Wagner and the Effects of Music'. *Victorian Studies* 35: 4 (1992): 385–408.

Calloway, Stephen. *Aubrey Beardsley*. London: V & A Publications, 1998.

Castle, Terry. *The Apparitional Lesbian: Female Homosexuality and Modern Culture*. New York: Columbia University Press, 1993.

Caedel, Martin. *Pacifism in Britain 1914–1945: The Defining of a Faith*. Oxford: Clarendon Press, 1980.

Caedel, Martin. *Semi-Detached Idealists: The British Peace Movement and International Relations, 1854–1945*. Oxford: Oxford University Press, 2000.

Caedel, Martin. *Thinking About War and Peace*. Oxford: Oxford University Press, 1987.

Chotia, Jean. *English Drama in the Early Modern Period, 1890–1940*. London & New York: Longman, 1996.

Clark, Kenneth. 'Thoughts of a Great Humanist'. *Burlington Magazine* 554, XCI (May 1949): 144–5.

Clark, Kenneth. 'Bernard Berenson'. *Burlington Magazine* 690, CII (September 1960): 381–6.

Colby, Vineta. 'The Puritan Aesthete: Vernon Lee'. *The Singular Anomaly: Women Novelists of the Nineteenth Century*. New York: New York University Press, and London: University of London Press, 1970. 235–304.

Colby, Vineta. *Vernon Lee: A Literary Biography*. Charlottesville and London: University of Virginia Press, 2003.

Collins, L. J. *Theatre at War, 1914–18*. Basingstoke: Macmillan, 1998.

Colton, W. K. 'The Effect of War on Art'. *The Architect* XLV (17 March 1916): 200.

Connerton, Paul. *How Societies Remember*. Cambridge: Cambridge University Press, Pa: 1989.

Constable, Liz, Dennis Denisoff and Matthew Potolsky. eds. *Perennial Decay: On the Aesthetics and Politics of Decadence*. Philadelphia: University of Pennsylvania Press, 1999.

Corbett, David Peters. *The Modernity of English Art*. Manchester: Manchester University Press, 1997.

Craig, Edward Gordon. *The Art of the Theatre*. Edinburgh: T. N. Foulis, 1905.

Crawford, Robert. 'Pater's *Renaissance*, Andrew Lang, and Anthropological Romanticism'. *English Literary History* 53 (1986): 849–79.

Creech, James. *Closet Writing/Gay Writing: The Case of Melville's Pierre*. Chicago and London: The University of Chicago Press, 1993.

Davis, Whitney. *Replications: Archaeology, Art History, Psychoanalysis*. University Park: Pennsylvania State University Press, 1996.

Dellamora, Richard. *Masculine Desire*. Chapel Hill and London: University of North Carolina Press, 1990.

Dellamora, Richard. Introduction. *Victorian Sexual Dissidence*. Chicago and London: The University of Chicago Press, 1999. 1–17.

Dellamora, Richard. 'Productive Decadence: "The Queer Comradeship of Outlawed Thought": Vernon Lee, Max Nordau, and Oscar Wilde'. *New Literary History* 35 (2005): 1–18.

Demoor, Marysa. *Their Fair Share: Women, Power and Criticism in the Athenæum, from Millicent Garrett Fawcett to Katherine Mansfield, 1870–1920*. Aldershot: Ashgate, 2000.

Denisoff, Dennis. 'The Forest Beyond the Frame': Picturing Women's Desires in Vernon Lee and Virginia Woolf'. In Talia Schaffer and Kathy Alexis Psomiades, eds. *Women and British Aestheticism*. Charlottesville: University of Virginia Press, 1999. 251–69.

Denisoff, Dennis. *Sexuality and Visuality from Literature to Film, 1840–1940*. London: Palgrave-Macmillan, 2004.

di Robilant, Andrea. *A Venetian Affair*. London and New York: Fourth Estate, 2004.

Dowling, Linda. 'Victorian Oxford and the Science of Language'. *PMLA* 97. 2 (1982): 160–78.

Dowling, Linda. *Language and Decadence in the Victorian Fin de Siècle.* Princeton: Princeton University Press, 1989.

Dowling, Linda. 'Ruskin's Pied Beauty and the Constitution of a "Homosexual" Code'. *Victorian Newsletter* (Spring 1989): 1–8.

Dowling, Linda. *Hellenism and Homosexuality in Victorian Oxford.* Ithaca and London: Cornell University Press, 1994.

Duclaux, A. Mary F. Robinson. 'In Casa Paget (A Retrospect. In Memoriam Eugène Lee-Hamilton)'. *Country Life* (28 December 1907): 935–7.

Duclaux, A. Mary F. Robinson. 'Souvenirs sur Walter Pater'. *La Revue de Paris* 1 (15 January 1925): 339–58. Translated as 'Recollections of Pater, 1880–94'. In R. M. Seiler, ed. *Walter Pater: A Life Remembered.* Calgary: University of Calgary Press, 1987. 63–78.

Eksteins, Modris. *Rites of Spring: The Great War and the Birth of the Modern Age.* London: Bantam, 1989.

Eliot, T. S. *The Waste Land: A Facsimile and Transcript of the Original Drafts including the Annotations of Ezra Pound.* ed. Valerie Eliot. London: Faber, 1971.

Ellmann, Richard. *Oscar Wilde.* London: Hamish Hamilton, 1987.

Faderman, Lillian. *The Ladies from Llangollen: A Study in Romantic Friendship.* Harmondsworth: Penguin, 1971.

Felski, Rita. *The Gender of Modernity.* Cambridge: Harvard University Press, 1995.

Fish, Stanley. *Is There a Text in This Class?* Cambridge: Harvard University Press, 1980.

Fraser, Hilary. 'Women and the Ends of Art History: Vision and Corporeality in Nineteenth-Century Discourse'. *Victorian Studies* 42: 1 (1999): 77–100.

Fraser, Hilary. 'Vernon Lee: England, Italy and Identity Politics.' In Carol Richardson and Graham Smith, eds, *Britannia Italia Germania: Taste and Travel in the Nineteenth Century.* Edinburgh, VARIE, at the University of Edinburgh, 2001. 175–91.

Fraser, Hilary. 'Regarding the Eighteenth Century: Vernon Lee and Emilia Dilke Construct a Period'. In Francis O'Gorman and Kathleen Turner, eds, *The Victorians and the Eighteenth Century.* Aldershot and Burlington VT: Ashgate, 2004. 223–49.

Freud, Sigmund. *The Standard Edition of the Complete Psychological Works of Sigmund Freud.* 24 volumes. ed. James Strachey London: Hogarth Press and the Institute of Psycho-Analysis, London, 1953–1974. Volume VII: *A Case of Hysteria, Three Essays on the Theory of Sexuality, and Other Works* (1953), 125–245.

Fussell, Paul. *The Great War and Modern Memory.* London and New York: Oxford University Press, 1975.

Galliard, Françoise, '*A Rebours* ou l'inversion des signes'. *L'esprit de decadence.* Paris: Librarie Minard, 1980. 129–40.

Galsworthy, John. 'Art and War'. *The Atlantic Monthly* CXVI (5 November 1915): 625.

Gardner, Burdett. *The Lesbian Imagination (Victorian Style): A Psychological and Critical Study of 'Vernon Lee'.* New York and London: Garland, 1987.

Geffroy-Menoux, Sophie. 'L'enfant dans les textes de Vernon Lee'. *Cahiers Victoriens & Edouardiens* 47 (April 1998): 251–63.

Geffroy-Menoux, Sophie. 'La musique dans les textes de Vernon Lee'. *Cahiers Victoriens & Edouardiens* 49: 'La musique' (April 1999): 57–70.

Geffroy-Menoux, Sophie. *La voix maudite: Trois nouvelles fantastiques de Vernon Lee*. Traduction, préface, postface, notes et une nouvelle inédite de S. Geoffroy-Menoux. Rennes: Terre de Brume, 2001.

Gettmann, Royal A. Introduction, *The Handling of Words*, by Vernon Lee. Lincoln: University of Nebraska Press, 1968. vii–xxiv.

Gettmann, Royal A. 'Vernon Lee: Exponent of Aestheticism'. *Prairie Schooner* 42 (September 1968): 47–55.

Gilbert, Pamela. *Disease, Desire and the Body in Victorian Women's Popular Novels*. Cambridge: Cambridge University Press, 1997.

Greenblatt, Stephen. *Shakespearean Negotiations: The Circulation of Social Energy in Renaissance England*. Berkeley: University of California Press, 1988.

Gregory, Horace. 'The Romantic Inventions of Vernon Lee'. Introduction to *The Snake Lady and Other Stories by Vernon Lee*. New York: Grove, 1954.

Grosskurth, Phyllis. *John Addington Symonds: A Biography*. London: Longmans, 1964.

Grosskurth, Phyllis. *Havelock Ellis: A Biography*. London and Melbourne: Quarter Books, 1981.

Gunn, Peter. *Vernon Lee: Violet Paget 1856–1935*. London: Oxford University Press, 1964.

Hannoosh, Michele. *Parody and Decadence: Laforgue's Moralités legendaires*. Columbus: Ohio State University Press, 1989.

Hodgson, Willliam B. *Errors in the Use of English*. Edinburgh: David Douglas, 1881.

Holland, M. and R. Hart-Davis, eds. *The Complete Letters of Oscar Wilde*. London: Fourth Estate, 2000.

Horne, Philip. 'Introduction'. *The Tragic Muse* by Henry James. Harmondsworth: Penguin, 1995. vii–xxix.

Huysmans, Joris-Karl. *A Rebours*. Paris: Gallimard, 1977.

Inman, B. A. 'Estrangement and Connection: Walter Pater, Benjamin Jowett, and William Money Hardinge'. In Laurel Brake and Ian Small, eds. *Pater in the 1990s*. Greensboro, N.C.: ELT Press, 1991. 1–20.

Iser, Wolfgang. 'Do I Write for an Audience?' *PMLA* 115: 3 (2000): 310–14.

Jackson, Holbrook. *The Eighteen Nineties: A Review of Art and Ideas at the Close of the Nineteenth Century*. Revised edition. New York: Alfred A. Knopf, 1922.

James, Henry. *Henry James: Letters*. ed. Leon Edel. 4 vols: London and Basingstoke: Macmillan, 1974–1984. Volume III: *1883–1895*. 1980.

James, Henry. *Literary Criticism*. New York and Cambridge: Library of America, 1984.

James, Henry. *The Complete Notebooks of Henry James*. eds. Leon Edel and Lyall H. Powers. New York and Oxford: Oxford University Press, 1987.

James, William. *The Principles of Psychology*. New York: Holt and Company, 1890.

Kane, Mary Patricia. *Spurious Ghosts: The Fantastic Tales of Vernon Lee*. Rome: Carocci, 2004.

Ledger, Sally and Scott McCracken. 'Introduction'. In Sally Ledger and Scott McCracken, eds. *Cultural Politics at the Fin de Siècle*. Cambridge: Cambridge University Press, 1995. 1–10.

Lee-Hamilton, Eugene. *Poems and Transcripts*. Edinburgh and London: William Blackwood, 1878.

Lee-Hamilton, Eugene. *The New Medusa, and Other Poems*. London: Elliot Stock, 1882.

Lee-Hamilton, Eugene. *Apollo and Marsyas, and Other Poems*. London: Elliot Stock, 1884.

Lee-Hamilton, Eugene. *Sonnets of the Wingless Hours*. London: Eliot Stock, 1894.

Lee-Hamilton, Eugene. Selection introduced by John Addington Symonds. In *The Poets and the Poetry of the Nineteenth Century*. ed. Alfred H. Miles. 11 vols. 7: *Robert Bridges and Contemporary Poets*. London: Routledge, 1915. 241–56.

Lee-Hamilton, Eugene. *Selected Poems of Eugene Lee-Hamilton (1845–1907): A Victorian Craftsman Rediscovered*. ed. MacDonald P. Jackson. Lewiston and Lampeter: Edwin Mellen Press, 2002.

Leighton, Angela. 'Ghosts, Aestheticism, and "Vernon Lee"'. *Victorian Studies* 28: 1 (2000): 1–14.

Leighton, Angela. 'Resurrections of the Body: Women Writers and the Idea of the Renaissance'. In Alison Chapman and Jane Stabler, eds. *Unfolding the South: Nineteenth-Century British Women Writers and Artists in Italy*. Manchester and New York: Manchester University Press, 2003. 222–38.

Letley, Emma. *Maurice Baring: A Citizen of Europe*. London: Constable, 1991.

Lewis, Wyndham. 'A Lady's Response to Machiavelli'. *The Lion and the Fox: The Role of the Hero in the Plays of Shakespeare*. New York: Barnes and Noble, 1927. 111–14.

Lodge, David. *The Novelist at the Crossroads*. London: Routledge & Kegan Paul, 1986.

Lyon, Harvey T. 'The Deep Reverberation of a Bell: The Life and Poetry of Eugene Lee-Hamilton'. PhD dissertation, Harvard, 1955.

[MacColl, Norman]. 'Novels of the Week'. *Athenæum* (6 December 1884): 730.

Mallgrave, Harry Francis, and Eleftherios Ikonomou. eds. *Empathy, Form, and Space: Problems in German Aesthetics 1873–1893*. Santa Monica: The Getty Centre for the Humanities, 1994.

Mallon, T. 'A Boy of No Importance.' *Fact: Essays on Writers and Writing*. New York: Pantheon, 2001.

Maltz, Diana. 'Engaging "Delicate Brains": From Working-Class Enculturation to Upper-Class Lesbian Liberation in Vernon Lee and Kit Anstruther-Thomson's Psychological Aesthetics'. In Talia Schaffer and Kathy Alexis Psomiades, eds. *Women and British Aestheticism*. Charlottesville: University of Virginia Press, 1999. 211–29.

Mannocchi, Phyllis F. ' "Vernon Lee": A Reintroduction and Primary Bibliography'. *English Literature in Transition, 1880–1920* 26: 4 (1983): 231–67.

Mannocchi, Phyllis F. 'Vernon Lee and Kit Anstruther-Thomson: A Study of Love and Collaboration between Romantic Friends'. *Women's Studies* 12 (1986): 129–48.

Mariano, Nicky. *Forty Years with Berenson*. London: Hamish Hamilton, 1966.

Marin, Louis. 'The Figurability of the Visual: The Veronica or the Question of the Portrait at Port-Royal'. *New Literary History* 22 (1991): 281–96.

Markgraf, Carl. ' "Vernon Lee": A Commentary and an Annotated Bibliography of Writings about her'. *English Literature in Transition, 1880–1920* 26: 4 (1983): 268–312.

Mattheisen, P. F. and M. Millgate, eds. *Transatlantic Dialogue: Selected American Correspondence of Edmund Gosse*. Austin and London: University of Texas Press, 1965.

Maxwell, Catherine. 'From Dionysus to Dionea: Vernon Lee's Portraits'. *Word & Image* 13: 3 (July–Sept 1997): 253–69.

Maxwell, Catherine. 'Vernon Lee and the Ghosts of Italy'. In Alison Chapman and Jane Stabler, eds. *Unfolding the South: Nineteenth-century British Women Writers and Artists in Italy 1789–1900*. Manchester: Manchester University Press, 2003. 201–21.

Meisel, Perry. *The Absent Father: Virginia Woolf and Walter Pater*. London and New Haven: Yale University Press, 1980.

Meisel, Perry. *The Myth of the Modern: A Study in British Literature and Criticism after 1850*. London and New Haven: Yale University Press, 1987.

Nicolson, Benedict. 'In Honour of Bernard Berenson'. *Burlington Magazine* 628, XCVII (July 1955): 195–6.

Nordau, Max. *Degeneration*. Lincoln: University of Nebraska, 1993.

Nunokawa, Jeff. *Tame Passions of Wilde: The Styles of Manageable Desire*. Princeton: University of Princeton Press, 2003.

Ormond, Leonée. 'Vernon Lee as a Critic of Aestheticism in *Miss Brown*'. *Colby Library Quarterly* 9: 3 (1970): 131–54.

Paglia, Camille. *Sexual Personae: Art and Decadence from Nefertiti to Emily Dickinson*. New York: Vintage, 1991.

Pater, Walter. *Studies in the History of the Renaissance*. Oxford: Macmillan, 1873.

Pater, Walter. *Marius the Epicurean*. 2nd ed. London: Macmillan, 1885.

[Pater, Walter.] Review of 'Amiel's Journal: The Journal Intime of Henri-Frederic Amiel'. *Guardian* (17 March 1886): 406–7.

[Pater, Walter.] 'Vernon Lee's "Juvenilia"'. *Pall Mall Gazette* (5 August 1887), 5.

[Pater, Walter.] Review of 'Robert Elsmere' by Mrs Humphry Ward. *Guardian* (28 March 1888): 468–9.

Pater, Walter. 'Vernon Lee's "Juvenilia"'. *Pall Mall Gazette* (5 August 1887): 5.

Pater, Walter. *New Library Edition of the Works of Walter Pater*. 10 vols. London: Macmillan, 1910.

Vol I. *The Renaissance*.

Vol II. *Marius the Epicurean Part 1*.

Vol III. *Marius the Epicurean Part 2*.

Vol IV. *Imaginary Portraits*.

Vol V. *Appreciations*.

Vol VI. *Plato and Platonism*.

Vol VII. *Greek Studies*.

Vol VIII. *Miscellaneous Studies*.

Vol IX. *Gaston de Latour*.

Vol X. *Essays from The Guardian*.

Pater, Walter. *Letters of Walter Pater*. ed. Lawrence Evans. Oxford: Clarendon Press, 1970.

Plain, Gill. 'The Shape of Things to Come: The Remarkable Modernity of Vernon Lee's *Satan the Waster* (1915–1920)'. In Claire Tylee, ed. *Women, the First World War and the Dramatic Imagination. International Essays (1914–1999)*. Lewiston, New York and Lampeter: Edwin Mellen Press, 2000. 5–21.

Poole, William Frederick. *Poole's Index to Periodical Literature: the first supplement from January 1, 1882 to January 1, 1887.* Vol II. London: Rubner & Co., 1888.

Preston, Harriet Waters. 'Vernon Lee'. *Atlantic Monthly* 55 (February 1885): 219–27.

Psomiades, Kathy Alexis. *Beauty's Body: Femininity and Representation in British Aestheticism.* Stanford CA: Stanford University Press, 1997.

Psomiades, Kathy Alexis. ' "Still Burning from This Strangling Embrace": Vernon Lee on Desire and Aesthetics'. In Richard Dellamora, ed. *Victorian Sexual Dissidence.* Chicago and London: The University of Chicago Press, 1999: 21–41.

Pulham, Patricia. 'The Castrato and the Cry in Vernon Lee's Wicked Voices'. *Victorian Literature and Culture* 30: 2 (2002): 421–37.

Pulham, Patricia. 'A Transatlantic Alliance: Charlotte Perkins Gilman and Vernon Lee'. In Ann Heilmann, ed., *Feminist Forerunners: (New) Womanism and Feminism in the Early Twentieth Century.* London: Pandora Press, 2003. 34–43.

Reed, Christopher. *Bloomsbury Rooms. Modernism, Subculture, and Domesticity.* New Haven, Conn. and London: Yale University Press, 2004.

Robinson, Mary. *The End of the Middle Ages.* London: T. Fisher Unwin, 1889.

Rosenblatt, Louise. *Literature as Exploration.* New York: Appleton-Century, 1938. Repr. New York: Noble & Noble, 1968.

Rosenblatt, Louise. *The Reader, The Text, The Poem: The Transactional Theory of the Literary Work.* London: Feffer and Simons, 1978. Repr. With a new preface and epilogue. Carbondale: Southern Illinois University Press, 1994.

Ryan, Judith. *The Vanishing Subject: Early Psychology and Literary Modernism.* Chicago and London: University of Chicago Press, 1991.

Samuels, Ernest. *Bernard Berenson: The Making of a Connoisseur.* Cambridge, Mass., and London: Belknap Press, Harvard University, 1979.

Samuels, Ernest, with the collaboration of Jayne Newcomer Samuels. *Bernard Berenson: The Making of a Legend.* Cambridge, Mass., and London: Belknap Press, Harvard University, 1987.

Schaffer, Talia. *The Forgotten Female Aesthetes: Literary Culture in Late-Victorian England.* Charlottesville and London: University Press of Virginia, 2000.

Sedgwick, Eve Kosofsky. *Between Men: English Literature and Male Homosocial Desire.* New York: Columbia University Press, 1985.

Seed, David. 'Introduction'. *The Handling of Words and Other Studies in Literary Psychology, by Vernon Lee.* Lampeter: Edwin Mellen, 1992. i–xxx.

Seiler, R. M. *Walter Pater: A Life Remembered.* Calgary: University of Calgary Press, 1987.

Semon, Richard. *Mnemic Psychology.* Trans. B. Duffy. New York: Macmillan, 1923.

[Sharp, William] 'Literature'. Review of *Marius the Epicurean. Athenæum* (28 February 1885): 271–3.

Sharp, William. 'Some Personal Reminiscences of Walter Pater'. *Atlantic Monthly,* 74 (December 1894): 801–14.

Sinfield, Alan. *The Wilde Century.* London: Cassell, 1994.

Small, Ian. 'Vernon Lee, Association and "Impressionist" Criticism'. *The British Journal of Aesthetics* 17: 2 (Spring 1977): 178–84.

Small, Ian. *Conditions for Criticism: Authority, Knowledge, and Literature in the Late Nineteenth Century.* Oxford: Clarendon Press, 1991.

Smedley, Constance. 'The Greenleaf Theatre'. *The English Review* XXXV (July 1922): 58–60.

Smedley, Constance. *Crusaders: The Reminiscences of Constance Smedley (Mrs Maxwell Armfield).* London: Duckworth, 1929.

Spackman, Barbara. *Decadent Genealogies: The Rhetoric of Sickness from Baudelaire to D'Annunzio.* Ithaca: Cornell University Press, 1989.

Spackman, Barbara. 'Interversions'. In Liz Constable, Dennis Denisoff, and Matthew Potolsky, eds. *Perennial Decay: On the Aesthetics and Politics of Decadence.* Philadelphia: University of Pennsylvania Press, 1999. 35–49.

Sparshott, Francis Edward. *The Structure of Aesthetics.* London and Toronto: Routledge and Kegan Paul and the University of Toronto Press, 1963.

Staten, Henry. *Eros in Mourning: Homer to Lacan.* Baltimore and London: The Johns Hopkins University Press, 1995.

Stearns, Peter N. *Be a Man! Males in Modern Society.* New York: Holmes and Meier, 1990.

Stetz, M. D. and M. Samuels Lasner. *The Yellow Book: A Centenary Exhibition.* Cambridge, MA: The Houghton Library, Harvard University, 1994.

[Stillman W. J.] Review of *Euphorion. Being Studies of the Antique and the Mediæval in the Renaissance.* By Vernon Lee. Boston: Roberts Bros., *Nation* 40 (22 January 1885): 76–7.

Stutfield, Hugh E. M. 'Tommyrotics'. *Blackwood's Edinburgh Magazine* (June 1895): 833–45.

Swinburne, Algernon Charles. 'Notes on Designs of the Old Masters at Florence', *Essays and Studies.* London: Chatto & Windus, 1875. 314–57.

Symonds, John Addington. *Studies of the Greek Poets: First Series.* London: Smith, Elder, & Co., 1873.

Symonds, John Addington. Review of Eugene Lee-Hamilton's *Apollo and Marsyas. The Academy* 27 (31 January 1885): 71.

Symonds, John Addington. *In the Key of Blue and Other Prose Essays.* London: Elkin Mathews & John Lane, and New York: Macmillan, 1893.

Symonds, John Addington. Introduction to Eugene Lee-Hamilton. In *The Poets and the Poetry of the Nineteenth Century.* ed. Alfred H. Miles. 11 vols. 7: *Robert Bridges and Contemporary Poets.* London: Routledge, 1915. 241–56.

Symonds, John Addington. *The Letters of John Addington Symonds.* eds. Herbert M. Schueller and Robert L. Peters. 3 vols. Detroit: Wayne State University Press, 1967–69.

Taylor, Dennis. *Hardy's Literary Language and Victorian Philology.* Oxford: Clarendon, 1993.

Thirlwell, Angela. *William and Lucy: The Other Rossettis.* New Haven and London: Yale University Press, 2003.

Thornton, R. K. R. *The Decadent Dilemma.* London: Edward Arnold, 1983.

Trench, Richard Chevenix. *English, Past and Present.* 1855. ed. A. Smythe Palmer. London: Routledge; New York: Dutton, 1905.

Vanita, Ruth. *Sappho and the Virgin Mary: Same-Sex Love and the English Literary Imagination.* New York: Columbia University Press, 1997.

Vicinus, Martha. 'The Adolescent Boy: Fin-de-Siècle Femme Fatale?' *Journal of the History of Sexuality* 5 (1994): 90–114. Rpt. in Richard Dellamora, ed. *Victorian Sexual Dissidence*. Chicago and London: The University of Chicago Press, 1999. 83–106.

Vicinus, Martha. *Intimate Friends: Women who Loved Women, 1778–1928*. Chicago and London: The University of Chicago Press, 2004.

[Ward, Mary] M. A. W. Review of *Marius the Epicurean'*. *Macmillan's Magazine* (June 1885): 132–9.

Waugh, Arthur. 'Reticence in Literature'. *Yellow Book* (April 1894): 356–7.

Weber, Carl J. 'Henry James and his Tiger-Cat'. *PMLA* LXVIII: 4 (Sept. 1953): 672–87.

Wedgwood, Julia. 'Fiction'. *Contemporary Review* 47 (May 1885): 747–54.

Wilde, Oscar. *The Picture of Dorian Gray*. 1890–1. Rpt. *The Picture of Dorian Gray*. ed. Donald L. Lawler. New York and London: W. W. Norton & Company, 1988.

Wilde, Oscar. *Lady Windermere's Fan*. 1892. Rpt. in *The Picture of Dorian Gray and Other Writings by Oscar Wilde*. ed. Richard Ellmann. New York: Bantam, 1982. 195–259.

Wilde, Oscar. 'The Young King'. In *A House of Pomegranates*. London: James R. Osgood, McIlvaine, 1891. 1–26. Rpt. in *Oscar Wilde: Complete Short Fiction*. ed. Ian Small. London: Penguin, 1994. 83–96.

Williams, Gordon. *British Theatre in the Great War: A Reevaluation*. London: Continuum Intl Pub Group, 2002.

Winter, Jay. *Sites of Memory, Sites of Mourning: The Great War in European Cultural History*. Cambridge: Cambridge University Press, 1995.

Woolf, Virginia. *A Room of One's Own*. London: The Hogarth Press, 1929.

Woolf, Virginia. *To the Lighthouse*. Harmondsworth: Penguin, in association with The Hogarth Press, 1964.

Woolf, Virginia. *The Diary of Virginia Woolf*. 5 vols. ed. Anne Olivier Bell. New York and London: The Hogarth Press, 1977–1984. *I: 1915–1919*. Introduction by Quentin Bell. New York and London: The Hogarth Press, 1977.

Woolf, Virginia. *The Letters of Virginia Woolf*. ed. Nigel Nicolson and Joanne Trautman. 6 vols. London: The Hogarth Press, 1975–80.

Zorn, Christa. 'Aesthetic Intertextuality as Cultural Critique: Vernon Lee Rewrites History though Walter Pater's "La Gioconda"'. *The Victorian Newsletter* 91 (Spring 1997): 4–10.

Zorn, Christa. *Vernon Lee: Aesthetics, History, and the Victorian Female Intellectual*. Athens, OH: Ohio University Press, 2003.

Index